YORK

ALSO BY LAURA RUBY

York: The Shadow Cipher

YORK

—BOOK TWO—
THE CLOCKWORK GHOST

LAURA RUBY

WALDEN POND PRESS
An Imprint of HarperCollinsPublishers

For my father, Richard Ruby

1939–2018

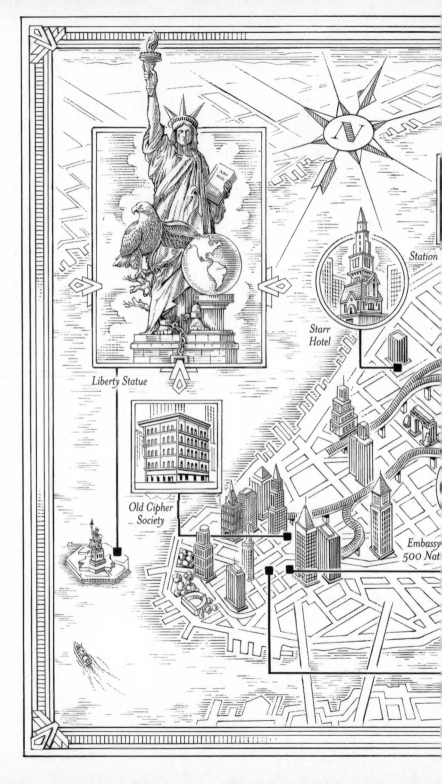

Station

Starr
Hotel

Liberty Statue

Old Cipher
Society

Embassy
500 Nat

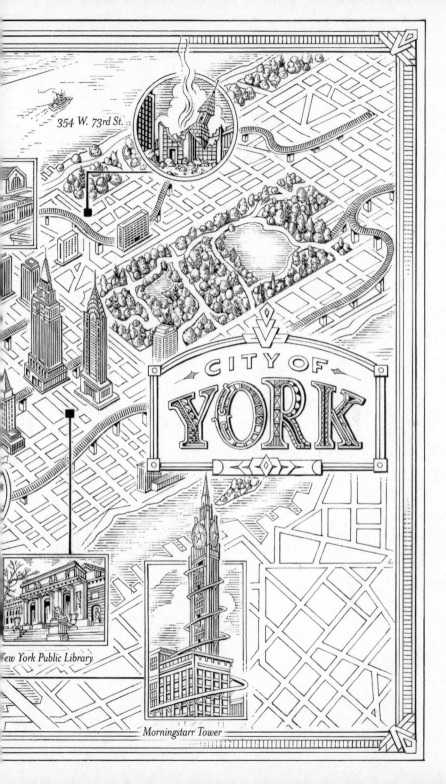

354 W. 73rd St.

CITY OF
YORK

New York Public Library

Morningstarr Tower

What strange phenomena we find in a great city,
all we need do is stroll about with our eyes open.
Life swarms with innocent monsters.

—CHARLES BAUDELAIRE,
Paris Spleen: Little Poems in Prose

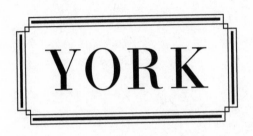

YORK

—BOOK TWO—

THE CLOCKWORK GHOST

New York City
April 12th, 1844

If money could buy happiness, then the very richest New Yorkers should have been among the happiest people in the whole city. Or the whole world. Instead, they were often the most dissatisfied—those with the biggest and best things are always clamoring for something bigger and better. They scrambled for properties with the best views of the river, tickets to the best performances, meals in the best restaurants, invitations to dine with the most important people.

And no one in New York City was more important than the Morningstarr twins: engineers, inventors, geniuses with a reputation for serving delectable food and inviting the most eccentric guests to their table. At the Morningstarrs', you never knew who might be sitting next to you: a fiery abolitionist, a circus soothsayer, a Swiss opera singer, a Chinese dignitary, a lady cellist, a lady *pirate*. You might hear Theodore Morningstarr arguing religious doctrine with a bishop, while Theresa Morningstarr championed the education of women with a university president, all while a mechanical suit of armor spooned out whipped potatoes. No matter who was on the guest list or what was planned for the evening, one thing was certain: Anyone who attended one of the Morningstarrs' rare dinner parties was sure to have a story to tell.

But unlike most of the Morningstarrs' guests, Miss Millicent "Millie" Munsterberg wasn't thinking about the stories she would have to tell. No, the fifteen-year-old was pushing buttered carrots around her plate, wondering why she had to spend a perfectly nice Saturday evening with a bunch of bores and crackpots. Why, even the pretty young woman seated diagonally from her, wearing a plain but expensive silk dress, prattled for an hour about math and the design of some engine with an old man named Mr. Cabbage.

Math! An engine! What was wrong with these people?

"Millicent, dear," said her mother from across the table. "Mrs. Hamilton asked you a question."

"Who?" Miss Millie said.

Her mother's mouth tightened. With her knife, she pointed to the wrinkled lady on Millie's right.

"Oh," said Miss Millie, turning to the sad old thing. "Yes. I'm so sorry, Mrs. Hammerston, I was concentrating on these most delicious root vegetables. You were saying?"

The woman opened her mouth to speak, but Millie's mother said, "Mrs. *Hamilton* asked if you were interested in visiting her orphanage," she said, in the tight voice she used when she wanted nothing more than to banish Millie to her room without supper forever.

"Me? Visit orphans?" exclaimed Miss Millie, horrified. She had peach-pink cheeks and a tumble of gleaming golden curls. Many claimed that Miss Millicent Munsterberg looked just like an angel, but then they'd never observed her curling her lip at the prospect of spending time with orphaned children.

"Oh, I doubt the orphans would care to suffer your company, either, young lady," grumbled the man seated on her left. He had pale skin, restless gray eyes, a silly dark mustache, and a forehead so large that Miss Millie felt he should apologize for it.

"I beg your pardon," Miss Millie said.

"I'm sure you do not," said the man, whose name Miss Millie had forgotten almost immediately after he'd introduced himself. Earlier in the evening, he'd been babbling some nonsense about ravens, and about how sometimes he was awakened at night by the sound of his own heart pounding in his ears. Miss Millie thought he was quite mad.

But that could have been said about any one of the people at the table, including their hosts, the infamous Morningstarr twins. Miss Millie could not understand why two doddering old fools were the objects of such fascination. Why, Mr. Theodore Morningstarr, in an uproar over the upcoming presidential election, banged his fists on the table so hard his roast quail hopped off his plate and into his lap. And Miss Theresa Morningstarr clearly paid no attention to the current fashion at all, with the graying tower of her hair listing precariously to the left and her gown sagging on her tall, thin frame. Here she was, one of the richest women in America, and the only jewelry she wore was a tarnished old locket on a chain around her neck. Where were her diamonds? Where were her rubies and emeralds and gold? Miss Millie's own mother was positively dripping in jewelry, but no one so much as glanced at Mrs. Munsterberg's sparkling rings or bracelets. What good was being rich if you couldn't be bothered to show it off?

What good was being rich if people refused to admire you for it?

But perhaps the Morningstarrs weren't so rich as they pretended. Miss Millie knew many families who weren't so rich as they pretended. (The biggest cocktail ring her mother wore was made of paste.)

"Millicent!" hissed her mother.

"Oh, what now?" said Miss Millie. Her mother had been *so* peevish since her thirty-fourth birthday the week before, when Millie had given her a cane as a joke.

"I was saying," said her mother through gritted teeth, "that perhaps Miss Morningstarr might excuse you from the table so that you can take in some fresh air, as it seems you don't have much of an appetite?" Mrs. Munsterberg looked around at the assembled guests. "She's been ill lately."

"I haven't been—" Miss Millie began, but snapped her mouth shut at her mother's warning frown.

"It is the wise person who knows when *not* to speak, don't you agree, Mr. Poe?" said Mrs. Hamilton.

"Quite," said the man with the offensive forehead. He and Mrs. Hamilton clinked glasses over Miss Millie's plate, which Miss Millie thought was exceedingly rude.

"I'd be happy to excuse Miss Millicent," said Miss

Theresa Morningstarr, gesturing with a bony hand. "Through those French doors you'll find a parlor with a balcony, my dear. Please, take in as much fresh air as you like."

"Thank you," said Miss Millie as meekly as she was able, which was not meekly at all. On her way out of the room, she almost crashed into the clanking suit of armor. "Lance," according to the engraved panel on his iron lapel, stepped aside and swept a creaking arm out, welcoming her to pass. As she did so, she heard the pretty young woman in the plain dress ask if she could see Lance's insides after dinner.

It was all extremely vexing.

But once Miss Millie found the parlor, she didn't bother opening the doors to the balcony. Instead, she threw herself in an overstuffed velvet chair to sulk. It simply wasn't fair of her mother to drag her here against her will and force her to converse with such odious people about such tedious things. It wasn't as if her mother enjoyed the company. Both Miss Millie's parents had dined with the Morningstarrs once, years ago, before Miss Millie was born, and her mother had claimed that the evening was a perfect horror.

"Why would you want to repeat it, then?" Miss Millie asked.

"Because your father needs their support," said her mother. "One good word from them and investors will come flocking."

Dr. Munsterberg was a great scientist but a mediocre businessman. "He's not even coming to dinner with us!"

"All the more reason to be on your best behavior."

Miss Millie thought she was behaving rather well, considering.

She cast her eyes about the room. It was a grand enough parlor, with a marble fireplace, a large crystal chandelier overhead, an ornate carpet at her feet. Next to her, on a claw-footed table, sat a small silver cube. She picked it up to examine it more closely, and then gasped. *Here* were the jewels missing from Miss Theresa Morningstarr's fingers and wrists: The surface of the cube was studded with sparkling rubies and sapphires, emeralds and diamonds, pearls and onyx. If these stones were real, the cube was worth a fortune. Who would leave such a priceless item just lying around for anyone to pick up, especially with all these strangers in the house? At the dinner table in the other room, there was an Arab sheik, a Cherokee trader, an Indian rug maker, and an *actor*! Even Miss Millie knew you could never trust an actor.

A voice behind her said, "It's a puzzle."

Miss Millie leaped to her feet, fumbling with the cube. "What? Who's there?"

Sitting in the farthest corner of the room was a young woman close to Miss Millie's own age, perhaps a year or two older, holding a quill. The girl set the quill aside and, in no great hurry, fanned the pages she had written before closing her book. She got up from her chair and walked toward Miss Millie. She was small and lithe, brown-eyed and brown-skinned, wearing a simple gray gown that complemented her so well that Miss Millie was even more vexed than before.

"You could have said something so I knew you were there," snapped Miss Millie.

"I believe I just did," said the girl.

"Then why don't you make yourself useful and fetch me a . . . a . . . sherry." Miss Millie wasn't yet allowed to have sherry but this servant wouldn't know that.

"You look healthy enough," the girl said, one side of her mouth quirking up. "Fetch it for yourself."

"Well! I never!"

"Are you certain?" the girl said.

"*What? I*—"

The girl set her book on the seat of the chair, held

out her palm. "Give me the cube and I'll show you what it does."

Reluctantly, Miss Millie pressed the cube into the other girl's hand. The girl started twisting the cube. "This cube is made up of twenty-six smaller cubes attached in the center. The object is to spin the blocks until each face of the cube has all the same color stones." She rotated the cubes faster and faster, left and right. After a few minutes, she handed the cube back to Miss Millie.

"The stones on each face don't match," Miss Millie said.

"Not yet. I got you most of the way there. You can solve the rest easily, I'm sure."

Miss Millie slapped the cube back on the tabletop. "I have no interest in silly games."

"No?" said the girl. "You seemed quite interested in that one a few moments ago."

"Who *are* you?"

"Who are *you*?"

"Miss Millicent Magdalena Mariah Munsterberg," said Miss Millie.

"Oh, dear," said the girl.

"So you know who I am," said Miss Millie, lifting her pointed chin.

"No earthly idea," the girl said. "But your name is quite . . . alliterative." She fingered a large silver pin on the bodice of her dress. A butterfly, or perhaps a moth. The wings fluttered lazily at her touch.

All of a sudden, Miss Millie worried that this girl wasn't a servant at all, that she'd insulted someone . . . important. "You're a guest of the Morningstarrs?" she asked. "I don't recall you from dinner."

"I don't much care for parties. I'd rather read a good book."

No matter how important this particular girl was, Miss Millie couldn't stop herself from blurting, "You prefer reading to parties? How peculiar!"

"So I've been told," said the girl, scooping up her book from the seat of the chair. "Well, then. It's about time for me to retire. I'll leave you to your private contemplation."

The girl turned to go, and then she paused, turned back. "If you do choose to solve the puzzle, be warned: It likes to play tricks."

And then she was gone.

Miss Millie frowned at the now-empty room, frowned at the silver cube, vexed once again. The girl's words made no sense. This whole evening made no sense. There seemed to be only one way to redeem it. Miss

Millie snatched the cube from the table and tucked it into her reticule. The gemstones couldn't be real, so the Morningstarrs wouldn't miss the cube. But even if the cube was real, and the Morningstarrs did miss it, they had only themselves to blame. You can't just invite *anyone* into your home. Maybe they'd think the girl in the gray dress had stolen it, whoever she was.

Now, that would be a clever trick.

Cheered, Miss Millie rejoined the dinner party in time for dessert, a lovely chocolate pudding. She forgot all about the puzzle cube in her purse until much later, when she was getting ready for bed. As she reclined in her soft feather pillows, she rotated the cubes, trying to match the stones on each face. After some time, she almost launched the useless thing against the wall, convinced it wasn't a puzzle at all, when every gem clicked into place. She waited for the trick that the girl had mentioned, but nothing happened. She set the puzzle cube on the side table, imagining all the rings and bracelets and brooches she'd make once she had the cube melted down, and then fell fast asleep . . .

. . . and was awakened in the middle of the night by the strangest sounds. Clicking sounds. *Scuttling* sounds.

"Hello," said a tiny voice.

Miss Millie sat up, gathering the sheets to her neck,

trying to focus in the darkness. "Who is that?!" she said.

Giggles. "Hello."

With trembling fingers, Miss Millie reached for the solar lamp on her bed table, flicked it on.

Hundreds of tiny silver spiders scuttled across her ceiling, over the furniture, on the floor. On the thinnest gossamer chain, a single spider inched down to dangle in front of Miss Millie's shocked, white face. It had three emerald eyes, slightly off-kilter.

"Hello?" it said.

Miss Millie screamed. The spider zipped back to the ceiling. The other spiders raced in crazed circles on every surface of the room, *hello, hello, hello.*

The door flew open. Hair wild, Dr. Munsterberg stood with Mrs. Munsterberg right behind him. As they took in the scene, Mrs. Munsterberg screamed right along with her daughter, while Dr. Munsterberg grabbed at the spiders. He caught one in his fist, a ruby-eyed creature the size of a penny.

"Hello!" it said, and hopped to the floor. The army of spiders ran for the window and disappeared through the cracks between the panes, giggling the whole way.

Miss Millie had stopped screaming and was now sobbing, because she knew where the spiders had come from. "She said it would play tricks, but she didn't say anything about spiders!"

"What? Who?" said Dr. Munsterberg. "Miss Theresa?"

"No," wailed Miss Millie. "The other girl."

"What other girl?" demanded Mrs. Munsterberg.

But Dr. Munsterberg wasn't listening anymore. He had walked to the window and was searching the grounds outside for any hint of metal gleaming in the dark. Everyone in New York City had lived alongside Morningstarr Machines for years, but Dr. Munsterberg had never seen machines so small. And now he had to wonder how very small the Morningstarrs could make their machines.

Or, he thought, how very big.

NEW YORK CITY

Present Day

CHAPTER ONE

Tess

There are cats, and there are Cats.

Your typical lowercase cat is fascinating enough. Alternately elegant and ridiculous, liquid and solid, here and gone. But Cats, well, Cats are *more*. Slinkier and sassier, bigger and bendier, a concentration of Catness, a *multiplicity* of cats in a single body. A Cat is every cat, and no cat at all.

If you asked Tess Biedermann, her cat Nine was such a Cat.

Not that Tess was biased or anything.

"It's science," she said.

"I wish science had given Nine some flashlight eyes," said Tess's friend Jaime Cruz. "It's dark as deep space in here."

Tess, Jaime, and Tess's brother, Theo, were standing inside a building on West 73rd Street in Manhattan. This nondescript structure had once stood next to their old apartment building, an original Morningstarr building, managed by Jaime's grandmother. It was the building they'd all called home.

A home they loved. A home they'd hoped to save. A home they'd helped to destroy.

They were trying hard not to dwell on that last part.

Outside, it was a bright and steamy August day, but here, inside the closed door, a door that had been hidden from the world for over a century and a half, the cool air was thick with dust, the darkness impenetrable. It was the third time they'd tried to explore this place. The first time, they were so disappointed not to find the treasure they were seeking right behind the door, they'd turned around and marched out again. The second time, they'd been stopped outside by an overly ambitious security guard who told them he'd have them arrested if he ever saw them again.

Now Jaime sniffed. Theo sneezed. Tess rubbed her eyes, willing them to adjust. They were perched on some sort of landing. In front of them appeared to be nothing but the entrance to a stone tunnel leading . . . well, who knew where? Nine tugged at her harness, trying to pull Tess forward, though Tess held her back. This would have been easier on Tess's arm if Nine didn't weigh forty-five pounds.

Nine was definitely an Uppercase Cat.

"Well," said Theo. "I don't see the greatest treasure known to man, do you?"

"Nine can see," said Tess. "And she wants us to keep moving."

"Well, as long as the *cat* thinks it's safe to keep moving," said Theo.

"You mean the Cat," said Tess.

"That's what I said."

"No, you didn't."

"I think the Cipher wants us to keep moving, too," said Jaime. "Look down."

Tess looked. At their feet, painted onto the stone floor, a phosphorescent-green arrow pointed straight into the tunnel. As if it had already anticipated their hesitation.

"Not particularly mysterious," said Theo. "You'd think the Cipher would make things harder."

"Haven't things been hard enough?" said Tess. They had. Just over a month ago, a developer named Darnell Slant had finally persuaded the city to sell him all five Morningstarr buildings, the kids' building among them.

And just over a month ago, Tess and Theo and Jaime had decided that the only way they could save their building was to solve the greatest mystery of the Morningstarrs: the Morningstarr Cipher, the puzzle that the enigmatic twins had embedded in the streets and the monuments and the artifacts of New York City more than a hundred and fifty years before. A puzzle that people had been try-ing—and failing—to solve for all that time, because they had missed the most important aspect.

It hadn't wanted to be solved. Until now.

At least, they hoped so.

"For all we know, the Cipher is leading us right into some kind of trap," Jaime said. "It's not like it would be the first time. Remember the Underway puzzle? When we almost died?

Theo said, "That's comforting."

"Always here to help," said Jaime. Tess could tell that Jaime was trying to keep his tone bright, but he only sounded stressed. But then they were all stressed. And confused. They'd thought they solved the Cipher when the clues led back to their building. They'd thought they'd understood the Morningstarrs better than anyone. But the memories of their beloved building crashing down right before their eyes haunted them. It showed them that no one, not even they, really understood the Morningstarrs, and that the Cipher remained a cipher.

"Remind me why we're doing this again?" Theo said.

"You know why," Tess said. What Tess did not say, did not *have* to say, was that Slant was all over television and social media telling people how he would reshape New York City into the "city of the future"—whatever that meant. That he was talking about starting his own school so that he could "imbue the minds of the future with the values of the future"—whatever that meant. That he was backing political candidates and research groups that Tess's dad claimed were "shady as all get-out"—whatever *that* meant. That Slant seemed to be more powerful than ever. That they had not managed to save their own home, but maybe they could save someone else's. That the destruction of 354 W. 73rd Street had to mean *something*. And it wouldn't mean anything if they didn't solve the Cipher.

After a few moments, Jaime said, "We can't let him win."

They all knew who "he" was. They started to move, slowly, carefully, while Nine urged them along. With each step, tiny lights overhead sputtered to life, casting a dim green pall over everything, as much good as that did. Nothing to see but endless walls of stone. They seemed to be in some sort of tunnel running underneath the building.

"Do you guys feel that? There's a slight pitch in the floor," said Theo. "This passageway is leading us down."

"Awesome," said Jaime. "I'm sure that's nothing to worry about."

Tess stayed quiet, even though the questions were itching to burst from her mouth. Leading them down *where*? What if the tunnel collapsed on their heads? What if it led them straight through the island and then out to sea? What if a battalion of Underway conductors or Rollers or Lances or moths were lying in wait for them?

What if they failed again?

Nine turned and gave Tess's fingers a gentle nip. She always knew when Tess's mind was churning. She was a Cat, after all. But despite Nine's calming presence, Tess shivered. "It's cold."

"Yeah," said Jaime. "And quiet. I don't hear the Underway trains. Do you?"

"No," said Theo. "Walls and floors must be too thick."

Jaime touched the stone on the walls. "There's something written here." He ran his fingers over the faint markings. "A name. Sam."

"No last name?" Tess asked.

"Just Sam."

They kept walking, the pitch of the stone floor getting steeper. From time to time, Jaime stopped and read another name etched into the stones. Beulah. James. Sissy. Solomon. Patrick. More often, there were simple Xs scratched into the stone, as if someone had only wanted to leave a mark.

"So many," Tess said. "But if the door we came through was the only entrance to this tunnel, and that door was hidden until now, how did anyone get into this tunnel?"

"Maybe the people who built it signed their names," said Theo.

"Hmmm," Jaime said. "What's that?"

"What?" said Tess.

"That," said Jaime, pointing. A few feet in front of them, something crowded the tunnel. They stopped short, but Nine wasn't having it. She jerked her leash out of Tess's hand.

"Wait! Nine!"

Nine didn't wait. She bounded forward, nearly swallowed up by the darkness. Her stripes and spots seemed to float in the air, her snuffles echoing off the stone. After a few moments, she chirped softly, calling to them.

"Wait!" said Theo, but Tess felt along the walls till she reached the large something that filled the tunnel. Which, when she ran her hands over the wheels and the sides, turned out to be some sort of carriage, the kind that you'd see in Central Park, drawn by sleepy, clopping horses. But when Tess peered around to the front of the carriage, there were no horses hitched there. There wasn't anything hitched there. Unless? She felt along the reins, which tapered as they stretched all the way to the ground, where there were . . .

Tess jumped back.

"What?" said Theo.

"Ants," said Tess.

"Ants?" said Theo.

"Four mechanical ants. They're each about the size of a thumb," said Tess.

"Are they moving?"

Tess crouched and squinted in the gloom. The antenna of one ant was swiveling their way, as if listening. "Maybe?"

Jaime crouched next to her. "Yep. Ants. Because why not ants?"

"The real ones can carry more than a thousand times their body weight," said Theo. "Who knows what the mechanical ones can carry?"

"A fully loaded carriage, I'm guessing," said Jaime. "Shall we?"

They got into the carriage. As soon as they'd sat down, the ants began to march forward. Or rather, scuttle. Despite the scuttling and the cobblestone tunnel floor, the ride was surprisingly smooth. Nine the Cat positioned herself at the front of the carriage, letting the slight wind ruffle her whiskers, like the captain on the prow of a ship.

They didn't scuttle far, however. Or at least, the ride didn't seem to be that long. But they did pass other openings in the tunnel, lefts and rights they didn't take. Who built this tunnel? How did the ants know where to go?

The ants weren't saying.

Tess wished she could talk to her grandpa Ben, wished he was here, right now, riding along with them. But Grandpa Ben had been moved from 354 W. 73rd Street to a place on Long Island, and to a fancy facility uptown immediately after that. Grandpa Ben forgot more than he remembered.

And then, as suddenly as they had begun, they stopped moving.

"We're here," said Tess.

"Great. Where's here?" Theo said. The ants' antennae

twitched, seemed to point to a set of rough stone steps chopped into the nearest wall.

"Thanks!" Jaime said to the nearest ant. He held out a finger as if he wanted to pat the ant's silvery thorax, then thought better of it. He patted Nine instead, who meowed her approval.

They left the ants behind and started to climb the narrow stone staircase that zigged and zagged. The first five minutes were easy enough, the second five were harder. The next ten were torture.

"This is an inordinate number of steps," Theo said.

"I rebuke these steps," said Jaime.

"I rebuke the Cipher," Tess said, wiping the sweat from her brow.

"No, you don't," said Theo.

"Sometimes *I* do," said Jaime. "Like when I look around our new apartment and everything is so white it hurts my eyes."

"And maybe when you have to climb ninety bazillion stone steps to nowhere?" said Tess.

"That, too."

But the Cipher wasn't leading them to nowhere. Just when they thought they would never stop climbing, when they thought their hearts would burst, they reached the top stair. And a door with no knob. Just a metal loop with the hasp of a combination lock threaded through it. The lock appeared to be old, something from another century. It had an oddly jagged steel hasp with three brass dials, each dial stamped with numbers one through nine. Tess tugged on it, but of course it was locked.

"Okay, we need a combination," she said.

Nine meowed.

Theo's brows scrunched. "Three dials would give us . . . seven hundred and twenty-nine possibilities."

"Better than a million possibilities," said Jaime. "But worse than, say, one."

"There has to be a clue around here somewhere," Tess said.

They examined the stones all around the doorway, looking for any kind of sign or symbol, but found nothing. They examined the door itself, but the surface had no writing they could find. Tess dropped to her knees and ran her fingers along the stone floor. Jaime and Theo did the same. Jaime went so far as to study the last ten risers leading to the door.

"Maybe the clue was in the number of steps?" Jaime said. "Did anyone count them?"

"I didn't," said Tess.

"I didn't, either," said Theo, sounding extremely disappointed in himself.

"So, how are we supposed to open the lock without any sort of clue?" said Tess.

Nine scratched at the door, meowed again.

"Maybe there isn't any clue this time. Maybe there's just work," Theo said. "Start with one combination and go through them until we get it right."

Nine twirled around their ankles, pausing only to give Tess a tiny nip on her ankle. Tess bent to pet her.

"We should have brought snacks," Jaime said. "And some water. Because we could be fooling with this thing till next Thursday."

Theo started with 1-1-1, then 1-1-2, then 1-1-3. Jaime kept a record in his sketchbook. Tess sat on the stone steps, her hand on Nine's back.

She'd always had what her parents called "a prodigious imagination," but she never could have imagined what had transpired over the summer. The fact that all five original Morningstarr buildings would be sold to Darnell Slant didn't surprise her at all; she'd been worried about that since she was little. But she didn't anticipate the fact that her grandfather would be sent a clue to the Morningstarr Cipher that no one had ever seen before. Or that the letter would lead to a whole new set of clues, a sort of shadow cipher operating independently from the original, a shadow cipher that Tess was convinced was the *real* Cipher. Or that solving the clues in the shadow cipher would lead to a horrible betrayal on the part of one of her grandfather's oldest friends and the destruction of the Morningstarr building they were trying so hard to save. The fact that Theo and Tess would be forced to live with their great-aunt Esther in Queens and Jaime with his grandmother in a brand-new building all the way in Hoboken, New Jersey. The fact that they had no idea where else the Cipher would take them. The fact that solving the clues seemed to have awakened something at the very heart of the city itself, something that Tess wanted to trust, but . . .

Nine mrrowed again, rubbed her big face against Tess's leg.

"My thumb is going numb," said Theo.

"I'll take a turn," said Tess. She and Jaime switched so that Jaime was trying the combinations on the lock and Tess was keeping track. Theo sat on the step scratching Nine's ears until her purr was a soothing rumble. When Jaime's thumb went numb, Tess took over trying combinations and Theo took notes. Jaime sat on the steps to rest, and Nine licked his knees.

They switched places, and switched again. Hours went by. Or days. Tess couldn't be sure.

Jaime flexed his fingers, rolled his wrist. "What if it's

a number we know already?"

Their old building was 354 W. 73rd Street. Perking up, Tess said, "Try three-five-four!"

Jaime did. No luck. They also had no luck with other addresses, birthdays of the Morningstarrs, or the month and the day the Morningstarrs disappeared.

"Let's just keep working," said Theo. "We'll get there."

Jaime sighed, hefted the lock again. Then, he frowned, ran his thumb over the hasp.

"What?" said Tess.

"The hasp isn't a loop, but it's not straight, either."

"Yeah, I noticed that," said Tess.

"It looks like cat ears."

"What?"

"The way a little kid would draw cat ears. Triangle, straight line, triangle. See?"

Nine mrrowed softly, wound herself around Jaime's feet.

"A cat," Theo repeated.

"Or a Cat," Tess said. "Like Nine."

"Or nine," said Theo.

For a moment, they were all silent. Nine stopped winding and licking and nipping, instead groomed the end of her long tail. Jaime said, "But Nine is just one number." He tried 9-9-9, but that didn't work, either.

"Nine isn't her full name," Tess said.

Jaime said, "What do you mean?"

Theo tucked Jaime's pencil into his own overlarge, bushy hair. "When Aunt Esther gave her to us, she said, 'I have brought you an animal. The animal's name is Nine Eighty-Seven. I have also brought you some Fig Newtons, but not for the animal.'"

Jaime stared at Theo, at his pencil in Theo's hair, then down at Nine. Nine peered at him, still and watchful, the answer to her own riddle.

"If this works, I think maybe we need to have a conversation with your aunt Esther," said Jaime, before turning the first dial to nine, the second to eight, the third to seven. He tugged.

The lock popped open with a click.

And something small and whitish, the size of a pain capsule, dropped to the floor. Nine batted at it.

"Must have been hidden inside the lock." Theo stooped down, scooped it up.

Tess peered over Theo's shoulder. "What is it?"

"I think it's a scroll," Theo said, unwinding it. In Theo's hand was a thin strip of yellowed paper on which was written:

TICKET #3152—TLJ. THE 17TH OF JUNE.

"Ticket #3152? TLJ? A ticket to what?" Tess said.

"Maybe we'll find out when we open the door," said Jaime. He plucked his pencil from Theo's hair, wiped it on his pants, and put that and his sketchbook in his back pocket. Then he unhooked the lock and tucked it into the other pocket. With both hands, he took hold of the only available handle on the door, the small metal loop through which the hasp had been threaded.

"Ready?" Jaime said.

No, Tess thought. "Yes," Tess said.

Jaime pulled. The heavy door opened just a crack. Tess and Theo got their fingers around it, and together they all wrenched the door wide. A shaft of bright light hit them. Before they could stop her, Nine slipped through the opening.

And that was when someone started to scream.

CHAPTER TWO
Theo

The woman was extremely tall, blue-haired, and brown-skinned, with hoop earrings so large that Theo thought they could serve as perches for parrots. She wore a black dress with lots of complicated straps crisscrossing her shoulders and a belt with at least three buckles that perhaps doubled as weapons. She loomed like a goddess, both hands on her hips, glaring down at them. Another woman, shorter and Asian, looking more surprised than angry, stood on a pedestal in the middle of the room in a half-pinned white wedding gown or caftan or muumuu or bedsheet—Theo wasn't up on the latest fashions—both hands clapped on the sides of her face like Edvard Munch's painting *The Scream*. If Theo had to guess, and he had to, the door from the tunnel had led them into the back of some sort of fancy shop. There were mirrors all around and plush armchairs. Several large stalls for changing. Some glasses and a pitcher of water with lemon slices floating in it sat on a marble table next to one of the chairs. Theo thought about asking for a sip of the water, but had a feeling the tall woman might dump the whole pitcher over his head.

"What," boomed the tall woman, "in the name of all that is good and right do you think you children are doing?"

"I'm sorry, ma'am, we were just—" Jaime began, but the woman cut him off.

"Child!" the woman said. "This is a place of business, not a public park! Not a movie theater! Not a library! Not a school! Not your living room!" She peered at Nine, who had dropped down to her belly as if to appear smaller. "And not a zoo!"

"We're so sorry," Tess said. "We didn't know where—"

"You just opened a door in my gorgeous *stone wall*, a door I didn't know was there," the woman said. "How did you get it open? Where did you come from?" She stalked to the wall they'd just burst through and peered down the stone steps. "What in the world . . . ?" she said, her voice echoing off the stone.

The Asian woman stepped off the pedestal on which she'd been standing, carefully gathering up the hem of the dress/muumuu/caftan, trying not to disturb the pins studding the bottom. "What's down there, Janice?"

"I have absolutely no idea," said the taller woman. "Perhaps the children would like to explain it to us before I call all their parents."

Theo didn't even bother opening his mouth because he knew he'd say the wrong thing, like asking if this woman had any parrots, or if she was planning on getting some, because they would look really great with her earrings, in his inexpert opinion on fashion. Tess opened her mouth and closed it several times, as if conjuring up then discarding one lie after the other, lies that maybe other people might believe but this tall goddess wouldn't buy for a second.

Jaime said, "I think we found part of the Underground Railroad."

"What?" said the tall woman and the smaller woman simultaneously.

"We did?" said Theo and Tess simultaneously.

Jaime told the women that he and his friends had been exploring a construction site and found a way into the basement of the building next door. In that basement, hidden behind a pile of rocks, there was an opening to a very old tunnel leading down underneath the building. They knew they shouldn't, but they decided to enter the tunnel. They walked that long, stone tunnel and noticed that there were names scratched into the stone on the walls, names like Sam and Beulah and Solomon, but also a lot of Xs. He couldn't be sure, Jaime said, but somehow he got the most powerful feeling that those were the names and marks of people trying to escape something terrible, and they wrote their names and made their marks just in case they didn't make it, even if it was a risk to do so.

For some reason, the story didn't sound vague or even that strange when Jaime told it. It sounded right, and true.

The tall woman, Janice, considered Jaime for what seemed like a very long time.

Finally, she said, "What's your name, young man?"

"Jaime Cruz, ma'am."

"You wouldn't be lying to me, Jaime Cruz, would you?"

"No, ma'am."

"So if I were to walk down those stairs and into that tunnel, I would find those names and those Xs scratched into the stone?"

"Yes, ma'am. You might find a lot of other things, too."

Janice took a deep breath, brushed some of her curly, smoky-blue hair back from her face, hair that seemed elegant rather than silly or shocking on her. "A part of the Underground Railroad leading straight to Jennings. I shouldn't be surprised at all. And I've always wondered why we were so far east. So near the docks."

"Wait," said Jaime. "*This* is Jennings?"

"Where else?" Janice said, as if Jennings were the only good and right place the tunnel could have led them. Except Theo had no idea what Jennings was, even though the name sounded familiar.

"My grandmother has talked about this place," said Jaime. "She said that she's going to come straight here to have a dress made when I get married." Jaime's brown cheeks went the slightest bit rosy.

Janice laughed. "You getting married anytime soon?"

"I'm twelve, ma'am. I'll be thirteen in September."

"So that would be a no," said Janice.

Jennings, Jennings, Theo thought, turning the name over in his head. "Jennings as in *Thomas* Jennings? The guy who invented dry cleaning?"

"Thomas L. Jennings, the *tailor, businessman,* and

abolitionist who invented dry cleaning," said Janice, her voice clipped.

"The first African American to receive a patent!" Theo said. "In 1821!"

The woman's big brown eyes got bigger, then her expression softened. "Well!" she said, now considering Theo. "You know your history."

Theo almost said, "Yes," because he *did* know his history, or always thought he did. But then he remembered how many times he'd been surprised over the last few weeks. Instead he said, "I know some history. You still have dry-cleaning shops all around the city. My mom goes to one."

"Then you know the TLJ headquarters is right next door, in the same building. Opened in 1837."

Ticket #3152, TLJ, the 17th of June, Theo thought. Could it be?

Jaime said, "Anyway, I'm very sorry we burst in on you both."

"No harm done, I suppose," said Janice. The smaller woman in the white muumuu was sitting on the floor petting Nine. "Except for the cat hair you're getting all over that dress, Bibi."

"What?" said Bibi. "This is a good kitty."

Janice rolled her eyes. "That," she said, "is a saber-tooth."

"A good sabertooth, then," said Bibi, shrugging. Nine licked her hand.

"She belongs in the Bronx Ecological Park with the rest of the chimera."

"She's not a chimera," Tess said. "She's a Cat."

"Uh-huh," said Janice, one thin eyebrow raised so high it almost disappeared into the cloud of blue hair. "She'd scare all the hamster-hogs and fer-rabbits and panda-quoks. Or eat them. They should make some a little bigger."

"The big chimera are illegal," said Theo.

"Like that's stopped people before," said Janice.

"The only thing Nine eats is her kibble," Tess said. Then toed the expensive carpet. "You're not really going to call our parents, are you?"

Janice put her hands on her hips again. "Are any of your parents professional historians who could date that tunnel? Or perhaps journalists who could write about it? Powerful lawyers or ex-presidents who will make sure this building isn't ripped out right under us and sold to some rich man who doesn't care about anyone's history or future but his own?"

Tess was quiet for a moment. "No," she said. "No one like that."

"Then I'm not going to call them," said Janice, flashing a hint of teeth—a smile or a grimace or both.

"If you do decide to call some lawyers and historians, maybe you could say *you* were the ones who found the tunnel?" said Jaime.

"What if you discovered something amazing?" said Bibi. "You don't want credit?"

"I'd rather have my grandmother not find out that I was doing things she wouldn't like than get any credit," said Jaime. Tess and Theo nodded.

"I have a grandmother like that," said Janice. "All right. No mention of you to anyone, right, Bibi?"

"I'm thirty-three years old, and my parents are still mad I didn't take John Park to my senior prom," said Bibi. "My lips are sealed." She planted a kiss on top of Nine's head. Nine received this kiss as if it was her due.

Janice peered once again down the stone steps. "Until I decide what to do, I'm going to close this door. A little help, please?"

Theo, Tess, Jaime, and both women heaved the jagged stone "door" closed. Once it was shut, the stones met so seamlessly you couldn't tell there was ever an opening there at all. Which, thought Theo, was likely the point.

"Well, children, it has been interesting meeting you," said Janice the Goddess, "but my afternoon is booked solid. I think it's time for you and your saber-tooth friend to get on home."

"Thank you, ma'am," said Jaime. "We appreciate that."

"I'm sure you do," said Janice. She pointed to one end of the grand room, where yet another door was marked Exit. "The storefront is that way. Walk straight through to get to the street. You can see yourselves out. But don't touch anything!"

They all turned to go when Janice added, "And maybe don't hang around construction sites from now on. You don't want to get in trouble, do you?"

"Too—" said Tess.

"—late," said Theo.

Theo, Tess, Jaime, and Nine got to the front door of Jennings's Fine Designs without destroying any of the handmade clothing, knocking over any of the racks, exploding anything, or getting cat hair on any of the patrons. (That is, the patrons who didn't want to get cat hair on themselves; some of the people were terrified of Nine, some were helpless in the face of her and couldn't keep their hands off her, that is, when she wished it. It was her superpower. Among many.)

Once they were out on the street, Theo pointed to the dry-cleaning shop next door. He whispered, "The paper we found said—

"—TLJ," Tess finished for him.

Jaime pushed his glasses up the bridge of his nose. "Let's go in."

The place was warm and bright, packed with customers handing in tickets despite the late hour. Thomas L. Jennings memorabilia hung all over the brick walls and under the glass countertop at the front of the store. When Theo handed his ticket to the harried, red-faced clerk, the clerk glanced down at it, then looked up at Theo.

"Is this is a joke?"

"No joke," said Theo.

"We're closing in a few minutes and I got customers, kid," said the clerk, handing back the slip. "Can I help who's next?"

"But—" Tess said.

"NEXT!" shouted the clerk. A pale woman carrying three identical red business suits scowled at Tess before not-too-gently elbowing her aside. Nine growled, and the woman dropped her suits on the floor, startled. Nine sniffed at the suits, tossed her striped head, and dragged Tess and Theo over to Jaime, who had been waving at them from one end of the store.

"What?" said Theo.

"That," said Jaime. He pointed to a black gown in a glass case displayed in front of the alterations desk. "Read the plaque at the bottom."

TICKET # 3152, TLJ, THE 17TH OF JUNE.

A TICKET WRITTEN BY THOMAS L. JENNINGS HIMSELF SOMETIME IN THE 1840S. BELIEVED TO BE A GOWN WORN BY NONE OTHER THAN MISS THERESA MORNINGSTARR, THE ITEM WAS NONETHELESS NEVER PICKED UP. SOME SAY THAT IT WAS LEFT HERE BY MISTAKE AND FORGOTTEN; OTHERS INSIST THAT LEAVING THE DRESS WAS MEANT AS AN INSULT, THOUGH MR. JENNINGS WAS A GUEST AT SEVERAL DINNER PARTIES AND EVENTS THROWN BY THE MORNINGSTARRS BEFORE AND AFTER THE TICKET WAS WRITTEN. STILL OTHERS BELIEVE THE DRESS ISN'T CONNECTED TO MISS MORNINGSTARR AT ALL, AND INSTEAD BELONGED TO SOMEONE ELSE ENTIRELY. THE TRUTH, ALAS, IS LOST TO TIME.

NO MATTER THE PROVENANCE OF THE DRESS, NOTE THE QUALITY OF THE SILK, THE AUSTERE DESIGN, AND THE ONE EMBELLISHMENT: THE LACE AROUND THE COLLAR. MR. JENNINGS'S REVOLUTIONARY CLEANING PROCESS DID NOT DAMAGE EITHER THE SILK OR THE DELICATE LACE.

Theo peered at the lace around the collar of the dress. Instead of dots or flowers, the lace was decorated with tiny hearts. Jaime took out his phone, took a picture of the dress. Then he pulled out his sketchbook and drew a sketch, because he didn't quite trust technology. In his sketch, where a woman's face would be, Jaime drew a blank oval, which Theo thought was just a bit creepy.

Tess frowned at the creepy blank oval, then glanced around the busy shop. She kept her voice low when she said, "I think we have to figure out whose dress this is. She's probably the key to the next clue."

"It's late and if we don't get home soon our parents and your grandmother will start freaking out. Let's go back to Aunt Esther's," said Theo. "We can look through some of Grandpa Ben's notes. He researched a lot of the people who hung out with the Morningstarrs, or did business with them. Maybe we'll find something."

Jaime sighed, tucked his sketchbook back into his pocket, but didn't say anything cheerful or sarcastic or cheerfully sarcastic.

"Are you okay?" Tess asked him.

Jaime tugged at a loose 'loc. "You guys ever wonder when this will end? Or how?"

"It will end when we find the treasure," Tess said,

enunciating each word, as if she were telling herself this as much as telling Jaime.

"Yes, but sometimes I wonder if my idea of treasure and the Morningstarrs' idea of treasure are two different things," Jaime said.

In the past few weeks, Theo had been thinking along the same lines, but Tess looked so crushed by Jaime's lack of enthusiasm that Theo kept his own mouth shut. Whether Theo wanted to admit it or not, he needed Tess's relentless energy, her strange certainty, to keep going. Otherwise, they had destroyed their own building for nothing. And that was nothing Theo could stand.

They left the dry-cleaning store on West 34th Street and had to walk nearly fifteen minutes to the nearest Underway. Taking the Underway was an entirely different experience than it used to be, ever since they'd found out that the Guildmen running the trains might not be human but Morningstarr Machines, ever since they had nearly died while riding a runaway Underway train, ever since they had found out that some of the Morningstarr Machines—maybe all of them—could have their own agendas.

The ride to Queens was long, but the three of them sat rigidly in their seats. Nine, however, was calm and quiet at their feet as the passengers loaded and unloaded at the various stops. The Guildman managing the train car was tall and thin, with spidery limbs and a pale face so expressionless that he could have been one of Jaime's blank ovals. But he paid the three of them no mind, sweeping cold blue eyes over all the passengers, making sure no one was eating anything or littering anything or otherwise causing trouble. Instead of cleaning the floors the way it normally would, a silvery caterpillar curled up in one of the seats across from them, as if it were sleeping. Theo jerked his chin at it.

Jaime murmured. "Yeah, I noticed."

"Think it will turn into something else?" Tess said. "A butterfly? A moth?"

Theo shrugged, a frown tugging his features down. He hated not knowing things. Lately, it had been happening all too often.

They hopped another train over to Astoria. During the ride, Theo tried hard not to look at the Guildman or the caterpillar or especially the other passengers, blissfully bouncing along as if nothing in the world had changed, though so much already had.

Finally, they arrived at their station. They walked the rest of the way to Aunt Esther's modest house, now Theo's and Tess's as well. The twins' aunt Esther was a small, sturdy woman of indiscriminate age who had worked every kind of job and traveled all around the globe amassing the unusual items that decorated her home. And her home was as unique as she was. Jaime perked up when they entered, delighted by all the masks and the weird puppets and the plants and the tiny mechanical spiders that kept those plants pruned and watered. As much as it had pained them to move from 354 W. 73rd Street to Queens, Theo had to admit Aunt Esther's house was pretty cool. And so was Aunt Esther.

"Ah, you're back," Aunt Esther said, as they piled through the door. "Luckily, I have just plated some Fig Newtons."

Nine meowed plaintively.

"Stop complaining," said Aunt Esther. "You know I have treats for you, too, Nine Eighty-Seven."

"About that . . . ," said Tess.

"The treats? They are one hundred percent organic. I get them from a small shop in Kansas. I do miss Kansas. Did I tell you about the time I worked as a wheat thresher? One does enjoy a good threshing."

"No, I was talking about Nine's name," said Tess.

"A perfectly suitable name," said Aunt Esther briskly, setting the plate of cookies on the dining room table. She had to shoo several silver spiders away, and they giggled as they scooted from the tabletop and scattered on the floor. Nine pawed at them, and they giggled some more.

"Did you name Nine?" Jaime asked, already on his second cookie.

"Me? Oh no. She already had a name when I picked her up," Aunt Esther said. She held up a pitcher. "Lemonade?"

"Yes, thank you," said Jaime. "So who named her?"

"Why, I'm not sure," said Aunt Esther. "Perhaps she named herself."

Theo tried not to roll his eyes, failed.

"I see you and your cynical eyeballs, Theodore," Aunt Esther said, plunking a glass of lemonade in front of him. "They're going to get stuck that way."

"No, they won't," said Theo.

"They *could*," said Aunt Esther. "Stranger things have happened, as you well know." She reached into her pocket, pulled out a small, fish-shaped treat. She tossed it to Nine, who caught it in her mouth. "Cats have a very strong sense of self. Have you ever noticed that when their people name them things the cats don't approve of, they refuse to respond? What kind of creature with any dignity would answer to Floofykins or Boo Boo?"

Jaime took a long sip of lemonade, swallowed. "I don't know, I'm kind of partial to Boo Boo."

"Boo Boo?" said Theo.

"Perhaps you're right. Something banal like Mittens or Patches would be much worse." Aunt Esther shivered, as if the thought of banality were perfectly dreadful.

"If you didn't name her, where did you get her?" Theo asked.

"I answered an ad in the paper. A nice young woman uptown. Very nice. She had kittens and puppies and some other animals that were more difficult to identify, including a few chimera. The number has been disconnected since, though. I called again because I wanted one of her puppies. Looked like wolves with absolutely enormous feet. No telling how big they'd get." She smiled brightly, as if the thought of ginormous puppies were as delightful as the thought of banal cat names was awful.

"So the ad just said something about pets?" Theo asked.

"No, of course not," said Aunt Esther.

"Of course not," said Jaime, one side of his mouth quirking up.

"The ad said, 'Esther, we have what you've been looking for,' with a phone number. So I called."

Tess dropped the cookie she'd been holding. "Wait, the ad had *your* name in it?"

"Why wouldn't it? I'm quite well-known about the city."

Theo and Jaime exchanged glances. Theo said, "But Aunt Esther, how—"

"It certainly wasn't the first personal ad I've ever read directed at me. I met my second husband through the personal ads. He was a trapeze artist. Very flexible joints." Aunt Esther looked at the plate. "Oh, dear. You are all quite the ravenous monsters, aren't you? I'll get you more Fig Newtons. It's a good thing I purchase in bulk." She swept from the room, leaving them with an empty plate and more questions than answers.

CHAPTER THREE
Jaime

The twins' aunt brought two more plates full of cookies and more cryptic answers to their questions about Nine, her name, and where she came from. No, Aunt Esther said, she didn't remember much about the place she picked her up except that it was clean, or remember much about the young woman with the overlarge animals except that she and the animals were clean as well. Cleanliness, said Aunt Esther, was a virtue. Along with curiosity, tenacity, and punctuality. Her third husband wasn't punctual, and that, she said, was the end of that. Tess reminded her that technically she'd never been married, but Aunt Esther waved this off.

Jaime wondered aloud if being concerned with

technicalities was a virtue or a vice and earned a smile and several more cookies.

Even though talking with the twins' aunt was frustrating, it was also fascinating to Jaime. Aunt Esther was like a character from a novel. Someone ageless and magical like Dumbledore or Gandalf or Galadriel, someone who had lived so many lives that sometimes they got the details mixed up. Or rather, chose very carefully which details they wanted to reveal, because they had learned the hard way to trust no one.

Trust no one. The thought flared in Jaime's head as he and the twins finished their snack and headed for the attic room, where many of Benjamin Adler's notebooks were crammed in boxes. The letter that had started it all, the letter that had been sent to the twins' grandpa Ben and intercepted by Tess had had the words TRUST NO ONE scripted on the envelope. And they hadn't trusted anyone with their discovery of the shadow cipher—until Edgar Wellington. Jaime could still feel the Atlantic Tunnel vibrating under his feet, still see the mandibles of the giant metal machine punching through the wall, smell the dust in the air, feel the horror as the machine mowed Edgar Wellington down mere moments after he had betrayed them. The fact that Edgar had lived, the fact that he didn't seem to remember that day in the tunnel or the days preceding it, the fact that he'd visited the twins and chattered at them as if nothing had ever happened didn't lessen the strangeness of it, the dread that sometimes backed up in Jaime's throat, that woke him up in the dead of night.

Jaime shook the thoughts from his head and tried to focus on what Tess was saying.

"Grandpa kept a lot of notes on the Morningstarrs' associates and guests in this notebook, though I'm sure it's not a complete list. And sometimes there are just descriptions of people instead of their names." She dug around in a box and pulled out several leather-bound journals. "I wish they'd had cameras back in the day. Maybe we would have had a picture of someone wearing the dress."

They each took a journal and started combing through the pages. Some names scrawled in Benjamin Adler's tiny, crabbed script were familiar. Eliza Hamilton. Edgar Allan Poe. Charles Dickens. Other names weren't familiar at all, and they had to look them up on the twins' computer or Jaime's phone. Still other people were described by what they did.

"'According to the *Sun*, a lady cellist, apparently quite talented, played in the drawing room after dinner, September 18, 1849,'" read Jaime. "'Unusual for the time because the way the cello had to be held was considered inappropriate for ladies.'"

"What *wasn't* considered inappropriate for ladies?" Tess said sourly.

Jaime used his phone to search for female cellists of the nineteenth century and found a Portuguese cellist named Guilhermina Suggia, but she was born in 1885, too late to have been a guest or a friend of the Morningstarrs. He also found a French cellist named Lisa Cristiani, who was born in 1827 and died of cholera in 1853.

"She toured all over Europe and Russia. Mendelssohn wrote the 'Song without Words' opus 109 for her because he was so impressed by her playing. But I can't find any information about her being in New York City or even in the US."

"I'll write her name down anyway," Tess said.

They kept reading. Jaime found a mention of a lady pirate. He used his phone for another search and found the story of one Sadie Farrell, aka Sadie the Goat, who had earned her nickname because she would head-butt her marks in the stomach before robbing them. She lived in New York City until another woman, Gallus Mag, allegedly over six feet tall, bit off Sadie's ear. Sadie stole a sloop in the spring of 1869 and raided houses along the Hudson and Harlem Rivers.

"Oh, and occasionally, she kidnapped people," Jaime said. "But I'm not sure if she's a real person or just a legend."

"Plus," said Tess, "would a lady pirate wear a silk gown?"

"Maybe she would if she was visiting the Morning-starrs," Theo said.

"I have a feeling the Morningstarrs weren't that concerned with what was appropriate for ladies," Tess said.

They kept scouring the notes, looking for any other mentions of women. They found lady chemists and lady writers and lady blacksmiths and lady poets and lady socialites—sometimes with names, sometimes without, as before. When there wasn't a name, Jaime and Theo continued to do a little research to figure out some likely suspects. Tess dutifully wrote down all the names, as did Jaime, in his sketchbook.

After a while, they had a long list of names, but didn't seem any closer to figuring out the provenance of the dress. Any one of the women on their list could have owned it. Or none of them.

"The heart on the lace has to be some kind of clue," said Tess.

"Or maybe it's just decoration?"

"It's the only decoration on the dress."

"We didn't examine the whole dress, though," Jaime pointed out. "For all we know, there's something hidden in the fabric or sewed into the hem or something."

"Great. So now we have to break into a dry-cleaning shop," said Theo.

Jaime checked the time on his phone, stood, stretched. "We don't have to break into anything because I have to go back to Hoboken or Mima will kill me." He couldn't bring himself to use the word *home*.

Tess tossed the journal she'd been reading aside and stood, too. "Okay. Maybe we can take this up again tomorrow? Want us to come to you this time?"

The twins still hadn't seen Jaime's new apartment, but Jaime wasn't ready for that. "Your grandpa's notes are all here. It's not like I'm going to ask you to drag them all the way out to New Jersey."

Tess bit her lip, but didn't say anything. At the door, she gave Jaime a hug. Nine gently nibbled at his fingertips, as if he were the one who needed comfort.

"Be careful," Tess said, as he put his hand on the knob.

"You sound like my grandmother," Jaime said.

"I'm going to take that as a compliment."

Jaime texted his grandmother to tell her he was on his

way home. Then, he took the Underway back to Grand Central Station in Manhattan, but instead of hopping another downtown train, he did what he'd been doing more and more of lately: He walked. There had been days during which Jaime walked for hours and hours, taking in as much of the city as he could. Ever since 354 W. 73rd Street had come down—ever since they had brought it down—every single store and monument and building seemed fragile somehow, too easily razed, too easily broken. He'd sit on a bench in Washington Square Park or under the cover of a bus stop or on the stoop of a pizza shop, penciling the buildings in his sketchbook. Then he'd go home and ink them, trying to make them all feel real again, whole again, impervious to every-thing and everyone, the people who meant to do ill and the ones who meant do well, because, sometimes, the result was the same.

Today, he walked all the way from Grand Central Station down to Broadway and Liberty Street. He sat on a bench and stared up at the Morningstarr Tower, once the tallest building in Manhattan. Not too long ago, you could tour the building. Ride one of the ever-shifting escalators. See the writing desk of Theresa Morning-starr, the portrait of a scowling Theodore Morningstarr hanging over one of the grand fireplaces. Take an elevator all the way to the top of the tower, look out upon the whole of the city, the blue-gray water all around. Jaime opened his sketchbook and drew the elegant lines of the building, the Underway tracks spiraling up the tower.

He did not draw the fences around the building. The caution tape. The CLOSED UNTIL FURTHER NOTICE signs. The name SLANT plastered everywhere.

He sketched until his hand ached and his stomach rumbled for dinner. So he put his sketchbook away. Instead of taking the PATH train, he walked back up to 39th Street, where he could catch the ferry. He bought his ticket and joined the crowds of commuters piling onto the boat. Instead of taking a seat inside, he wound his way through the throngs of people and found a place for himself outside along the guardrails. He didn't mind the wind; he didn't mind the fine spray. Despite the late hour, the air was still warm, the evening sky bright with the light of the silvery moon. When he leaned over the railing and looked closely, the water below was alive with darting silvery fish. The moon and the water and the fish soothed him, reminded him of the good things in the world, the city they were trying to save, even if the city didn't know it needed saving.

In the distance, the ferry slips hunkered under a huge sign that said ERIE-LACKAWANNA. The boat slowed as it approached the slip, finally docking to disgorge its passengers. Jaime had to walk only a few minutes to get to his apartment, in a brand-new building with views of the Manhattan skyline.

Jaime hated it. Hated the white walls and the spotless carpets and the windows so clear that birds sometimes flew right into them. He hated the blare of the giant televisions coming from the enormous gym downstairs, the helpful security guards, the happy children running through the hallways. He had never once swum in the rooftop pool no matter how hot it got, refused to even get a muffin at the shop on the ground floor. Mima said he was being ridiculous, but Jaime knew she didn't like the place any better than he did. She was, however, much better at making the best of things.

Jaime got on the perfectly normal elevator that traveled only up and down, and punched the perfectly normal-looking button, and grumbled to himself as he did. The elevator door was about to close, when he heard a high voice pipe, "EXCUSE ME, PLEASE."

Jaime put a hand between the closing doors, and they opened to reveal a small girl, about six, on a blue tricycle. The girl had light brown skin and high pigtails that stuck up like antennae. She was wearing a knee-length white smock splattered with neon paint, black leggings printed with tiny dinosaurs, and red rubber galoshes. A large raccoon-cat sat in the basket of the tricycle, brandishing a cheese curl.

"*Cricket?*" Jaime said.

"Who else would it be?" Cricket said, pedaling the tricycle onto the elevator.

"What are you doing here?"

"What are *you* doing here?" said Cricket.

"I live here," Jaime said.

"No, *I* live here."

"Since when?"

Cricket dug around underneath Karl, causing him to chitter in protest. She pulled out a large watch and consulted it. "Since a hundred minutes ago."

"A little over an hour?"

She scowled. "A hundred minutes."

"Okay, but—"

"Eleventh floor, please," Cricket said, jamming the watch back under Karl, who squawked.

"That's my floor!" Jaime said.

"No," Cricket said, "it's mine."

Jaime pressed "11" again, and the doors closed.

"Well, maybe it's both of ours."

Cricket thought about this for a second. Then she said, "It's mine, but I'll let you live there."

Jaime couldn't help it, he laughed. Cricket's scowl deepened, and he laughed again.

"I'm not laughing at you. I just think you're funny."

Cricket shook her head. "I'm not funny. I am very serious. For example, I have been exploring this building and it's all wrong. It's PECULIAR."

Even though Jaime, too, thought it was all wrong and also PECULIAR, he asked, "What's wrong with it?"

"Way too white and shiny," she said.

"You might be right about that."

Cricket cut her eyes to him. "I painted my bedroom walls with pictures of aliens and flowers and pizza. It's much better now, but my mom didn't think so. She BURST INTO HYSTERICS."

Jaime swallowed hard. His own mother had died when he was very young, and he would give anything to have her here, bursting into hysterics over something he'd done. "Some moms do that, I guess."

"Hmmph," said Cricket. "And I don't like all the wiggle worms."

"The what?"

"The wiggle worms. Haven't you seen them?"

Jaime didn't have a clue what she was talking about. "No. But I'm glad to see *you*."

Now she narrowed her eyes, peering at him with suspicion.

"I really am."

Her face relaxed a little. "I'm glad I'm not living with Cranky Cousin Gordon in Bayonne, New Jersey, anymore. His whole house smells like nachos. He doesn't even eat nachos. That doesn't make sense and I don't like NONSENSICAL things."

There was a sharp *ding!* and the elevator doors opened. Cricket pedaled out into the hallway. Before reaching the end of the hallway, she turned. In a quiet voice she added, "I'm glad to see your famous hair." Then she disappeared around the corner.

Jaime smiled to himself as he unlocked the door of the new apartment, heartened to find someone familiar in the building, even if it was an extremely cranky six-year-old who didn't enjoy being nice to people unless she was guilted into it, and who really should have been getting ready for bed. As soon as he opened the door, the scent of pork, onions, and peppers filled his nose. A pile of fried plantains sat on a plate next to the stove. His stomach grumbled loudly in response.

"Ah, there's my hungry boy, just in time," said Mima.

"I think your belly has a sixth sense." She was still wearing her white coveralls that said THE HANDY WOMAN on the back.

"Busy day?" said Jaime, as Mima spooned healthy portions of pork and vegetables onto a plate and set the plate on the counter for him.

"There are a lot of bungling maintenance men in this tiny little city. How these bungling men still have jobs, I don't know. People like to give bungling men a lot of chances. My parents would tell me that these men have families, they have to have work! As if women don't have families."

Jaime's grandmother, who he called Mima because she had raised him as if she were his mother, wasn't like some of the more traditional people in her large Cuban family, uncles and aunts and cousins who'd told Mima that managing a building was beneath her, and repair work was even worse. "Great-Aunt Sylvia said, 'Manual labor should be left to men. Otherwise, why would they call it *man*-ual?' Can you believe that?" Mima coughed in disgust. "Anyway, I have enough work to last me till next year. Jaime, why aren't you eating? It's going to get cold!"

Jaime tucked into the pork, which melted in this mouth. No matter what she made—traditional Cuban dishes or a just a plain old bugburger—it was always delicious. "I think your fingers have brains in them," Jaime said, "because they make the most incredible things."

"My brains are in my brains, silly boy," said Mima, smiling. She spooned out some food for herself and sat next to him at the counter.

"You won't believe who I just saw," said Jaime.

"Cricket and Karl," said Mima.

Jaime stopped shoveling his food for a moment. "How did you know?"

"The brains in my brains?" said Mima. "I helped the Morans get an apartment here."

"You did?"

"Of course I did. A lot of people didn't have a place to go after, well . . . after," said Mima, taking a delicate bite.

"That's nice of you," said Jaime.

"You don't mean that," said Mima.

"Yes, I do!"

"You don't like this place."

Jaime put a bite of food in his mouth, chewed, swallowed. "Do *you* like it?"

"Once we get it painted . . . ," Mima began, but didn't finish the thought. Their apartment, with its large windows and white walls and huge rooms and two sparkling bathrooms, was spacious and new and terrible, which was why Mima spent most of her time driving around town, doing repair work for everyone else in Hoboken. Sometimes, she called it Broboken, on account of all the bumbling old repairmen and the roving bands of cocky young men who pushed and shoved their way onto the trains and the ferry every morning. She couldn't stand to be here, either.

But that didn't mean either of them wanted to talk about it.

After dinner, Jaime helped his grandmother clean up the dishes and then went to his room. Like all the other rooms in the apartment, his room was large, with a giant window facing Manhattan. He pulled out his sketchbook and sat down at his desk. He leafed through the pages, examining the drawing he'd made of the dress in Thomas Jennings's shop, the featureless oval in place of the face, the list of women who could have owned the dress, the sketch of the Morningstarr Tower. He pulled another sketchbook from the packed shelf along the wall. Unlike his other sketchbooks, this book was filled with drawings of the same character. Page after page showed a beautiful brown-skinned woman wearing different costumes: a blue unitard with high red boots; green camouflage cargo pants and a matching green

T-shirt; a flat, gold breastplate, thigh and shin guards, a helmet with little wings on it. In some, she carried a sword, in others, she carried a staff, in still others, she had a belt studded with ninja stars.

None of them were right.

Yet.

He turned back to the sketch of the plain dark dress from the Jennings shop. Maybe he would try a simple costume this time. Something old and timeless that wouldn't compete with the woman wearing it.

Jaime turned to a new white page, licked the tip of his pencil. With the view of the city he loved filling the window in front of him, he tried, once again, to conjure a superhero to help him save it.

CHAPTER FOUR

Duke

Five miles away from Jaime's Hoboken apartment, in a glass tower in Manhattan, a tall, pale man with a vague resemblance to a smug turtle leaned back in a leather chair, his feet up on his huge mahogany desk. The man's name was Jackson "Duke" Goodson, and he was having a good day.

First, he was having a good day because he wearing a brand-new hat. It was, like all his other hats, a cowboy hat—this one a soft, mushroom-y beige with a brown leather band. When he'd walked into the office that morning, his secretary, Candi, said, "Good morning, sir! Love the hat!" She said it every morning about every hat, but he never got tired of it. He was quite well-known for his cowboy hats. In any one of the newspaper profiles written on Duke Goodson—and there were many—you could always find a line that went something like: "Duke Goodson was easy to spot in the crowd due to his trademark cowboy hat," or, "Goodson, clad in one of his customary hats, is a good son of the South, born and raised in Oklahoma." That his real name wasn't Jackson "Duke" Goodson, that he hadn't grown up anywhere near Oklahoma, that he just wore the hats to distract from his four-thousand-dollar Italian suits, well, that just made the profiles all the more enjoyable to read.

He was just starting the latest profile when his fancy new cell phone erupted with the song "All My Exes Live in Texas." He took his feet off the desk, scooped up the phone, clicked the green button.

"Goodson here," he barked.

"Sir, we're having a little trouble getting Mrs. Chopra to sign the—"

"If I don't have those papers on my desk tomorrow morning, signed and notarized, you're fired. Understand that will be the least of your problems. And your family's." He clicked off the phone.

Sometimes his people needed a little encouragement, and he was all too happy to provide it.

He went back to his newspaper. He didn't have to read

the profile to know what it said, though he read it anyway. The writers of the newspaper profiles would always
mention Duke Goodson's hats, but then they moved
on to what Duke Goodson actually did to deserve all
this attention (and it wasn't wearing hats). Duke Goodson was a fixer. When rich and powerful people had a
problem, they called Duke Goodson to fix it. Has your
wayward teenage son taken up burglary out of boredom
and ended up in jail and, worse, in the papers? Call
Duke. Need a loan for your brand-new casino but the
banks don't want to give you the cash? Call Duke. Want
to be mayor or senator or governor or dogcatcher but
everyone including your own spouse hates your guts?
Call Duke. And, true to his (false) name, Duke was
very good at fixing things. So good, in fact, that Duke
Goodson was nearly as rich and powerful as his clients.
Something the writers never failed to mention, too.

The headline of this article was "The Fixer's Fixer."

Not bad for a good ol' boy from the South. He would
have giggled, except he wouldn't be caught dead giggling.

The phone sang about exes in Texas again. He picked
it up and said, "Well?"

"It's done," said a voice on the other end of the call.

"Better be," said Goodson, and rang off. Goodson
tossed the phone to the desk, one side of his mouth

yanked into a satisfied smirk. And here was the second reason he was having a good day: He had finally wrapped up some loose ends on the 354 W. 73rd Street project. Loose ends by the names of Mr. Stoop and Mr. Pinscher. Not their real names either, but it didn't matter. Stoop and Pinscher were much worse at concealing themselves than Duke Goodson was. Much, *much* worse. After they'd been released by the police, Stoop and Pinscher had disappeared. It took a few weeks of searching, but he'd found the two of them holed up in a motel in some Podunk town in the middle of an Illinois cornfield. Pinscher had even gotten a job at the local gas station in order to keep himself and his stooped friend in bugburgers and Pop-Tarts. Wrappers everywhere in that motel room. It was disgusting. Also disgusting: Pinscher blaming his and Stoop's failures on a bunch of kids. Stoop tearing up over his dead mutant pet as if it had been a golden retriever instead of a scuttling scrap of trash grown in a lab.

Useless, the two of them. Like blundering minions in a comic book.

So Duke did what one does with useless, blundering minions. He had Stoop and Pinscher dispatched to an outpost in Siberia. Duke knew lots of fine folks there. Hardy fellows, Siberians. Didn't take any guff. Not that

Stoop and Pinscher were in any condition to give any guff.

It was sad, really.

Ha, no, it wasn't.

Goodson pushed the newspaper and the phone aside, pulled out a file labeled Morningstarr, made some notes. The third reason Duke Goodson was having a good day was because he'd grown curious about the kids who had allegedly gotten in Stoop and Pinscher's way. Not curious because he actually believed Pinscher, but curious because he believed in being thorough. (How could mere children get in the way of grown, competent adults? They can't! They're children! Small, hungry, silly, helpless, overrated things, children. Duke didn't understand why anyone would have them. He himself had never been a child, even when he was a child.)

Though the children weren't interesting in and of themselves, Duke had discovered that they did have rather intriguing relatives. Two of them were the offspring of a New York City detective and the grandchildren of one Benjamin Adler, and the third child was the son of an engineer *and* the grandson of the former manager of 354 W. 73rd Street. Duke imagined that that police detective knew quite a bit about the Old York Cipher, maybe her father had even given her a clue or two before he lost his mind to dementia. And Duke imagined that the former building manager knew quite a bit about the building she'd managed for half her life. Including its secrets. Well, if it had had any secrets—which Duke wasn't sure it did, but his client was sure—and his client was the one paying. Who was Duke Goodson to argue with a man willing to pay through the nose for a little information? So information Duke's client would get. No matter what Duke Goodson had to do to get it.

He might start small, or rather, big: with that cat. Can't have an oversized feline like that just wandering around the city, free as you please. Eating Stoop's lab-grown monster was one thing, but *people* could surely be harmed by such an unnatural creature. That really would be too bad. (Well, depending on the person.) Besides, Duke had some ideas for that cat.

"Candi!" Duke shouted.

His gorgeous blond assistant appeared in the doorway. Like all his girls, she was a former cheerleader, all red lipstick and lean muscle. "Yes, sir?"

"I might have a job for you later."

"Anything you need, sir."

"Right now, I need my nap. Hold my calls for twenty minutes," Duke told her, tossing her the cell phone.

She caught it with one hand, slipped it into the pocket of her red dress. "Certainly, sir. Shall I close the door?"

"Yes, thank you, Candi."

Once the door was closed, Duke Goodson leaned back in his chair, put his feet back up on the desk, and tipped his new hat so that the brim shaded his eyes against the fluorescent lights. As he did right before every nap, he let his mind roam over the accomplishments of the day. The hat, the blundering minions squared away in Siberia, his delicious plans for some pesky, squirming children and their various pets and relatives. The delight on Darnell's face when Duke cleaned up this whole silly situation, the bonus added to Duke's Swiss bank account.

Duke's last thought before he fell asleep: What the reporters never put in their profiles about him, what they never figured out, was his *real* specialty, his true talent, the motto he lived by.

In order to fix things, you first had to break them.

CHAPTER FIVE

Tess

For the next few days, Tess, Jaime, and Theo assembled names for their list of possible owners of the Jennings dress. Tess was as eager to figure out the mystery of the black gown as she'd been every other aspect of the Old York Cipher, and her mind churned with questions. Whose gown could it be? Did it belong to Eliza Hamilton (who mourned her husband for fifty years)? Or to someone like Anna Ottendorfer (a widow-turned-owner of a mid-nineteenth-century German-language newspaper in New York)? Or maybe it belonged to the elusive Ava Oneal (a puzzle of a whole different kind)?

But as eager as Tess was during the day, her nights were different. Ever since she began reading about the people of New York whose lives were wrapped up in the mystery of the Morningstarrs, Tess's sleep—when she could actually sleep—was fitful and filled with monsters.

Sometimes the monsters took recognizable shapes. Tess floated alone in a vast ocean, the water cold and inky, as a fin raced toward her. Tess careened down a city street, as a Komodo dragon the size of a truck sprinted behind. Tess tiptoed around the hallways of 354 W. 73rd Street, Mr. Stoop and Mr. Pinscher lurking around every corner. Tess was strapped to a chair while Darnell Slant ranted about progress from a TV and the walls of her home collapsed around her.

And sometimes there were no monsters in her dreams, and that was worse. She dreamed it was 1851 and she was waiting with Elizabeth Blackwell, the first woman doctor in America. Dr. Blackwell had put out a sign at her office in Manhattan, advertising her services as a physician, but even women were too angry and afraid to see a woman doctor. In the dream, Tess kept asking what was wrong with a girl being a doctor? Why was everyone so angry? What was everyone so afraid of? But no one had any answers.

And then it was 1793, before the time of the Morningstarrs, and she was sitting with black and white and brown orphans in the home of Catherine "Katy" Ferguson, who had invited the orphans inside for lessons in life and scripture. The daughter of an enslaved woman, Katy herself never learned to read or write, but she remembered what her mother had taught her about the Bible when she was little and wanted to pass on this knowledge. Tess asked her who had stolen her mother from her homeland, who had enslaved her, who had kept Katy from learning to read, who was keeping her from her mother in Virginia, but Katy kept shaking her head. There was no single monster, Katy said. Or too many monsters to count, which amounted to the same thing.

The very worst nightmare: Tess watching in horror from her bed while the bruise-colored shadows coalesced into a creature vaguely human-shaped but something both more and less human. The monster blocked her doorway, her only escape, filling the space, hulking there, waiting for her to make a move. Tess told herself it was nothing, she was imagining things, she was only dreaming; but the monster told her that she was awake and utterly alone, that everyone else in the world was gone, that it been saving her for last. It was patient, it been around forever, it was made of lies and deception, rage and resentment, bitterness and oblivion, and it would wait as long as it took. It would wait her out. And it would win, because it always did.

When she had this last, worst nightmare, Nine would climb up into her bed and nibble on her fingers and lick her face until she woke with a shudder. Then Tess would hold on to the Cat as if Nine were a buoy in a storm-tossed sea all the way till the morning.

"Well, you look perfectly terrible," Tess's mother said, when Tess shuffled into the kitchen after hours of tossing and turning. "Nightmares again?"

"Probably," said Tess, grabbing a cereal bowl from the cabinet. "I don't always remember."

"Do you want to talk about it?"

"I'm fine." Tess plunked the bowl on the table and filled it with cereal, though she wasn't that hungry. "Still thinking about 354 West 73rd is all."

"That's understandable," her mother said. "We all are." Her mother's tone was neutral, but her eyes were shrouded with worry.

With the sun coming through the windows burnishing her mother's face, the terror of the nightmares faded a little. Tess began to feel foolish that she'd been so scared. She had her mom; she had her dad and brother and Aunt Esther. She wasn't alone. "It's okay, Mom. I'll keep trying my meditations. And Nine helps a lot."

At this, her mother smiled and glanced down at Nine. "I'm glad you have her."

"I'm glad *we* have her," said Tess. Nine mrrowed, brushed up against Tess's legs, then wound herself around Tess's mom's, getting fur on Miriam Bieder-mann's suit pants.

"Is Dad already at the office?"

"Yep," said her mother. "He needs to prep for the new school year."

Tess's dad was a school social worker, and he took the "worker" part as seriously as Tess's mom did. "He's there already? It's not even seven o'clock!"

"He's got a lot of kids to take care of. You know him."

"And you're going to work early today, too?" Tess asked.

"Have to. New partner," said her mother, grimacing.

"Really? What happened to Syd?" Tess had liked her mom's old partner, a man with silver hair but the big biceps of a body builder.

"The stress and the tedium finally got to him. He's quitting to become a park ranger."

"Seriously?"

"Seriously," said her mother. "He said that he'd rather deal with bears stealing food from campers than with the police brass. No idea how this new guy is going to work out. He's really green. Just out of uniform."

Tess took spoonful of cereal, chewed. "Is it hard to be a cop, Mom?"

Her mother poured herself more coffee and sat down at the table with Tess. "It's hard, but probably not for the reasons you're thinking. Not that many people know this, but when the police department was created in the 1830s, it was to protect rich people and rich people's stuff. That usually meant rich *white* people and their stuff. And even though 1830 sounds like a long time ago, it's really not. Hard to shake that legacy. Hard to get some people to trust me when I say I want to help them find the things they've lost, the things that have been stolen from them. Why should they believe me?"

"Because you *are* trying to help?"

"Sometimes, that's not enough," her mom said. Then she suddenly laughed. "Wow, I sound grumpy. Maybe I should join Syd and the bears."

"Sounds like a band name," Tess said.

Theo shambled into the kitchen, yawning. "What sounds like a band name?"

Tess ate another spoonful of cereal. "Syd and the Bears."

"What kind of band name is that?" said Theo, grabbing the cereal box and pouring himself a bowl.

"Maybe it does need a little more oomph," their mother agreed. "Syd and the Felonious Bears."

Theo splashed milk all over his cereal and a little on the floor. Nine moved in to lap it up. "I like 'The Felonious Bears.' No Syd."

"What have you got against Syd?" said Tess.

"Who's this Syd, anyway?" Theo said.

"Mom's old partner, remember? But she's getting a new one today."

"Let me guess: a felonious bear?"

Their mom ruffled his bushy hair. "You're the felonious bear."

An hour later, Tess and Theo had finished their breakfasts and showers, and their mom had left. While they waited for Jaime to arrive, they consulted their list of possible owners of the Jennings gown—society wives, writers, poets, musicians, daughters, pirates, thieves, actresses, educators, mathematicians, scientists.

It was a very long list.

Theo said, "Mom might be right about the felonious bear thing, because if we don't narrow this list down, we're not going to have a choice but to break into the dry-cleaning shop and steal that dress to see if there's anything hidden in it." Theo dug around in his hair as if there were something hidden in *there*. "Maybe the dress isn't a clue at all."

"Has to be. The ticket numbers matched up," Tess said. She combed through the list of names, but the dress could have belonged to any of them and none of them. "Okay, so the only embellishment on the gown was that lace with the little hearts."

"Uh-huh," said Theo, who didn't care about lace or hearts.

"Maybe it means something."

"What does?"

"The hearts."

"As in, we should have counted the hearts? Maybe the number of symbols is important."

When Jaime finally arrived, he used his phone to send the photos of the dress to the twins' computer. They blew up the images on the screen. They counted the number of hearts on the lace and got one hundred and eleven.

"Doesn't mean anything to me," said Theo.

"Me, neither," Jaime said.

Theo continued to root around in his shaggy hair, scratched. "I don't think the lace is important. It's just lace. Lace is lace."

"Like I said the other day, there's got to be something else hidden in that gown. In the hem or the undercoat or whatever you call what goes under these old-fashioned dresses," Jaime said.

But something was itching at Tess's nightmare-exhausted brain. She'd been so scared during the night, and even in the morning. But then she saw the sun on her mother's face. And felt . . . love.

Maybe the gown wasn't important, the number of symbols wasn't important, but the symbol itself was.

Hearts. Love. Hearts. Love.

"Love!" she said. "Love is the thing!"

"Okay," said Jaime, looking at Tess as if she'd grown another nose.

"No, you don't understand. The heart means love."

"We're aware of the symbolism, Tess," said Theo. "We all got the same Valentine's cards in the first grade."

"The only Valentine's Day cards you got were from Mom and me," Tess retorted. "I'm saying that what's important is the symbol of love on the lace. Love on the lace, love on the lace." Her eyes went wide. "Lovelace! *Ada* Lovelace!"

Jaime frowned. "Ada Lovelace? I don't remember that name on our list."

"She's the daughter of Lord Byron, the poet. She was

a mathematician. Studied computers in the 1840s."

"I thought that the Morningstarrs were the only ones working on computers and robots and that kind of thing," Jaime said.

"No, said Theo. "A guy named Charles Babbage was working on them, too. Ada Lovelace worked with him."

"And she was ignored for a long time. A lot of people said she was delusional," said Tess.

"Huh," said Theo.

Tess's excitement illuminated the foggy corners of her mind, brightening everything. "What do you want to bet she corresponded with the Morningstarrs? She must have. They were building machines unlike anyone else. Maybe she even came to New York City."

"I've never read anything about that," said Theo.

"Doesn't mean it didn't happen," Tess insisted. "We don't know everything about the Morningstarrs."

"That's my point," said Theo. By his expression, however, Tess knew he believed she was onto something.

"Let's do some searches on Ada and see if there's any mention of her being in New York City."

They spent a couple of hours searching both the web and Grandpa Ben's notebooks, but didn't find any evidence that Ada Lovelace had ever come to New York

City or any indication that there was correspondence with the Morningstarrs. Theo wanted to risk a call to the Cipherist Society to ask them, but Tess didn't.

"Remember what happened the last time?" she said.

"Okay, but—"

"I don't want to ask for help unless we absolutely have to," Tess said. "I don't want anyone else hurt or . . ." She trailed off.

"We get it," Jaime said, giving her shoulder a friendly bump. "We don't want anyone else to get hurt, either. But if Ada Lovelace never came to New York City and never wrote to Theodore or Theresa, or if she did and we can't find the evidence, then where are we going to look for the next clue?"

They surveyed the piles of notebooks and reams of notes they'd taken in silence for a moment. Then Theo said, "Well, there are a lot of Ada Lovelace's writings where she discussed the potential of Charles Babbage's Analytical Engine."

"A computer?" Jaime asked.

"Yeah, early one," Theo said. "He was developing the Analytical Engine around the same time that the Morningstarrs were building their machines, though the Morningstarrs' work was much more advanced. But maybe *he* came to New York? Maybe he wrote the Morningstarrs?"

They spent another hour combing the notebooks and the web for Charles Babbage and his various engines in New York City. They found out that Babbage had made some discoveries in cryptography, breaking something called the Vigenère cipher, that he was a sought-after dinner guest because he was such a good storyteller—it even said he'd met Ada Lovelace at one of his own parties.

"I can't find anything that says he came to New York City, though," said Theo.

Jaime, who had been scrolling through his phone, suddenly looked up. "Maybe Ada or Charles never came to New York City, but some of their letters did."

"What letters?" said Tess. "Where are they?"

"My favorite place. Well, my favorite place besides the comic-book store."

"Your grandmother's kitchen?"

"Okay, my third favorite place."

"Where?"

"Where all the best mysteries are. The New York Public Library."

CHAPTER SIX
Theo

To get to the main branch of the library, Theo, Tess, and Jaime took the 7 train, and walked the rest of the way. The day was hot and humid, so by the time they arrived at the library steps, they were eager to get into the cool air inside the building. Still, they stopped to admire Patience and Fortitude, the stone lions that decorated the entrance of the library. As Jaime did a quick sketch of Patience, and Nine imitated the lion's posture, Tess said, "Wouldn't it be amazing if the lions were Morningstarr Machines, too?"

"The Morningstarrs didn't build Machines that looked like mammals," said Theo.

"I sometimes wish they had," said Tess. "No one would mess with those lions."

Theo said, "If you believe the rumors, the library doesn't need lions for protection."

Though the building itself had been built long after the time of the Morningstarrs, it was said that Morningstarr Machines roamed the library at night. What *kind* of machines, no one could say. Once, a man had hidden in a bathroom after closing time and tried to steal a map from one of the collections. Two days later, the police found the map in its proper place in the collection and the would-be thief locked in a maintenance closet in a Bug's Burgers on Staten Island. All the man would say about his time in the library was "So shiny. So, so shiny."

But the only thing that was shining right now was the sun. Theo scratched at his head, where the sweat trickled in his thick, bushy hair. "Can we go inside now?"

"Why? Are you losing Patience?" Tess said.

Jaime tucked his sketchbook into his pocket, looked Theo over. "Definitely a loss of Fortitude."

"You're both dorks," said Theo, and charged up the steps, nearly running over a pale, blond woman in a red dress and matching shoes who swerved into his path. She tossed a dirty look over her shoulder, then pushed through the library doors.

Theo still heard her candy-apple heels click-clacking

on the stone as they entered the cool cave of the library. Light poured down from the high windows over the doors and washed the cream-colored walls and floors in gold. Huge archways led into grand staircases. As much as he loved the archives of the Old York Cipherist Society, Theo loved the library even more. Not only had Grandpa Ben and Grandma Annie taken him to the library when he and Tess were small, his parents had, too. It even smelled like home to him.

Jaime said, "Okay, we have to find the Pforzheimer Collection. I think it's on the third floor. There should be letters to Babbage from Ada. Did you know that her real name was Ada King, Countess of Lovelace?"

"Ha! The Countess of Lovelace. The *Countess*! Get it?" Theo said. "She was a mathematician!"

"Wait, who's the dork now?" said Tess.

"Just because you don't have a sense of humor," Theo said.

They climbed the steps to the third floor and approached the information desk. The librarian was a youngish woman with short black hair, tan skin, and huge green glasses that swallowed most of her face.

"Sure, you'll find plenty of material under the heading 'Sioux,'" she was saying to the teenager in front of her, "but the word *Sioux* is a colonial word, a mispronunciation. I would also look up the Lakota and Dakota."

The teenager, a white kid wearing a wool hat that made Theo itch just looking at it, said, "Why are there so many different names for the same people?"

The librarian shrugged with one shoulder. "What other people call you is not always what you call yourself. Sometimes it's out of disrespect. Sometimes it's out of misunderstanding."

"Huh," said the kid. "Never thought of that. Thanks for the info."

"Happy to help," said the librarian.

The kid tipped his woolen hat and turned to leave. His eyes widened at the sight of Nine, but then he tipped his woolen hat at her, too, before walking away. The librarian waved Theo, Tess, and Jaime forward.

Jaime said, "Hi! We're here to see some letters in the Pforzheimer Collection?"

"Ah! Fabulous! Which letters would you like to see?" the librarian asked.

"The letters from Ada King to Charles Babbage?"

"The Countess of Lovelace! Isn't that perfect title for a mathematician? *Countess*? Get it?" said the librarian.

"You have an excellent sense of humor," Theo

announced, mostly for Tess's benefit.

"That's very true, though not everyone appreciates it," said the librarian.

"Tell me about it," said Theo. "I mean, you don't have to tell me about it because I know. Uh, unless you want to." Tess and Jaime turned to stare at him. Theo's face got hot, as if he were outside in the humid air instead of inside of the library.

The librarian didn't seem to notice his awkwardness or had so much experience with awkwardness that his wasn't remarkable.

Theo liked her eyeglasses.

"There are some procedures you have to follow if you want to see the letters," she told them. "You can't take them out of their sleeves. And you can't take them out of the library. And I'm sorry, I know your kitty is a therapy animal, but fur doesn't always agree with old documents. I'd like her to stay out here with me, if that's okay with you. And her."

Nine peered up at the librarian and meowed.

"That's okay with her," said Tess.

"Great," said the librarian, whose name tag said Dr. Deborah Little Crow. "I'll show you to room 319 and retrieve the letters for you."

Dr. Little Crow walked them to room 319 and

unlocked the door with a key card. She opened the door and turned on the lights. It was a medium-sized room with various shelves and filing cabinets around the perimeter, and a round table with some chairs in the center. A portrait of Ada Lovelace hung over one of the filing cabinets. Dark curls framed her face. Hooded eyes seemed to stare at him.

"She was only thirty-six when she died," said Dr. Little Crow, when she saw where Theo was looking. "And she had been really ambitious, too. She saw more potential for Charles Babbage's designs than he did." She bent and let Nine sniff her hand before scratching the cat between the ears. "Okay, Kitty, you stay right here while I get these guys set up." Nine sat and stared peacefully into the middle distance as if that had been her plan all along.

The librarian entered the room and pulled a binder off the shelf. She opened the binder on the table and paged through the plastic-covered letters until she came upon what she was looking for. "The King–Babbage letters begin right here. You can have a seat and examine them for as long as you want."

"Thank you!" said Tess.

"No problem," said the librarian. "I'll be at the desk with your kitty."

"Her name is Nine," Tess told her.

"Is it?" Dr. Little Crow said. "What a great name!" To the cat, she said, "Come on, you beautiful thing. I'm sure I can scavenge up some treats for you. Crows are good at that." She laughed at her own joke and closed the door behind her, leaving Theo, Tess, and Jaime alone with the Countess of Lovelace.

A mathematician called "Countess."

It was still funny.

Maybe one day he'd marry a librarian.

"Theo, are you going to stand there daydreaming about Dr. Little Crow or are you going to help us look at these letters?" Tess said.

Theo sat down at the table. There were six letters in total, all sent between 1843 and 1844. They took turns reading the letters out loud, taking notes and pictures, trying to figure out if there were any hidden messages or codes.

"It is an omission not to have sent me the drawings to which continual reference is made throughout your packet of papers . . . ," the first one began.

Then: "The solution was (as you supposed) of the simplest description."

"I have just told Weatstone that I cannot consent to

your making the reuse of the remaining notes. So send them to me at once, pray."

"In consequence of the enclosed, I am starting for Town; & I shall send this to you immediately on my arrival . . ."

"We are quite delighted at yr (somewhat unhoped for) proposal, this mor.g received. . . ."

On the surface, none of the letters seemed to hint at any particular clues. It was only when they reached the sixth letter, sent in October 1844, that things got more interesting:

"'I so enjoyed the symposium last April and am eager to arrange another such trip. I am still mourning the loss of my gift, however,'" Theo read. "'I was looking forward to solving the puzzle.'"

"The puzzle!" said Tess. "What puzzle?"

Theo read through the rest of the letter. "She doesn't say. And she doesn't give any specifics about this symposium, either." He pushed the binder away, rubbed his forehead and the bridge of his nose, and caught the knowing eyes of Ada King, Countess of Lovelace, in the portrait on the wall.

Jaime said, "I know it's just a picture, but it feels like she's in the room, staring down at us."

"It really does," said Tess. "It's as if she's willing us to find something. Or knows we're missing something."

Theo glanced at the closed door, then got up to grab a couple of tissues from a box on top of a cabinet. He sat down again and pulled the binder closer. Using the tissues to cover his fingertips, he reached into the plastic pocket and slid the letter out. "Sorry, Dr. Little Crow," he muttered.

The three of them held their breath, but there was nothing on the back of the letter, nothing lightly scratched between the lines.

"Maybe it's written in invisible ink again?" Jaime suggested.

"We didn't bring any solvents," said Tess. "Some cipherists we are."

Theo used the tissues to remove the other King–Babbage letters, but again, there was nothing on the back of any of them, nothing to indicate any clues. "Maybe we took a wrong turn somewhere," he said. "Maybe the gown has nothing to do with Ada at all." Starting with the first letter, he carefully returned each to their protective sleeves. But when he lifted the sixth letter, he paused.

"What?" said Jaime.

"The paper feels heavier than the rest." He covered his palm with one of tissues and laid the paper on top of it to examine the edge. "It's thicker, too." He sighed when he realized what he had to do. "I'm *really* sorry, Dr. Little Crow." He used the tip of his index finger to dig at the corner of the paper.

"Theo," Tess warned.

"I know," he said, but he kept digging, as gently as he could. Soon, a little flap of paper had come away from the original. Someone had pasted an extra piece of paper over the back of this letter so neatly that no one had detected it.

Until now.

When the flap was big enough, Theo peeled the two pieces of paper apart to reveal what had been written on the back of Ada's sixth letter to Charles Babbage.

First, she had scrawled two small drawings:

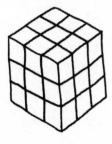 

"Isn't that a Rubik's cube? I didn't know they existed in the 1800s," said Jaime.

"I don't think they did," said Theo.

Underneath the drawings, Ada had written:

The puzzle fit in the palm of my hand. Made of silver and gemstones. I believe I left it in the M.s' drawing room. I wonder if that empty-headed little girl with the yellow hair stole it. She was clutching her reticule quite tightly when she returned to the table, if I recall.

If she doesn't melt it down out of sheer frustration, I can imagine she will deposit it in a spare box in her attic, to be found by a descendant and displayed in some museum or another a hundred hundred years from now. One more mysterious relic among many.

Oh, we have much work to do to, Mr. Babbage. Much work.

Yours,

A.A.L.

Below the text, someone—Ada? Someone else?—had scrawled this:

FCHBMFWSHFUVWSXLJSMCBHWJU

"Does that look like the same handwriting to you?" Jaime said. "Because I'm not sure it is."

"Someone could have added this cipher and hidden the text on the back with that second sheet of paper," said Tess.

"But when? This collection has been here for only twenty years," Jaime said. "And how or why would they do that?"

"That's a good question," said Theo.

Tess pointed to the writing. "She writes here about 'the M.s' drawing room.' She has to be talking about the Morningstarrs."

"She could be talking about anyone whose name begins with *M*," Theo said.

"Come on, Theo!" Tess said. "It's too adorable."

"I hate when you say that."

Jaime copied the text of the letter into his sketchbook and then took a photo for good measure. He was just slipping the phone back into his pocket when there was a brief knock on the door. Theo barely had time to close the binder before the door opened and Dr. Little Crow appeared. "How are you guys doing?" she said.

"Great!" said Jaime calmly, smoothly, innocently. "We're almost done."

"Whew! I think Nine's gained nine pounds on all the treats I've given her. She's napping them off now."

"Well, Nine eats for ten," said Tess.

Dr. Little Crow's eyes fell on the closed binder. "You guys find anything?"

"Ada was very passionate," Tess offered.

"She was," agreed the librarian. "You know, I never asked you why you guys were so interested in her."

"Isn't everyone?" said Tess.

Dr. Little Crow laughed. "Not as many as should be! But school isn't in session yet. Shouldn't you be out swimming or biking or generally causing your parents grief?"

"We're overachievers," Theo said. He was dead serious, but the librarian laughed again, as if he'd made a joke. Lots of people thought he was making jokes when he wasn't and didn't realize he was making jokes when he was. It was irritating.

Maybe he should keep his options open when it came to marriage.

Then again, her glasses were really awesome.

"Well, let me know if you need anything else," Dr. Little Crow said. She shut the door.

"We should clean up and go," said Tess. "She's been really nice, but I feel bad saddling her with Nine all this time."

"So should we erase the cipher on the back of this letter?" Theo said.

"I vote that we take some pictures and then cover up the back," Jaime said. "We put it in the sleeve the way it was. I don't want anyone else to find it, and I don't want Dr. Little Crow to get in trouble for what we did."

Jaime pulled the binder toward him and opened it to the sixth letter. He pressed a thumb against the edge of the two papers, the letter and the false back. "Still sticky," he said. He laid the original letter on the table, placed the false back on top of it, and pressed all around the edges with his thumb. He held up the letter. "Good as . . . old?"

"Ha," Theo said. He held the plastic sleeve open while Jaime slid the letter in. Once the paper was inside the sleeve, you couldn't tell that there was anything strange about it at all.

Theo put the binder back on the shelf and lined up the edges. Once he was done, he said, "Ready?"

"Ready," Tess said.

Theo went to the door and opened it.

Standing right outside was the pale blonde in a red dress—the same blond woman Theo had almost bumped into on the library stairs earlier, or was it a different one? She stared at the three of them for a long, tense moment, a stare so cold and calculating that it made Theo's skin prickle. Then she smiled suddenly—a tensing of the face, a baring of too-white teeth. "Oh, sorry, children," she said. "I think I have the wrong room."

As she click-clacked away, Jaime said, "I don't think that woman had the wrong room."

Theo rubbed the back of his neck where the hair was standing on end. "And I don't think she was sorry."

CHAPTER SEVEN
Jaime

Sometimes, Jaime's father would say he was sorry. "I'm sorry your mother isn't here to see this new drawing." "I'm sorry your mother isn't here to watch you get this award." "She loved you, more than anything. I'm sorry she isn't here to tell you herself."

Sometimes, Jaime went looking for his mother. She was in many of the photos on the walls of his apartment, of course, so that was often the first place he found her. But she haunted his father's drawings, too, the ones he sent from Sudan or wherever he was on assignment. His father drew her everywhere—in the desert, in the rain forest, on a beach with the surf lapping at her toes. Even when she wasn't smiling in the drawings, it seemed as if she were about to. Jaime kept most of his father's drawings in a folder on his nightstand. He would go through the drawings one by one, sometimes for hours.

But since his mother had been a scientist, and an important one, she also lived in the heads of other people; on the web, Jaime had to share her with anyone and everyone. All Jaime had to do was type her name into the search box on his phone, and there she was: her towering hair; the easy confidence that shone through on the screen no matter where she was pictured, no matter what she was doing. It was like seeing a ghost. He would forget and touch the screen—expecting to feel the skin of her arm or her cheek—and be surprised by the cool glass under his fingertip.

Even more eerie than the images that popped up on his screen were the videos. The interviews and the lectures, the conversations and panel discussions. When he was younger, he watched these videos incessantly, memorizing everything his mother said, though he didn't understand much of the complex physics that was her specialty. His favorite video clip had less to do with physics and more to do with the challenges of being a young black girl with an interest in science.

"Oh, there were certain people who tried to talk me out of it. Tried to persuade me to do everything else, anything else," she said in the clip. "I was tall and athletic, so I should take up basketball or track and get a scholarship, these people said. I could study accounting or nursing. Something more practical than all this pie-in-the-sky stuff, they said."

The interviewer said, "And what did you say?"

"I said that those are fine dreams to have, but they weren't my dreams. Occasionally, those same people would get angry."

"They would argue with you?" the interviewer said.

"Not always. More often they would just give you a long look. You could feel them taking in your skin color and your hair and your size, you could see them deciding that all problems in the world are caused by people like you, people who want things they shouldn't want, who have dreams they aren't supposed to have. People get strangely angry about things like that, have you noticed? That's something I hope my son never has to feel. The weight of that look. But even if he does, I hope that he'll never let it stop him. I hope he dreams dreams bigger than any star in the universe. I hope he dreams pie-in-the-sky dreams."

Jaime *had* felt the weight of that look his mother spoke about, chilly eyes that scraped him up and down, left and right, eyes that said there were so many problems in the world and he just might be the cause of them. But he was always able to shake off the feeling in a second or two. Those people didn't know him; they didn't matter. His dreams mattered. The people he loved mattered.

But now, as he stood here in the New York Public Library, the blond woman's icy stare lingered. It weighed on him like the lead blanket they put over you at the dentist's, but it was something that exposed you rather than protected you.

Tess's voice broke through Jaime's reverie. "That woman was too creepy. Like she brushes her teeth with bleach. Let's get out of here before she comes back."

They returned to Dr. Little Crow's desk. The whole time Theo and Tess chatted with the librarian, Jaime was scanning the library for another glimpse of light hair, a red dress the color of fresh blood. But she was gone.

Whiskers tickled his fingertips, and a thick purr hummed in his bones as Nine rubbed her face against his leg and hand.

"Jaime?" Tess said. "Are you okay?"

"Fine," he said, not quite fine. He had never been a nervous person, but here he was, practically shaking in his Converses because some wacky lady with a bad dye job had given him the evil eye. He wished Mima were here to stare that lady down, flay her in a dozen different languages. He wished he were big enough and strong enough to hold his head high like his mother always had, to have the quiet dignity and nobility of his father.

But then, Mima taught him to trust his gut, and his gut was telling him that the discovery of the Shadow Cipher gave them power, but the kind of power more powerful people covet, the kind of power more powerful people would do almost anything to get.

He waited until they were outside of the library before he said, "We have to come up with a better cover story for what we're doing. We can't just keep running around the city, telling everyone what we're looking for."

"But we're not," Tess said.

"We just told that librarian about the letters we wanted to see. We could have found them ourselves. What if the librarian mentions it to someone else or writes it down in some log or something? What if . . ." He paused, all sorts of horrible scenarios straight out of stories and movies racing around his skull. "What if somebody questions her? Or threatens her?"

Theo shook his head, but his eyes widened with alarm. "That's why we hid the clue."

"Someone else could find it. We're not the only ones trying to figure out the Cipher."

"Yes, but we never were," said Tess.

Jaime jammed his hands in his pockets, trying to explain. "Ever since 354 West 73rd came down, I don't know. It's been different. *I've* felt different. And don't tell me it's because I live in Hoboken."

"It's because you live in Hoboken," Theo said, almost automatically. Then he held up his hands in surrender. "No, I know what you mean. Things have been . . . strange."

Tess swallowed hard, and Nine licked her fingers to soothe her. "That blond woman was the strange one," she said. "Who do you think she is?"

"Probably nobody," said Jaime. "But I don't want to meet her again."

"No more run-ins with icky strangers," Tess said. "Agreed." She reached behind her and tightened her braid with a quick tug. "Let's get out of here. We need a break. Want to come back to Aunt Esther's? We can grab something to eat."

"Fig Newtons?" said Jaime.

"Theo makes a mean sandwich," Tess said.

Theo said, "I make a *good* sandwich."

Later, in the twins' attic room, Nine sprawled like a rug on the rug. Remnants of a too-late lunch—plates and balled-up napkins and blobs of cheese hardened to adhesive—littered the floor all around them. Jaime liked this room, cozy and messy as it was. He peeled off a stamp of cheese from his plate and popped it in his mouth, reminded of something else Mima always told him: When you're feeling nervous and out of sorts, eat something. You might just be hungry.

Mostly, it was true.

"Well," Jaime said. "That sandwich was both good and mean."

"Theo, himself, is both good and mean," said Tess.

"Mean," said Theo, "is usually a matter of perception."

"You sound like a comic-book villain," Jaime told him.

"Yeah, when they're monologuing about how they and the hero are really a lot alike," Tess said. "Two sides of the same coin."

Theo pulled a Fig Newton off a platter. "About this clue."

"Grumpy," said Tess, tossing the crust of her bread to Nine. But she turned her attention to Jaime's sketchbook with the sketch of Ada's letter. "Okay, what do we have?"

The puzzle fit in the palm of my hand. Made of silver and gemstones. I believe I left it in the M.s' drawing room. I wonder if that empty-headed little girl with the yellow hair stole it. She was clutching her reticule quite tightly when she returned to the table, if I recall.

If she doesn't melt it down out of sheer frustration, I can imagine she will deposit it in a spare box in her attic, to be found by a descendant and displayed in some museum or another a hundred hundred years from now. One more mysterious relic among many.

Oh, we have much work to do to, Mr. Babbage. Much work.

Yours,

A.A.L.

FCHBMFWSHFUVWSXLJSMCBHWJU

"We have some drawings of a cube, some sort of puzzle box. And some talk about it being stolen in 1844. And there is this string of characters along the bottom, which could be a cipher," Jaime said.

"I wonder if we're supposed to be solving this cipher or looking for this puzzle box."

"Or both," said Jaime.

"Or neither," said Theo.

"You know it's totally okay to stop telling us our ideas are stupid," Tess said.

"When did I say that?" Theo said.

Tess sighed so hard a loose spiral of hair flew up, then floated back down to rest against her temple. "Let's start with the cipher along the bottom. Maybe it's something we can crack," she suggested. The three of them looked at the string of letters and then they all took another cookie for fortification.

Jaime said what the three of them were thinking, and probably Nine, too. "If it's just some word scrambled up, a substitution cipher, there are going to be so many possible permutations."

"Millions and millions," said Theo. But they tried it anyway, putting the characters into cipher solvers on the web, coming up with all sorts of meaningless words and phrases.

"Maybe the string of characters refers to something in the letter," Tess said. "Like, say, the letter *F* refers to the sixth line or the sixth word of the letter, and so on."

"There aren't that many lines in the whole letter," Theo said.

"The individual words, then," said Tess.

They tried the sixth word. *Palm*. Then the third word, *fit*. The eighth, the second, etc.

"Palm, fit, my, puzzle, and," Jaime said. "It doesn't sound like it's forming a new sentence as much as repeating what the letter already says."

"We could try frequency analysis," said Theo.

"What's that?" Jaime asked.

"There are certain letters in the English alphabet that are used more often in English words than other letters, like *e* and *a*. If this is a substitution cipher, and we figure out how often each letter appears in this cipher, we might be able to figure out what it says. There are tools on the web to do the calculations."

While Theo found a tool and punched in the characters from the cipher, Jaime lay back on the rug with his hands behind his head, thinking. Any other day, Jaime might have been excited about Theo's suggestion and eager to see what the tool came up with. And yet, though the food had made him feel better, he still got the feeling they were missing something obvious, that they were taking the long way around when there was a simpler solution. He mentally retraced the steps that had gotten them to the library in the first place. Lovelace, Babbage, the Analytical Engine, the—

Wait.

"Babbage!" he blurted.

"What about him?" said Theo.

"When we read about him before, wasn't there something about him solving a specific *kind* of cipher?"

Tess grabbed his wrist. "Yes! But I can't remember what it was called."

Quickly, Jaime searched for the terms *Babbage, cipher* and found what he was looking for. "The Vigenère cipher," he read, sounding out the unfamiliar word.

"To encipher a message, you use twenty-six different cipher alphabets instead of just one."

Theo stopped what he was doing. "Really? That's awesome."

"Here's a table with the different alphabets," Jaime said, holding up the phone. The twins leaned in to look:

Plain	a	b	c	d	e	f	g	h	i	j	k	l	m	n	o	p	q	r	s	t	u	v	w	x	y	z
1	B	C	D	E	F	G	H	I	J	K	L	M	N	O	P	Q	R	S	T	U	V	W	X	Y	Z	A
2	C	D	E	F	G	H	I	J	K	L	M	N	O	P	Q	R	S	T	U	V	W	X	Y	Z	A	B
3	D	E	F	G	H	I	J	K	L	M	N	O	P	Q	R	S	T	U	V	W	X	Y	Z	A	B	C
4	E	F	G	H	I	J	K	L	M	N	O	P	Q	R	S	T	U	V	W	X	Y	Z	A	B	C	D
5	F	G	H	I	J	K	L	M	N	O	P	Q	R	S	T	U	V	W	X	Y	Z	A	B	C	D	E
6	G	H	I	J	K	L	M	N	O	P	Q	R	S	T	U	V	W	X	Y	Z	A	B	C	D	E	F
7	H	I	J	K	L	M	N	O	P	Q	R	S	T	U	V	W	X	Y	Z	A	B	C	D	E	F	G
8	I	J	K	L	M	N	O	P	Q	R	S	T	U	V	W	X	Y	Z	A	B	C	D	E	F	G	H
9	J	K	L	M	N	O	P	Q	R	S	T	U	V	W	X	Y	Z	A	B	C	D	E	F	G	H	I
10	K	L	M	N	O	P	Q	R	S	T	U	V	W	X	Y	Z	A	B	C	D	E	F	G	H	I	J
11	L	M	N	O	P	Q	R	S	T	U	V	W	X	Y	Z	A	B	C	D	E	F	G	H	I	J	K
12	M	N	O	P	Q	R	S	T	U	V	W	X	Y	Z	A	B	C	D	E	F	G	H	I	J	K	L
13	N	O	P	Q	R	S	T	U	V	W	X	Y	Z	A	B	C	D	E	F	G	H	I	J	K	L	M
14	O	P	Q	R	S	T	U	V	W	X	Y	Z	A	B	C	D	E	F	G	H	I	J	K	L	M	N
15	P	Q	R	S	T	U	V	W	X	Y	Z	A	B	C	D	E	F	G	H	I	J	K	L	M	N	O
16	Q	R	S	T	U	V	W	X	Y	Z	A	B	C	D	E	F	G	H	I	J	K	L	M	N	O	P
17	R	S	T	U	V	W	X	Y	Z	A	B	C	D	E	F	G	H	I	J	K	L	M	N	O	P	Q
18	S	T	U	V	W	X	Y	Z	A	B	C	D	E	F	G	H	I	J	K	L	M	N	O	P	Q	R
19	T	U	V	W	X	Y	Z	A	B	C	D	E	F	G	H	I	J	K	L	M	N	O	P	Q	R	S
20	U	V	W	X	Y	Z	A	B	C	D	E	F	G	H	I	J	K	L	M	N	O	P	Q	R	S	T
21	V	W	X	Y	Z	A	B	C	D	E	F	G	H	I	J	K	L	M	N	O	P	Q	R	S	T	U
22	W	X	Y	Z	A	B	C	D	E	F	G	H	I	J	K	L	M	N	O	P	Q	R	S	T	U	V
23	X	Y	Z	A	B	C	D	E	F	G	H	I	J	K	L	M	N	O	P	Q	R	S	T	U	V	W
24	Y	Z	A	B	C	D	E	F	G	H	I	J	K	L	M	N	O	P	Q	R	S	T	U	V	W	X
25	Z	A	B	C	D	E	F	G	H	I	J	K	L	M	N	O	P	Q	R	S	T	U	V	W	X	Y
26	A	B	C	D	E	F	G	H	I	J	K	L	M	N	O	P	Q	R	S	T	U	V	W	X	Y	Z

"That is cool," Tess said.

"The problem is that we need a key word in order to decipher the message," Jaime said.

"Whomp-whomp," said Tess.

Jaime checked the time on his phone, stood, stretched. "I'm going to be late for dinner if I don't get going. Work on this tomorrow?"

"Tomorrow," said Tess, holding up her fist. Jaime bumped it. Theo saluted. Nine wound herself around Jaime's legs three times, as if she were casting some sort of spell. Maybe she was.

Jaime walked down the stairs and found Aunt Esther watering her plants while the mechanical spiders darted away from the streams.

"Jaime!" she said. "I thought I heard your dulcet tones wafting down from the attic."

Jaime laughed. "I don't think anyone's called my voice 'dulcet' before."

"They should," said Aunt Esther. "Back when I was a casting agent, I heard plenty of non-dulcet tones, believe me."

"When was that?"

"Oh, years ago," she said, shooing away a spider. "If you wanted to, you could get voice-over work when you're older."

"Thank you. I'll keep that in mind," said Jaime, heading for the front door. "Gotta get home now."

Aunt Esther added, "Or you could keep on doing what you're doing."

Something about *her* tone made him pause with his hand on the knob. When he asked her the question, he felt as if he were asking every question he'd ever had, would ever have. "And what am I doing?"

"Why, everything you can, dear," Aunt Esther said. "Everything you possibly can."

CHAPTER EIGHT
Karl

Miles away, in the Hoboken building Jaime was not yet able to call home, a determined little girl raced her tricycle down an empty hallway, a security guard hot on her heels.

The little girl's legs pumped, her breath came sharp and fast.

"Stop!" yelled the guard.

She did not stop. She would not stop. Her name was Zelda "Cricket" Moran, and she was unstoppable.

The security guard would learn this soon enough.

Karl the raccoon clutched the rims of his basket with one of his tiny but strong hands. With the other hand, he held up the empty bag of cheese curls, hoping to catch Cricket's attention, but she was currently preoccupied.

Alas.

Karl wedged the empty bag in the side of the basket, closed his eyes, and let the breeze waft through his whiskers. Even with all the shouting, it was a pleasant-enough ride. Karl enjoyed these little adventures with Cricket. Never a dull moment, that was what he always said. Well, he would have said it, if he could talk. Too bad that the people who engineered him hadn't bothered to shape the fine muscles of his tongue and jaw so that he could form words. How surprised everyone would be. He had so many delightful stories to tell, so many opinions on a wide variety of topics. Child-rearing! Horticulture! Cookery! Politics! One day, he would figure a way to write his thoughts down. But he was the patient sort and was willing to wait until Cricket got her own computer. In the meantime, being her traveling companion was a fine occupation. He was well cared for, happy and comfortable, and there were cheese curls aplenty.

Just not at the moment.

Karl scratched his furry belly, rolled over to look behind Cricket's shoulder. The security guard was still chasing them, red-faced and furious, stomping like a movie monster. He was making quite the spectacle of himself. Cricket had a talent for bringing out the—what was the term?—ah yes, the *berserker* in people. She said something or did something, and suddenly they snapped, gibbering gibberish and jerking their arms around like broken toys.

For example, just this afternoon, Cricket and Karl were exploring the building, taking note of all entrances and exits, suspicious persons and/or happenings, as was their habit. While the security guard was making his rounds, Cricket took the opportunity to search his desk, which was when she found what she called a "wiggle worm." Cricket declared the thing EXTREMELY SUSPICIOUS and confiscated it, telling Karl that she was going to bring it back to their apartment for further study. But before they could do that, the security guard came back, saw the wiggle worm in Cricket's hand, and the berserking—and this not-so-merry chase—began.

Now Cricket took a right turn so hard that the back wheel of the tricycle came off the ground, then slammed back down, rocking Karl in his basket. They careened past startled residents in bathing suits heading for the rooftop pool, a pack of glum teenagers with black makeup reminiscent of Karl's own raccoon mask, a pair of dads in unfortunate Bermuda shorts. Cricket jerked the handlebars right again, and they circled back around to the lobby, where they almost ran over a tall boy with short, tidy dreadlocks and glasses. Jaime, his name was.

"Hey, hey, hey," Jaime said, catching the handlebars. "Where are you going so fast, Cricket?"

Cricket didn't have time to answer, because the security guard came chugging up behind them, shoes squeaking on the marble floor.

"Thanks, kid," the guard said. "I'll take it from here." He reached out to grab Cricket's arm, but Jaime stepped in front of her.

"What are you doing?" he said to the guard.

"My job," the guard said. "Now, you listen to me, little girl, you need to—"

"Excuse me, sir, but I asked you what you think you're doing," Jaime said. "Why were you chasing her like that? She's just a baby."

Cricket began, "I am *not* a—" but Jaime held out a hand to keep her from finishing her sentence. Karl was surprised when Cricket snapped her mouth shut.

The guard scowled and wiped sweat off his pale forehead. "She stole something from my desk."

"What did she steal?" Jaime asked.

The man scowled even more deeply. "Something."

"Something," Jaime said, his tone flat.

"Something important."

"A sandwich? A cup of coffee? Your diary? A million dollars? What?"

"No need to be rude," said the guard.

Jaime whipped off his eyeglasses, suddenly seeming much older than he was. "Rude is chasing a baby around an apartment building. Rude is *scaring* a baby."

"That girl does not look scared," the guard insisted. But people in the lobby were starting to stare. The guard shifted from one foot to the other, as if his pants were too tight. Well, they were too tight, in Karl's opinion, though he himself had never worn pants.

"I was just trying to get my important, um, thing back."

"Uh-huh," said Jaime, putting his glasses back on. "Well, maybe if you can tell me what it is, I can ask Cricket if she took it."

The guard looked from Jaime to Cricket to the furrowed brows of the residents in the lobby, then his shoulders seemed to sink in surrender. "You know what. I guess it doesn't matter. I could get another, uh, another—"

"Very Important Something?" Jaime said.

Now it was the guard's turn to snap his mouth shut. He marched back to his desk and dropped into his seat, his expression—what was the term?—ah yes, murderous.

Jaime turned to Cricket. "Are you okay?"

Cricket stared up at him as if she'd never seen him before. "Yes. I'm fine."

"What about your friend here? Karl, are you okay?"

Thank you, yes, I'm perfectly well, Karl chittered. *It's been quite an adventure and I've built up something of an appetite.* He held up the empty cheese curl bag.

Jaime took the empty bag, balled it up in his fist, and tossed it in the nearest trash can. "I think Karl needs some more cheese curls."

What a smart boy, Karl thought. Good and kind. Some might even say heroic. By the way she was gazing up at him, Cricket might say exactly that.

If she had been anyone but Zelda "Cricket" Moran, that is.

"I don't like that man," Cricket said. "He's PECULIAR."

"I don't like him, either," said Jaime. "But you should probably avoid him from now on. I'll talk to your parents. You didn't take anything from his desk, did you?"

"Hmmph," Cricket said.

"Cricket?"

"I don't take things, I CONFISCATE them."

"Okay, did you confiscate anything from his desk?"

"I might have confiscated a wiggle worm," Cricket said.

"A what?"

"A WIGGLE WORM."

"Yes, but—"

"It's a WORM and it WIGGLES," Cricket said.

"Okay?" said Jaime, clearly confused. "Where's the wiggle worm now?"

"I gave it to Karl. He ate it."

Karl chittered, *The child did indeed give me said wiggle worm, Kind Sir, but I did not eat it. I would much prefer a cheese curl.*

"Well," Jaime said. "Don't take any more, uh, wiggle worms from anywhere."

Cricket crossed her arms. "I don't *take* anything."

"Confiscate, then," said Jaime.

"I'm not making any promises," Cricket said. "This place is too PECULIAR."

Karl was growing weary of this kind of talk; he was hungry and in need of a snack and a nap, in that order. He wished he could simply ask for these things in a tongue they could understand. It would be so much simpler.

Instead, he was forced to wait as Jaime informed Cricket that she should be more careful and Cricket informed Jaime that she wasn't scared of anyone, etc. Karl's gaze wandered from Jaime and Cricket to the front of the lobby, where enormous glass windows showed a view of the street outside.

And the man and the woman in the strange coats that stood watching them with dark and unreadable eyes.

Karl opened his mouth to warn Jaime and Cricket, and was more disappointed than usual when no words came out.

CHAPTER NINE
Tess

Tess was in the middle of a rare and perfectly pleasant dream when her dad bellowed, "Rise and Shineth, for Thy Father Hast Made Thy Breakfast!"

Theo rolled over and fell unceremoniously out of bed with a thud. "Have you been reading Shakespeare again?"

Tess opened one eye and said, "Dad! I was having a good dream for once."

Her dad peered down at her. "What kind of dream?"

Tess frowned. "I'm trying to remember. There were cats, though."

Theo sat up. "There's always a cat."

Nine mrrowed agreeably and leaped from her spot on Tess's bed.

"Nine is ready to eat," said her dad, who was wearing a T-shirt that said WHO'S YOUR LLAMA? with a picture of an alpaca. Theo seemed to be too tired to critique it.

Her dad said, "What about you two? Ready to eat?"

Theo scrubbed at his hair. "What did you make?"

"It's a surprise."

"That doesn't exactly instill me with confidence."

"Oh, Cry for Him, for He Is Full of Doubt," their father sang at the top of his lungs. "Come downstairs. You've overslept."

"It's summer. You can't oversleep during the summer," Tess grumbled.

"You most certainly can. Especially when your loving father has prepared a surprise breakfast and it's getting cold."

Tess and Theo fought over who got the bathroom first—Tess won—and then dragged themselves downstairs to the kitchen to find stacks of pancakes shaped like . . .

"Uh, Dad, what are these supposed to be?" said Theo.

"What do you mean? You can't tell?"

He looked so sad that Tess said, "He's just joking."

Theo said, "I'm—" but Tess kicked him under the table.

"They're Morningstarr Machines," their father said. He pointed at various-sized blobs of pancake arranged on different plates. "See, this one is a Roller, this one is Squeegee, and this one is that new one, that big moth. I wonder where that one went. They had another sighting in the Bronx a couple of weeks ago but that was the last I heard."

"Looks just like them, Dad," Tess said.

Theo blinked. Said, "Dad, your shirt says 'Who's your llama?' but I'm pretty sure that's an alpaca."

Their dad looked down. "I love this shirt."

Theo relented, ate a bite of pancake. "Delicious."

Their father beamed. "Is Jaime coming over? I'm going to make him some spiders."

Tess ate her pancakes, which were blobby but tasty.

"Have you been thinking about it?" Theo said, voice lowered so their father couldn't hear.

"About what?" said Tess.

"The clue," Theo said, biting the head off a Roller. "We'll have to try Ada, Lovelace, Babbage, Morningstarr, or all or any combination of those. It's probably something more obscure. Maybe a word or phrase from the letter."

"Hmmm," said Tess.

"What?" said Theo. "You think we should try something else?"

"I don't think anything. I'm still asleep."

"Let me know when you're awake, then."

Tess took another pancake, soaked it in syrup, and tried to remember her good dream. Tess had been walking in a garden with an elaborate topiary, with hedges trimmed in the shapes of numbers. Cats darted in and out of the hedges. One of them was small and white, with one blue eye, one green. She led Tess to a table where a woman with a familiar face was drinking tea. The woman wanted to tell Tess . . . something about the clue. That they were looking in the wrong direction. That they had to back up a bit. She said she was the queen. No, that wasn't it. She was a princess? No. Duchess? No.

Oh.

OH.

Of course.

Seems like Ada Lovelace had a bad sense of humor as well.

"Not more obscure," Tess said.

"What?"

"The key word isn't more obscure. It's obvious."

"How do you know that?"

"*You* know it."

"What do you mean?"

"You know what the key word is."

Theo paused, pancake dangling on the end of his fork. "I do?"

"It's only thing it could be."

"You know," Theo said, scowling, "it's at times like these that I remember that I never liked you."

"You love your sister," said their father.

"What does that have to do with liking her?"

The doorbell rang. Theo dropped his pancake and ran to get it, brought Jaime back into the kitchen.

"Jaime!" said Tess's dad. "Have a seat. I've made you some spiders."

"Thanks?" said Jaime, sitting at the table. "Oooh! Morningstarr Machines!"

Tess's dad said, "I'm glad someone appreciates my work."

"We appreciate you," Tess said.

Her dad said, "You haven't tried the Rollers yet.

They're blueberry." He went back to the stove and poured more batter into a pan.

Theo wiped his mouth with a napkin and whispered, "Tess knows the key word."

"It's obvious," Jaime said.

"It is?" said Theo.

"Yes," Jaime and Tess said at exactly the same time.

Theo couldn't help but shake his head. "It's weird when you guys do that."

"Do what?" Tess and Jaime said, and laughed. For one moment, it was as if the tragedy of 354 W. 73rd Street never happened, that they were the same as they used to be. Tess tried to hold on to the feeling.

After they finished their breakfast and helped wash the dishes, they went upstairs. Jaime pulled out his sketchbook and wrote the word COUNTESS across the top of the page.

"HA! Told you it was an awesome joke," Theo said.

"If this actually is the key word, it's no joke," Jaime said.

They consulted the Vigenère table they had found the day before:

Plain	a	b	c	d	e	f	g	h	i	j	k	l	m	n	o	p	q	r	s	t	u	v	w	x	y	z
1	B	C	D	E	F	G	H	I	J	K	L	M	N	O	P	Q	R	S	T	U	V	W	X	Y	Z	A
2	C	D	E	F	G	H	I	J	K	L	M	N	O	P	Q	R	S	T	U	V	W	X	Y	Z	A	B
3	D	E	F	G	H	I	J	K	L	M	N	O	P	Q	R	S	T	U	V	W	X	Y	Z	A	B	C
4	E	F	G	H	I	J	K	L	M	N	O	P	Q	R	S	T	U	V	W	X	Y	Z	A	B	C	D
5	F	G	H	I	J	K	L	M	N	O	P	Q	R	S	T	U	V	W	X	Y	Z	A	B	C	D	E
6	G	H	I	J	K	L	M	N	O	P	Q	R	S	T	U	V	W	X	Y	Z	A	B	C	D	E	F
7	H	I	J	K	L	M	N	O	P	Q	R	S	T	U	V	W	X	Y	Z	A	B	C	D	E	F	G
8	I	J	K	L	M	N	O	P	Q	R	S	T	U	V	W	X	Y	Z	A	B	C	D	E	F	G	H
9	J	K	L	M	N	O	P	Q	R	S	T	U	V	W	X	Y	Z	A	B	C	D	E	F	G	H	I
10	K	L	M	N	O	P	Q	R	S	T	U	V	W	X	Y	Z	A	B	C	D	E	F	G	H	I	J
11	L	M	N	O	P	Q	R	S	T	U	V	W	X	Y	Z	A	B	C	D	E	F	G	H	I	J	K
12	M	N	O	P	Q	R	S	T	U	V	W	X	Y	Z	A	B	C	D	E	F	G	H	I	J	K	L
13	N	O	P	Q	R	S	T	U	V	W	X	Y	Z	A	B	C	D	E	F	G	H	I	J	K	L	M
14	O	P	Q	R	S	T	U	V	W	X	Y	Z	A	B	C	D	E	F	G	H	I	J	K	L	M	N
15	P	Q	R	S	T	U	V	W	X	Y	Z	A	B	C	D	E	F	G	H	I	J	K	L	M	N	O
16	Q	R	S	T	U	V	W	X	Y	Z	A	B	C	D	E	F	G	H	I	J	K	L	M	N	O	P
17	R	S	T	U	V	W	X	Y	Z	A	B	C	D	E	F	G	H	I	J	K	L	M	N	O	P	Q
18	S	T	U	V	W	X	Y	Z	A	B	C	D	E	F	G	H	I	J	K	L	M	N	O	P	Q	R
19	T	U	V	W	X	Y	Z	A	B	C	D	E	F	G	H	I	J	K	L	M	N	O	P	Q	R	S
20	U	V	W	X	Y	Z	A	B	C	D	E	F	G	H	I	J	K	L	M	N	O	P	Q	R	S	T
21	V	W	X	Y	Z	A	B	C	D	E	F	G	H	I	J	K	L	M	N	O	P	Q	R	S	T	U
22	W	X	Y	Z	A	B	C	D	E	F	G	H	I	J	K	L	M	N	O	P	Q	R	S	T	U	V
23	X	Y	Z	A	B	C	D	E	F	G	H	I	J	K	L	M	N	O	P	Q	R	S	T	U	V	W
24	Y	Z	A	B	C	D	E	F	G	H	I	J	K	L	M	N	O	P	Q	R	S	T	U	V	W	X
25	Z	A	B	C	D	E	F	G	H	I	J	K	L	M	N	O	P	Q	R	S	T	U	V	W	X	Y
26	A	B	C	D	E	F	G	H	I	J	K	L	M	N	O	P	Q	R	S	T	U	V	W	X	Y	Z

F C H B M F W S H F U V W S X L J S M C B H W J U

"So," Jaime said. "The key word *countess* gives us the order of the different alphabets. First, the *C* alphabet; next, the *O* alphabet; after that, the *U* alphabet." He wrote the key word three times plus one extra *C*. Underneath that, he wrote the ciphertext:

```
C O U N T E S S C O U N T E S S C O U N T E S S C
F C H B M F W S H F U V W S X L J S M C B H W J U
```

On the chart, Tess went to the *C* alphabet. "In the *C* alphabet, the letter *F* represents the plaintext letter *D*," she said.

Jaime wrote *D* underneath the ciphertext.

```
C O U N T E S S C O U N T E S S C O U N T E S S C
F C H B M F W S H F U V W S X L J S M C B H W J U
D
```

"In the *O* alphabet, the cipher character *C* gives us a plaintext character of *O*," said Tess.

Jaime wrote that down as well.

```
C O U N T E S S C O U N T E S S C O U N T E S S C
F C H B M F W S H F U V W S X L J S M C B H W J U
D O
```

They went through the whole cipher like this. Once they were through, Jaime read the message out loud:

COUNTESSCOUNTESSCOUNTESSC
FCHBMFWSHFUVWSXLJSMCBHWJU
DONOTBEAFRAIDOFTHESPIDERS

"'Do not be afraid of the spiders,'" Jaime said. "Well. That's helpful."

"I don't see how that's helpful," Theo said. "Who's afraid of spiders? You might as well say 'Do not be afraid of the vacuum cleaner.'" He plucked a tiny mechanical spider from the nearest plant.

"Not everyone likes those so much," said Jaime, watching the little robot leap back into the plant and scurry up the stalk.

"You don't have houseplants?" Theo asked.

"Mima likes to prune her own plants."

Tess said, "Forget about the spiders and the houseplants for a minute. Let's back up. Maybe we were on the right track yesterday when we thought the clue was in the text of the letter Ada wrote. Remember, someone bothered to cover up the whole thing, not just the ciphertext."

"It was easier to cover up the whole thing rather than a little part of it," Theo said absently, but he stuck his hand in his bushy hair and held it there, his thinking pose.

Jaime turned the pages in his sketchbook to the text of the letter he had copied. "She says that she can imagine the puzzle displayed in a museum. One more relic among many."

"The Morningstarrs set these clues back in 1855. Old things end up in museums. At least, old things that aren't streets or graves or entire buildings end up in museums."

"Yes, but the Morningstarrs couldn't have predicted whether the objects or paintings or whatever these things are stayed in the area. Old things get shipped to other places. Old things get sold to collectors," Theo said.

"The Morningstarrs had faith," said Jaime.

"Huh?"

"They had faith that these items were so important that someone would preserve them."

Tess didn't say it out loud, but she thought it: Or, the Morningstarrs *knew* that someone would preserve them. But maybe that was the definition of faith. Something that you can't prove but you know in your heart is true even when you can't explain it.

"We can search museum collections online," Tess said.

"And we can call the museums, too," Jaime said.

"*Talk* on the *phone*?" Theo said. "That sounds horrible."

"Some people still do it," said Tess.

"*Old* people still do it," Theo insisted. "Mom does it."

"Theo has phone anxiety," Tess explained to Jaime.

"I do not!"

"It's nothing to be embarrassed about," she said.

"I'm not embarrassed," Theo said, blushing.

"But there have to be hundreds of museums in New York City," said Jaime.

They spent the rest of the morning searching museum collections online, took a break for lunch; Aunt Esther ordered a pizza for them, and then had to order another one when Tess complained she was still hungry. Then, they spent the afternoon calling big museums with enormous art collections dating back to the ancient Greeks and odd little museums that exhibited things like toothpastes from around the world and a shoe once thrown at the head of a former president of the United States. They got switched from department to department, and told repeatedly that they would just have to visit the museum themselves if they wanted more specific information, or informed that crank-calling museums was "a seriously silly thing to do," or directed to current exhibits of other things they might be interested in, like elevator plaques from the Elevator Historical Society, a trivet from the Cast-Iron Museum, a tricycle with square wheels from the Museum of Mathematics, a giant butterfly called a "dogface" from the Staten Island Museum's Wall of Insects.

The ache in Tess's shoulders moved to her head. She wished the Morningstarrs had simply drawn a treasure map like normal people. But then, if they had done that, someone probably would have found it years and years and years ago, and grabbed the treasure for themselves. And Grandpa Ben might have never grown up in 354 W. 73, and neither would her mother, and if her mother hadn't lived there, would she have ever met her father? Would Tess and Theo have ever been born? Grandpa Ben once told her about something called the butterfly effect, where one tiny event could affect a million bigger things, like the flapping of the wings of a butterfly could influence the formation of a hurricane weeks later. If you started reimagining the past, you could change your own existence, or undo it completely, which was just too weird to contemplate.

Tess consulted the list of museums for the next one to call. "The 2nd City Reliquary," she said aloud.

"2nd City?" said Theo. "Isn't that what they call Chicago?"

"Reliquary," Jaime said. "A place they keep relics. Like Ada said in the letter."

Why would there be a museum dedicated to Chicago relics in Brooklyn? Tess dialed the number anyway.

A rumbly voice said, "2nd City Reliquary."

"Hi. I'm doing a group project for school about puzzles and I was just wondering if—"

"School? Isn't school out for the summer?"

"It's a very special school. We go all year round."

"Cool!" said the rumbly voice. "What are you looking for?"

"I'm looking for a certain kind of puzzle. It's a cube made up of a bunch of smaller cubes, and you have to rotate them to—"

"Oh! Yes! We have one of those around here somewhere."

"You do?"

"Yep!"

"Okay, then," said Tess.

"Okay!" said the rumbly voice.

"One more question," Tess said.

"Sure."

"Why do they call your museum the '2nd City Reliquary'?"

"Because it's the second one."

"Was there a first one?"

"Sure!" said the rumbly voice. "Until one day it disappeared."

"Uh . . . disappeared?"

"One day it was here, next day the whole thing was gone. And I don't mean the shelves were cleared out, I mean the entire building was just . . . gone. Poof! As if it had never been built. Weird, huh?"

"Not as weird as you think."

CHAPTER TEN
Theo

Brooklyn was only a half hour away, but it might as well have been another country. The streets around the place were packed with tattooed girls in denim shorts over tights, and boys who dressed like farmers from 1825. Beards were long and lush, mustaches wide and waxed.

A skinny brown guy in striped pants and roller skates twirled around Theo twice. "Dope 'fro," he said, then skated off into the crowd.

The 2nd City Reliquary itself was a storefront in the neighborhood of Williamsburg, a tiny place packed with all sorts of odds and ends. Old Underway tokens, soda bottles, maps, posters, baseball cards, miniature Liberty Statues, a display of porcelain unicorns, and a very old shovel labeled VERY OLD SHOVEL.

"This is a museum?" said Jaime. "Kind of looks like my great-aunt Sylvia's house."

A man stepped out from behind the counter. He had long curly hair that matched a bushy curly beard. He wore a SpongeBob SquarePants T-shirt and shiny running pants with flip-flops.

"Welcome to the Reliquary, my dudes and Ms. Dude. You looking for something in particular?"

"Just visiting," Tess said.

"We like visitors who are just visiting. Especially cat visitors who are just visiting," the man said, when Nine sniffed at his feet and then nudged his knee with her nose. "Hey there, cat friend."

"She must like you," Jaime said.

"Thus, I am truly blessed," the man said. "So let me point out some stuff to you and your kitty, here. We've got lots of cool stuff. Some Liberty Statues over there. Baseball cards back there. Old Underway maps. Some different pieces of rock and schist from all around the city, some of them we think date back to the time when the Underway was first excavated. Ridiculous, right?" He was grinning, so Theo assumed he meant *ridiculous* as in "awesome" as opposed to *ridiculous* as in "ridiculous," because what was ridiculous about schist?

"Ridiculous," said Theo.

"Obvi," the man said. "Oh, and the Community Collection on display is an array of animal bones."

Tess's head snapped up. Nine stopped sniffing.

The clerk held up both hands. "No animals were harmed to make the collection! All the bones were found on hiking trails and in barns and parks and attics and the like. City bones, the bones of history! You should check it out for yourselves, young ones."

"Why would you want to display a bunch of mouse bones?" Tess said.

"Maybe because there's beauty even in things we associate with endings," the man said, "Or maybe the point of the collection is that there is no end, not to us, not to anything. Anyway, feel free to take a look around." The clerk went back behind the counter and starting flipping through a comic book.

Before Tess could ask all the questions clearly piling up in her head, Theo and Jaime steered her toward the VERY OLD SHOVEL.

"We don't have time for you to ask the four thousand questions you want to ask," Theo said before Tess could open her mouth. "We have to find the puzzle and figure out the next clue."

"Let's split up," Jaime suggested. "This place isn't

that big but we can cover it quicker that way."

So they did. Tess and Nine went to explore the back of the museum, Jaime stayed in front by the door, and Theo wandered the maze of shelves and display cases in the middle. It didn't take long for Theo to find what he was looking for. On a rickety metal shelf in the center of the Reliquary sat the puzzle in Ada's drawing. A dirty, tarnished thing. The tag on it said VERY OLD PUZZLE.

Theo glanced around, but no one was watching. He picked up the puzzle. At one point, the puzzle must have had different-colored stones set into the smaller cubes, but many of the stones were missing now. If their challenge was to solve the puzzle, how would that even work? Do they collect all stones of the same color on a side like a Rubik's cube? Form some sort of other pattern? That would be difficult. Maybe impossible. It could take days, weeks, months. They might never work it out.

And then another thing occurred to him, knotting up his gut: He couldn't take months or weeks or even days standing in this museum, trying to solve this puzzle.

He would have to steal it.

With one hand, he yanked at his own bushy hair, trying to pull himself back to himself. His mother was a detective. A *burglary* detective. He couldn't steal this puzzle.

He had to steal this puzzle.

How was he going to steal this puzzle?

How was he going to steal *anything*?

What if this wasn't the only thing they had to steal?

He thought about the relics and the artifacts in the other museums, not just in New York City, but around the world. So many of those artifacts were stolen, too—from graves, from houses of worship. Did it matter that this was just a lost and damaged old puzzle? Did it matter that someone had already stolen it long ago? Did it matter that, now, they were trying to do something good?

He felt the way he imagined Tess felt all the time, mind spinning with question after question, enough questions to make a person sick. And sure enough, as if she were able to sense his spinning mind, Nine came charging around the corner, dragging Tess behind her.

Nine nibbled at his fingers. Tess whispered, "You found it."

"Yeah," he said.

"What's wrong?"

"It's damaged. It will be hard to solve."

"Not impossible, though," she said.

"Maybe impossible."

"Not."

"Even if we can solve it, it will take forever."

Tess thought a moment. "We're going to have to borrow it."

"You mean steal it."

"No, I mean borrow it. We'll take it home, solve it, figure out the next clue, and then bring it back."

"But what if they figure out it's missing? What if they have a camera in here and they're taping us right now?"

"I don't see a camera in here," Tess said.

"*Hidden* cameras," Theo said.

"This doesn't look like the kind of place where they have hidden cameras."

"I don't want to steal stuff," Theo said. "It's not right."

"I know," said Tess. "But we won't keep it. We'll return it."

"What if we have to keep it? What if—"

"Hey, I thought I was the one with all the questions."

"I guess not," Theo said, tugging on his lip.

"You're doing that lip thing again," Tess said.

Theo let go just as Jaime appeared. Nine rubbed against Jaime's knees.

"How are you at diversions?" Theo asked Jaime.

"I could pretend to have a tantrum in the middle

of the store," Jaime said. "I could keep yelling for the manager."

Tess laughed. "Subtle."

"The guy at the counter was reading a comic book. I'm sure I can distract him for a while." Jaime's big brown eyes narrowed. "You guys are not going to get yourselves arrested, are you?"

"Obvi," Tess said.

Jaime went to the front counter and said, "Hey. Is that Batman number ninety-two?"

"Yeah," said the counterman. "An oldie but a goodie."

"I have that one! Has Ace the Bat-Hound, right?"

While Jaime and the counterman talked about Batmen and Bat-Hounds, Tess pretended to examine the exhibits all around the puzzle. Theo stood behind her, blocking her from view so that she could slip the puzzle into her bag. When Theo glanced at the front of the store, Jaime and the counterman were still communing happily over comics.

"Did you hear about Len Wein?"

"Tragedy," said the man, shaking his head.

"He helped create Storm," Jaime said.

"Wolverine, too."

"He's cool but Storm is cooler."

"*Cooler*, I get it," the man said.

Theo tugged at his lip as Tess shifted around some of the exhibits on the shelf so that it wouldn't appear as if anything was missing.

"Done," whispered Tess.

His nerves balled up in his stomach like bad takeout. "The Cipher was a lot more fun when we didn't *have* to solve it."

Jaime's nerves must have gotten to him, too, because he ended his conversation and walked back to where Tess and Theo were whispering. "We ready?"

"As we're ever going to be," said Theo.

"Mrrow," chirped Nine.

On their way out, they thanked the man for his help.

"No problem, young ones," he said. "Come back anytime!"

They slipped out the door, all of them breathing a sigh of relief when they weren't followed. They had just reached end of the street when a woman whipped around the corner and slammed right into Tess. Before Tess could say anything, the woman started to scream.

"It bit me!" she shrieked. "Help!"

"What?" said Tess. "She didn't—" And then she took a step back—they all did—because the woman looked so familiar. She had icy-blond hair and wore a red dress and matching shoes.

The woman held up her arm, which was suddenly dripping with blood. "Look at this!"

Tess's face went pale. "My cat didn't do that. She didn't touch you!"

"That is no cat!"

"Of course she's a cat."

"That is some kind of monster! Oh my Lord, that's a *machine*, isn't it?" the woman yelled.

"No!" said Tess.

"It is! It's a machine!" the woman wailed. "Some kind of malfunctioning machine! Help! Won't someone help me?" But she didn't look scared, and she didn't back up. Her dark eyes gleamed with something that appeared to Theo to be . . . amusement?

She was enjoying this, whoever she was.

People in the street stopped to stare. Jaime grabbed Tess's arm, and Theo grabbed the other.

"Put your heads down," Jaime muttered. "Don't run."

"But—" Tess began, but Jaime cut her off.

"Walk to the train. Pretend you can't hear her, that she isn't talking about you at all."

They walked, behind them a rising torrent of murmurs along with the shrieking of the woman. One man's voice rumbled, "Is that blood?"

Once they hit the stairs to the Underway, they walked

faster, hopping the nearest train. They sat in a row, stiff and nervous, Tess muttering, "Nine didn't even get near that woman. She bumped into *me*. And why would she say Nine is a machine? Why would she lie like that?"

Nine nudged her fingers, and Tess buried her face in the cat's fur. Theo studied the passengers one by one. None of them seemed to be watching them; all of them seemed to be watching them.

"We're okay," Jaime said.

"I want to know who that woman is," Theo said, keeping his voice low. "She must be following us."

Jaime shook his head. "It was a different woman. The one at the library was taller and had light eyes. This one was shorter and had brown eyes."

"There are two of them?" said Tess. "A team? But whose team?"

"I don't know," Jaime said grimly. He pulled out his sketchbook and quickly drew the woman holding up her arm and shrieking while a cold glee made her eyes glint.

Theo shivered at the drawing. "That's almost too good."

They were quiet the rest of the ride to Aunt Esther's house, as if they were afraid that any more talking would somehow summon another person shrieking like a banshee. When they finally made it through Aunt Esther's front door, Tess closed it and leaned upon it.

"Whew," she said. "That was really close."

Jaime said, "We need to lie low for a while."

"The cube will keep us busy enough," Theo said.

Aunt Esther appeared in the doorway to the kitchen. "What will keep you busy enough?"

"Helping you with dinner, Ms. Esther," said Jaime.

Aunt Esther beamed. "You are always such a gentleman, Mr. Jaime. I was thinking of putting together a lasagna."

"That's convenient, because I love lasagna," Jaime said.

"Then you'll have to stay and eat with us. Why don't you call your grandmother and ask her."

Theo wondered what it must be like, to have a gift for people, to say the kinds of things they wanted to hear without ever sounding fake, because you didn't need to fake things. Theo didn't fake things, either, but people didn't always seem to like him for it. Most of the time he didn't mind, but once in a while, he did.

But he was grateful to Jaime for distracting the counterman from their thievery, distracting Aunt Esther from their conversation, and distracting Tess from her run-in with the banshee. They spent the next two hours in the kitchen with Aunt Esther, helping to chop onions and tomatoes, boiling noodles, layering a giant lasagna into a giant pan. Nine helped by eating the cheese that they accidentally dropped to the floor. And after they had put the lasagna into the oven, Lance helped by serving everyone cookies and milk in the living room. ("Dessert first," Aunt Esther said. "Dessert *always*," said Tess.)

They were in such a good mood, the weirdness of the day pushed to the backs of their minds, that Theo was unprepared for the sudden appearance of his mother, who was supposed to be home much later. When she came into the living room, she didn't smile, she didn't say hello, she didn't comment on the cookie crumbs or the scent of tomato sauce in the air. She put her hands in her pockets and said, "Who wants to tell me what happened today?"

Immediately, Theo thought of the puzzle, how they had stolen it. He opened his mouth, but couldn't think of a thing.

"You have something you want to say, Theo?"

"I—" he began. But then didn't know how to finish. Even Jaime seemed at a loss for words, his usual grace erased at the sight of Mrs. Biedermann's stern expression.

Mrs. Biedermann pulled out her own phone,

punched a few buttons. Then she turned it around so they could see. "Maybe this video will jog your memories? It's all over the internet."

On the phone they saw the woman shrieking, waving around her bloody arm. And they saw themselves, all four of them, Nine seeming larger than ever.

Tess leaned forward, "Mom, that woman bumped into me. Nine never touched her. She wouldn't bite anyone like that. The woman was lying."

Their mother sighed, put the phone back in her pocket. "Why would she lie?"

"I don't know!" Tess said.

There was a sharp rap on the door. Mrs. Biedermann yelled, "Come in," and a pale, doughy man stepped inside.

"My new partner, Detective Clarkson," Mrs. Biedermann said, gesturing at the man.

Tess stared. They all did. Because the pale, doughy man was one of the officers who had discovered the three of them climbing down from an abandoned Underway track last month, a man who knew who Tess and Theo's mother was but agreed not to tell her so they wouldn't get in trouble (and so he wouldn't have to do extra paperwork).

If he remembered them now, and Theo was sure he

did, he didn't show it. Clarkson simply nodded, his face as grave as Mrs. Biedermann's.

"They're here, Detective," he said.

"Who's here?" said Tess,

"Listen, sweetheart," said Mrs. Biedermann. "I believe you. I do. But the woman in the video filed charges."

"Nine didn't do anything, Mom," Theo said.

Jaime agreed. "She didn't, Mrs. Biedermann. Really."

"Be that as it may, I have to take Nine." When Tess's jaw dropped open in shock, she said, "Just for a little while, just until we get this straightened out."

"No!" Tess said, grabbing Nine around the neck, hugging her. "No! It's not fair. That woman was lying!"

"What were you doing in Brooklyn?" their mother asked.

"What does that matter?" Theo said, his tone sharper than he'd intended. His mother just stared at him, and so did Clarkson. "We were at a museum. That woman bumped into Tess. We didn't do anything. *Nine* didn't do anything. She faked that bite. I don't know why, but she did."

At this, Clarkson's face softened. "I talked to that woman and her story was full of applesauce." His eyes cut to Theo's mom and he added, "In my opinion."

"I know. But because you're my kids, and because I got you that license for Nine, I can't show any favoritism. I have to go by the book."

Aunt Esther, who had been quiet during this whole exchange, said, "Whose book, Miriam?"

"You know what I mean."

"I'm not sure I do," said Aunt Esther. "You know that Nine wouldn't hurt a fly. And the children told you what they were doing. That woman must have some sort of agenda. Perhaps she's trying to get to you."

"Why would this woman want to get to me?"

"I don't know, Miriam. You should ask her about that."

"I will," Theo's mom said. "And the sooner I figure it out, the sooner we'll get Nine back. But right now, the city pound is going to have to take her. They're here right now."

At this, Tess started to cry. Next to Theo, Jaime squeezed the couch cushions so hard his knuckles went white. Theo's whole body itched, as if his skin were coming loose.

His mother crouched in front of Tess. "It's going to be okay. I've talked to the guys at the pound; they'll look after her, they'll make sure she's cared for."

"I can't," said Tess, "I can't." Maybe she meant she

couldn't bear to see Nine go or she couldn't live without Nine even for a little while or she couldn't stand something so unfair or all of it.

But his mom took hold of Nine's harness, setting her mouth at the sound of Tess's cries. Nine hunched, trying and failing to make herself smaller. She emitted a confused "Mrrow?"

Aunt Esther stood. "Don't do this, Miriam."

"I have to," said Theo's mom. But she didn't meet anyone's eyes as she led Nine from the living room and out the door.

Clarkson lingered one moment more. "I know this whole thing seems corn nuts, but your mom is really smart. She's going to figure out what the butterscotch that woman is about, and get your kitty back banana split, don't you worry."

Theo could have told him that the only person who could persuade Tess not to worry wasn't a person at all, but the very large cat they had just taken away.

Tess put her face in her hands and sobbed.

Soon after, Tess went up to her bed. Aunt Esther slammed pots and pans around the kitchen, her lips stitched tight in disapproval. Lance cowered in the corner. Theo and Jaime picked at the lasagna, but couldn't eat much. They finally gave up, wrapped the pan in foil, and put it in the fridge for a time they weren't feeling so sick. Jaime told Theo he had to get home, and Aunt Esther said she would walk him to the train station.

"If I don't get some air I might spontaneously combust," she announced.

Before they, too, disappeared out the front door, Jaime said, "Tell Tess I said good-bye."

"I will," Theo said.

"Tell her . . ." He seemed about to say something more, but didn't.

"Tomorrow," Theo said. "You'll see her tomorrow."

"Yeah," said Jaime.

And then they were out the door.

Theo's dad came home. He'd heard what happened and went upstairs to check on Tess while Theo cleaned the kitchen. Theo left a plate with a square of lasagna for his dad on the table, but when his dad came back downstairs, he didn't seem to have much of an appetite, either. He helped Theo with the dishes, and then the two of them watched TV for a while, avoiding all the news reports of a giant cat, likely a machine disguised as an animal, terrorizing innocent blond ladies in Brooklyn.

Theo lasted another hour and then he went to bed. Somehow, he fell asleep. He was awakened by Tess's soft cries, too much like the cries of a lost kitten. He crawled out of his bed and knelt next to hers. Her eyes twitched under her lids, and her limbs thrashed as if she were trying to run. He caught hold of one of her hands and whispered, "It's okay. Everything's okay," even though it wasn't, and he wasn't sure how they were going to fix it. He talked to her and squeezed her hand until her thrashing slowed, then stopped.

Without letting go, Theo shifted so that he was sitting against her bed, head resting on the mattress. He held his sister's hand all through the night, till the sky split against the rising sun, black and gold as Nine's fur.

CHAPTER ELEVEN
Nine

Miriam Biedermann had not lied to her children. The men who loaded Nine into their van and drove her to the large, dank facility in Manhattan were gentle with her. They did not yank on her harness or yell. They talked to her in low, soothing voices. The cage they put her in was clean, with a comfortable bed in one corner and a bowl full of water.

But a cage was still a cage, something Nine knew well. When she was only a kitten, and just another number, Nine had spent most of her time in one.

She hadn't minded the cage, not back then. She had been small enough that the expanse of the enclosure seemed vast as any universe. Eyes and ears closed, barely able to walk, she nosed along the padded bottom of the cage, trying and failing to find its edges. All she could be certain of were the smells: the papery scent of the padding beneath her paws; the sharp tang of the metal bars; the musk of her brothers and sisters, each one distinct; and the smell of her mother, milky and strong.

As she and her siblings grew, so did the size of the cage. With their eyes and ears open, the kittens wrestled and chased, leaped and pounced, napped in a giant, twitching heap. Occasionally, a gloved hand would open the cage and one of the kittens would be lifted out despite Mother's loud protests. Once outside the cage, the kittens were weighed and measured. Mouths were pried open so that teeth could be checked. Needles. Too many needles. Other indignities that Nine didn't like to recall.

What she did recall: She was always the hardest to catch.

No matter how quick the hand that reached in to grab her, she was quicker. It was a game, her favorite, evading the gloved hand. She charged around the cage, banking off the sides, darting and dodging, using the backs of her siblings for stairs. It often took two and three pairs of hands to corral her. Once caught, she hissed and wriggled, twisted and slipped, leading her captors on a merry chase around the other cages in the facility.

There were many cages. Sometimes the musk of the creatures in the cages was familiar; sometimes it was puzzling and strange. Sometimes the creatures were friendly, meowing and yipping and howling their approval, and sometimes they were hostile, trying to stick snouts bristling with teeth through the bars to snap at her as she raced by. She was too fast for them all.

That was how her early life went: She played with her siblings and nuzzled her mother and evaded capture as best she could. And then, one by one, her siblings were taken and never returned. There were nine, eight, then seven, six, five, four, three, two. One day, while she was sedated, they took her mother.

And Nine was alone in the cage.

Like she was now.

She didn't have to nose along the bottom of this particular cage to find its boundaries; she had enough room to take five steps but no more. The smells of this place were too numerous to absorb: so much rage and sadness, desperation and despair. She didn't touch the food the men offered her, though they offered it kindly. She was too busy testing the limits of the lock on her cage door. She leaned against it, pawed it, bit it. Was disappointed when it held. Was more disappointed when one of the men, not so kindly, reinforced the lock by wrapping it with wire.

This would not do.

She didn't understand how or why she had ended up here, but she knew that whatever the reason, it was a tragic mistake. She had a family and a job. She could not stay trapped in this prison for the lost and the abandoned and the stolen. She waited until dark, when the men left these wailing creatures to endure the lonely night in whatever way they could, and used a claw to tease open the knot of wire. She grasped the wire between her teeth and patiently unwound it from the lock. Then she turned her attention to the lock itself. It wasn't a complicated contraption. It was merely a lever on the outside of the cage. She worked one paw between the metal bars and lifted the lever as she leaned on the door. It opened with a barely audible creak. Well, barely audible to humans, but the other creatures heard it well enough. As Nine sauntered down the empty hallway, past cage after cage, the creatures muttered and sang, howled and growled, mewled and cried. She wanted to help them; she didn't have time to help them. She steeled herself against their plaintive wails and headed straight for the large swinging door at the very end of the hallway, the door to freedom.

But just before Nine reached the door, it swung open, a long shadow looming behind it. Nine's nails scratched for purchase as she scrambled backward and raced back down the hallway. The long shadow followed her, footsteps eerily quiet on the cement floor. At the sight of the intruder, the other animals grew frantic, the air filling with the rattling of their cages, the sounds of their barks and mewls and shrieks. Nine found herself on the opposite side of the building, a brick wall in front of her, cages to her left and right.

No way out.

Nine turned around and lowered her head, gathering herself to spring.

The woman stopped just a few feet from Nine, smiling, unafraid. She crouched to meet Nine's eyes and smiled wider when Nine answered her steady gaze with a warning growl.

"Well, well, well," the woman murmured. "Just the kitty I was looking for."

CHAPTER TWELVE

Jaime

The morning after the twins' mom took Nine away, Jaime woke up far too early with a strange, hot pressure in his head, like someone was squeezing his brain from the inside.

He got up and tried to shake off the feeling, and when that didn't work, he massaged his temples. He was distracted from the pain by his hamster-hogs, Napoleon and Tyrone, both girls, who began sniffing around their cage for breakfast. He opened the top of the cage, grabbed their food bowl, and poured some fresh kibble. As usual, Napoleon ran over and munched, but Tyrone, much pickier, took one sniff of the kibble and charged over to her wheel. She jumped on and ran as fast as she could, squeaking her displeasure with the kibble, with Jaime, with a heartless universe that had saddled her with an unfeeling, selfish owner who did not serve adequate food.

"Okay, okay," Jaime huffed, shuffling to the kitchen to find some bit of fruit to please her. It was only when he returned with a couple of cubes of watermelon and watched Tyrone run that he recognized the source of the pain in his head: He was angry. So angry he could have sprinted ten miles on a Jaime-sized exercise wheel, if someone had invented such a thing.

Jaime was not an angry person. He was chill, he took things in stride, like his mother before him. He liked that about himself. As a baby, he was so calm and quiet that his parents took to poking him in his crib every hour to make sure he was still alive (or so Mima said). But that guard chasing Cricket, that woman faking her bite, Detective Biedermann taking Nine away from Tess, her own daughter, ate at him.

It just wasn't right.

It wasn't right when he got dressed; it wasn't right when he sat at the breakfast table, dully shoveling Mima's eggs into his mouth; and it wasn't right when he lied to Mima, telling her that he was fine, and that Tess would be fine, that Detective Biedermann would get Nine back.

An hour later, he left for the twins' house, the headache still squeezing his skull. He glared at the security guard on duty, even though it wasn't the same one who had chased Cricket, earning a confused "Good morning?" from the poor guy. It made Jaime feel guilty, but not guilty enough to apologize. Which wasn't like him, either. This quest to solve the Old York Cipher was not only taking over his life, it was turning him into a whole different person. Or maybe he would have turned into a whole different person anyway, he couldn't be sure.

What he was sure of: They had to get Nine back, and immediately, as in today. And at the moment, he didn't care who he had to glare at to make it happen.

Oddly, this thought cheered him a little, and on the Underway ride out to Queens, the hot pain in his head cooled, receded. By the time he arrived at the twins' house, he felt almost as chill as he normally did, as he used to, before all of this Cipher stuff happened. Though it was still quite early, Aunt Esther seemed pleased to see him, and so did Mr. Biedermann, who was at the kitchen table eating a bagel.

"Ah, Jaime," said Mr. Biedermann. "How's your morning been?"

"As good as yours, probably," said Jaime. "Any news about Nine?"

Aunt Esther harrumphed and banged a mug on the counter. Mr. Biedermann frowned at her back. "No, not yet. But my wife is working on it."

Aunt Esther grabbed a handful of silverware and jammed them into a drawer. "She could work a little faster."

"It's been twelve hours, Esther."

Aunt Esther sniffed. "Like I said."

Mr. Biedermann closed his eyes as if taking a moment to pray for patience, then opened them again. He ate the last bite of bagel and got up. "I have to be off to work. Feel free to have a bagel, Jaime, or anything else you want. The twins are already up and should be downstairs in a few minutes." Before he left, he placed a hand on Jaime's shoulder. "I'm always glad to see you, but I'm especially glad today. Tess is going to need a friend."

Jaime didn't know what to say, so said nothing. He nodded instead. It was enough for Mr. Biedermann, who gathered a stack of file folders and headed out of the kitchen. As he walked, his pocket started ringing. Literally ringing, like the bell between classes at school. Mr. Biedermann fumbled with his folders and his phone. "Hello?" he said.

Then he stopped in his tracks.

"What? Well, where is she?"

Pause.

Mr. Biedermann stiffened, and his voice did, too. "And *why* are you asking me this?"

Another pause.

"My daughter has been home all night. *Crying*, I might add. She is utterly devastated. A little girl, utterly devastated."

Pause. A quick glance over his shoulder at Aunt Esther.

"No one from this house has been anywhere near that place. And I don't appreciate your accusations. I'm calling my wife. Also? You better send some people out to look for her, because if you don't . . ." Mr. Biedermann turned off the phone, came back to the table, dropped the phone and his files on top.

Aunt Esther said, "What is it, Lawrence?"

"Nine," said Mr. Biedermann.

"What about Nine?" said a voice from the doorway.

Tess. Her eyes red. Still in a nightgown. Theo right behind her.

"Honey," said Mr. Biedermann. "Why don't you sit—"

"What about Nine?" Tess repeated.

Mr. Biedermann took a deep breath, then said, "She's missing."

Theo put a hand on Tess's shoulder. But if they

expected Tess to collapse, to scream, they were surprised. Because she did none of those things. Tess blinked, then a slow grin spread across her face.

"Tess?" said Mr. Biedermann.

"She got away," said Tess. "She'll come home now."

"Tess."

"She's always been good at that. Escaping. And hiding. Like that time when she was a kitten and she got out of the apartment. She ended up in Mr. Perlmutter's cereal cabinet. She ate all his Wheaties."

"Tess—" Mr. Biedermann began again.

"And that time she decided to ride the dumbwaiter. She was gone for hours. I was so worried. But I was worried for nothing! I'm always worried for nothing!"

"Honey."

"Remember, Dad? Remember how she likes to escape? How she likes to hide?"

Mr. Biedermann pressed his lips together. Then he said, "I remember."

"She got away," Tess said firmly. "She'll come home."

"Tess, are you—"

"I'm fine, Dad," Tess said.

"But—"

"Honestly. I'm fine."

Jaime didn't think she was fine. He didn't think

anything was fine. But Mr. Biedermann picked up the cell. "Well. I'm going to let your mother know what happened."

"If she doesn't already," Theo said.

"Yes. Well. I'll call her anyway," said Mr. Biedermann. He scooped up the phone and the files. He seemed about to say something else, but decided against it. They heard the front door slam as he left.

Jaime and Theo looked at Tess. She put her hands on her hips, her eyes and her smile overbright. "So. What's for breakfast?"

Tess kept it up all morning, the smiling. All through breakfast—slowly munching her way through a bagel. While she bounced down the stairs wearing jean shorts and a Wonder Woman T-shirt. During the Underway ride to Manhattan, to the place where they'd taken Nine. Through their search of the surrounding blocks, hoping to find Nine hiding in an alley or napping in a doorway.

And she kept it up all the way back to Aunt Esther's, all through their lunch of empanadas from a joint down the street. It was like a wall, Tess's brightness, a spell she encased herself in, a safe place where she was Not Worried About Anything and Nine was Most Certainly Just

Fine and On Her Way Home Right Now. Every once in a while, Theo would touch Tess's arm or her fingers the way Nine used to nudge—to reassure her, to bring her out of herself, or to tell her to take as long as she needed. Early that morning, Jaime had been so sure that he, that they, could bring Nine home; he was at a loss now that Nine had decided to free herself. But he couldn't help but worry that Nine hadn't done any such thing. That she'd been taken. That the woman who had accused the cat of attacking her might have had something to do with it. That Nine wasn't coming home, not without assistance. But he couldn't bring himself to say it out loud. Not yet. Instead, he drew sketches of Nine: unlocking a cage; slipping between the bars; sliding under a cracked window; vanishing into the night. He drew dozens of variations and showed the pictures to Tess. With each variation, she smiled her bright smile and squeezed his wrist as if he were actually doing something, as if there were something to thank him for.

Aunt Esther seemed out of sorts herself, deflated somehow, like a magician robbed of magic. She announced that she was off to the market and that she would leave them a plate of Fig Newtons. At Tess's answering grin, Aunt Esther harrumphed again, added another stack of cookies to the plate before she, too, left.

Theo fetched the metal puzzle from his room upstairs and brought it down to the living room, where they went through the motions of examining it under a magnifying glass. The surface was studded with the occasional stone here or there—a red one, a blue one, but there were far more empty settings than stones.

"There are a lot missing," said Theo.

"We can solve it," said Tess, smiling, smiling, smiling.

"Maybe," said Theo, careful not to mention what he normally would—that is, that the puzzle would be very difficult to solve with a few stones missing, let alone most of them. But Theo, being Theo, tried anyway. And then Jaime took a turn. Tess, surprisingly, or unsurprisingly, worked at it the longest, until she, too, gave up. She passed the cube back to Theo and peeked out the front windows, just in case Nine was home and wanted to get in the house.

Jaime watched her look left and right, watched her shoulders sink just the slightest bit when she didn't see the cat, when she sat back down on the couch. "Maybe we're not supposed to solve it," Jaime said. "Maybe we're supposed to take it apart."

"That's interesting," Theo said, actually sounding intrigued by something other than Tess or Nine for the first time that day. "Maybe we can build something else out of it."

"Good idea," Tess said, smiling. Jaime wished she would stop that. It was starting to freak him out.

Theo fetched a small tool kit, and they went to work on the puzzle with a screwdriver. Then with a hammer and chisel. But if they were supposed to take it apart and build something else with it, it was going to be a challenge. Not one of the tiny cubes budged even a millimeter.

"This isn't working," said Theo, shoving a hand in his hair. Then, "Ouch!" because he'd forgotten he was still holding the chisel.

"Don't chip your head," said Jaime, but it came out wrong. Not chill or cheerful, not funny at all.

"Hello," said Tess.

"Sorry?" said Jaime.

"I'm talking to the spiders," she replied. She pointed at the plants hanging by the window. "They're looking at us. See?"

Jaime was afraid to turn his head for fear that Tess was hallucinating, but she wasn't hallucinating. A little crowd of spiders had gathered at the lip of one of the potted plants. And they did seem to watching with their strange, kookoo-bunny eyes.

They had too many eyes, Jaime thought. It wasn't right.

"Do they . . . do they do this a lot?" Jaime said. "Watch you like that?"

"Well," said Theo. "Ours mostly laugh."

"Giggle," Tess said. "It's more like a giggle."

"Okay?" said Jaime. Another couple of spiders joined the bunch at the lip of the pot. Then, a tiny voice said, "Hello."

"And say 'hello,'" Theo added.

"Uh-huh," said Jaime. And flipped right off the couch when one of the spiders suddenly leaped from the potted plant and landed on the table in front of him.

"Don't be afraid," Tess murmured.

". . . of the spiders," Theo finished.

"*Don't be afraid of the spiders,*" Jaime repeated after them, heart thudding anyway.

"The Vigenère cipher," Tess breathed. "That was the solution to it. Don't be afraid."

The little spider giggled. "Hello, hello, hello." It scuttled toward the center of the table, toward the puzzle, climbed on top of it.

Another spider leaped from the plant to the table, circled the puzzle. Then another. Spider after spider gathered. Jaime knelt in front of the table, brought the magnifying glass over the puzzle to better see what the spiders were doing. They swarmed the silvery cube, their bodies almost blending into the surface. Their tiny legs clicked and worked. Together, they flipped the puzzle over, and once again swarmed the surface. Then, they dropped the cube to the surface of the table with a thud. A shimmering wave of spiders raced across the table, off the edge, and across the floor.

The last spider crouched under the magnifying glass. "Hello!" it warbled. It seemed to Jaime that it had one less eye now—two shimmering green eyes rather than three. Then it giggled, before it jumped from the table and raced away, leaving the puzzle in front of them studded with gleaming, multicolored jewels, just like new.

CHAPTER THIRTEEN

Tess

Tess heard Jaime and Theo exclaim over the puzzle, examine it, wonder aloud if anyone's spiders would have done what Aunt Esther's had done or if Aunt Esther's spiders were special, and what that meant. If the colored stones were real jewels, and if they were, how much the puzzle would be worth. And she saw them scramble to solve it, turning the individual cubes this way and that, trying to match up the stones on each face.

But she didn't really hear them and she didn't really see them because she wasn't really there. She was eleven years old again, and she'd had Nine for only six months. Nine was only twelve pounds then—still just a kitten, really—smart and fast and mischievous. Though she got Nine a license from the city, Tess's mom hadn't been convinced that Nine would make a good therapy animal until she saw the cat in training, how attentive and alert she was, how very clever and very strong, how she kept Tess from stumbling into traffic, how she kept Tess from spiraling into an anxiety attack, how she comforted Tess during her endless nightmares. When Nine went missing one snowy winter afternoon, Tess was frantic, but her mother wasn't worried. Nine was too smart to get lost, she said. She's playing a game, she said. Until they searched the whole building, the elevator, the roof, and the basement. Until the hours started to tick by, and darkness fell like a rough blanket over their heads as they roamed the alleys outside. Then the expression on her mother's face moved from concern to alarm to resignation to acceptance, ticking through the emotions quick as the minute hand of a clock.

"Tess, it's freezing. I need to get you inside. I'm sure Nine has found a place to . . . hide."

"No," Tess had said. "She'll find us. Wherever she is. I know it. We just have to keep calling."

Her mother touched Tess's shoulder, must have felt the deep shiver that started at Tess's knees and vibrated all the way up to Tess's head. But her mother relented, stayed out with Tess another half hour anyway, shouting over the sounds of cars and Rollers and madly barking dogs until both their voices went dry and hoarse. And even after she forced Tess inside to warm up, she let Tess roam the building, let her search the basement and the elevator and the halls and the roof one more time.

When Tess got back to her apartment, she found her father cooking dinner, Theo doing homework, and her mother folding laundry in front of the TV. Then, it was the rage rather than the radiators that warmed her.

"What are you doing?" she'd shouted at them.

They all stopped, staring.

"She's out there, and you're just . . . making stew and folding underwear as if nothing's wrong!"

"Tess," her mother began, but Tess roared, "NO!" as loud as she could. With renewed determination, she turned and ran back into the hallway, calling Nine's name. She knocked on every apartment door, explored every nook and cranny of the building she could think of, including every inch of Grandpa Ben's place, while Grandpa and Lance watched her, both of them wringing their hands. When she got down to the lobby, she pressed her face to the glass, tears turning to frost on her cheeks, stinging there. Through the glass, she could still hear the incessant barking and whining of the dogs. Why? Why did they keep barking? What were they barking at?

What were they barking at?

She burst from the building, followed the sound of the barks. It led her down the alley along one side, where rows of now-empty cans and dumpsters squatted in the darkness. A lone man pulled at the leashes of a half dozen dogs who were frantically sniffing and barking at one of the dumpsters.

"Will you guys cut it out! LEAVE IT!"

Tess ran up to the man. "What are they barking at?"

"What else? Dog pee, table scraps, garbage. I don't know! What do you expect from animals with brains the size of baseballs." He tugged at the leashes again. "I SAID, LEAVE IT!"

The dogs, who ranged in size from teacup to pony, were trying to stick their heads under the dumpster. Tess pushed the pony aside and peered underneath.

"Nine?" she said.

The answer was a frighteningly weak "Mrrow."

"Oh, Nine!" Tess reached under the dumpster and discovered that Nine was wrapped up in some kind of old net. Volleyball or badminton or something. The more the kitten had struggled against it, the more it must have gotten tangled around her paws and her neck, the tighter it must had bound her. When Tess ripped off the net and pulled her out from underneath the dumpster, tucked the cat inside her coat, the cat was so cold, so, so cold, far more cold than a living thing should ever be and still live.

She ignored the dog walker and his dogs, who yelled and yipped at her back. She ran all the way from the alley to the lobby, from the lobby the elevator, from the elevator to her apartment, could barely speak after she threw open the door, showed her parents what was stowed in her coat. The entire family packed into a cab and raced to the nearest emergency vet. The vet said that if Tess hadn't found Nine when she did, the cat could have died in the freezing cold.

"You saved her life," the vet said. "Maybe one day, she'll return the favor."

Traffic, anxiety attacks, nightmares. Tess had said, "She already has."

"Who has what?" Theo and Jaime, both of them huddled around the puzzle, stared at her from their perch on Aunt Esther's couch.

"Nothing," Tess said. She got up and went to the window. She nudged the thin curtains aside. On the street, groups of women pushed strollers, kids ran for the nearest park or basketball court, men hung out on stoops, laughing. A blond woman in a red dress walked by, bright hair bouncing.

Tess bolted for the door.

"Tess!" Theo shouted, but Tess was already outside, already chasing the blond woman. She caught the woman's arm just as she reached the corner.

"What do you think you're doing here?" Tess yelled. "Where's Nine? What did you do to my cat?"

The woman turned, wide-eyed. "What? What do you mean?"

She was younger than Tess had expected. Acne dotted her chin. Tiny printed flowers covered the red dress. She looked about as dangerous as a daisy. "Why would I do anything to anyone's cat? I'm allergic to cats!"

"I . . . ," Tess started. "I think I might have the wrong person."

"No duh," said the girl, rubbing her arm. Footsteps thundered behind them. Theo and Jaime, breathing hard.

"Is everything okay?" Jaime said.

"Your friend needs serious help," said the girl, before turning and flouncing away.

Tess hugged herself. "I saw the red dress and I thought . . ."

"We know," said Jaime.

Theo said, "Let's go back inside. We almost solved the puzzle."

Who cares? Tess thought, but she didn't bother to say it.

"Tess," said Theo. "She'll be back. I know it."

Tess dragged her gaze to her brother. "*How* do you know?"

Theo thought about this for a moment, searching his brain for evidence to back up his statement, then shrugged helplessly. "I just know."

"That's my line," Tess said.

"Yeah, well, maybe I'm learning to trust my gut sometimes."

"Trust your gut? Who *are* you?"

"Your brother," said Theo, holding out his hand.

There was nothing else to do but take it.

Inside, the puzzle sat on the table, just a few stones out of place. Tess tried to trust her own gut, tried to pay attention as Theo and Jaime passed the puzzle back and forth, each of them trying different twists and turns. She watched as Theo tested different maneuvers, talking out loud about how logical and beautiful the puzzle was as he did. Her gaze, however, kept drifting to the window.

Until Theo said, "Got it!"

He placed the silver cube in the center of the table and then sat back. They waited for something to happen. And waited. And waited.

Jaime said, "Should we ask the spiders for help?" A joke, or maybe not.

"What if the spiders didn't help?" Theo said. "What if they put the jewels in random places and we haven't really solved anything?"

Jaime shrugged. Theo tugged at his lip. Tess wondered whether she should check behind the house. Maybe Nine was stuck behind one of the cans back there, or tangled in one of the bushes. But then, how would she have gotten across the water from Manhattan? She would have had to hitch a ride somehow. Taxi or car or Underway train. Or Underway *tunnel*. What if Nine was beneath the city right now? What if she was wandering in the dark? What if she ran into one of those giant ants? Or something much bigger?

Theo squeezed her hand again. Tess squeezed back. He'd done this last night, she remembered suddenly. Sensed when she was spinning, touched her arm, or talked to her. How long had he done that? An hour? All night? *Theo?* He didn't look any different—same bushy hair, same frown, same skinny frame, same annoying habits of pulling on his lip and burying his hand in his unruly curls, one elbow sticking out. And yet, in his profile, in the rough, awkward squeeze of his fingers, she got a glimpse of someone older, someone wiser, someone who could focus on whatever technical problem presented itself but who also could tear himself away from technical problems, sense the brokenness in people, and try his best to fix that as well.

The cube rattled. It settled for a few minutes, then rattled again.

"I hope it doesn't explode," Jaime said. Another joke. Or not.

"It won't explode," said Theo.

It might, Tess thought.

It didn't. It rattled, then bounced, thudding on the table's surface. They all jumped.

"It sounds like when Mima makes popcorn," Jaime said, right before the cube burst, then pulled in on itself, combining and recombining. Two short "arms" shot out from its sides, two "feet" erupted from the bottom. A tiny, boxy head, complete with two jeweled blue eyes, popped from the top.

"What is that supposed to be?" Tess said.

"A toy?" Jaime said.

"Doesn't look like something the Morningstarrs would build," Theo said.

Jaime knelt next to the table. "Maybe they didn't build this one. Hey, there, robot. What are you about?"

The little robot shuddered, then spat out what looked like an overlarge jack from a game of jacks. It hit Jaime in the nose.

"Oh, man," said Theo. "How are we going to return the puzzle now?"

"We can put it back the way it was later," said Tess.

Jaime picked up the larger silver jack-like piece. "This must be the center axis of the cube."

Theo said, "Save that. We might need it."

"I wasn't going to eat it," said Jaime, tucking it into one of his many pockets.

But Tess wasn't looking at the axis; she was watching

the robot. It was completely still for a moment, but then the blue eyes flared. It lifted one tiny arm in the direction of the front door. In a tiny, tinny voice, it said, "To the Land of Kings!"

"The land of what?" Jaime said.

It turned its tiny, boxy head and marched its tiny, boxy body across the circular table, a trip that took a rather long time. When it reached the edge of the table, it stopped, looked down.

"Oh no," it said.

It swiveled, marched in another direction, reached the edge.

"Oh no," it said again.

A third trip across the table yielded the same result.

"Oh no."

"This is going well," Jaime said. He scooped up the robot.

"Don't touch it! What if it's dangerous?" Theo said.

"It's not dangerous," Jaime said, placing the robot on the floor. "Are you?"

The robot marched across the living room. It reached the door with a little *thunk*, but kept marching in place, saying "Oh no, oh no, oh no," the whole time.

"I think it wants us to follow it out the door," Tess said.

"Yeah," said Theo, "but we can't run around outside, not yet. We don't want more trouble."

All Tess wanted to do was run around outside. What if Nine was outside? What if she needed help?

"I don't want to lie low," Tess said. "I'm tired of lying low."

"It's only been a day, Tess," Theo said.

"I don't care."

"We're already all over the internet with that creepy woman's video," Jaime said. He walked to the robot and picked it up, cradled it in the crook of his elbow.

"Oh no," said the robot forlornly.

At that moment, Aunt Esther opened the door, her arms full of groceries. She regarded the three of them, the little robot in Jaime's hands. "Have a new friend, I see. What's its name?"

"Name?"

"Everything has a name."

"Oh no," said the robot.

"That's its name, Aunt Esther," Tess said, taking one of the grocery bags. "Ono."

"It's original at least," said Aunt Esther. "Any word about Nine?"

"Not yet," Tess said. "We were thinking of looking for her but . . ."

"But?"

"We don't want to end up in another video," said Tess.

"Well, that's an easy problem to solve," said Aunt Esther, heading for the kitchen.

"It is?"

"Certainly," Aunt Esther said. "All you need is the right disguise."

CHAPTER FOURTEEN
Theo

Theo was not one for disguises. For example, his last seven Halloween costumes were ghost, ghost, ghost, nerd, ghost, nerd ghost, and a bushy-haired TV painter named Bob Ross who liked to paint "happy little trees." Every October, Theo argued that he didn't actually need a costume because no one outside of his apartment building knew who he was anyway, so why bother when, technically, he was a mystery to everyone? Which was when his dad draped a sheet over his head and told him to say thank you even if stores on the block gave out candy bars with nougat.

Theo hated nougat. But Tess loved candy bars with nougat, and she loved Aunt Esther's idea.

"What kind of disguises?" Tess asked, as they all piled into the kitchen to unload the groceries.

"Whatever kind you like," Aunt Esther said. "I've still got three trunks full of costumes from my days in the theater. I could never bring myself to part with them."

"When were you in the theater?" Theo asked automatically—and pointlessly—because Aunt Esther never explained herself.

"Oh, a long time ago," Aunt Esther said. "When we're done putting away the food, we'll take a look and see." She eyed the little robot still tucked in Jaime's arms. "We might even find something for your friend, there."

Later, after lunch, they traipsed up the stairs to the attic where Aunt Esther kept her trunks. She had dozens and dozens of them in various shapes and sizes and colors. She'd even given Tess her own trunk as a Hanukkah present some five years ago, an old-fashioned brown leather thing that Tess called "The Magix." Tess would never tell Theo what she kept in there.

Aunt Esther had no such qualms. She threw open a large red trunk and pulled out dresses and suits and leotards and props from it, tossing them to the floor or at Theo, Tess, and Jaime.

She pulled out an elaborate gold gown with a huge

skirt. "One of you could go as Lady MacBeth."

"I think that might call a little attention to us, Aunt Esther," Tess said.

"You might be right. Well, I have this army uniform from our production of *Hurricane Hall*."

"*Hurricane Hall*? What's *Hurricane Hall*?" Not that Theo really cared, but he hated not knowing things.

"You don't know *Hurricane Hall*? A novel published in 1848. A comedy of manners in the style of Jane Austen. A young black heroine is taken in by her rich, white New York City relatives when her white father dies. You really should know this, Theo."

"It sounds familiar," Theo grumbled. It didn't.

"Oh, never mind. You'll probably read it in high school. We set our production during World War II. Though I suppose this might call too much attention as well." She set the uniform aside and pulled out a white satin shirt with big blue pom-poms down the front. "Hmmm . . . a clown? Perhaps too frightening. How about a woodland sprite? No, the leaf crown is far too itchy. No, not this. Not this, either." She pawed through the costumes in one trunk and moved to the next. "I don't suppose you want to dress as members of a chain gang? No, that wouldn't be appropriate. I do have a giant ham sandwich costume around here somewhere."

Just when Theo was certain that Aunt Esther would insist they dress up as candy bars with nougat, she said, "Aha! How about this?" She unrolled a nondescript set of slate-gray coveralls, shook them out. On the front pocket were the words ACME REPAIR CO.

"That could work," Jaime said. "No one notices repair people."

"Exactly," said Aunt Esther. "And if you tuck your hair under a cap and put on a pair of these"—she held up a pair of mirrored sunglasses—"then no one will recognize you. I've got coveralls for the three of you." She gave each of them a pair, plus glasses and a matching baseball cap. "And for your little friend, I have this!" She handed something diaphanous and crumpled to Jaime.

Jaime unfolded the rumpled item. "What . . . what is this?"

"It's a Tinker Bell costume! Onstage, we put it on a parakeet, complete with this red wig. Oh, dear, I think the moths got to the wings. They're looking a little chewed up."

"Oh no," said the robot.

"Uh, I think we might be okay if I just put Ono in my pocket," Jaime said. He slipped on the coveralls and zipped up, and tucked his hair into the cap as he slid the glasses on. Then he gently slid the robot into the pocket on the front of his shirt.

"How do I look?"

"About twenty-five," said Tess, impressed.

"Eighteen, tops," Theo said.

Jaime grinned. "Not sure the hat is going to fit over your hair, Theo."

"Maybe Theo could wear Tinker Bell's wig," Tess said.

"It would just float on top of his hair like a cherry on a sundae," said Jaime.

"Maybe we could all dress as ghosts instead," said Theo.

Tess pulled on the coveralls. "It's not Halloween. Besides, everyone knew the ghost was you."

"They did not."

"Yes, they did," said Jaime. "The whole block knew."

"Even when I went as the nerdy ghost?"

"Especially then."

Aunt Esther patted Theo on the shoulder. "Next time, I'll lend you the giant ham sandwich."

Aunt Esther loaded them up with real sandwiches for lunch and then waved good-bye as they sneaked out the back door, just in case anyone was, in Tess's words, "casing the joint." Once they were out on the street, no one seemed to give them a second glance.

Jaime patted his front pocket and whispered, "Okay, Ono, do your thing."

"To the Land of Kings?" the robot said.

"That's right."

The robot reached one arm out of Jaime's pocket and pointed. They started walking.

"Let's hope the Land of Kings isn't in Canada," Theo said.

"What do you have against Canada?" Tess said, but she said it absently, as if she weren't the one making the joke, as if the answer didn't matter in the least. Her mirrored gaze swept side to side. As they walked, she would occasionally turn around and walk backward, scanning the street behind them. Maybe she was looking for blondes in red dresses. But more likely she was looking for one ginormous Cat.

When they reached the bus stop, the robot pointed at it and said, "To the Land of Kings!" They got on the Q19.

"Maybe it's not in Colorado or Canada," Jaime said.

"Maybe it's on the Canary Islands," Theo said.

"The Q-19 is going to drop us off on the Canary Islands?"

"No, but maybe your friend will walk us right into the Atlantic Ocean," Theo said.

"So it's *my* friend now."

"Oh, shut up," Tess said. "You two are bickering like, like . . ."

We normally do? Theo thought, but didn't say it. Jaime didn't say it, either, just watched the landscape outside shift from the tightly packed houses and delis and shops of Astoria to Sunnyside Gardens, through Woodside and Jackson Heights. When they reached Flushing, the robot pointed again. "To the Land of Kings!" it said.

"I think this is our stop," said Jaime.

They got off the bus. Wherever the robot pointed, they walked, until they reached Bowne Street and a sign that said KINGSLAND HOMESTEAD.

"Well! The Land of Kings," Jaime said.

The robot's jeweled eyes flashed, and it beeped with primitive robot joy. Jaime tucked it down into his pocket and buttoned the flap over its head.

"Oh no," it said, its voice small and muffled.

The trees surrounding the homestead were spectacular, but the homestead itself was not. It was a rather plain yellow house, smallish and modest.

"Built around 1785," said Jaime.

"You know about this house?" Theo asked.

"No, I'm reading the plaque," Jaime said, pointing to the wrought-iron fence that surrounded the property.

Tess swore.

"Language," Theo said.

"Look at the porch," Tess said.

On the porch was a sign that said OPEN TUES, SAT, SUN. 2:30—4:30.

"Considering the fact that it's not Tuesday, Saturday, or Sunday, and it's not between two thirty and four thirty, I think we made the trip for nothing."

"To the Land of Kings," mumbled the robot.

"Your pocket is talking," Theo said.

Jaime unbuttoned his pocket, and spoke into it. "Kingsland isn't open."

"To the Land of Kings!"

"Sorry, little buddy. Not today."

Theo couldn't be sure, but the robot sounded just the slightest bit ticked off when it said, "Land. Of. Kings."

"You can keep saying that, but it's not going to change the fact that it's noon on Wednesday," Jaime said.

Theo's stomach rumbled. "Speaking of noon, maybe we should have those sandwiches before we go back. Plus it's hot in these coveralls. I need to sit down."

They found a bench in the park surrounding the homestead and laid out their food. Sandwiches, apples, and Fig Newtons (of course). As they ate, Jaime read about the house on his phone.

"Built around 1785 by a dude named Charles Doughty. It's called 'Kingsland' because of Doughty's son-in-law, British sea captain Joseph King, who bought the home in 1801," he read. "And it's been moved a few times before ending up here."

"Land of Kings!" said his pocket.

"Uh-huh," Jaime said. "That's what I'm talking about."

Theo popped a cookie into his mouth, chewed, swallowed. "We could come back on Saturday, though it might be more crowded then."

"Do you think a lot of people come to some old house in Queens on a Saturday?" Tess said.

"More than there are now," said Jaime. "It would really be better if we could get in the house when it's closed."

"LAND OF KINGS," the robot insisted.

"I think your robot is cranky," said Tess.

"It's not my robot," Jaime said.

"He likes you," Theo said.

Jaime stood and brushed the crumbs from his lap. "Let's just try the door to see if it's locked."

"Of course it's locked."

Jaime shrugged. "Let's try anyway. We can look through the windows. Maybe it will prompt the robot to give us another clue."

They circled the house and stepped up onto the porch. Jaime opened the screen door and tried the knob.

"Locked, like I said."

"You really love being right," Jaime said.

"I do," Theo said. He did. Didn't everyone?

Jaime cupped his hands around his face and peered into one of the darkened windows.

"See anything?" Tess asked, though she wasn't even facing the right way. She was scanning the surrounding grounds as if Nine were going to suddenly appear any moment.

"LAND OF KINGS," the robot squawked.

Jaime hooked a finger in his pocket. "I told you, the house is closed and the door is locked. We don't have a key."

"LAND OF KINGS LAND OF KINGS LAND OF KINGS."

The robot was so loud that Jaime slapped a hand over his pocket, glanced all around to make sure no one was watching them. No one was. There were no cars in the small parking lot, no kids in the nearby playground.

Tess fixed her mirrors onto Jaime, her brows creasing. "I think he might be trying to tell us something."

"What?"

"That we might have the key."

"But we don't," Theo said.

Jaime patted his various pockets. Then, he unbuttoned the top button of the coveralls, reached inside. He pulled out the overlarge silver jack and showed it to the robot. "You mean this?"

"LAND OF KINGS LAND OF KINGS LAND OF KINGS."

"I think that's a yes," said Tess.

Theo tried not to feel bad about being wrong. Again. Grandpa Ben would have noticed, would have reminded him that being right was not the point. The process of discovery was the point. The journey was the point. And journeys don't always feel comfortable. Sometimes, Grandpa Ben would say, journeys are downright painful, like Frodo's long trip to Mordor to destroy the ring in *The Lord of the Rings*. Theo hated those books. All that talking and fighting and dying, when the eagles could have flown them to Mordor all along.

Where were the eagles when you needed them?

Lazy eagles.

They returned to their bench, balled up the paper bag that had contained their lunch, and went back to the homestead. Jaime pulled off the mirrored glasses and replaced them with his own pair. "That's better. I couldn't see anything." He took one more look around, then inserted the jack into the lock.

The inner door swung open.

By this point, they weren't even surprised.

Inside the house, it was gloomy and dark, but a little cooler than it was outside in the sun. The bottom floor was arranged like a museum, with historical displays and racks of postcards. Jaime pulled Ono from his pocket and set it on the floor. The robot marched across the room as fast as it could, which was not fast at all. Still, it seemed to know where it was going. When it reached the bottom step of the staircase, it said, "Oh no!" It backed up and hit the step again. "Oh no!" And again, "Oh no! Oh no! Oh no!"

Jaime scooped up the robot, and they climbed the steps. Upstairs was much different from downstairs. Instead of museum displays and postcards, the rooms up here were decorated with Victorian furniture, as if a family still lived here, a family stuck somewhere in the 1850s. The fancy parlor had pinkish-red drapes, a fireplace, gold wallpaper everywhere.

"What do you think, Ono?" Jaime said. "A little gaudy?"

"THE LAND OF KINGS," Ono said.

"That's where we are, all right," Jaime said. "Do you know what the next clue is, or what?"

"LAND OF KINGS, LAND OF KINGS."

Jaime sighed. "I'll have to teach you some new words."

"What if he can't learn any new words?" Tess said, as she ran her hand across the fireplace mantel.

Theo went to the writing desk between the two windows and leafed through the ledger that was open there. Columns of handwritten figures filled the pages. Just as he was turning away from the ledger, Ono yelled, "OH NO, LAND OF KINGS, OH NO, LAND OF KINGS."

"What's he going on about?" Theo asked Jaime.

"No idea," Jaime said.

"Maybe he's saying that you're close to the next clue, Theo," Tess said. She was still wearing the mirrored sunglasses that Aunt Esther had given them, and it gave her an inscrutable look. As if she were an FBI agent or a spy or something. As if she were someone completely different, a girl who had never lost anything.

Theo turned back to the desk. It had a couple of ledgers on it, some books and papers on a shelf above. He put his hand on the ledger. Ono said, "LAND OF KINGS." Theo took his hand away. Ono said, "OH NO."

Tess took off the glasses and came to stand next to him. She shut the ledger. There were no words on the cover. She turned to the front page. On the top, someone had written, "Land of the Kings."

"Is it this book, Ono?" Tess asked the robot.

"LAND OF KINGS, LAND OF KINGS," the robot said.

"The clue must be in here somewhere," Tess said. She paged through the book.

"There are a lot of numbers," Jaime said, joining them. "Some kind of code?"

"Could be," Theo said. "The whole book could be one elaborate cipher."

"Well, we can't stay here all night trying to figure it out," Tess said. When Tess picked up the ledger and tucked it into her coveralls, the robot beeped and squealed. It almost sounded happy.

Theo was not happy. "We can't *take* the ledger."

"Sure we can," said Tess. "We'll borrow it."

"We 'borrowed' the silver puzzle from the 2nd City Reliquary and look what happened. Now he talks. Sort of."

"I like this robot," said Jaime. "He's kind of cute."

"What I'm saying is that the ledger could be valuable."

Tess said, "It could be. Or it could only be valuable to *us*. Besides, we'll return anything we take."

"We're going to have to start keeping a list," Theo grumbled. He moved the other book to the center of the desk and rearranged an inkpot and a feather pen so it didn't seem as if anything was missing from the display.

But this was a museum, so someone would notice at some point. And when they did, who would they call? Theo closed his eyes and imagined his mother fingerprinting this whole room, only to discover that her children were the thieves. What if the 2nd City Reliquary also called the police? What if his mother got that call, too? What if she thought the three of them were some kind of artifact-stealing gang or something? What if she was forced to arrest them and put them in jail because she couldn't appear to be playing favorites?

Tess slipped her hand in his. "Theo? Are you okay?"

Her eyes were still red from crying over Nine. He wondered if that's what his eyes looked like, too. But then he remembered the mirrored glasses he still wore and knew she would see her own red eyes reflected there.

He squeezed her hand. He didn't know which one of them it was for.

CHAPTER FIFTEEN
Jaime

The twins were abnormally quiet on the bus back to their aunt's house, not that Jaime blamed them. He'd be furious if someone had come into his house and pretended that Tyrone bit her. Tyrone wouldn't bite anyone! Well, unless they deserved it. And some people deserved it, didn't they?

But Nine hadn't bitten that blond woman in the red dress. So what was her deal? Why did she look so much like the other blond woman, the one they saw at the library? Was it a uniform? A disguise? Even now, wearing his own disguise, the cap pulled low, he felt conspicuous, watched. Stupid, because this was a New York City bus and the passengers were making it a point not to make eye contact with anyone else. Besides, what would he do if the blond woman were sitting behind him? Yell at her? Accuse her of faking or lying or spying? Tess told him that he looked twenty-five. *He'd* be the one to get in trouble. And then what would happen? Would Mrs. Biedermann arrest *him*? Have him taken away?

He slid down in his seat, trying to shrink. Which wasn't fair. Why should he be the one to make himself smaller?

To distract himself, he rummaged inside the coveralls and pulled out his sketchbook and a pencil. He turned to a fresh page and started to sketch without thinking too much about what he was doing. Sometimes, he liked to let his hand figure out what he was drawing before his head could catch up.

Jaime had a friend named Adam whose mother was also from Trinidad, like Jaime's mother was. Adam's mother, Ms. Tracey, told Adam stories about the strange spirits and creatures called jumbies that lived alongside the people there, and had even written some books about them. Once, when Jaime stayed over at Adam's house for a birthday party, Ms. Tracey turned out the lights and told all the boys there about the spirits of Trinidad. Ghosts that roam the island at night. Mermaids who can lure men to their deaths in the blue water of the sea. Douens, the souls of lost children, spirits who have no faces and their feet on backward, spirits who like to take other children into the forest where they can be lost, too.

Not one boy slept that night.

It was the best birthday party Jaime had ever been to.

Now, in his sketchbook, Jaime drew ghosts, mermaids, douens. In one sketch, a lovely woman appeared at the edge of a frothy shore. Not the superhero he usually drew, but someone taller and paler, wearing a tight dress. Her feet were bare. He turned the page and drew the woman unzipping her skin and slipping out of it headfirst. She had the face of a wild boar. She reminded him a bit of another Trini spirit Ms. Tracey had talked about, the soucouyant, a woman who made a pact with the devil so that she could shed her skin and become anything she wanted, from a wild boar to a monkey to a ball of fire. The drawing made him both scared and sad. Scared because he had to wonder if his hand knew something about the blond woman that his brain didn't, and sad because his own mother wasn't around to tell him scary stories, or nice ones. That Adam couldn't stay over at his own house, call his mother "Ms. Renée," and listen to her stories. How many stories get lost when a single person is lost?

Again, he turned the page. This time, he drew more

thoughtfully and intentionally. The superhero he kept drawing over and over. Dark and beautiful, dense, curly hair piled loosely on her head, she wore nothing flashy—no armor or unitards or masks. Just a plain gray coat that fell nearly to her ankles, a cane in her hand.

She looked a little like his mother. And yet she also looked like herself, whoever she was.

"Who is that?" Tess asked.

"I don't know yet," Jaime said.

Tess tapped the coat. "Reminds me a little of Ada's dress. Plain like that."

"Without the hearts," Jaime said.

"She doesn't need hearts?"

"She doesn't need to wear them on her clothes."

On a whim, probably because Tess was watching, Jaime drew a companion for the woman. A large cat. Sleek and black, like a panther, with a long tail. She— and he knew the cat was a she—had a brazen expression on her feline face. *Just try to catch me*, the expression said.

Tess reached under the mirrored glasses and wiped at her eye.

"I'm sorry," Jaime said. "I didn't mean to make you upset."

"No, no. I love it," Tess said. "It's just . . ."

"I know." He did.

Tess readjusted the mirrored glasses. "Nine will be home when we get back."

"I bet she will."

A ghost of a smile touched Tess's mouth, and then she turned from him, staring out the bus window again.

Jaime added more stray curls around the woman's face and a sideways sweep to the coat, as if a strong wind were blowing, as if something were coming. One eyebrow was quirked. Dark eyes glinted. She stared right at him. Challenging him.

Why *should* he make himself smaller?

He pulled himself up in the seat, sat straight and tall the rest of the way.

Back at Aunt Esther's, Tess ran around the house calling Nine's name. She knocked on the neighbors' doors and asked if they'd seen the spotted cat with striped ears. They hadn't. She called her father at work and asked if there was any news about Nine, and then she called her mother. Her mother said that somehow Nine had escaped her cage, but they had no idea how she could have gotten out of the building, or where she'd gotten to. Someone was sure to see her and report it, however, because the video was still all over the news. She was sure Nine would show up. Tess just had to be patient.

Tess hung up Aunt Esther's ancient wall phone, a yellow plastic thing with a long curly cord, but she kept her hand on it, as if hoping it would ring again, and someone would be on the other end with different news.

"Tess," said Aunt Esther, "why don't you all take those coveralls off and throw them in the wash. I'll answer the phone if it rings."

They peeled off the coveralls and put them in the washing machine as Aunt Esther suggested, and then took Ono and the stolen ledger upstairs to the twins' room. They set it on the floor between them to examine it more carefully. Jaime let Ono roam around the room as they tried to make sense of the endless columns of numbers. "Oh no oh no oh no oh no," the robot whispered softly to itself, as it bumped into walls and dressers and bed frames.

"So," said Jaime, "we've got lots of lists of purchases. Feed for farm animals and food for the household. But I'm not seeing a pattern."

"Nothing jumps out," Theo said. "But it could be hidden the way all the other ciphers have been hidden. Invisible ink, or maybe there's an address on every third page or—"

Tess cut him off. "Or every fifth page or maybe

there's something hidden in the binding or glued to one of the pages."

"Yes, but I think if—"

"Or maybe if you take the first figure of every page and add them or multiply them or divide them, you get a number of a house somewhere in Brooklyn or the East Village or something."

"I—"

"Or maybe we went to the wrong house and stole the wrong book. Maybe we were never meant to follow the robot at all. Maybe it's a decoy built by the Morningstarrs' greatest nemesis."

Theo pulled his lip. "Who was the Morningstarrs' greatest nemesis?"

"Take your pick. Charles Dickens. Charles Babbage. Any Charles. All the Charleses."

"Why would all the Charleses—"

Jaime put a hand on Theo's arm to stop him, to save him from pitching himself into Tess's endless questions, her endless possibilities. "The puzzles are always hard at first," Jaime said to Tess. "But we've figured them out so far. And didn't you say that the Cipher is figuring us out, too? That maybe it wants us to understand it?"

Tess got to her feet and moved to the window. She

hooked a finger around the curtain and peeked out at the postage-stamp-sized backyard. "That was before."

Theo stopped pulling on his lip. "The Cipher didn't take Nine. For all we know, solving the Cipher has nothing to do with Nine."

"Her name was a clue!" Tess said. "And why else would anyone lie about her? Why would someone say she was a machine and not a real animal? The Morningstarrs designed all the machines. And they also created the Cipher. What if someone has figured out what we're doing? What if that someone wants to stop us from solving the puzzle?"

Jaime said, "Are we going to let them?"

Tess pinned him with dark, angry eyes. "And weren't you the one who said that we should lie low for a while?"

"Yes," Jaime said. "*That* was before."

"Before what?"

Before they made me feel small. "Before they took Nine."

The little robot marched into the open closet and tipped headfirst into a sneaker. "Oh no," it said.

"'Oh no' is right," said Tess. The anger in Tess's face dulled and she let the curtain drop. She sat back on the floor.

"Okay. So let's look at this thing one page at a time. Theo, where's your magnifying glass?"

✦ ✦ ✦

They spent hours scouring the pages of the ledger, examining the binding, looking for hidden ciphers and patterns in the rows of figures. They read mind-numbing numbers of grocery purchases for the household—flour, molasses, sugar, brandy, provisions of pork and beef. Salaries for gardeners and smiths. They combed through lists of construction costs: masonry, wood, wages, dwellings for apprentices and servants. They found payments for shoes for Young Bob, Old Bob, and Wiley Dan, and imagined a comic book based on all three.

But it was fruitless.

Jaime took off his glasses and rubbed the bridge of his nose. "I can't see anymore. Take this up again tomorrow?"

"Tomorrow," Tess and Theo agreed.

"Mind if I take Ono with me? I've kind of gotten attached."

They all looked at the robot, which had been trying to communicate with the stuffed teddy bear in the corner for at least ten minutes. "To the Land of Kings," it said to the bear. "Kings. KINGS."

"Come on, Ono," Jaime said. "We're going to take a ride on the Underway."

"To the Land of Kings?"

"To the Land of Broboken. You'll love it," Jaime said.

"Oh no," said the robot.

He said good-bye to the twins and to Aunt Esther, said he hoped that Nine would return by the morning. Then, he and Ono walked to the Underway station and boarded the train bound for Manhattan. He held the little robot close and murmured, "If I let your head peek out of my pocket, will you promise to be quiet?"

In a tiny voice, Ono whispered, "Land of Kings."

"Good," said Jaime.

Ono didn't say another word for the whole trip. Not on the first train, not on the walk to catch the next. And Ono didn't say anything when they finally reached Hoboken, though the robot did beep irritably when they were almost mowed down by a clutch of suited young bros who apparently didn't see Jaime at all, or maybe expected him to step aside.

"Watch where you're going," said one of the bros, a shiny-faced, sallow young man in a too-tight suit.

"Watch that your pants don't split when you sit," said Jaime.

"What?" the bro shouted. But Jaime didn't turn around, kept walking, straight and tall. Maybe Ono was some kind of magical Transformer, and would turn into a monster truck or a rocket launcher with a face if the bro dared to challenge Jaime further. Jaime really didn't think so, but the thought was funny enough to be comforting.

His good mood lasted only till he reached the lobby of his building, because Cricket was standing there, talking to the security guard, with an expression he had never before seen on her face. If he didn't know better, he would have said it was fear.

"Cricket? What is it?" Jaime said. "What's wrong?"

Cricket managed to choke out one word: "Karl."

Then Cricket—fierce, determined, opinionated, impossible-to-break Cricket—burst into tears.

CHAPTER SIXTEEN
Duke

Duke Goodson drummed his fingers on the armrest as his limo inched through Harlem's late-afternoon traffic. He'd already berated his driver for not taking 278, but apparently the woman needed another thrashing.

He rapped on the glass.

"Yes, sir?" said Candi, the driver.

"This traffic is a nightmare. Why are we on Seventh Avenue?"

"Because 278 is worse, sir."

"No, it certainly isn't. I told you to take 278. I expect when I tell you to take 278 that you'll take 278."

Candi's expression in the mirror didn't change. "You *suggested* I take 278. But 278 is worse. So I took Seventh."

"My suggestions aren't suggestions."

"I'll remember that, sir."

"Don't be cheeky."

"I'm never cheeky, sir."

"You are always cheeky, Candi. One day I'm going to have you sent somewhere terrible."

"Yes, sir."

"When I say terrible, I mean terrible. I mean hard labor. I mean surface of the moon conditions. I mean bread and water minus the bread."

"Anything to get out of New York City traffic, sir."

See? Cheeky.

But Candi could get away with it because she was the best driver Duke had, and knew all five boroughs and most of the Eastern Seaboard like she knew the back of her own hand. Plus she was as discreet as a Swiss banker and had black belts in mysterious fighting disciplines she wouldn't discuss.

Not many drivers like Candi. And, irritatingly, Candi knew it.

Duke soothed his nerves by checking out the neighborhood. Harlem was bustling, packed with people. They passed an old-fashioned-looking barber shop, restaurants, brownstones. Lots of nice property here. Might be a useful investment. Clear out the old, bring in the new, and then charge the new five thousand dollars a month for a one-bedroom apartment. Close down the chicken place that's been there for who-knows-how-long and open up a fancy cheese shop instead. Or an artisanal salt store. A café where they grind coffee beans imported from Hawaii and Jamaica and Vietnam. Duke had heard the most expensive coffee in the world was weasel coffee—coffee beans eaten by civets and then collected from their scat. Poop coffee. You could charge anywhere from $35 to $100 for one cup of that coffee. Duke was sure that the rich bozos from the Upper East Side would risk New York City traffic to get it just to say they'd gotten it.

Rich bozos were Duke's favorite kind of people.

Candi turned onto 158th Street and the traffic eased. Candi didn't say "I told you so," didn't even flick her eyes to the mirror. She didn't have to. She wouldn't have a job working for Duke Goodson if she pulled that cheeky garbage and then didn't get Duke where he needed to be. But it looked as if they would be early. Duke hoped the doctor wouldn't mind. Not that he cared about how the doctor felt. It was just that people were so much easier to handle when they weren't cranky.

Except the doctor was bound to be cranky when he heard what Duke had to report.

Oh, well. If things got out of hand, Duke could always try out his new favorite toy, the fizz gun. He'd been itching for an opportunity to test it.

And if it didn't work, he'd let Candi handle it.

Candi guided the limo into the Bronx Ecological Park. Not the front entrance, the back entrance, for employees only. They parked right next to the farthest structure—the research building. She got out of the car and opened the door for Duke.

"Here you are, sir," said Candi.

"I can see that for myself."

"Of course you can, sir."

Duke waved Candi away. "Go to the snack bar and get yourself a smoothie or whatever it is you eat. I might be a while."

"I do love smoothies, sir."

"Stop that."

"What, sir?"

Duke made a disgusted noise in the back of his throat and went to the door. He punched in some numbers on the keypad, a temporary access code he'd been granted for today's meeting. He entered the cold, white building that smelled vaguely of lemons, dog kibble, and compost heap. He swept past groups of people wearing lab coats. They peered at him curiously, but he didn't bother to glare at them. He was in too much of a hurry. He'd decided that being a little early, rather than a disadvantage, was an advantage. He could see what the doctor was up to, if he was doing any experiments on the side, so to speak, instead of the ones he'd described.

But when Duke reached the second to last lab on the left, and burst through the door, he didn't find anything remotely interesting. The doctor, who was peering into a microscope, simply said, "You're early."

"Only a few minutes."

"Twenty-three minutes, to be exact."

A fussy one. Duke couldn't stand the fussy ones. Always scrubbing out fingerprints on the countertops. Complaining about every line of the contract. Probably had an obsession with fonts, for Pete's sake. Duke made a mental note to use Comic Sans for all future communications. Just to irk the man.

Right now, though, Duke was the only one irked. "What are you looking at?"

"A skin cell from a cuttlefish."

"Fascinating."

"Quite," said the doctor. "I'm thinking of introducing the cells of this mollusk into rats."

"Why rats?"

"Why not rats?"

Duke didn't have an answer to this question, except to say, "Who wants a cuttle-rat?"

Finally the man straightened and looked directly at Duke. Not many people were brave enough to look directly at Duke, especially not skinny doctors with bulbous, greenish-brown eyes the color of pond scum. You'd think a doctor would want to do something about those eyes. They seemed to be about to fall out of his head.

He looked like a newt.

The doctor said, "I'm not making pets here, Mr. Goodson. No one will be custom-ordering a cuttle-rat."

"Call me Duke," said Duke, with a flash of his white teeth. He would refer to the doctor as "Dr. Newt" to anyone who asked.

"I'm researching the properties and features of certain animals, and whether those properties and features can be successfully transferred to other species while maintaining the health of the test animal. In this case, I want to see if rats can manifest the ability to change the color of their fur the way a cuttlefish can change the color of its skin."

"How would that work?" Duke said. "Fur is dead and skin is—"

"I don't have the time to explain the science, Mr.

Goodson." The doctor looked at his watch. "And I don't see the specimen I was promised."

The gall of the little salamander, to interrupt Duke Goodson, the fixer's fixer, as if he were a nobody. Duke was tempted to fizz the man and leave him on the floor to be eaten by his cuttle-rats. But Slant wanted to work with the doctor, and it was Duke's job to arrange such things, no matter how irritating a job it was. And he'd had a lot practice working with cold-blooded creatures. Possibly more practice than the doctor himself.

So Duke took a long, slow stroll around the lab. Small cages lined the periphery and he took his time scrutinizing each one. There was a guinea pig with a strange, long-furred tail rather like a monkey's. A snake with a dozen tiny pink feet. The smallest mice that Duke had ever seen that flew around their cage on bright blue butterfly wings. And then, there was a cage full of rabbits that looked perfectly normal.

"What's with the rabbits?" he asked. "They don't look any different to me."

The doctor sighed a dramatic, overlong sigh and marched over to the wall. He flipped off the light. The bunnies that had appeared normal glowed green in the dark. "I injected a naturally glowing jellyfish protein in the embryos of rabbits. Now they glow."

"That's quite—"

"Nothing. It's nothing. Or rather, it's something that impresses investors but nothing more than that. Not yet." He flipped on the light, and Duke Goodson squinted at the sudden brightness.

"All of these hybrids are on the small side," Duke said.

"You know the larger chimera are illegal," the doctor said. "The ecological park has some of the last known ligers and grolar bears in the United States. And once they're gone, they're gone."

"Seems a shame," Duke said, though he preferred his animals on a plate.

"A shame?" the doctor said, his voice testy. "It's to keep quacks from making monsters, as you well know."

Monsters could be quite useful, Duke thought. Especially the human ones. But he didn't say it.

The last cage had a series of large cocoons suspended from the top with some sort of biological resin. But they weren't shaped like cocoons. They looked more like eggs of some sort, mottled and gray. "And what will these be?"

The doctor tapped a pen on the lab table, *tap-tap-tap*. "The specimen, Mr. Goodson. Where is the specimen I was promised?"

"We're working on it."

"What do you mean, you're working on it? I thought you had captured it."

"We did. But it seems it escaped."

"Escaped? How could it escape?"

"It's a smart little bugger," Duke said.

"It's not little, and that's the point. There are very few of the larger chimera available to work with, particularly not chimera made up of more than two species. I need that specimen."

"More than two species? What are you talking about? I thought it was a cat mixed with another cat."

The doctor's newt eyes seemed to glow the way the rabbits had. "Oh, it's much more than a cat, Mr. Goodson. Much more. I *need* to study it."

"I have my best people on the job. It won't be long."

"Your best people? Candi?"

If newts could have crushes, Duke might say that the good doctor had a crush on Candi. Most men did. And almost everyone believed her. Candi, like all Duke's ladies, disarmed people, soothed or inflamed them, depending on what she wanted them to feel. Her blandly pretty face—with hair bleached to the color of spun sugar, black spiky lashes, the lipstick applied just so—was arresting, mesmerizing. She could say almost anything and people took it as gospel. "Science has proven that to get rich, you just have to have the right attitude!" "Lazy, good-for-nothing thieves raid your fridge when you're at work!" "The president is a spy for Greenland!" "Are *your* neighbors stealing your Wi-Fi?" Quite extraordinary when you thought about it. But that was the point. Many folks simply didn't enjoy thinking. It was far too much effort. They preferred to have someone else doing their thinking for them. And who better to tell you what to think than someone who looked like a more accessible version of a movie star or the Barbie doll you played with as a child?

"Yes, Doctor, Candi is on the job. Along with many others. They'll get it done."

The doctor's face hardened. "I hope so. Otherwise, I don't think I'll be able to fulfill your friend's other requests."

Friend? *Requests?* Duke laughed. "He is not my friend. He isn't yours, either. And he doesn't make requests. You have an arrangement."

"That's right. We have an arrangement. An arrangement that includes the specimen. Delivered here to me, safe and unharmed."

Well. The doctor had steel in his spine, Duke had to give him that.

He would also have to give him a good crack on the head when the time came.

But not just yet. The doctor had a reputation and a history. He came from a long line of men known for their brilliant scientific discoveries, their flexible sense of morality, and their penchant for professional disaster and financial ruin. In the middle of the nineteenth century, one of the doctor's ancestors had abandoned promising experiments in the treatment of infections in order to study spiders, of all things. He emptied his bank account and drained his wife's inheritance traveling the world to gather as many species as he could. He was killed by the bite of a black widow. When his wife found him, the story went, his body was covered in the numerous tarantulas he kept as pets. To repay his considerable debts, his wife had to sell his lab, his equipment, his papers, and his creatures to the highest bidder, who didn't have to bid very high to get them. That same bidder went on to develop medicines and even weapons derived from spider venom, and made a killing.

Ha, killing.

Duke smiled at the doctor. "You will have your kitty as soon as possible. I give you my word."

"Your word," said the doctor. He blinked slowly,

slowly, as if ticking off the seconds. Then he went to the glass cage in which hung the oversized eggs. He tapped the glass. One of them twitched, then twitched again.

The doctor did not peel his eyes away from the eggs when he said, "I'm afraid you'll have to leave now, Mr. Goodson. I have a birth to attend to."

"Of course," said Duke. "I'll be in touch."

"Yes, you will," said the doctor.

Before heading out the door, Duke took one last glance over his shoulder at the man, at the twitching cocoon-eggs that were gestating who-knows-what. The doctor was *murmuring* to the things. "Hello, there," he whispered softly to the mottled, gray husks. "Welcome to the world."

Not for the first time, Duke wondered if the name you were born with shaped you from the very beginning, or you defined the meaning of your name through action and experience. Whatever the case, the doctor's name suited him perfectly.

"I'll speak to you soon, Dr. Munsterberg," Duke said. But the man didn't even hear him.

CHAPTER SEVENTEEN

Tess

Tess's grandpa Ben always said that if you want to know the future, read about the past.

Mohican historian Hendrick Aupaumut once wrote:

> A great people traveled from the north and west. For many, many years they moved across the land, leaving settlements in rich river valleys as others moved on. Reaching the eastern edge of the country, some of these people settled on the river later renamed the Delaware. Others moved north and settled in the valley of a river. . . . They named this river Mahicannituck and called themselves the muh-he-con-neok, the people of the waters that are never still.

He was writing, of course, about the migration of his own people. One wonders what the Mohicans, the

Munsee, and the Lenape thought when they saw the first European ships sailing up the Hudson or blundering over the sharp rocks toward Manhattan. What did they make of the unwashed white people who stank of sweat and beer piling onto the shore? Did they realize that the Puritans, so persecuted in their own countries, believed that this rich, forested land was theirs for the taking, and that they did not have to ask or share?

And what did the natives make of Dutch explorer Adriaen Block in 1614, as he maneuvered his ship through Hell's Gate, up the East River and into the Long Island Sound, to become the first white man to view Astoria? Were they more curious than scared? Perhaps it was the storytellers among them, the wives and mothers, the ones who would tear the world apart for the sake of their children, who got a bad feeling in their guts, who were haunted by uneasy dreams. Perhaps they were visited by their ancestors, and warned of a coming storm. But then maybe even the storytellers couldn't anticipate how many colonists would arrive, and how quickly. Who among them could know they would soon be forced to migrate west, or stay and wrestle for slivers of the land they had inhabited for thirteen thousand years? How could they have guessed that the treacherous rocks and reefs in Hell's Gate would be dynamited, or that thousands upon thousands more strangers would pile onto the shores of Queens to join them: Italians, Greeks, Colombians, Chinese, Guyanese, as well as Indians, Dominicans, Ecuadorians, Romanians, Filipinos, and Koreans?

Most of whom were asleep at four in the morning.

All except Tess Biedermann.

She must have drifted off for a little while, at least, and had a nightmare she didn't want to remember, because Theo was slumped next to her bed, snoring, his hand around her wrist. Gently, she unclasped his fingers and pulled her arm away. She slid down to the end of the bed and slipped into her sneakers and a sweatshirt. Then, she crept downstairs as quietly as she could.

The house was dark and still. Well, mostly still, as the spiders that cared for the plants never slept. A faint giggle followed Tess out the front door.

On the street, only Tess and the Rollers were up and at work. The Rollers picked delicately at any stray trash that littered the sidewalks and the glass cobbles, rolling the rubbish into balls, the same routine they'd been performing for over 150 years. Tess barely took notice of them as she walked one block, two blocks, three—searching yards and alleys, in bins and under dumpsters. New York City, which always felt so small and familiar to her, was enormous and odd at four a.m. She imagined it filled with hidden dangers and lurking strangers, ready to take what wasn't theirs. Finders, keepers, the strangers might say, unmoved by the fact that what they found had been stolen, not lost at all.

After searching till dawn for any sign of Nine, Tess sat on Aunt Esther's stoop, defeated. Someone must have taken her. That was the only explanation. Someone knew she was special and was keeping her for themselves. Instead of tears, frustration burned Tess's eyes dry, and she scrubbed at them with angry fists. That was how her mother found Tess—eyes itchy and red, her hands curled on her lap.

Her mother sat down next to her in the pink light of the early morning. "Were you out looking for Nine?"

Tess didn't answer, simply tracked a nearby Roller as it scraped a banana peel from the walk in front of the house.

"I guess you're not talking to me yet, huh?"

Tess most certainly was not.

"Okay, you don't have to talk to me. Maybe you could just listen?"

Again, Tess said nothing.

"Look, sweetheart. I'm sorry. I'm so sorry," her mother said. "I've called in favors at animal control.

They're on the lookout for her."

Tess pressed her lips shut.

"They're searching everywhere. They know how special she is. How important."

At this, Tess said, "You shouldn't have done it."

Because Tess's mother was her mother, she knew Tess meant that Nine should never have been given up in the first place. That this was the mistake Mrs. Biedermann should be sorry for. "I know you're upset. But what I shouldn't have done is pulled strings to get you a license for Nine in the first place."

At this, Tess gasped. *"What?"*

"If other people couldn't get large chimera licenses, why should we get one? It wasn't fair to use my influence. I was wrong."

"That's not what you were wrong about!" Tess shouted.

"Isn't it? Don't you think there are other people who deserve a companion like Nine, but couldn't get one? What I should have done is lobby for new city regulations instead of skirting them for the kid I love."

Tess was so angry she thought she might burst, but she wasn't sure what or who to be angry at. Her mother was wrong, but she was right, too. Everyone should have a Nine.

"If it helps, my new partner agrees with you."

Tess remembered her mom's new partner had said that the blond lady's story did seem to be full of applesauce or custard or something like that.

"Oh, he can't say it directly because I'm his superior," said Tess's mom. "I'm supposed to be training him and he's not supposed to question my judgment. But I can tell he thinks I was wrong."

Tess unclenched one of her fists. "I like your new partner."

"I do, too," said her mother. "Even when he mutters under his breath that he doesn't know what the peanut brittle I thought I was doing."

"So what the peanut brittle *did* you think you were doing?"

Her mother rubbed her forehead. "Beats me. You're supposed to be wiser when you're older. Doesn't always work that way. But listen, I'm doing everything I can. Seriously. I won't stop looking, okay?"

Tess couldn't help the tears that made her vision glassy. "Okay."

"So maybe you can come inside now and eat breakfast with me before I go to work? Aunt Esther is too angry with me to cook, so she sent Lance into the kitchen. He made enough flapjacks for an army and it doesn't appear as if he's going to quit anytime soon."

They went inside and tried their best to make a dent in Lance's pile of pancakes. Soon, Tess's dad came downstairs to help. And then Theo. Aunt Esther grudgingly sat with them, nibbling the crispy edges off a single pancake. The doorbell rang, and the twins' mom got up to get it. She came back into the kitchen with her new partner, Detective Clarkson.

"Ooooh! Pancakes!" he said.

"Please have some," said Tess's mom. "Lance won't stop cooking them."

Detective Clarkson saw Lance clomping around the kitchen, so he stuffed a pancake into his mouth, as if he were afraid Lance would attack if he didn't.

They were almost through with their breakfast when the doorbell rang again. Not just once though, three times—frantic and insistent.

"Okay, okay," Tess's dad shouted. "Hold your zebras."

This time, Jaime appeared in the doorway, breathing hard, as if he'd run all the way from Hoboken.

"It's Karl," he said.

"What about him?" Tess said.

"He's missing!"

"Wait," said Detective Clarkson. "So this Karl is a raccoon?"

"A raccoon-cat," Jaime said. "I think. Maybe there are bits of other animals in there, too, hard to tell. Mostly, he looks like a raccoon. With antlers."

"Antlers?" said Detective Clarkson.

"Not real ones. Cricket puts him in a lot of hats with horns or antlers. Things like that."

Detective Clarkson frowned so hard his eyes nearly crossed. "Who's Cricket?"

"My neighbor," said Jaime.

"Your neighbor is . . . a cricket?"

"She's a girl."

Tess said, "First Nine, then Karl. I don't think this is a coincidence."

"Hmmm," said Theo, pulling on his lip. "Felonious bears."

"What bears?" said Detective Clarkson.

"No bears," said Tess's mom. "Just felonies."

"Mom, I think someone might be stealing hybrids," Tess said.

Tess's mom nodded. "Could be." She turned to her partner. "Clarkson, I want you to check with animal control and see if they've gotten any calls about missing chimera."

"I thought the bigger nutter butters were outlawed," Clarkson said.

"They were, but people who already owned them were grandfathered in. That's why we could keep Nine. But these bigger chimera are valuable. And it looks like whoever is doing this believes the smaller chimera are valuable, too. Who knows why they were taken."

"Or who took them," said Tess.

Clarkson nodded. "I'm on it." He pulled his phone from his pocket and punched in some numbers. "Connect me with AC, would you, Nancy? I don't care if the phone system is confusing, just do it, okay? It's not for me, it's for Biedermann. I don't know where in the Wheaties the cat is, that's why I'm calling. It's not just the cat anymore. We could have a gang of felonious bears running around. What? I meant thieves. Felonious *thieves*. I'm not repetitive, *you're* repetitive." His voice trailed off as he marched out to the back porch to take the rest of the call.

"That's my cue," said Tess's mom. "I have to get to work." She stopped to kiss the top of Tess's head. "I know you're worried, I'm worried, too, but I promise I'll get to the bottom of this. And, Jaime, we'll ride out to Hoboken and talk to Cricket and her parents and anyone else we can get ahold of. We'll find out if anyone saw anything strange."

"All of Hoboken is strange," Jaime said.

"Then I guess we'll get a lot of statements," said Tess's mom. "But I want you kids to try to relax. Maybe do something fun today. Go to the park. See a movie. Rent some exos and play some ball. Get your mind off of this for a while."

"Sure," Tess said, who had no intention of doing any such things.

After both her parents had left for the day, Tess, Theo, and Jaime went upstairs to tackle the ledger again. They figured that if they couldn't do much to help locate Nine or Karl, they could at least figure out the next clue to the Cipher.

But as it turned out, figuring out the next clue was as difficult as figuring out what had happened to the animals. Maybe more so.

Days passed. Tess's mom and Detective Clarkson interviewed people and made calls and conducted searches, while Tess, Theo, and Jaime looked through the ledger. They analyzed the figures in every possible way, they tried to find some sort of relationships between the lists of words, they examined each page, and came up with nothing. Jaime, who now carried Ono everywhere, would take the little robot out of his pocket and set it on the floor as they worked. Sometimes, Ono would seem to follow their analysis, its eyes shining, other times, it would explore the twins' room, bumping into boxes and shoes and walls. Still other times, it would fall over with a *thunk* and appear to sleep, making a slight buzzing noise like a fridge.

"Tyrone adores it," Jaime said. "And she doesn't like anybody. I think it speaks hamster-hog. Or she speaks Ono."

One afternoon, more than a week after Nine first vanished, Tess, Theo, and Jaime were sprawled on the floor with the ledger in the middle. They had researched the families who'd owned the Kingsland house and surrounding properties; they had studied lumber outputs of mills in the early 1800s; they had tried to pin down the identities of Young Bob, Old Bob, and Wiley Dan; they had racked their brains and racked them some more, and could still not come up with a way to make the clue reveal itself.

"All right. It's official. I hate this book," Jaime said.

"Me too," Tess said.

Jaime took off his glasses and cleaned them on his T-shirt. "Maybe we took a wrong turn somewhere?"

"Yeah, but where?" Tess said. "Maybe every turn was a wrong turn. What if the wrong turn wasn't with this clue, but three clues ago?"

Theo put his hands behind his head. "We need a

fresh pair of eyes," he said. "A different perspective."

"I don't know about you," Jaime said, "but my eyes are shot."

Ono, who had been dozing in a pile of Tess's stuffed animals, roused itself. It sat up, then got to its feet. As if it had taken Theo literally, its jeweled eyes flashed, then glowed. It marched over to the ledger, turning its tiny head this way and that. "To the Land of Kings!" it said.

"Been there, done that, bro," Jaime said.

"To the Land of Kings!" the robot insisted. It marched in a circle: "To the Land of Kings to the Land of Kings to the Land of Kings." It marched so fast it tripped and fell on its face. "Oh no," it said.

"Hmmm," Jaime said. He crawled to where the robot lay and then pressed himself to the floor to observe the ledger from Ono's point of view. He pressed down on the pages, fanning the edges. Then *his* eyes snapped wide.

"The pages!" he said. "There's an image on them! Look!" He picked up the ledger, closed it, and showed them the edges of the pages, which were a dull-iron gray. But when he opened the cover and slightly fanned the edges, a picture appeared.

"It's a fore-edge painting!" said Tess.

Theo smacked himself in the head. "The one kind of hidden cipher I didn't think of."

"You can't think of everything," said Tess.

"I should have," Theo grumbled. Normally, Tess would have made fun of him, but since he'd been trying to do Nine's job, soothing Tess during her nightmares—and during her daymares—she'd been as nice as she could be. Which was mostly nice. Though, sometimes, when she despaired she'd ever get Nine back again, she wasn't very nice at all.

They gathered around the book. The painting depicted a grand hall with elaborate ironwork arches and columns and a large clock suspended from the ceiling.

"I know where that is. That's the inside of Station One," Jaime said. "When we visit my aunts in South Orange, we take the train from there."

Underneath the image was a message:

Stop the clock in dead of night
To wake what sleeps and stir their flight

"Well, that doesn't sound too ominous," Jaime said.

Theo said, "Dead of night. Station One is open twenty-four hours a day, but our families' apartments aren't. How are we going to sneak out in the dead of night? And what time, exactly, is the dead of night?"

"When it's darkest, I'd say," Jaime said.

Tess ran a finger over the words. "'To wake what sleeps.' But what is sleeping at Station One?"

"That's what I'm saying. Ominous."

"Maybe mice are sleeping," Theo said. "Doesn't have to be something scary."

But by this time, Tess had a strange feeling. That whatever the Morningstarrs had left sleeping at Station One was no mouse.

And if they woke it up, there was a chance they would never get it to sleep again.

CHAPTER EIGHTEEN

Theo

They decided that staying at Jaime's overnight was too risky. That his grandmother would surely hear them if they tried to sneak out of Jaime's apartment in the middle of the night. But since Tess had so many nightmares, Theo's parents and aunt were used to hearing some noise from upstairs, especially lately, since Nine wasn't around. The three of them would stay in the twins' room and sneak out the window at midnight. Theo told his parents that they didn't have to worry about anything, that he would take care of Tess if she had a nightmare. Which seemed to surprise them.

But it wasn't the first time Theo had surprised them. His parents didn't understand why Tess had so many more nightmares than Theo did. Once, however, Theo had something that Tess had not. When Theo was very small, he'd had an imaginary friend.

"Can you set a place for Pink?" he'd asked his mother, as she set the table for dinner.

"Who's Pink?" asked his mother.

"Pink. My friend. He's right there." He pointed to a chair.

His mother frowned, but his dad nodded. "Okay, here's a plate for Pink. I hope he likes brisket."

"He loves brisket," Theo said. "And mashed potatoes. Mashed potatoes are his favorite."

"Good to know," Theo's mom said.

"Mashed potatoes don't get stuck in his teeth. He has a lot of teeth."

"Really?" asked Theo's mom. "Is he a shark?"

"What? No!" Theo said.

"A tiger?"

"No."

"A lion."

"No! He's a *wolf*."

"Is he a pink wolf?"

"Why would a wolf be pink?" Theo said.

"Right, I'm sorry. Sometimes I get confused," said Theo's mom, smiling in that way that grown-ups smile when they think you're doing something cute instead of something serious. Pink was a big, bad wolf, who could get bigger anytime he wanted to, and that was serious business. Very serious. The reason Theo didn't have as many nightmares as Tess was because Pink watched over him. No one would have a nightmare if they had a Pink.

Anyway, it was not something to smile about.

"Why are you smiling?" Theo demanded.

"Mom is smiling because you have a friend," said Theo's dad.

"That's not why she's smiling," Theo muttered.

"It is," said Theo's mom.

"Never mind. Pink doesn't want brisket anymore." As he stomped away, Theo overheard his parents talking about his "imaginary" friend, which only made him angrier. Grandpa Ben said that all sorts of things—stories and machines and medicine—started as ideas in people's imaginations. Pink was not imaginary, and even if he was, that didn't make him any less real.

Later, at night, after he had read Theo one last story, Grandpa Ben told Theo not to be angry, not to be sad, because when Theo's mom was little, she'd had an imaginary friend, too.

"Was it a wolf?" Theo asked.

"No. Not a wolf."

"A shark?"

"No, not a shark. It was a girl."

"That's boring," said Theo.

From the other side of the room, Tess yelled, "Girls are NOT boring!"

"You're boring," Theo said.

"HA!" said Tess, who was not boring at all, and knew it.

"Your mom's friend was named Ms. Trixie. And Miriam—your mom—liked for us to set an extra place at the table, too. And Ms. Trixie came with us to the library and to the park and even on vacation. Your mom didn't like to go anywhere without her."

"What did she look like?"

"Unfortunately, I couldn't see her. But your mom said she wasn't very tall, but she seemed tall, if that makes sense. She could do cartwheels and other tricks. And when your mom was sad, Ms. Trixie would sometimes smooth her hair."

That didn't sound very interesting to Theo, at least, not as interesting as a ginormous wolf with too many teeth, but he was pleased to hear that his mom had had a friend once, too. Everyone needed friends.

Now the only one awake at eleven p.m., Theo wished he still believed in Pink, still believed he had a wolf to watch over him while he caught some sleep. But it seemed that he and Tess had switched places again. They had gone to bed early, at nine thirty, and she hadn't twitched once. Ono was cradled in one arm. Jaime was sprawled out over the top of his sleeping bag, breathing softly, one 'loc on his forehead lifting up and then dropping down with each breath. But Theo could not get comfortable. He worried that his mother wouldn't be able to find Nine and Karl, that they were gone forever. He worried that Tess wouldn't be the same after. Maybe Cricket, too.

Theo worried until eleven forty-five, and then he woke Tess and Jaime. They zipped themselves into Aunt Esther's coveralls, figuring that the station was bound to have workers wandering around and there might be a chance they could blend in. They stuffed tools—a wrench, a screwdriver, a chisel, a small hammer—in their pockets. They arranged their bedding and the sleeping bag so that it appeared they were still in them. Then, they eased open the window screen and climbed out to the small deck off the third floor. Even though Theo's parents slept with a dragonfly fan whirring overhead to drown out the noise of the street, the three of them crept down the wooden stairs as slowly and quietly as they could. They waited in the backyard for a few moments, just in case, but no lights went on in the house, and nobody came rushing out to ask them why in the corn nuts they were out of bed, for peanut butter's sake?

They hopped on the N train. Anywhere else, you might expect the trains to be empty at midnight, but New York was as alive at night as it was during the day. Plenty of people still packed the Underway cars all the way from Queens and into Manhattan. In their shapeless uniforms, no one looked at them twice, not even the Guildman manning the train. Ono watched the caterpillar drift across the wall of the car, and whispered, "Oh no, oh no, oh no," to himself.

They got off the train at Station One. Theo had been here before, but he was always awed by how magnificent it was. When this was all over, he would build a replica of the station, complete with every stone pillar and all of the twenty-two stone eagles that graced the frieze on the front of the building. In that moment, he realized how weird it was to contemplate a future without the Cipher. In the few short months they had been working to solve it, it had consumed every waking minute and most of their sleeping ones. Who would they be without this grand puzzle to solve?

"Theo!" said Tess.

"Huh?"

"You were having a spell."

"What? I was not."

"I've been calling your name for a full minute."

"I was thinking."

Tess considered him, opened her mouth to say something salty, he was sure. Instead she said, "Okay. We should find the clock, though. We have to be back before anyone else gets up, otherwise Mom will never let us out of the house again."

Inside, the station got more magnificent, and Theo was awed all over again. Ironwork arches decorated the ceiling of the enormous atrium. The moon poured silver through the framed skylights overhead, turning the polished marble floors to elaborate chessboards. Grand staircases were tucked in every corner, delivering travelers upstairs to the waiting room and restaurants and downstairs to the trains that could take them as close as Queens and as far as the Pacific. And, all throughout the atrium, there was the hiss of giant gears, the murmur and thud of the machines that powered the Underway, hammering like so many hearts.

"Theo!" said Tess. "Snap out of it!"

"Clocks, Theo," Jaime said.

Though there were a number of clocks in the station, each grander than the next, the largest and grandest hung in the middle of the lobby, over the widest tunnel leading to the train platforms.

"That's got to be it," Jaime said. "Looks just like the one in the picture on the ledger."

"A good place to start, anyway," said Theo. "But that's pretty high up there. How are we going to get to it?"

"We need a ladder," said Tess. "A really tall ladder. Where are we going to find a really tall ladder?"

"I'm sure I've got one in my pockets somewhere," Jaime said.

"So now your pockets are Hermione's pocketbook?" said Tess.

"Whose pocketbook?" said Theo. He wondered why a purse was called a pocketbook, and then why it was called a purse.

"There's got to be a janitor's closet around here," said Tess.

They stood there, looking up at the clock in frustration. Jaime's pocket beeped. Since there weren't as many people in the lobby, he unbuttoned the pocket and let Ono peek out.

"To the Land of Kings," Ono said.

"Uh-huh," said Jaime. "We have to get up there but we need a ladder."

"To the Land of Kings," Ono repeated.

"Do you know how we can get a ladder?" Tess asked the robot.

"How would the robot know where we could get a ladder?" Theo said, irritated again, though he had been trying to be as patient with Tess as she had been with him. Ono reached up with its stubby robot arms. Except they weren't so stubby anymore. The ends of the robot's arms burst with new silver blocks, adding to their length with a tiny *snap! snap! snap!* Theo glanced left and right and left again. The few people in the lobby were slumped on benches or staring bleary-eyed at the board that listed the incoming and outgoing trains. No one was paying attention to these "workers." The three of them might as well be invisible.

"Wait, is it me or are its arms getting longer?" Jaime said, peering into his pocket.

"Try putting it on the ground for a minute," said Tess.

Jaime set Ono on the ground. As soon as he did, Ono's arms grew and grew—*snap-snap-snap-snap*—and so did its legs—*snap-snap-snap-snap*. Between the arms and the legs, horizontal rungs burst and bolted themselves across the verticals. Jaime caught both of Ono's "feet" and held them as Ono's limbs extended until they reached the clock, then another set of verticals extended back to the floor, making it into a standing ladder.

Jaime shook his head in wonder. "I shouldn't be surprised by anything by now, but . . ."

Again, Theo glanced around, but still, no one was looking at the three of them and their magical Morningstarr ladder. Maybe workmen dragged ladders out here all the time.

"Do you think it will hold the weight of a person?" Tess said.

"Yes," said Theo and Jaime at the same time. Nobody laughed.

"I'll go," said Jaime. "I'm the strongest."

"You're the strongest, but I'm the lightest," said Tess.

"*I'm* the lightest," Theo said.

"We're about the same size," Tess said. She was trying to be kind. She knew he wasn't one for heights or tricks or acrobatics or skinny robot ladders reaching up a story or two or or or or. But Theo and Tess were not about the same size, not anymore. Tess had grown a lot, but Theo's height was still mostly in his hair.

"Theo might be the best person to stop the clock," Jaime said.

"So let me try," said Theo. "If I can't make the climb, then one of you can."

"Are you sure?" Jaime asked.

"No," he said. "Give me all the tools you've got. I might need them."

Tess and Jaime gave him everything they had and he stuffed them into his own pockets. Then, he carefully put a foot on the first rung of the ladder. He pressed, testing, and then he placed his second foot on the rung and waited to see if the rung gave.

"To the Land of Kings!" Ono squeaked, seemingly impatient. The robot's "face" and "body"—if you could call them his face and his body—were way up in the middle of the ladder. Just a couple of tiny boxes, one stacked on top of the other.

"I'm coming," Theo said. The first few rungs were no problem. One foot after the other, he told himself, don't look down. But the higher he got, the harder it was *not* to look down.

He looked down.

Oh no.

His calf muscles cramped, his hands locked around the rungs. He squeezed his eyes shut, tried to control his breathing. His ragged exhalations seemed to echo all around him, the marble floors and the metal arches and the shiny skylights bouncing them right back at him.

"You're doing great," Tess said. "Just a little more."

Theo was not doing great.

And it was not just "a little more."

But he willed himself to keep going. A little farther, and a little farther after that, and again and again. And then he bonked the clock with his head, and he almost fell off the ladder, his stomach feeling like it'd dropped somewhere around his feet.

Keeping one hand tight on the ladder, he stared into the face of the clock. A quiet but persistent *tick–tick–tick* emanated from it, like the chirp of some relentless insect. Theo tried opening the glass front of the clock. Didn't work. He reached around to the back of the clock and found a latch. He opened the latch to expose the works. The ticking grew louder. Swallowing hard, Theo glanced down. None of the passengers roaming around seemed to be paying attention. He steeled himself and gingerly felt around the movement of the clock, his fingers brushing against gears and weights. A weight-driven clock that didn't need to be wound, a weight-driven clock powered by . . . what? The light pouring in from the ceiling? The movement of the air? The energy of atoms spinning? The verse from the fore-edge painting ticked in his mind:

Stop the clock in dead of night
To wake what sleeps and stir their flight

How was he to stop an unstoppable clock? Smash it with a hammer? Eviscerate it with a crowbar? And even if he could stop it, *should* he? The clue sounded ominous. The last time a clue sounded so ominous, he and Tess and Jaime managed to take down their whole building, and instead of stopping Slant, Slant was more powerful than ever. Not for the first time, Theo wondered exactly what the Morningstarrs really wanted, what the *Cipher* really wanted.

Down below, Tess coughed with impatience. They had come so far. He had to know. He had to.

Theo felt around the works again, his nimble fingers finding a wire. He didn't need any of the tools that Tess and Jaime had given him to yank it away from its connection.

The ticking stopped.

Theo waited for something else to happen, anything else to happen, but nothing did. He glanced down at Tess and Jaime and shook his head.

"Come down," Tess shout-whispered.

Theo took a deep breath and willed himself to take a step.

"You're not moving," said Jaime.

"I'm getting ready to move," Theo muttered. "Give me a second."

Just as his foot hit the rung below, he heard a strange rumbling sound. He gripped the ladder and looked around, but he didn't see anything except for a bunch of sleepy train passengers doing exactly what he was— looking for the source of the noise.

Another rumble and more cracking sounds like tumbling rocks. Coming from outside somewhere. But where?

And what?

"Oh no," said Ono.

"Hurry!" Tess said.

Theo made it a quarter of the way down the ladder when there was a bone-rattling crash. Across the lobby, an enormous window shattered, glass raining to the floor below. People covered their heads as something large and silvery darted through the air, circling, showering everyone with bits of rock and dust. Another huge silvery thing crashed through the window and circled the other way.

Theo froze on the ladder as one of the large silvery creatures passed so close to him that he could have jumped on its back and ridden the thing straight to Mordor.

He had just enough time to say, "Well, the eagles are finally here," when the tip of a huge wing hit the ladder, knocking Theo right off.

CHAPTER NINETEEN

Jaime

Jaime stood there in shock as the great silver eagle knocked Theo off the ladder, and Theo fell and fell and fell. It took so long, the falling, so, so long. Ono was shouting, "Oh no!" and Tess was shouting, "Oh no!" and Jaime was, too. It seemed like hours before Jaime could make himself dart forward, arms out, as if he could catch Theo without both of them being smashed to pieces on the marble. "This is so stupid," he said to himself. "You're not Superman." But just then, another eagle swooped down, caught Theo by the collar. The eagle landed only long enough to drop Theo to the floor before it launched itself into the air once again.

Snap! Snap! Snap! Snap! Ono changed again. Every comic book and every action movie swirled in Jaime's mind. He was sure he'd see Ono transform into some sort of fighting robot, sure he'd see Ono take on the eagles one by one. But Ono was only Ono, and it wasn't growing but shrinking, pulling its elongated limbs back in. It was little Ono that Jaime caught in one hand.

"Land. Kings," Ono said. If Jaime didn't know better, he would have thought the robot was breathing hard.

Jaime pressed Ono into his pocket and skidded over to where Theo lay dazed. Tess was crouched next to him, pressing on his arms and legs.

"Theo? Theo! Are you okay? Is anything broken?"

"What?" said Theo. "No, I don't think so. What happened?"

"One eagle knocked you over, and another eagle caught you," Jaime told him.

"Caught me?"

"Yeah."

All three of them turned their heads toward the ceiling. Not one, not two, but many eagles darted in and out of the shattered window, swooped and dived. Underway passengers, so sleepy and uninterested before, were screaming, throwing themselves under benches or over countertops, running in crazed circles.

"How many do you think there are?" Tess said.

"Twenty-two," said Theo.

"You counted?" Jaime said.

"There were twenty-two eagles on the stone frieze on the front of the building," said Theo.

"And we woke them up," Jaime said.

"This isn't going to be pretty," said Tess.

"It's not pretty now," Jaime said. "We should get out of here."

"Not before we get the next clue!" Tess said.

"Maybe we need to follow the eagles like we followed Ono," Theo said.

"Yeah, but they're not going anywhere in particular," Jaime said. "They're just flying around in circles terrifying people."

"They're good at it," said Theo.

Right in front of them, an eagle landed with a *BOOM!* on sharp metal claws. They all screamed and scuttled backward. The eagle lowered its silvery head, fixed them with a gaze like some sort of fire, red and jewel-like. *BOOM! BOOM! BOOM! BOOM!* It walked toward them, the claws scratching the marble floor, the metal beak clicking.

"Oh no, oh no, oh no," they all said when the eagle emitted a metallic shriek, clicked and clicked again. When they hugged one another and squeezed their eyes shut, the eagle only shrieked louder, clicking, clicking, clicking.

Jaime opened one eye and jumped. The eagle's beak was only inches away, but its clicking beak wasn't biting, the claws were not tearing.

Jaime opened the other eye and sat up. The eagle reared back and, instead, held out one of its legs. And that was when Jaime saw something strapped there, right above the ginormous metal claw. Some kind of band or bracelet knotted to its leg. Despite his terror, Jaime leaned closer, trying to see. Someone grabbed the back of his uniform, someone said, "No!" But what if it was one of those bands like messenger birds wear; what if the eagle was trying to tell them something?

Or maybe it was just doing a dance before it ate them.

No, the eagles didn't hurt Theo, and this eagle wasn't attacking him. Jaime crawled forward reached for band. Vaguely, he heard people screaming, "Don't touch it, man! Get away! It's going to bite your arm off!" Jaime ignored them. When he touched the band, it felt like leather, dusty with rock. He untied it, and the eagle clicked its beak, flapped its wings, as if to say, "Finally." The eagle launched itself into the air, crashing through the ceiling. One by one, the other eagles followed, silvery rockets in the dead of night.

◆ ◆ ◆

Mesmerized as they were by the eagles, it took Ono shrieking "OH NO!" to shake them out of their trance.

Other people were starting to crawl out from under their benches, peer over countertops, pull phones from pockets to take pictures of the shattered windows and ceiling.

"Come on, we've got to move," Jaime said.

"But we need the clue!" Tess said.

"I've got the clue," Jaime said. He really hoped he did. But that didn't matter, because if they didn't get out of here soon, they would be stuck here when the police showed up, and then they would wish the eagles had swallowed them all.

"Theo," Jaime said. "Get in between us. Put your arms around our shoulders. Pretend you're hurt. Everybody keep your heads down."

They did as Jaime asked. With Theo limping between them, Jaime and Tess hobbled as fast as they could toward the stairs that led to the trains.

"Will they still be running?" said Tess.

"Hopefully, for the next few minutes they will," Jaime said. "Still faster than a bus."

They made it to the N just as a train was pulling into the station. Down here, on the platforms, passengers were glancing curiously at the stairs, but no one was truly alarmed. Not yet. The three of them hopped on the train and slumped down in their seats, caps pulled low over their faces. No one spoke to them; no one seemed to notice them at all.

Miraculously, they made it back to Queens before four in the morning. They climbed the stairs back to the twins' room. Nothing seemed different, nothing had been disturbed. They emptied their pockets on the night table. Ono beeped at the various tools as if they, too, could come to life; it was a relief when they didn't.

Jaime, Theo, and Tess peeled off the uniforms and Tess hid them in a trunk in her closet, a trunk that had THE MAGIX written in gold along the top. Jaime reminded himself to ask her what that meant some other time.

They got back in their respective beds and tried to sleep. Which was ridiculous, because they were all way too keyed up. Jaime had the tether or strap or whatever it was tied around his wrist like a bracelet. He traced it with his fingers. Something was tooled in the leather, some kind of code maybe, some kind of cipher. And the eagle had offered it to them, to him. Why? Because he was the first person it saw? Because it saw something in him that seemed trustworthy? But that was dumb. How could some mechanical eagle decide he was the one to take the bracelet rather than anyone else?

Unless it somehow knew that they were the ones who had awakened it.

The day broke cool and rainy. Bleary-eyed, Jaime, Tess, and Theo dragged themselves from bed and went downstairs, where Mr. Biedermann was making scrambled eggs and bugbacon and Lance was sitting in the corner, sulking. Jaime didn't know a suit of armor could sulk, but then he hadn't known that a puzzle game could turn into a robot and then a ladder and back again, or that stone eagles could be dormant for more than a hundred years until someone stopped a clock. It felt as if he were in a comic book. *Living* a comic book.

Jaime pinched himself and yelped.

Tess frowned at him, confused. He shrugged. "Just checking."

She nodded, as if this made perfect sense. Maybe she'd been pinching herself a lot, too.

Mr. Biedermann held up a spatula. "So who wants bacon?"

All three of them raised their hands; all three of them yawned.

"Stayed up a little too late last night, I guess?" said Mr. Biedermann, scooping slices of bugbacon and putting them on each of their plates. "You can nap later."

Tess moved her bacon around her plate, but didn't eat. "Where's Mom?"

"Where else? Work."

"Anything about Nine and Karl?"

Mr. Biedermann scooped eggs onto her plate. "I'm sorry. Not yet. But she is following some leads."

"What leads?"

"She wasn't specific. You know how she is."

Tess took this news without changing expression, though under the table her leg started to bounce. Theo touched her arm, mouthed: *Breathe.* She took a deep breath, held it, let it out. The bounce quieted a bit. Not much, but a bit.

Jaime ate his eggs and bugbacon hungrily, angrily. He didn't know whether they should keep trying to solve the Cipher or if they should be out combing every one of the five boroughs for Nine and Karl. He remembered that Mrs. Biedermann was going to go out to Hoboken to interview Cricket and her family. He wanted to know what she learned.

It was easy to convince the twins that they were better

off trying to figure out the new clue—if the strap now around his wrist was a new clue—the next day, after they'd had a chance to rest.

Tess said, "Let us come to you next time. It's not fair that you're the one that has to go back and forth."

He didn't tell her that he hadn't wanted them going back and forth, that if no one visited him at the new place in Hoboken, it would keep only being temporary, it wouldn't become real. But he didn't argue. He told her which trains to take and then headed to the place he didn't want to call home.

He pushed open the doors of his building at around noon to find Cricket and her brother, Otto, in the lobby. Both of them were dressed in green camo. Both were on foot—no tricycles or scooters. And both of them were inspecting every corner of the place, every nook and cranny. Cricket even had a magnifying glass. She used it to inspect the security desk. The guard, a large black man with a shiny bald head, smiled indulgently as she turned the magnifying glass on him and declared that he had a mole that he should probably get looked at.

"Cricket," said Jaime. "What are you looking for?"

Cricket turned the magnifying glass on Jaime, instead, one of her eyes about the size of a baseball.

"Clues," she said. "What do you think?"

"What kind of clues?"

"The clue kind of clues."

"Okay. Can I help?"

"I don't know," said Cricket, lowering the magnifying glass. "Can you?"

Otto ran over, holding a candy bar wrapper. "Is this a clue, Zelda?"

"Don't call me Zelda. And no, that's just a piece of trash."

"It could be a clue," Otto insisted. "What if the person who took Karl dropped it?"

"What if he did?" Cricket said.

"We can dust it for fingerprints!" Otto said.

"No, we can't," said Cricket.

Otto's face got all red, the way Otto and Cricket's father's did before he started yelling about something or another. "Can, too!"

"That's a great idea, Otto," Jaime said. "Why don't you let me hang on to that while you check for more clues?"

Otto grinned and gave Jaime the wrapper. "Okay! I'm going to look by the elevators." He dashed off.

Cricket crossed her arms, then uncrossed them. "You are good with children," she told him.

Jaime made sure he didn't crack a smile. "Thank you, Cricket."

"But that isn't a clue."

"It's okay if Otto thinks so. Speaking of clues, though, I'd like you to tell me again about yesterday, and when Karl disappeared."

"I already told everybody! And no one has found him!"

"I know. And I'm sorry. But people are looking."

"LIP SERVICE," Cricket announced loudly, recrossing her arms.

"Not this time. This time, people really are looking. You know Tess's cat?"

Cricket nodded. "The big one?"

"Yes. She's missing, too. I think they're connected."

Cricket dropped her arms. "COLLUSION. CONSPIRACY."

"Maybe. So do you think you could go over it again? Just for me?"

"Yes. But I'm going to need REINFORCEMENTS."

To Cricket, reinforcements consisted of a grilled cheese sandwich followed by her mother's fudge brownies and a tall glass of milk. Mrs. Moran offered lunch to Jaime, too, and he couldn't refuse, so he ate for the second time in two hours. Ono began beeping in his pocket, so Jaime took it out and set it on the table. Otto could not stop giggling when Ono paraded across the table and said, "Oh no," every time it reached the edge.

"Thank you, Mrs. Moran," Jaime said. "These brownies are delicious."

"You're welcome, Jaime. It's nice to see you again. And it was so nice of your grandmother to find us this beautiful place. I can't thank her enough. We love it here. My husband has his own office now. And the rooms are so spacious." Mrs. Moran raised her coffee cup, gesturing to the living room beyond. She had painted it a soft gray color, and decorated with low modern furniture in shades of burnt orange and red. Jaime had to admit the place looked good. Not sterile at all. She had always been a pretty woman—brown-skinned with large, soulful dark eyes and a short, tidy 'fro—but now she glowed like a woman in an ad for face cream. She was happy.

At least someone was.

But not completely. "I'm worried about Karl, though. Cricket has been devastated."

"What's devastated?" asked Cricket.

"Upset."

"I'm not DEVASTATED," said Cricket. "I'm AGGRAVATED."

"Either way," said Mrs. Moran. "She hasn't been herself."

"I'M NOT SOMEBODY ELSE," said Cricket.

"That's not what I . . . Cricket, would you like another brownie?"

"I want another brownie!" said Otto.

Cricket raised a brow at her brother. "You've had four. Don't you think that's enough?"

"You're not the boss of me," said Otto. "Why are you always pretending to be the boss? You're too small."

"I am the Small Boss," Cricket said, taking another brownie.

Otto pounded the table. "MOM!"

"Oh no," said Ono.

While Mrs. Moran soothed the kids with more milk, she told Jaime that Cricket had been out riding her tricycle with Karl as usual when she stopped to talk to the security guard. She parked the tricycle by the wall, with Karl still in the basket. When Cricket turned around, Karl was gone. He wasn't anywhere in the building. The local police thought that maybe Karl had simply escaped out the front door or the back, but that wasn't like him at all. He was too attached to Cricket. Plus there were always crowds of people passing through the lobby during the day, Mrs. Moran said, so anyone could have taken him.

"I heard him," said Cricket.

"What, darling?" her mom said.

"I heard Karl. He said my name."

"Honey, Karl can't—"

"HE DID. HE SAID MY NAME." Cricket swiped angry tears from her cheeks. "What if they don't have Cheez Doodles where he is? What will he eat? Where will he sleep?"

"Detective Biedermann is working really hard, Cricket. And so am I," said Jaime.

Cricket frowned. "What are you doing?"

Jaime thought about what the twins' aunt Esther had said about him. "I'm doing everything I possibly can, Cricket. And so are Tess and Theo."

"I want to help, too," said Cricket.

"You are," Jaime said. "You already have. By telling Detective Biedermann what happened yesterday, and by telling me again today."

Cricket got a sulky look on her face. "That's not helping. You should make me a sheriff."

"A Small Sheriff," said Otto, his mouth smeared with brownie.

"Anything else you remember about yesterday?" Jaime asked. "Were there any unusual people in the lobby?"

"Everyone's unusual here. They wear weird shorts."

"Okay, anyone you haven't seen around before. Anyone who seemed to be paying a little too much attention to you or to Karl?"

Cricket thought about this. "There was one lady."

"What lady?" said Mrs. Moran.

Cricket played with the brownie crumbs on her plate, arranging them in a circle. "She wore a red dress."

CHAPTER TWENTY
Karl

If you had asked Karl, and if Karl had been able to answer, he would have told you that he had been lounging in Cricket's basket, enjoying another Cheez Doodle, when someone had unceremoniously thrown a bag over his head, scooped him up, and carried him off without so much as a "please" or "excuse me" or "my deepest apologies for this rude behavior." As he bumped along in the dark, he chittered and chattered, doing his best to shape Cricket's name with his rigid palate, but to no avail. He heard street noises—cars and Rollers and voices—and smelled the river. For one terrible moment he thought this desperado, whoever it was, was planning to toss him into the water. Instead, Karl was stuffed into a cage in the back of a van.

At least they took the bag off his head. But the view wasn't pleasant. There were several cages in this van. In the cage on Karl's immediate left was a cat-sized lizard with a ruff of red fur around its neck. A rather strange-looking fellow, but it didn't appear to be hostile. On Karl's right, however, was . . . well. Karl wasn't quite sure. A coyote, perhaps? But with too many legs. Far too many. Why, the creature was positively bristling with legs. And teeth.

Karl sidled to the left and addressed the lizard. *Hello, Kind Sir,* he chittered. *Would you mind terribly telling us where we are headed?*

The lizard turned a blue eye on him, but didn't make a sound. Not the talkative sort, Karl guessed.

The creature on the right, though, laughed. "Heh, heh, heh," it said.

Karl squished himself against the left side of his cage. *Would you mind telling me what is so amusing?* he chittered.

The creature lurched toward Karl on its numerous legs. It was a deeply unpleasant thing to watch. "Heh, heh, heh."

Keep your distance, please, Karl said, *I am in great need of personal space at this particular time, I'm sure you understand.*

The creature regarded him, tipping its furred head this way and that, just like a dog might. And then it launched itself at the bars of the cage. "HEH!"

Karl tried to scramble backward, but couldn't move any farther away. Furry legs poked through the spaces between the bars, trying to reach him. At the end of each leg was a long, curved claw. One of them swiped only inches away from Karl's nose. The creature kept this up—the laughing, the launching, and the swiping— the whole ride. It was perfectly traumatic.

So it was quite a relief when the vehicle stopped moving and the doors opened. Two men in white coats and heavy gloves hefted the cages and carried them into a strange building that smelled of cleaning solutions and something else. Deeper and more frightening. It smelled like the coyote with too many legs. It smelled like *many* coyotes with too many legs.

Karl yearned for a Cheez Doodle. He yearned for his comfortable bed with his favorite hand-crocheted afghan. He yearned for Cricket.

He and the other animals were taken into a large white room with other cages. He was placed on a shelf. One of the men opened the door of the cage and held Karl still as the other hooked a water bottle to one of the bars. A bowl of kibble was tossed in the corner, and a blanket was placed along the bottom of the cage. Then the door was shut. The men marched out of the lab and left the various creatures to themselves. The many-legged coyote kept up its insane laughter, and some of the other animals howled and burbled and yipped. A rainbow-striped octopus methodically tossed all the rocks from its aquarium onto the floor while a monkey-faced bird yelled, "SOS! SOS! SOS!" over and over. Karl pulled the blanket over his head to try to drown them out, but it didn't work. By the time the lights in the lab came on again, Karl was more exhausted than he'd ever been and hungry enough to eat the strange kibble that got stuck in his teeth. He was wiping his lips with his little hand when another man arrived, this one skinny with rather bulbous eyes. The man peered at Karl through the thin bars of the cage.

If Karl hadn't known better, he would have thought the man's gaze was . . . hungry. As hungry as some of the other creatures that populated the cages.

"Hello, there, Karl," the man said. "I'm very pleased to meet you, finally."

The man held up a syringe.

Karl was not pleased. Not pleased at all.

CHAPTER TWENTY-ONE

Tess

Tess's dreams were filled with giant eagles smashing through windows, darting through clouds. She dreamed she was on the back of one of the eagles, riding it to somewhere safe. But where was that? The safe place? She didn't know, but she hoped the eagle did.

She woke up the way she had for the last week, with Theo slumped by the side of her bed. She didn't say anything about what he was doing, and neither did he. She didn't know what to say about it. She hated that he felt he needed to do this for her; she hated that she needed it from anyone. She hated that Nine was gone and she was starting to adjust to life without her. That seemed to be the most horrible thing of all, that you could lose something so precious to you, something you loved, and still go on. Grandpa Ben would have said that life itself was about loving and losing and loving again, despite the risks, but she had lost Grandpa Ben, at least in a way, and she didn't want to lose any more. She hated that she would never be able to stop it.

She touched Theo's shoulder and he stirred. He yawned, stretched, and got up from the floor as if sleeping by your sister's bed was the most normal thing in the world, as if it was something that all brothers did. He got in the shower first so she went downstairs to forage for breakfast, as all the adults would already be out of the house. She didn't have to forage, though, because Lance had taken it upon himself to whip up a fresh batch of oatmeal cookies. They were as good a breakfast as any, so she helped herself to four of them, which seemed to please Lance. (Granted, it was difficult to tell when a suit of armor was pleased, but Tess thought she detected a bit of a spring in Lance's step when she reached for another cookie.) By the time Theo came downstairs, she had devoured a half dozen all by herself. Theo did the same, and then stuffed more into a bag for Jaime.

After Tess showered and dressed, they left the house to Lance and the giggling spiders, and headed for Hoboken. Tess was excited to see Jaime's new place. She knew that he wasn't happy with it, that his building in

Hoboken was strange to him, stranger even than Aunt Esther's house in Queens. It had taken him weeks—and the onslaught of twenty-two mechanical eagles—just to invite them.

As Jaime had suggested, they took the N train to the PATH train that ran underneath the Hudson River to New Jersey. The previous night's rain had cooled the air, so when the twins burst from the train station, the sun was shining brightly on bars and restaurants and brownstones. They followed Jaime's directions to his building, finally arriving at a tall bank of condominiums that faced the bright blue ribbon of the Hudson. It was a beautiful building, but unlike their beloved 354 W. 73rd Street in Manhattan, this building was only a year old. The stone outside was white and sparkling. The lobby smelled of new carpet, the walls of fresh paint.

At the security desk, Tess asked the smiling guard for Jaime's apartment, and the woman happily rang Jaime.

"I have a Bess and Thom Friedman for you," the guard said. "Bess and Thom." Her eyes flicked to Tess and Theo, assessing. "Yes, she has a braid. And his hair *is* a little big. Great! I'll send them up." The guard rang off and pointed to the elevators. "Eleventh floor," she said. "And have a nice day!"

"Thank you," said Tess. "You too."

Theo grunted, and punched at the elevator buttons.

"What's wrong with you?" Tess said.

"Bess and Thom?"

"It was a mistake, that's all," said Tess.

"She's too cheerful," Theo said. "Everything about this place feels weird."

"It's new."

"That's not it."

"I know," Tess said.

At this, Theo seemed even more grumpy and stabbed at the elevator buttons again.

"You know that doesn't make the elevator come any faster," Tess said, and smiled. It was Theo's usual line.

"I know it doesn't," Theo said, stabbing away. "I bet this elevator only moves up and down."

"You said that the old elevator was a waste of space. That the reason it could move every which way was because the elevator shafts took up so much room."

Stab, stab, stab. "Yeah, but I also said it was cool."

"Okay," said Tess. She was twitchy enough without all this punching and stabbing, but she didn't complain. He couldn't have slept well slumped next to her bed. He couldn't have slept well all week. She was used to getting only a few snatches of sleep a night, but it was a new thing for Theo.

Theo was right, the elevator only went up and down. They made it to Jaime's floor in one quick minute, and barely felt the elevator's movement. The elevator doors opened up onto a large hallway that also smelled of fresh paint. The solar glass on the hall window was clear as the very air. Tess recalled how the wavy old solar glass of 354 W. 73rd Street fractured the light into rainbows, and missed her old building so much that it hurt. She clutched her chest and Theo stopped walking.

"Are you all right?"

"I'm fine," she said, not fine, but what was there to do about it?

They knocked on Jaime's apartment door and Jaime's grandmother let them in. She was wearing coveralls much like the ones they had worn as a disguise their last few outings. But hers had the words THE HANDY WOMAN embroidered on the front pocket and written on the back.

She grinned at them. "Tess! Theo! Why has it taken you so long to visit me?" She gathered both of them into a hug. She smelled of something sweet, like jam, and also something woody, like oak. As if she had been cooking up a batch of marmalade while carving wands for wizards.

She led them inside the apartment. It was a large apartment, with a big open space that housed the kitchen and living room. Everything was white. The cabinets, the countertops, the walls. The few pieces of furniture that they had brought from their old place appeared small and worn in this brand-new space. They hadn't purchased anything new themselves. They hadn't painted. There were a few photos on some of the tables, but most must have been packed away, still. It was as if this place were staged instead of lived in.

Jaime's grandmother knew what they were thinking, the way she often knew what children were thinking. "We've been too busy to decorate," she told them. "One day we're going to paint everything."

"It's a very nice place," said Tess.

"No, it isn't," said Jaime's grandmother. "But maybe it will be. Someday."

"Someday," Jaime said, walking down a long hallway from where the bedrooms must have been. "Hi."

Theo handed him the bag of cookies. "A Lance special."

"Thanks," Jaime said. "You guys want a drink or something?"

"Maybe later," Tess said.

"Speaking of later," said Jaime's grandmother, "I'll see you later. I have a packed schedule today. Lots of jobs all over the place." She kissed Jaime's cheek, and then Tess's and Theo's. "I'm glad to see you both. There's lunch in the fridge. Keep an eye on this boy for me. And don't do anything silly while I'm gone."

Since everything they'd done for the last few months could be considered silly or dumb or even life-threatening, they all merely nodded as Jaime's grandmother disappeared out the door.

"Well," said Jaime. "You want to see my room? It's about as thrilling as this one."

They followed him down the long hallway, which was as conspicuously absent of photographs as the living room was, and into a huge bedroom that faced the river.

"This view is amazing," said Tess.

"Hmmm," Jaime said. He fed his hamster-hogs. One of them jumped on her wheel and ran furiously. "I don't think Tyrone likes it, either," Jaime said.

"How would she decide?" Theo asked.

"She's very decisive," Jaime said.

Tess sat in Jaime's desk chair. On the desk itself, a sketchbook lay open. The pages were filled with sketches of the same woman in various outfits: armor, unitard, cargo pants, etc. Tess turned the page and found the woman wearing a plain gray coat that fell around her ankles.

Tess tapped the picture. "I like this one best so far."

"Me too," said Jaime. "But it's not right. Not yet. I'm working on it."

Theo sat on Jaime's bed. "So about the clue."

Jaime unwound the leather strap from his wrist. "I looked at it this morning but I don't know what it means."

He laid the strap on the bed. Tooled vertically into the leather, making one long strip, were these characters:

Jaime had copied the letters into his sketchbook horizontally:

E h h h x r l e e e H e d r c S o d e h l m s o r
i v a p n b d e l i b r e i l t l o s n p a u t t t o l e

"I figure it's the German word for 'Ach, this clue is going to give you a giant pain in your neck' or it's some sort of transposition cipher," he said, "but I didn't get much by using some of the tools on the web."

"There are some capital letters interspersed," Theo said.

Jaime wrote down the capitals: *E H S.* "Hmmm. I don't think that helps."

Tess tugged at her braid, let go. "Okay. Can I have a piece of paper, Jaime?"

They each took a stack of sheets and tried different arrangements of the letters. After a while, Tess lost herself in the work. That was what her grandpa Ben liked about puzzles—that you could forget yourself and your troubles for a while as you tried to solve them. Tess remembered when she was very small, only about four, sitting at her grandparents' kitchen table, legs swinging back and forth, doing her best to work the very first crossword puzzle ever invented. But it wasn't her grandpa Ben who had introduced her to crosswords, it was her grandma Annie. Though Grandma Annie didn't much care for the Morningstarr Cipher the way Grandpa Ben did, she did love her crossword puzzles.

"Arthur Wynne developed this puzzle more than a hundred years ago," Grandma Annie told Tess. "He called it a 'word-cross.'"

It wasn't like any crossword Tess had ever seen. This one was shaped like a diamond:

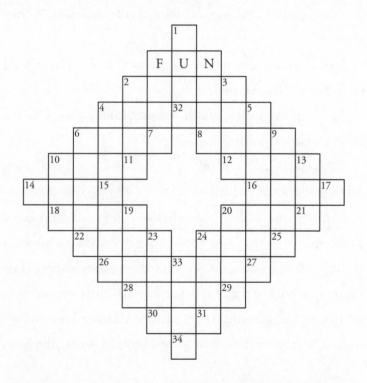

2-3. What bargain hunters enjoy.

4-5. A written acknowledgment.

6-7. Such and nothing more.

10-11. A bird.

14-15. Opposed to less.

18-19. What this puzzle is.

22-23. An animal of prey.

26-27. The close of a day.

28-29. To elude.

30-31. The plural of is.

8-9. To cultivate.

12-13. A bar of wood or iron.

16-17. What artists learn to do.

20-21. Fastened.

24-25. Found on the seashore.

10-18. The fibre of the gomuti palm.

6-22. What we all should be.

4-26. A day dream.

2-11. A talon.

19-28. A pigeon.

F-7. Part of your head.

23-30. A river in Russia.

1-32. To govern.

33-34. An aromatic plant.

N-8. A fist.

24-31. To agree with.

3-12. Part of a ship.

20-29. One.

5-27. Exchanging.

9-25. To sink in mud.

13-21. A boy.

Tess pointed at the squares. "I got 10–11. That's *dove*. And 24–25. That's *sand*. And I got F–7. *Face!* Also, 16–17. What artists learn to do. *Draw!* But I can't figure out the rest. It's hard, Grandma."

"You just figured out one more."

"What?"

"You've discovered the answer to 18–19. 'What this puzzle is.'"

Tess looked at 18–19, saw that there were four spaces. She wrote *h-a-r-d*. "This puzzle is hard!"

"See? You're doing great," said Grandma.

Grandpa Ben, who had been reading through a batch

of yellowed papers, looked over at the puzzle. "Oh, that thing. One of the clues is wrong."

"You always say that," said Grandma. To Tess, she said, "Ignore him, dear."

"Wait, which one is wrong?"

"Look at 22–23," Grandpa Ben said.

Tess read, "An animal of prey. That's an animal that other animals like to hunt, right?"

"What do you think?" said Grandpa.

Tess wrinkled her nose. She didn't like thinking about animals hunting animals.

"A deer?"

"What did I tell you?" He shook his head at Grandma Annie. "You're just confusing the girl."

"She's not confused."

"The answer is *lion*," said Grandpa Ben. "But a lion is a predator, not prey."

"The dictionary defines 'beast of prey' as a carnivorous animal," Grandma Annie said. "And anyway, a lion *could* be prey either way."

"Prey to what?" said Grandpa Ben.

"A bigger lion," Tess suggested.

Grandma and Grandpa both laughed, and Grandma reached for Grandpa's hand. That was how she remembered Grandpa Ben and Grandma Annie. Always laughing, reaching for each other, even when they disagreed.

After Grandma Annie died five years ago, they sat shivah. Though they weren't formal people, Tess's mom covered all the mirrors with black cloth, and they had visitors coming and going, bringing food and talking in low tones. Tess sat under a table and cried so hard she ran out of tears. Grandpa Ben gathered her onto his lap. He said that he hurt, too, but their pain was a measure of how much they loved Grandma Annie and how much joy she had brought them. He said he wouldn't trade his time with Grandma for anything, not even to stop his tears. And he said that he would try to laugh as much as he could, because that was how Grandma lived her life, and that was how he could honor her.

Tess hadn't felt like laughing much lately, but she thought that working this part of the Cipher honored her grandmother as well as her grandpa Ben. She pushed her papers away and focused on the leather strap itself. Something about the way the letters were tooled onto the leather nagged at her. Why were they vertical instead of horizontal? Why make a long strip of letters rather than tooling the letters across the strip so they could be read more easily? Were they supposed to read the letters differently somehow? Arrange the strip in a particular way?

Jaime tossed his pencil down, removed his glasses, and rubbed the bridge of his nose. "Your headache is catching, Tess." He put the glasses back on. "I liked this thing better as a bracelet."

"It would make a nice belt, too," said Theo.

"A belt?" Tess said, her thoughts racing, scratching for some bit of history. Who wore leather belts tooled with ciphers?

"What are you thinking?" said Theo, watching her.

"I know how to read it," Tess said.

"You do?"

"Yup. We just need someone with a bigger arm."

CHAPTER TWENTY-TWO

Theo

"Wait, what's wrong with my arm?" Jaime said.

"No, no, no," Tess said, "there's nothing wrong with your arm, that's not what I meant," but Theo knew what she meant. A long time ago, Grandpa Ben had told them of a method of encryption used by the ancient Greeks and the Spartans during war. They would wrap a strip of parchment or leather around a wooden rod of a certain circumference, write a message across the strip, and then unwind it from the rod. A messenger would carry the parchment strip or wear the leather strip as a belt, with the back side of the leather facing out, hiding the writing. The resulting cascade of characters on the strip would look meaningless until the recipient wrapped it around a rod of the same size.

Only then could you read the message.

"We don't need an arm, we need a scytale," said Theo.

"Or an arm," said Tess.

"Tyrone communicates more clearly than you guys do," Jaime said.

Theo explained how the cipher worked, that the rod used in the encryption method was called a scytale. "S-c-y-t-a-l-e. Rhymes with Italy."

"So I had the right idea wrapping the strap around my wrist," said Jaime. "The fact that it was wrapped around the eagle's leg was probably a hint."

"Yeah, one that we missed," said Theo.

"Till now," Jaime said.

They wrapped the leather around the upper part of Jaime's arm, then his bedpost, then Theo's leg, then Tess's. They tried some scraps of wood that Jaime's grandmother had stacked in the guest room closet. But with each thing they tried, the letters remained a jumble of letters.

"She's got some more stuff back here," Jaime said, digging around. Then he yelped and pulled his hand back. A silverfish skittered out of the pile and across the floor, scuttling under the bed.

"UGH," Jaime said. "I *hate* those things."

"Me too," said Tess. "They eat book bindings."

"And dandruff," Theo added.

Jaime made a gagging noise. "Let's get out of here."

"Those things are everywhere," Theo said.

"Let's get out of here anyway," Jaime said.

"Where do you want to go?"

"Somewhere where I can dream of a world free of dandruff-eating fish-bugs."

Theo thought the design of the bugs was rather elegant, and admired how quickly they moved, but also thought that mentioning this to Jaime right now might not be the best idea. Tess suggested they get some pizza for lunch, a much better idea. The three of them left the building and went to the pizza place on the corner, where they devoured a whole pie and two calzones by themselves. Then they took the train back to Aunt Esther's place in Queens. Which probably had way more silverfish than Jaime's building, another thing Theo didn't mention.

When they got off the train in Queens, the sun was hot and bright in the sky, covering everything in a kind of golden haze. Kids were playing in the parks and parking lots; parents and teenagers chatted and laughed on stoops. The fire department had opened a hydrant, and a group of little boys ran screaming through the spray. A man in an exo suit clomped down the sidewalk, but stopped to help another man carry a couch into an apartment building. The exos were huge and clumsy, and it was difficult to maneuver in them, but Theo knew that one day, someone would develop a suit just as light as clothes, or maybe lighter. One day, people might have exos installed just under the skin, so that that they could lift ten times more and run ten times faster. Faster, even, than a silverfish.

Since none of them wanted to rot inside on a day like this, they sat at Aunt Esther's small patio in the backyard. Jaime took Ono out of his pocket and set him in the middle of the table. Lance brought them a tray of cookies and milk, and for a little while, they all pretended that nobody's pets were missing and there was no puzzle to solve. Theo wasn't sure what he wanted out of the puzzle anymore. It wasn't to save his home; his home was here now. And though he still felt a little thrill every time they worked out a clue, he also felt a little chill. He had seen how dangerous, how destructive the Cipher could be. Who knows what else it had up its sleeve?

At this thought, Theo jammed a whole cookie in his mouth. He was thinking like Tess.

"Theo, maybe take human bites?" said Tess.

"What?"

"You weren't listening, were you?"

"I was listening."

"What was I saying, then?"

"These cookies could use a touch of salt," said Theo.

"I did not say that."

"No, *I'm* saying that. These cookies could use a touch of salt."

"Don't tell the suit of armor that," Jaime said.

"You've been watching those baking shows again, haven't you?" Tess said, pointing at him with a shard of cookie.

"They're informative," Theo said.

"*As* I was *saying*," Tess apparently continued, "Aunt Esther has a bunch of foam cylinders in the attic. All different sizes. We could try those."

"Good idea. Let's do that after we finish the cookies," Jaime said.

"If we keep eating them, Lance will just keep baking them," said Theo.

"And this is a problem for you?" Jaime said. He turned in the direction of the kitchen window. "THANK YOU, LANCE. THESE COOKIES ARE PERFECT—THEY DON'T NEED SALT OR ANYTHING."

"Funny," said Theo. It was. Also funny, when Jaime

wrapped the leather strap around Ono's middle, and Ono kept trying to back out of it, like Nine when Tess would put a hat on her.

So all of them were surprised when Ono suddenly grew about a foot wider—*Snap! Snap! Snap! Snap! Snap!*—and then his regular size again. The leather puddled around his feet. He tried to step over it, tripped, and fell.

"Oh no," he said.

"Oh yes!" said Jaime.

"Ono can be our scytale," Theo said.

Jaime set Ono upright. "Do you want to be our scytale?"

"Oh no?" said Ono.

"Just do what you did before. We're going to wrap this around you, and when we tell you, get a little wider. But just a little. Not all at once. You get me?" said Jaime.

"Land of Kings," Ono said. He stood still as Jaime wound the leather strip around him once again. But this time, he grew only a block at a time.

Theo laid his cheek on the table in order to read the characters. "A little more," Theo said.

Snap!

"More," said Theo.

Snap!

"More."

Snap! Snap!

"That's it," said Theo. "There it is."

Jaime picked up the little robot and held it on its back. Now the characters on the leather strip were aligned horizontally:

Elder brother hides the clue in the Smallpox Hospital red on blue.

"The Smallpox Hospital, red on blue." Tess said. "What smallpox hospital? And what's red on blue? And which brother? Are we talking about Theodore Morningstarr? And why are they getting so rhyme-y all of a sudden?"

Theo pulled on his lip, let go. "There was a smallpox hospital on Roosevelt Island, but I think they moved it in the 1850s."

"They moved the whole building?" said Jaime.

"Well," said Theo.

They looked it up on Jaime's phone. "'One of the

city's few landmarked ruins,'" Tess read, "'the hospital is often referred to as "the Renwick Ruin," one that could be imagined as the setting for a nineteenth-century Gothic novel.'"

The ruin in the picture *did* look like something out of the nineteenth century. Like someone dropped an old European castle on an island in New York.

"'The ruin is currently undergoing a five-million-dollar restoration.'" Tess said.

"I don't see anything in there about brothers," Jaime said. "Do you?

"Did Theodore have anything to do with building or funding that hospital? Did he have smallpox?"

"No, no," said Tess, stabbing at the screen, "this doesn't work. This particular hospital opened in 1856. That's too late to have anything to do with the Morningstarrs."

"Maybe there's another smallpox hospital some-where?" said Jaime. He took the phone from Tess, typed quickly with both thumbs. "It looks like there's a small-pox hospital on North Brother Island. *North* meaning 'above' or 'elder'?"

Tess unwound the leather strip from Ono. "That could be it!"

"Oh no," said Ono.

"You're right about that," Jaime said. "We can't get to

North Brother Island."

"Why not? Isn't there a ferry or something?"

"No," said Jaime.

"A water taxi."

"No."

"We could rent a boat, if we could get someone to do it for us. Though that's going to cost a fortune. I have some money I saved up. Not sure it will be enough."

"No."

"No?" Tess said. "What do you mean, no?"

"There are no ferries. No water taxis. No boats. No nothing. It's been abandoned for a hundred years. It's a bird sanctuary now." Jaime held up the phone, so Theo and Tess could see. "It says right here on the website. Visitors are forbidden."

"Where are visitors forbidden?"

They all turned to see Aunt Esther standing in the yard, waiting for an answer.

As it turned out, Aunt Esther didn't believe that people should be forbidden to visit public lands anywhere on God's green earth, if those visitors were responsible, cleaned up after themselves, didn't break anything or take advantage of anyone.

Which was how they ended up in a small solarboat

speeding toward North Brother Island, a cool spray dampening their hair and skin. Aunt Esther was wearing wading boots and had packed her fishing rod and tackle.

"I didn't know you had a boat," said Tess.

"Oh, this isn't mine. I'm just borrowing this from a friend. She won't mind."

Despite the splash of the water and the rush of the wind, Aunt Esther barely had to raise her voice, the solar engine was so quiet.

"One does miss the open ocean, though. I haven't been out on the ocean since I was the captain of the *Mrs. Cheng*. There's nothing like tuna fishing to get one's blood up. But we must make do with what we have. There are plenty of fish by North Brother Island."

"You've been here before?" Tess said.

"Many times," said Aunt Esther. "The island has quite a history."

Jaime took off his glasses to wipe away the water droplets. "What kind of history?"

"The Dutch India Company claimed North and South Brother Islands in the 1600s, though they didn't have a right to claim anything, as you know. The islands were called De Gesellen then. 'The Companions.' A friendly name, though this hasn't always been a friendly place. Mary Mallon was confined here for the last twenty years of her life."

"Mary Mallon?" Tess said.

"You might know her as Typhoid Mary. First documented asymptomatic carrier of typhoid fever. She worked as a cook. Sickened many people when she unwittingly passed the disease on to them. But she never got sick herself, and she refused to believe she was infected. So she kept moving from place to place, making people ill, until she was quarantined here."

The two islands—the companions—came into sharper view. Theo was good at being alone, liked being alone, but he couldn't imagine being trapped on a tiny island for twenty years with only doctors and nurses and birds for company.

"And that's not the only tragedy," said Aunt Esther. "In 1905, over one thousand people died when a steamship caught fire near the shore. They say that their ghosts haunt the island."

Tess's eyes went dark and wide as Underway tunnels. Aunt Esther laughed, her gray hair gleaming silver in the afternoon light.

"Oh, the ghosts aren't scary. They're just sad."

"I'd be angry," said Tess.

Aunt Esther regarded her. "Yes, I rather think you would."

Tess blinked, because of the spray or because she didn't know how to take Aunt Esther's comment. But with North Brother Island getting closer and closer, Tess stopped asking questions. The island was lush and green with trees and bushes, with just a few smokestacks or towers peeking through the top of the nearly impenetrable canopy. Remnants of what must have been a dock stuck like wooden teeth from the water.

Aunt Esther slowly maneuvered the boat toward the shore, where some small part of the dock still looked intact.

"Are you going to let us off on the dock?" Theo said.

"What dock? Oh! That? That won't bear your weight. We have to wreck ourselves on the beach. Well, not really. Mostly. A minor little shipwreck, that's all."

Tess tried to say something, but that something turned into a strangled yelp as Aunt Esther jammed the nose of the boat onto the scruffy sand. The boat bobbed and groaned in the water. Theo held on so that he wasn't pitched over the side. It wasn't deep, but something about the island was creeping him out already, and they hadn't even begun their search.

"I'll let you off here. You have"—Aunt Esther checked

her wristwatch—"two hours to explore while I do a little fishing. Then, I expect you back at this very place. Don't be late! If we get caught, we'll be arrested!" She said this with gusto, as if she'd been waiting for the right opportunity to be arrested and this was it.

Theo, Tess, and Jamie carefully climbed out of the boat and onto the sand, sloshing water all over their sneakers. Theo grabbed the pack that Esther had given them, filled with snacks, water, bug spray, a compass, and a rudimentary map of the island she'd printed off the web.

"Thanks, Aunt Esther," Theo said. "We really appreciate it."

"Of course!" Aunt Esther said. "Take lots of pictures, don't bother the nesting herons, don't eat any berries, and don't sit in any poison ivy. I did that once when I was doing field work for the museum. Awful. Give us a push, please!"

The three of them pushed the boat back into deeper water. Aunt Esther saluted, and turned the boat around. She followed the curve of the island and soon disappeared.

"Do you think she meant she ate berries or sat in poison ivy, or both?" said Tess, once she was out of earshot.

"Hard to know with Aunt Esther," said Theo.

Jaime consulted his phone. "Your aunt named her tuna boat after the most successful female pirate in history. Cheng I Sao ran a whole fleet of pirate ships and had a code of conduct for her pirates. They weren't allowed to abuse female prisoners. If they did, they would have their heads chopped off."

"That sounds like someone Aunt Esther would like," Tess said.

"Except for the whole pirating part," Theo said. "She doesn't approve of stealing."

"Let's hope we don't have to steal anything, then," said Jaime. He sealed his phone in a waterproof bag and put it in his pocket next to Ono, who beeped irritably. Then they turned to face the woods. From the pack, Theo pulled out the map. The map marked the general location of several buildings on the island, but it didn't say which building was which.

Jaime pointed at one of the structures. "Let's start with this one."

"Why that one?" Theo asked.

"We have to start somewhere."

It was as good a choice as any.

Stepping into the dense thicket of trees was like stepping into another country. Outside the forest, it was hot and dry and bright; inside, it was cool and damp and dim. Moss covered the bases of the trees; mushrooms fanned themselves against rotted logs. Branches and leaves cracked underfoot.

"This is amazing!" said Theo.

He had taken only a few dozen steps when he felt the ground give way, dropping him into the darkness.

CHAPTER TWENTY-THREE
Jaime

Theo was there, and then he wasn't.

"Theo?" Jaime said. "Theo!"

A thin voice seemed to warble up from the center of the earth. "Help! I'm down here!"

Jaime and Tess dropped to the ground. In the middle of a pile of leaves and vines, there was a dark hole—some kind of utility shaft or sewer—that dropped straight down into the dirt, all the way into the bedrock, for all Jaime knew. Theo was hanging from the strap of the backpack, which had luckily gotten caught on a jagged pipe jutting from the edge. Unluckily, the strap was in the process of tearing. It made a small but terrifying *shhhhhh* sound as it ripped.

Tess and Jaime plunged their hands into the shaft

and caught Theo's arm. They managed to haul him out just before the strap on the backpack tore.

"Thanks," said Theo, panting into the dirt. "That was close."

"Yeah," Tess said, panting just as hard.

"Everybody watch where they're walking," Jaime said. "This whole place could be riddled with these open sewers."

They dusted themselves off and kept walking, this time pushing the leaves and branches aside to make sure their feet would land on solid ground. They didn't have to walk for long when the ruins of the first building appeared like something out of a fairy tale. Or a horror movie. The building was brick and stone, but it was half-swallowed up by the thick green forest. Ivy climbed over the bricks, branches burst from the windows. The front door was long gone, and the house stood open like the mouth of a sleeping beast.

Who was hungrier, the house or the woods?

"Wow," said Jaime.

"It's cool, isn't it?" said Theo.

"That's not what I meant," Jaime said.

Tess flicked her braid from her shoulder so it flowed down her back. "I wonder what it is. Was. I mean, who lived here?"

"Ghosts," said Jaime.

"Let's take a look," Theo said. He marched toward the house as if he hadn't just fallen down a shaft and nearly died.

"You have no sense of self-preservation, you know that? Haven't you ever watched a scary movie?" Jaime shouted at his back, but Theo was already at the front door.

"He does have a sense of self-preservation," Tess said. "But it doesn't always kick in when he's curious."

"Great," said Jaime. "I hope there aren't any bears in that building."

"I think Aunt Esther would have told us if there were bears on the island," said Tess. She imitated Aunt Esther's no-nonsense tone. *"And remember not to pet the bears! I tried once when I was a tour guide at Yosemite and the darn bear bit my arm off!"*

"And that's how I got this metal hand!" Jaime added.

Tess laughed. It was a high, pure sound that echoed through the dense trees. A flock of birds hidden in the leaves shot up and broke through to the sky. Tess slapped a hand over her mouth.

"I hope those weren't the herons that Aunt Esther was talking about," Jaime said, and Tess laughed again, the sound muffled against her fingers.

They followed Theo into the house. As soon as they entered, Jaime could easily imagine ghosts lurking in every corner. Sad ones, angry ones, all kinds of ghosts. There were books and papers all over the floor of the front hall. Dust motes danced in the musty air. A crumbling spiral staircase led to . . . well, Jaime had no idea where the stairs led to and he wasn't sure he wanted to find out.

Theo, who had walked ahead, called back to them. "Come here. Take a look at this."

Tess ran to her brother; no sense of self-preservation there, either, thought Jaime. But Jaime was here, on an abandoned island, wandering around a ghost house, a house likely surrounded by bears and who knows what else, so he had to wonder about himself, too. He tucked a finger into his left front pocket, where Ono was dozing.

"We're okay, Ono," he muttered.

"Oh no," said Ono.

"Not helping," said Jaime.

Jaime came up behind the twins, looked over their heads into what was once an auditorium. The rows of seats had collapsed—or had been crushed—and layers of dirt and dust were thick on the floor.

"What kind of performances did they have here, do you think?" Tess said.

"*Hamlet*," said Jaime, backing away. He kept walking down the hallway until he reached the back door, still intact. The wood and the walls here were pockmarked with small tidy holes. He ran his hands across the divots. Then, he opened the door to look at the other side, where the holes were ringed with spiky shards of wood. What could have made these kinds of holes?

Oh no.

"Okay!" said Jaime. "This isn't the hospital. Let's get out of here."

"I want to look upstairs for a minute," Theo said.

Jaime pointed to the holes in the door. "I can't be sure, but I think these are bullet holes." He showed them the outside of the door, where the holes were splintered. "The guns were shot from the *inside*."

Theo examined the holes. "Those could have been shot decades ago."

"What's your point?" said Jaime.

"That whatever the people were shooting at is surely gone," Theo answered.

"How do you know that?" Jaime said.

The twins were quiet for a moment, then said, at exactly the same time, "You're right. Let's go."

They didn't run out of the house exactly, but they didn't walk, either. And they weren't as careful in the woods outside, stumbling and tripping over curbs hidden in the undergrowth and vines that snaked along the ground. When it seemed safe to do it, Jaime turned to take one last look at the house.

And he saw a face in the upstairs window.

He shuffled backward and fell, knocking the wind out of his lungs.

"Jaime!" said Tess. "Are you okay?"

"I saw a—" Jaime began, but when he pointed at the house, at the window where the face had been, there was nothing.

"A bear," he said. "I saw a bear."

"Very funny," said Tess, holding out a hand. He took it and she helped him to his feet. He checked the windows of the house one last time, but they were as vacant as they had been when they had first approached the house.

He was losing his mind.

"Let's look at the map again. Try to figure out which of these buildings is most likely the hospital," said Jaime.

"We could try this one," said Theo, pointing. "Looks like it's the biggest."

They headed for the next building. Branches clawed and grabbed at them, the dirt and leaves sucked at their shoes, willing them to stop, to lay down, to sleep, to stay, to stay here forever, to—

"Jaime!" said Tess.

"What!"

"Are you okay?"

"I'm fine."

"You seemed like—"

"—you were having a spell," Theo finished for her.

"This place is freaking me out," Jaime admitted.

"Me too," said Tess. "The sooner we find the next clue, the sooner we can get out of here."

But they made it to the next building with no more ghost sightings, no hint of bears. It felt huge, the stone towering over them. Here, too, ivy crawled all over the surface, small birds flew in and out of the broken windows. Between structures, there were tangles of pipes, portions of collapsed roofs or porches, rusting metal boxes that could have been generators.

As soon as they entered and saw the vast sheets of blue tile still affixed to the walls, they knew they'd found the right place.

"The blue," said Tess. "So the clue is here."

"We're looking for red on blue, whatever that means," said Theo.

"But where? This place is huge."

Theo said, "Maybe we should split—"

"Don't even say it," Jaime said, regretting every scary movie, every horror comic he'd ever read. "We are *not* splitting up."

"But we could—"

"No. We stay together, okay?"

Theo shrugged. "Okay." He checked the watch his aunt had given him. "We have an hour left."

"We'll go room to room. And nobody wanders off. You hear me, Theo?"

"Yes, Dad," Theo grumbled.

"Okay, then," he said. He started down one long hallway littered with piles of dust, rotting wood, and ceiling tiles. In one room, an old claw-foot bathtub and sink sat in the middle of a pile of bricks. In another, brown vines, bare of leaves, snaked across the walls and ceiling. Piles of books were randomly strewn, some rotting, some still intact. Tess picked up a book.

"Studies on the Effects of Tuberculosis," she read.

Jaime picked up another. *"Baltimore Catechism."*

They dropped the books and kept walking. In another room, they found an old bed, possibly an operating table, that looked more like a torture device. On the floor, in a soup of melted soap, they found a spray of copper keys turning green. In still another room, this one with tile yellow as old teeth, a large rectangular metal container squatted below a ferocious-looking spigot.

"Is this for washing clothes or washing people?" Tess said. Nobody answered her.

After they'd explored most of the bottom floor, they ventured upstairs. Some of the rooms still had steel bed frames in rows where the tuberculosis patients or typhoid patients were housed, some of the rooms had a single bed frame by a window. Graffiti covered many of the walls:

BERTRAND WAS HERE, 1898.

Tell Richard I will love him forever.

I AM ALREADY A GHOST.

Let me out, let me out, let me out.

Jaime stopped to look out of one of the windows. He had a perfect view of the sapphire-blue East River and Manhattan sparkling like a mirage on the other side of it. He couldn't imagine being quarantined here and seeing that city, knowing it was so close and understanding that you might never see it again. He shivered.

"I wish we knew what we were looking for," said Tess. "We don't have that much more time."

Theo said, "That's why I suggested we split—"

Jaime glared. Theo shut up.

They moved on. Pawing through books and papers, sifting through piles of wood and rubbish, reading the notes and graffiti. Just as he was beginning to despair that they would ever find what they were looking for, they came across more graffiti chalked or etched into the walls. One line curled around the blue-tiled room from one wall to the next, scrawled in chipped red paint:

BURY ME RIGHT NEXT TO LOUIS MG,
THE MOST TALENTED MAN IN THE WHOLE OF THE CITY.

"Who's Louis MG?" said Tess.

"I don't know," Theo said.

"Me, neither," said Jaime. He pulled out his sketchbook and wrote the message into it.

"Do you think it's any more important than the others?" said Tess.

"It's the only thing written in red. And it's the only writing we've seen that indicates a last name. And something about the word *bury*."

"Buried treasure?" Theo said.

"Maybe," said Jaime.

Just then, a loud crash made them all jump. Tess grabbed Theo's arm; Jaime grabbed Tess's.

"What was that?" Tess whispered.

"The house settling?" Theo suggested. "At least, that's what Dad always says."

They stood as still as they could, listening. Jaime couldn't be sure if it was his imagination, but he thought he heard footsteps somewhere down below. His skin prickled.

"Do you guys hear that?" he said. *Say no, say no, say no.*

"Yes," said Tess. "Someone else is here."

"Aunt Esther," Theo said, but he did not sound confident.

Jaime said, "There has to be another staircase on the other side of the building." He pointed, and the three of them crept as carefully and quietly as they could down the hallway toward a staircase they could only hope existed, and was still usable. But Jaime was right. At the end of the hallway, there was another staircase. They stood listening on the landing.

"Nothing," said Theo.

"I don't hear anything, either," Tess said.

"Maybe it was something else?" Jaime said, relieved. "An animal or—"

Another loud crash, like someone or something charging through a rotting wall. The three of them took the stairs so fast that Jaime bit his tongue as he ran. They burst from the building, stumbling through the vines and bushes, looking for the East River to come into view. But it was only when they'd been running for too long that Jaime realized that they were running in the wrong direction, moving away from water, from their meeting spot with the twins' aunt. He stopped, both hands on his knees.

"We have to go back the other way," he said. "This isn't right."

Tess turned in a circle. "Which way? Everything is the same!"

"What's that?" Theo said.

Jaime was afraid to look, afraid that he'd see a ghost or a bear or a ghost-bear lurking in the trees. Instead, he saw something large and squat and boxy. Another building, one not on the map, nestled in the undergrowth, painted green, almost indistinguishable from the surrounding foliage. But why do that? So that it wouldn't be visible from the sky? A brand-new fence surrounded the property, barbed wire spiky along the top.

"I thought the whole island was abandoned," said Tess. "I thought you could be arrested if you were discovered here."

They crept closer to the fence and then stopped abruptly when they heard more footsteps, these louder and heavier than the ones they'd heard before.

From around the building, a shape emerged, impossibly tall, dark-feathered but with spots along its neck. Its feet appeared to be on backward, and a long, vicious claw sprouted from each ankle.

"What is *that*?" Theo said.

"Jumbie," said Jaime. "It's a jumbie."

CHAPTER TWENTY-FOUR

Tess

At first, Tess did not, *could* not, move, as her brain tried to make sense of the creature approaching the fence. Feathers? she thought. Spots? Claws? Its knees bent the wrong way, and the tiny head upon its long speckled neck jerked like a chicken's. But it was the size of a rhino, if a rhino were perched on stilts. It stopped, stared at the woods where they were hidden, then broke into a trot, jumped, launched itself at the fence. Tess, Jaime, and Theo fell back at the same moment the creature hit the wire, bending it outward. It launched itself again and again, screeching.

Only one question churned in Tess's brain: What is it? What is it? What is it? What—

A beak snapped over their heads, tearing shrieks out of the three of them. The creature didn't care that the barbed wire bloodied its neck. It launched and screeched and snapped.

Movement behind the creature caught Tess's eye. A large black cat crept low and stealthy.

"Nine?" Tess breathed. "Nine?"

"Nine isn't black," said Jaime. "It looks more like—"

"What?"

The enormous creature snapped again, almost catching Tess in the nose.

"We've got to go," Theo said.

"Nine!" Tess yelled. "Nine!"

The cat glanced up, startled out of the hunt. Tess would have known those eyes anywhere.

"That's Nine!" Tess said. "That's her face, that's her tail, those are her eyes!"

"Tess," Jaime said.

"IT'S HER," Tess roared, over the screeching of the feathered creature. Tess had to save the cat, had to, had to free her from his place, from this creature, whatever it was. Nine was brave and strong, but she couldn't be a match for this sad and angry thing.

But the creature had noticed the cat now and had a new enemy. They circled each other warily. Tess yanked off her pack, searched. Held up the pair of wire cutters Aunt Esther had given them. Just in case.

"Tess!" said Theo.

"Are you *sure* it's her?" Jaime said.

"Yes," Tess hissed, going to work on the wire, sawing at it, squeezing with everything she had. Jaime grabbed at the edges of the cut wire and pulled to make a hole. As soon as it was big enough, Tess crawled through.

"No!" said Theo, "Let Nine come this way!"

But Tess wasn't listening. She waved her arms. "Hey! I'm right here!"

The creature whipped around, then around again, unsure who was the bigger danger—or the tastier meal—girl or cat.

Girl.

The creature lunged at Tess. The cat jumped, her own vicious claws unsheathed. She raked them against the creature's back, feathers flying. The creature screamed. The cat ducked and dodged, heading for Tess.

"Nine!" said Tess. She had just gathered Nine into her arms when a man in a green uniform came out of the building carrying some kind of weapon.

"Here!" said Theo. "Tess!" He and Jaime had their arms stuck through the hole in the fence. Tess dived for them. Theo and Jaime hauled her back through.

"Nine! Nine, come on!" said Tess, reaching for her cat.

The man shouted, "Hey! Who's there?"

His weapon was a crossbow. At least it looked like one. She had only seen them in movies.

Nine hissed. The creature snapped. The man took aim. Shot. The ginormous creature squawked, then drooped to the ground. Tess grabbed for Nine's collar, pulled.

And someone else—Jaime? Theo?—hauled Tess up by *her* collar and pushed her.

"Nine!" Tess said, reaching for the cat.

"Go!" a rough voice said. "All of you!"

They ran, crashing through the trees and bushes. Through the foliage, more green structures were visible, more fenced-in creatures. They were a blur of fur and claws and skin and teeth and teeth and teeth, but Tess didn't stop running. Behind them, a hum filled the air, a vibration that wriggled its way under Tess's skin and made her itch. Another weapon? Some sort of device that produced sound waves? But she didn't stop running until they hit the thin strip of scruffy sand at the edge of the island, the blue of the East River in front of them.

"Where's the dock?" said Theo. "Where's Aunt Esther?"

"Where's Nine?" Tess said.

"We ran the wrong way! The dock is around there," Jaime said, pointing to his left.

On the water, two shapes appeared. Boats, speeding toward them. The two boats split. One heading toward their left side, one heading right.

"They're trying to trap us!" Theo said.

"Police!" said Tess. "We can't be caught! Come on, we have to go back."

"Go back?" said Jaime, his eyes wide and incredulous.

"Through the woods," Tess said. "We can hide in there, at least."

"With all those jumbies?"

"With all those *what*?"

They dove back into the trees, jumping over fallen branches, bumping into ancient fire hydrants covered in ivy, slipping on once-paved roads hidden by vast slicks of wet leaves. In the darkest part of the forest, a pile of bricks and rotting wood appeared, once a cottage or storage house. The fallen roof and rotting wood formed a sort of cave.

"In there," Tess said. She crawled into the darkness. Theo followed, then Jaime. They hunkered as low as they could. The wood around them groaned, then settled. A million thoughts swirled and smashed in Tess's head, and she quivered with the strength of the collisions. What was that thing in the fenced yard? Who had built this facility? Who had told them to run? Who had taken Nine? What was she doing here? How would Tess get her back?

"A giraffe-owary," whispered Theo.

"Shhhh," said Jaime.

Of course, Theo was right. A giraffe and cassowary, made vicious through genetic manipulation.

But what for?

The growling and the barking grew louder, men shouted. If those were dogs barking, even if they weren't enhanced dogs, Tess and the others would be discovered. They would be captured. Maybe they would be *experimented* on themselves, turned into something else entirely, mixed with snakes or rhinos or lions or bears or spiders or lobsters or—

Jaime and Theo each gripped one of her arms to still her shaking. She closed her eyes and tried to breathe. When she opened them again, her gaze settled on scratches in the plaster in front of her. Crosshatches marking the days. So many crosshatches, years' worth. Next to the crosshatches, words:

I WILL HAUNT YOU TILL THE END OF TIME.

Outside, a dog—or something that was once a dog or like a dog—howled. Footsteps came close, closer.

"That way!" said a deep voice. "Under that wood pile!"

Tess, Jaime, and Theo went rigid with terror as the men and the dogs surrounded their hiding place. And then there was a confused "Hey! Who are you?" and another sound, "Ooof!"

A dog yelped. And then another. Tess risked a peek between the slats of wood and saw the animals vanishing into the trees. A man lay on the forest floor, holding his head. Tess looked out the other side of the structure. A small figure in a long silvery-gray coat, face hidden with a hood, kicked one man and then the next. The figure jumped up, banked off the trunk of a tree, and took down two more men in some sort of split kick. The figure swept the legs out from under another man and then brought a fist down on the head of the last. He fell as if an anvil had dropped upon him.

Then the figure turned, the long coat swirling all around like a cape. The figure stopped and called back to them in a low voice. "There's not that much time! Come!"

They didn't discuss whether they should follow, they simply scrambled after the figure, hoping they weren't making another terrible mistake. The figure led them through the trees, past structures new and old so fast that Tess's sides cramped and she had no time for terror, only the questions that propelled her forward. This time, when they broke through the trees to the beach, they saw the jagged wood of the old dock sticking out of the water, and another sight. The sight of Aunt Esther in her boat, wielding an oar, slugging a man trying to drag her out of her boat and into another one.

"I think NOT!" Aunt Esther bellowed, and bashed another man who attempted the same.

The figure in gray hummed, that hum that wriggled under Tess's skin, and suddenly, the men in the boat started shouting and pointing at the water, at something moving in the water. Dark shapes converged in the clear blue of the river, darting too fast to figure out what they were.

A thud and a crash. The boat lurched sideways.

"Go!" said the figure in gray. "Your aunt will take care of you. "

"But Nine—" said Tess,

An eruption of barking and snarling came from both sides.

"Nine has stripes and spots," Theo said. "Tess—it wasn't her."

"GO!" shouted the figure in gray. "They have other weapons. Things that could stun you, blind you, make you forget."

"Come on, Tess," said Jaime.

"Please," she said.

"I know, I hear you, but we have to go now," Jaime said.

Aunt Esther rammed the boat onto the shore, and they all climbed in. She didn't wait to greet the figure in gray, didn't seem to care who it was. She backed the boat away from North Brother Island and sped away as fast as she could.

But Tess turned to watch the shore. As she stared, the figure lowered her hood, exposing the beautiful—and familiar—face beneath.

CHAPTER TWENTY-FIVE
Cricket

While Tess, Theo, and Jaime were hurtling away from North Brother Island in Aunt Esther's borrowed solarboat, Zelda "Cricket" Moran was hurtling exactly nowhere. She was sitting in the middle of her blush-pink bed in the middle of her blush-pink room, staring at the mural she made the very first day she'd arrived here. Just this morning, she'd added a picture of Karl to it, eating his favorite snack. But that wasn't why she was trapped here on a perfectly good day, when she could be out investigating. No, her mother seemed to understand why she'd painted the picture of Karl on the wall, even if it didn't match the peachy pink of the paint her mother had chosen for her. "The color of dawn," her mother said. What her mother didn't understand, refused to understand, was that this building was filled to the brim with NEFARIOUS ACTORS performing NEFARIOUS DEEDS.

"You've been sneaking around, stealing things, drawing all over the walls! The only nefarious deeds being performed in this building are being performed by you!" her father had bellowed at breakfast, red in the face as he always was.

"'I don't think those words mean what you think they mean,'" said Cricket. It was a line from her favorite movie. She found it quite useful.

"WHAT?" Her father got redder in the face. Cricket thought he should see a doctor for that. It didn't look healthy.

"Cricket," her mother warned. To her husband, she said, "Go easy. She misses Karl."

Her father seemed about to yell something else, but swallowed the words (words that probably didn't mean what he thought they meant, either). He heaved a strangled sigh, then put a rough hand on Cricket's shoulder. "I know. I'm sorry about Karl. I'll call Detective Biedermann from the office and see if she has any more information, okay?"

Cricket, who had been expecting a fight, felt the tears well up in her eyes. She hated crying. But she did love her dad, as shouty and red as he could be.

"Okay," she said, barely able to get the words out.

But that didn't get her out of her punishment. She was grounded for two days for stealing the logbook from the security desk. Otto had created a diversion by throwing an epic temper tantrum in the middle of the lobby, and while the guard tried to soothe him, she swiped it. But some busybody had seen her do it, and here she was, sitting in this pink room with the pink comforter and the pink curtains and the pink, orange, and yellow pillows that her mother said looked like a sunrise but Cricket thought looked like pillows. Since Otto was two years younger than she, and more IMPRESSIONABLE, her parents said, he was grounded only for the afternoon.

It wasn't fair.

So many things in the world weren't.

The door creaked open. Her mother stood in the doorway sipping her coffee. "What kind of deeds, Cricket?"

Cricket swiped furiously at the tears that kept leaking from her eyes. Maybe she needed to go to the doctor, too, with all this leaking. "What?"

"You said this building is full of nefarious actors performing nefarious deeds. What kinds of deeds are you talking about?"

Cricket shrugged. She loved her mother, too, but Cricket had found that most people seemed to lose their minds somewhere around the age of eighteen or so. Suddenly, they don't believe in anything. Not ghosts, not intruders, not spies, not NEFARIOUS ACTORS performing NEFARIOUS DEEDS. Mention that you heard the monster scratching under your bed again, and some adult will tell you that there's no such thing, when you know perfectly well that there is, and they would, too, if only they paid attention. Mention spies, and a whole roomful of grown-ups will chuckle into their wine glasses—Cricket did not understand the point of wine, why would you want to drink something that made you silly?—and tell your mother how adorable you are and what an imagination you have and that maybe one day, you could be a storyteller or some person who makes cartoons or games for a living. Cricket didn't even like cartoons and thought most games were a waste of time. She listened to true-crime podcasts and watched the news. She knew the ways of the world. She knew how things worked.

"Cricket?"

Cricket struggled to come up with vaguely nefarious deeds her mother would find believable so that she would stop asking all these questions. "There are a lot of people wearing loud shirts and those shorts that come down to your knees."

"Bermuda shorts?"

"Is that what they wear in Bermuda?"

"I don't know."

"Then why do they call them Bermuda shorts?"

"Cricket."

"What?"

"I hardly think that people wearing silly clothes is nefarious. And I don't think *you* think it's nefarious, either. Why did you want that logbook?"

Not for the first time, Cricket wondered whether her mother was a double agent. Sometimes she seemed like a regular mother, interested in coffee and book clubs and her work as a freelance designer. But other times she seemed to look at Cricket as if she knew every one of Cricket's thoughts and intentions, as if Cricket's secrets weren't secret at all.

Moms were DISCONCERTING.

"I wanted the logbook because I wanted to see who had been to the building."

"Because of Karl?"

It wasn't the reason, or at least, it wasn't the whole reason, but her mother would think it was as good a reason as any. "Yes."

Her mother nodded, thinking. "What if I make you a deal?"

Now Cricket was suspicious. "What kind of deal?"

"If I take you to see the security chief of the building, and let you watch the recordings of the day Karl was taken—"

"But Detective Biedermann already watched those!"

"*We* haven't," said her mother.

Cricket could hardly believe her luck. "Yes!"

"Hold on, I'm not done. If I take you to see those recordings, will you promise—"

"I'll be good!"

"That wasn't what I was going to say, either. Let me finish."

"Okay," said Cricket, wishing she would finish a little faster.

"What I was going to say was that I'd like you to promise me that you'll tell me if you see something truly strange or scary or dangerous. I can help you. But I can't help you if I don't know what's wrong, if I don't know what you're truly up to. Do you understand?"

Her mother was being disconcerting again. Maybe she *was* a double agent—a mom, and more than a mom. A super-mom. A person who could still do depressing grown-up things like food shopping and taxes and laundry without screaming, but also hadn't lost her imagination and her curiosity and her brains. A person who knew the way the world worked, who knew how unfair things really were.

Maybe it would be okay to trust her.

Just this once.

Cricket reached under her bed, pulled out a box. She opened the lid and showed her mother what was inside.

Her mother backed up, her whole face screwing up in disgust. "Ugh, Cricket! What are those?"

"Not what you think," said Cricket.

CHAPTER TWENTY-SIX
Theo

Like his sister, Theo had been watching the island's shore, too. He saw the figure in gray lower her hood, saw the perfect oval face.

"It's a woman!" Theo said, impressed. He looked at Tess and Jaime, expected them to be as impressed as Theo was. But they were much more than impressed. They seemed utterly shocked. Jaime most of all.

"What?" he said. "What's wrong with you? I mean, I guess it's a little surprising that such a small woman could have fought off so many men, but she could have training in all sorts of disciplines. I would expect that you two would know that women can take care of themselves."

"That's not it," Jaime said.

"What then?"

"I know her. Sort of."

"You mean you recognize her?"

"I should," Jaime said. "I've been drawing her for months."

"Huh? What are you talking about?"

Jaime searched his pockets, found a drawing. He unfolded it for Theo, held it up with both hands so Theo could see. In the drawing, a pretty woman, small and brown-skinned, stood in a long gray coat that seemed to swirl around her.

"Where have you seen her before?" Theo said.

"I haven't. I made her up."

"*What?*"

"I made her up," Jaime said. Jaime's own skin had gone slightly grayish, and Theo wondered if Jaime would faint and tumble into the water. Theo didn't want Jaime to faint, and he definitely didn't want Jaime to tumble into the water. He'd seen the dark shapes moving under the surface; he'd witnessed the lurch of the guards' boat. Something terrible lived in the water.

And this woman had *called* to it.

But . . .

"You must have seen her somewhere," Theo said, feeling desperate. "In the newspaper, or online. Somewhere."

"No," Tess said. "I've looked at his drawings. He's done a ton of them. He's been developing her."

"I don't know what that means!" Theo heard the whine in his own voice but couldn't help it. He was starting to feel as if he were going mad.

"I was trying to create a superhero. A character for a comic," Jaime explained. "I've put her in a million different outfits and poses, but none of them worked. Until Ada Lovelace's dress gave me an idea. It was so plain. So I made a sort of coat-dress for my character. This is how I've been drawing her."

"A . . . superhero? Why?" Theo knew it was a stupid question; or rather, it was a bigger question than Jaime or anyone could answer. Why a superhero? Why would she show up now? Why the animals hidden on this island? Why would anyone create them? Why the Cipher in the first place? Why why why?

"I think the question is 'how,'" said Jaime.

"We'd get some answers if we went back to that island and questioned your superhero!" Theo shouted, his voice carrying over the splash of the water against the hull. Now he was starting to feel mad in the angry sense of the word.

Aunt Esther, who hadn't seemed to be listening to the earlier part of the conversation, heard Theo. She said, "No one's going back to that island. I don't know what we stumbled onto, but it's very dangerous."

"That woman, though—" Theo began.

"That woman saved us from being killed by that . . . that . . . thing," Jaime said. "What did you say it was?"

"A giraffe-owary," Theo said. "Cassowary and giraffe."

"She might have saved us from something worse," Tess said.

Theo stuck his hand in his spray-dampened curls, tugged to remind himself he wasn't in a dream. "What could be worse than being killed by a giraffe-owary?"

"I could think of a lot of things," Tess muttered.

"As far as I'm concerned," Aunt Esther said, "that woman was a very helpful person who escorted you safely to the beach and out of harm's way."

"She called to something in the water!" Theo said. "Some kind of . . ." He trailed off. He didn't know what was in the water. A shark-owary. A tiger-phin. A dolph-bear. Your garden-variety giant squid with eyes the size of dinner plates.

"Did she call to something?" Aunt Esther said. "Well. That is quite unlikely, but even if she did, it worked out for us. Those people aren't following our boat, and it doesn't seem as if the authorities have been called. Whoever is on that island, they want to keep what they're doing a secret."

"But what if they recognized us?" Theo said.

Aunt Esther frowned. "Why would they recognize you?"

Theo stuttered, searching for a reason. Tess filled it in.

"Because of the video with Nine. That lady who said Nine bit her," she said. "They could figure out who we are. We could get in trouble. You could get in trouble."

"Hmmm," Aunt Esther growled. "Then we will have to keep an eye out, won't we?"

"How?" said Theo.

"We'll call in our own reinforcements."

"What reinforcements?" Jaime asked.

Aunt Esther raised a brow. "You're not the only one who knows a few superheroes."

Aunt Esther returned the boat to her friend's boat slip in Flushing, anchored it. Then, she herded Theo, Tess, and Jaime onto the Underway to Astoria. Back at Aunt Esther's house, they found Theo and Tess's parents sitting in the living room, eating oatmeal cookies.

Theo's dad smiled. "Lance seems to be broken, Esther. He won't stop baking." He stood when he got a better look at them. "What happened to you?"

"Oh," said Aunt Esther, waving her hand breezily. "It was such a nice day, so I took the kids boating. Wouldn't you know it, everyone got a little bit seasick. So we cut our trip short."

"Seasick?" said Theo's mom. "You two never get seasick."

"It's mostly me, Mrs. Biedermann," said Jaime. "It's been a while since I've been on a boat."

"I'm so sorry. Seasickness is the worst," Theo's mom said. "Why don't you sit down and I'll get you some water. Or maybe some ginger tea? That could settle your stomach." She hustled into the kitchen.

Theo's dad said, "Where did you guys go boating?"

"Here and there," said Aunt Esther. "Mostly, we hung around the bay. Did a little fishing."

"Really? Were the fish biting?"

Theo remembered the dark shapes in the water, the lurching boat. "They weren't biting us, anyway."

"Glad to hear it," said Theo's dad, laughing. "Though I don't suppose you were fishing for piranha."

"They weren't biting *for* us, you mean, Theo," Aunt Esther said. "Still, it was a nice afternoon until the children started to feel a bit queasy."

"Ah," said Theo's dad. "I don't much care for fish anyway. We could have something else for dinner. Maybe order in. That is, whenever you're feeling better. And you're welcome to join us, Jaime. As always. Stay the night if you like."

"Thank you, Mr. Biedermann," Jaime said.

"You are looking a bit green around the gills, though," said Theo's dad. "Ha-ha. I'm going to get you a cool cloth for your head. That always helps me when I'm feeling a little sick."

After Theo's parents were out of the room, Aunt Esther said, "I probably don't have to tell you not to mention this to your parents. Not just yet, anyway."

It seemed odd to Theo that Aunt Esther would suggest that they not tell their parents that they were attacked by wild and probably illegal animals, threatened by strange men, and saved by a woman allegedly dreamed up by Jaime, but then Aunt Esther was deeply odd. And she seemed to understand that some things were better kept to yourself until the moment was right. If they told their mother what happened today, she would go to the ends of the earth to find the perpetrators. She would also put her kids under house arrest to keep them safe. As confused and angry as Theo was, as worried as he was, he didn't want to be trapped in the house. He still wanted to solve the Cipher if they could. And they wouldn't be able to do that sitting in Aunt Esther's living room, eating Lance's endless oatmeal cookies.

"We won't say anything," said Theo. Tess and Jaime nodded in agreement. Theo's dad came back with the cool cloth and laid it on Jaime's forehead. Jaime accepted this gratefully, leaning back in his chair and closing his eyes. Theo's mother set Jaime's tea on the table in front of him. She sat next to Tess, picked up Tess's hand.

"I do have some promising leads on the animals," she said.

"What animals?" said Tess.

"Nine and Karl. Are there others?"

"Oh! No! Well, probably," Tess said. "I mean, if they stole two animals, they're looking for more, right?"

"Yes," said Theo's mom. "That's what I was thinking. I watched the video taken from Jaime's building on the day Karl went missing. Clarkson is tracking down some people of interest right now."

"What people?" Tess said.

"I don't want to get your hopes up too much, but there were several people acting a bit strangely in the video. As a matter of fact, I should get going, too. I want to be there for the interviews."

"Thanks, Mom," Tess said.

"And to watch the other videos to see if that will help my case."

Theo said, "What other videos?"

"You don't know?"

"Know what?" Tess asked.

"I'm surprised. You kids seem to know what's going on in the city before I do. There was an incident at Station One. Apparently, there were machines concealed in the stone eagles on the front of the building. Possibly Morningstarr Machines, but that hasn't been confirmed."

"Huh," said Theo. Tess and Jaime said nothing.

"I have to say I would have thought the three of you would be more excited at this news. Previously unknown Morningstarr Machines in the shape of eagles? They weren't known to design birds."

"Fascinating," said Theo.

"About as fascinating as congressional hearings, I can see," said Theo's mom, standing up.

"I love congressional hearings," Theo said.

His mom laughed. "Right. Anyway, there were a bunch of people still at the station when the machines went bananas. They crashed windows and dive-bombed people and generally caused a lot of mayhem."

"No one was hurt, though, right?" said Tess.

"Luckily," said Theo's mom. "And no one has seen the eagles since. But there was else something a bit strange. Well, stranger than mechanical eagles flying around a train station scaring everyone, that is."

"What was a bit strange, Mom?" Theo asked.

"A witness said he saw some city employees fixing a clock. One of those employees was saved by an eagle. And one of the others of them took something from the eagle. The witness couldn't see what it was. But the city said that there was no scheduled maintenance on that clock. And the men weren't wearing the standard city uniforms. So we have to assume these men were working with the machines somehow. Maybe they did something to start them up. I don't know. We'll figure it out when we pull them in for questioning."

Theo's stomach dropped. Tess asked, "How will you find them?"

His mom smiled. "Easy. The witness got the whole thing on video. It's hard to make out their faces from the distance at which it was taken, but I'm sure our techs can enhance it."

"Great," said Theo. "That's really great."

CHAPTER TWENTY-SEVEN
Jaime

Theo and Tess and their mother were talking, but Jaime barely heard what they said. His drawing burned in his pocket, the woman's face burned in his mind. It was as if he'd conjured her, brought her to life himself from memories of his mother and every comic-book heroine he'd ever loved. Her existence was completely incredible, more incredible than all the incredible things that he had seen and done in the last month.

Or maybe Theo was right and he had seen the woman before. On TV or online and he'd forgotten.

He didn't know what to think, what to believe, what to do. All he knew is that he wanted to see her again, talk to her. Had she been looking for him? Following him? Did she recognize him, too?

He pulled the now-lukewarm cloth from his forehead and sat up. The twins were still talking with their mother, but now they were the ones that looked pale and gray. Their mom hugged them both, said good-bye to Jaime and headed out the door.

"What now?" said Jaime.

Aunt Esther said, "The eagles have landed."

"Okay," Jaime said.

"Nothing you three were involved with, I take it?"

Tess shook her head so that her braid swung back and forth like a pendulum. "Nooo," she said, drawing out the word. "No way."

"Good!" Aunt Esther said. "I will retrieve the take-out menus from the kitchen; you can pick what you'd like for dinner. Perhaps I can persuade Lancelot to stop making cookies for the next few hours." She swept out of the room.

Tess swore under her breath. Theo said, "Language!"

"Language, smanguage. If they got us on video again, we're sunk."

"Wait, what?" Jaime said. The twins explained what their mother had told them. Jaime put the cloth over his head. It didn't help.

"Maybe they didn't catch our faces in the video," said Tess.

"Mom seemed pretty confident that the 'workers'"—he put air quotes around the word—"could be identified. Even if our faces aren't clear, it's not like she won't recognize my hair from a distance."

"She was pretty confident about finding Nine, too, but she hasn't," Tess said, her tone sad rather than sharp.

Theo didn't answer, but his expression spoke for him. He wasn't feeling confident about anything. Losing Nine had definitely affected Tess—her knees were practically dancing her out of her chair—but working the clues had also affected Theo, made him less certain. Jaime wondered whether that was a good thing or a bad thing.

"Here are the menus," said Aunt Esther. "We have Chinese, Thai, Japanese, soul food, and Italian. Take your pick."

Nobody but Jaime was hungry, but they seemed happy enough when he picked soul food. Forty-five minutes later the food arrived: mac and cheese, collards, corn bread, shrimp and grits, ribs, and fried "chkn" made of cricket protein because Tess was feeling sad for birds at the moment.

"All the birds?" Theo asked.

"Yes," Tess said. "All of them. Even the scary ones. They didn't ask to be scary."

"Which birds are scary?" Mr. Biedermann wanted to know.

"They're the descendants of dinosaurs, for one," Theo said. "And certain birds retain memories of faces and will peck your head if they see you too often in their territory. Everyone thinks owls are cute but they'll pluck out your—"

"Theo," said Mr. Biedermann. "I am trying to eat here."

"Ostriches can be terribly aggressive," Aunt Esther said. "I had one chase me for a mile, once."

"Was that when you managed the game preserve in Africa?" said Mr. Biedermann.

"No. Why?"

"Never mind. These collards are delicious." Mr. Biedermann scooped up another mouthful.

Jaime stayed over at Aunt Esther's, mostly because he was too tired and freaked out from the day to think about traveling all the way to Hoboken. That night, he dreamed of the woman in gray, kicking and punching and swirling her way through whole battalions of bad guys. When she was through, she asked Jaime, "Don't you know who I am? Don't you?" right before a giraffe-owary crashed through a fence and chased Jaime through a dimly lit city. He woke up just as the monster backed him into an alley with no escape, razor-sharp beak poised to strike.

After that, he didn't get much sleep.

The next morning, he and the twins sat at the breakfast table waiting for Mrs. Biedermann to come downstairs and tell them they'd been identified on the video, that their adventures were over, that the blond lady had sung and they were all going to jail. But that was not what happened. Mrs. Biedermann shuffled into the kitchen looking as bleary-eyed and tired as her kids. Nobody asked her any questions until she'd finished one cup of coffee. (Every kid knew not to ask an adult any questions until that adult had had at least one cup of coffee. If you didn't, you might as well throw yourself into a giraffe-owary pen.)

As her mother poured her second cup of coffee, Tess ventured: "So did you identify the workers from the station attack?"

"Not yet. Techs are still working on the video. And I'm not sure if that will be my case, anyway. We can't consider the eagles stolen if they flew off by themselves, can we?"

"Guess not," said Tess, suddenly tucking into a pile of waffles with a gusto she hadn't shown before.

"What a weird week it's been," said Mrs. Biedermann.

"A weird month," Theo said.

"The whole summer has been weird," said Jaime.

"True, Jaime, true." Mrs. Biedermann added cream and sugar to her coffee, sat at the table. "What are you kids planning for today?"

Oh, breaking some more laws, risking death or dismemberment, Jaime thought. What every kid does in his spare time.

"Nothing much," Tess said. "Maybe we'll go to the movies or something."

"You should see that new one, the one they shot in Manhattan last year. What's it called? *Monster* something. Or *Robot* something. *Monsters and Robots*?"

Mr. Biedermann said, "You'll have to put up with Slant's old mug if you see that one. I heard he has a cameo in it."

"Ugh," said Mrs. Biedermann. "Then maybe you should see that other movie, the one that got all those awards. *The Lost Ones*, it's called. Based on an old book. Same author as *Penelope*, I think. Published in the 1860s. It's about the last people left on earth after some evil men destroy it."

"Sounds cheerful," said Mr. Biedermann. "Were the evil men named Slant?"

"Did you hear that he might run for office?"

"No!" said Mr. Biedermann. "Which office?"

"Mayor, I guess. Or senator. Whichever he can buy. He wants to 'move New York City forward' by cutting the budgets from things we don't need anymore, and investing in 'new technologies.'"

"What don't we need anymore?" Mr. Biedermann said.

"Libraries for one. Arts programs. Public schools."

"We don't need libraries?" said Theo.

"Or schools?" said Tess.

Mr. Biedermann put down his fork. "I think I just lost my appetite."

"Yeah, I'm sorry I brought it up," said Mrs. Biedermann. "Anyway, you kids were telling me what you were going to do today?"

"We could go back to my apartment," Jaime said. "We've got a pool on the roof. I've never used it, but it looks nice."

"What a great idea!" said Mr. Biedermann. "It's about eight thousand degrees outside, give or take a degree."

"Try not to wear yourselves out, okay?" said Mrs. Biedermann. "You're all looking a bit ragged."

"Theo always looks ragged," said Tess.

"Your brother, the hipster," Jaime said.

"I resent that," said Theo.

They helped clean up the breakfast dishes and said good-bye to the twins' parents and Aunt Esther. If the twins' aunt really knew some superheroes, they were stealthy ones, because Jaime didn't see anyone in costume rescuing kittens from trees or shooting webs at bank robbers or even following Jaime and the twins to Hoboken to make sure they were safe. They seemed to be on their own the way they always were. Jaime opened the button on his front pocket so that Ono could peek out. Better to have another set of eyes than not.

They got to Jaime's building with no trouble, possibly because it was so hot that everything and everyone was at risk of melting. Jaime broke his private promise never to use the facilities in the building and took the twins to the pool on the roof. He had to admit it was nice to swim in the cool, clear water, no threat of monsters anywhere.

After they swam for a while, they claimed several deck chairs for themselves and let the sun dry them. Tess slathered herself in sunscreen and offered some to Jaime, who paid special attention to his nose and the tops of his feet. A bunch of teenagers crowded a couple of lounge chairs next to them; the teens were all shapes and sizes and colors, like a box of crayons or a clothing ad. But they seemed to be wearing as little as possible, and the boys in particular flexed their pecs and biceps so often that it appeared they had medical problems. One of the teens, a pale, red-headed boy with a pimple in the middle of his forehead so large it looked like a third eye, observed Jaime applying the sunscreen lotion. "I thought black people didn't need sunscreen," he said.

"Only if they want to get sunburned." Jaime noted the boy's reddening nose and cheeks. "You want some of this? You're looking a little crispy already."

"I'm getting a tan," the boy announced.

"You're getting skin cancer," said one of his friends.

"No, he's just trying to clear up that pimple," said another.

"I am not," the redhead said.

"You don't want to clear up your pimple?" said a third teenager, this one dark-haired with so skin so white it was almost blue. "We should name it."

"Stop it," said the redhead, laughing.

"What about Percival?"

"Nah. How about Wilhelm? Willy for short."

"That's a name for a plant."

"Yeah, like a cactus or whatever."

"What are you talking about?"

The teens then got into a towel fight that ended up with all of them splashing around in the pool.

Theo said, "Since when is Wilhelm a name for a cactus?"

"Hormones must make you really dense," said Tess. "I wouldn't mind skipping that part."

"Yes, you would," Theo said.

"Not the growing taller and older part," Tess said. "Just the dense part."

"I'm not sure we can skip that," Jaime said. "They might go together." He had a sudden urge to flex his biceps, but fought it.

"I really don't want to be dense," said Theo. "Denser than I already am, anyway."

"You're one of the smartest people I know," Jaime said.

"I used to be," Theo said. "Now you might as well call me Wilhelm the plant."

"Stop feeling sorry for yourself," said Tess. "We do have a clue to figure out, don't we?"

Jaime didn't even have to look it up in his sketchbook. They all knew what the writing on the wall of the Smallpox Hospital said:

BURY ME RIGHT NEXT TO LOUIS MG,
THE MOST TALENTED MAN IN THE WHOLE OF THE CITY.

"We can start by identifying this Louis guy," said Jaime.

"If he was so talented, why haven't we heard of him?" Theo said.

"Remember that the clues mostly concern people and places and things that history has forgotten, right?" Tess said. "So maybe this guy was popular in the time of the Morningstarrs but has been overlooked or disregarded since then."

"Hmmm," said Jaime. "So if we do some searches for Louis online, maybe with 1850 dates, we can find something."

They left the pool to the splashing, flexing teens and went back to Jaime's apartment. By then, their suits were completely dry, so they pulled their street clothes over them and sat down to work at Jaime's computer. In the search box, they put "Louis MG" "New York City" and "1850." They came up with a Louis Vuitton exhibit, some comedian named Louis buying an apartment, and a whole bunch of listings on a whole bunch of other Louises, none of them particularly talented or even alive during the time of the Morningstarrs.

"'Bury me,'" said Jaime. "Maybe that's the clue."

"Could be," said Theo.

Jaime added "cemetery" to the search terms. They combed through the results, but nothing stood out.

"Maybe take out the date," said Theo. "It might be too specific."

So Jaime did. The first listing to pop up was an article called "The Most Famous Residents of New York City's Cemeteries."

"This might be something," Jaime said, tapping the screen.

Just then, there was a knock at the door. Jaime got up to answer it, weirdly expecting the group of teens to be standing there, asking him for the sunscreen or maybe wondering what they should call the redhead's pimple. (Roy, Jaime thought. Roy is a good name for a pimple.)

But it wasn't the teens—it was Cricket and her mother. Her mother was holding a box using only her fingertips, as if she would like to burn what was inside or maybe drop it from a plane into an active volcano.

"Hi, Jaime," Mrs. Moran said. "I was wondering if I could ask you a question."

"Sure," he said.

"What do you know about bugs?"

CHAPTER TWENTY-EIGHT
Candi/Ashli/Toni/Tammi/Lori/Laci/Lu

On the seventeenth floor in a glass tower in Manhattan, a group of women assembled to have their hair and makeup done for the day.

That morning, there were seven of them seated in a row, clean faced and dressed in identical red robes and slippers. Some mornings, there were just three of them; others, there were as many as fifteen women in the room. They had staggered appointments so that their favorite hair stylist, Anniq, and their favorite makeup artist, Belinda—along with their sundry assistants— could work their magic on them all. It was not every hair stylist who could achieve the exact shade of blond on so many different women with so many different hair textures, nor get the desired long banana curls that hung to the rib cage. And it was not every makeup artist who could affix false eyelashes with such dexterity, apply foundation so that each woman's skin was the color of peaches and cream, no matter what color peaches they'd been born with. Every time Anniq suggested that perhaps this woman or that one might like an update to her look—streaks of honey in the long locks, layers, a bob, a *pixie*—the women would smile sadly and say, "You know I can't." And if Belinda showed them a palette of new eye shadows they might want to try, or suggest a nude lip instead of the red lipstick they were so used to, the women would shake their heads ruefully. "You know I can't," they would say. "This is what they want." The women didn't specify who "they" were, they didn't have to. "They" meant everyone who watched their videos and listened to their commentaries, "they" were the police who were called when Duke wanted someone arrested, "they" were the investors who needed a little nudge in the right direction. Anniq and Belinda were professionals and would do their best to please their clients. Besides, the women didn't give off even a hint of their resentment of Anniq and Belinda, whom they claimed to love and appreciate so, so much, whom they would greet every morning with a kiss on one cheek and then the other, like the French. Anniq, dark and lush and mysterious, with her thick curly hair streaked with indigo, and Belinda, with her rich, coppery skin, full lips, and brown eyes shot with flecks of green and gold. Neither looked like anyone else, both shone like stars being born. In the blond women's more vulnerable moments—when they were overtired, or when they were just a bit too hungry—they would think to themselves, *Who does she think she is, putting those silly streaks in her hair?* Or, *Those have to be contact lenses, she had to have injections in those lips. Nobody really looks like that.* Or even, *Why do I have to look like this? Why do I have to dye my hair this color, style it this way? What's wrong with brown hair? Why do they believe me more when I wear this uniform? What am I doing here?* But more often, they would tamp down these unproductive thoughts by intense yoga breathing or snacking on the kale chips that the servers brought for breakfast. They had to be ready for battle at all times, and a soldier couldn't waste a minute feeling sorry for herself.

"Salty!" said Candi, biting into a kale chip. Her name really was Candi, short for Candace. She was technically the blondest, and the woman in charge of them all. She had the ear of the boss, and that was not anything the other blond ladies could boast. At least, not at the moment. The boss had a reputation for cycling the women. He would favor one for a while, until Belinda's magic couldn't quite hide the lines forming around the blonde's eyes and mouth, until the blond lady got too hungry and devoured whole boxes of doughnuts on the weekend and couldn't quite make up the difference by sipping bone broth the rest of the week. And then another blond lady would be looped in.

The blond women didn't know where the retired ones went. Perhaps to the Midwest somewhere. Kansas. Or Minnesota.

The blondes didn't like thinking about Minnesota.

So they didn't. Each of them thought she was special, not like the other girls, that she would be the one to stay, maybe even take the boss's place when he retired. Finally, get real power. But for now, they bided their time and did what was asked of them. Candi in particular.

But Candi had been asked to find a cat. And she was having some trouble.

She had never had trouble before.

"More tea, Ms. Candi?" asked an assistant.

"Yes, please," Candi said, holding out her cup. She frowned at her reflection in the mirror. She shouldn't even be able to frown. She would have to freshen the Botox soon. And maybe ask for some fillers around the mouth.

"You're looking especially beautiful this morning, Candi," said Toni, the blond girl to her left. She was new, and quite young, with the plump cheeks of a teenager that Belinda would shadow and sculpt with powders to make her look more like an adult.

"Thank you," said Candi, knowing full well that Toni was after her job. Well, she would have to get in line. Right behind Ashli, Tammi, Lori, Laci, and Lu. All of whom quickly joined in on the compliments.

Ashli: "Oh yes, Candi looks luminous without makeup."

Tammi: "She doesn't need it!"

Lori: "Maybe you should get a new haircut like Anniq suggested. A pixie! To show off those marvelous cheekbones."

Laci: "Oooh, a pixie would be so daring. But then Candi is the definition of daring."

Lu: "I think she should go for some layers. A pixie might be too much."

They all looked at Lu, quirking their carefully threaded eyebrows. Lu wasn't going to last. First of all, she called herself Lu. Not Luli or even Lulu. If you wanted a man's job, you couldn't have a man's name. You needed to call yourself the least threatening name think you could think of. If they even suspected that you had any ambitions beyond the roles they selected for you, if you were stubborn, if you stood out in the wrong way, you could be cut. Just like that.

Poor Lu. She was already on a plane to Minnesota, and she didn't even know it.

"Oh, you ladies are so kind," Candi said. "But I couldn't possibly get a pixie. I'm afraid I'm too attached to my hair as it is." In other words, *Don't come for me, and I won't come for you. And there are no guarantees I won't come for you anyway, because that's the way the world works.*

Toni smiled. "I don't blame you," she said. "You do wear it so well."

"Thank you, dear." Candi patted the younger woman's knee. "You might want to ask Belinda about her new eye shadows. She said those shadows can bring out even the smallest of eyes."

Toni tipped her head like a puppy, trying to sort out what Candi had said, then her eyes narrowed in recognition. No matter. Toni was no match for Candi, would never be. Candi sipped her green tea and fortified herself with another kale chip.

"How's the search going, Candi?" Lu asked. "Did you find that cat yet?" Again, the other women stared at her. You weren't supposed to be so direct, unless you were making a video to put online, a video in which you ranted rather prettily about the president playing too much golf, or maybe the secretary of state operating a tax scam out of a cupcake bakery in New Jersey. The blond women might answer to Duke Goodson, but they had roles as commentators and panelists for various news stations and internet companies. A girl had to make a living.

"The search is going as expected," Candi replied, her tone cool as the tea in her cup. "The cat is not just a cat, as you know."

"Looks like a cat," Lu said. "A big one, but still."

"Well, it isn't," Candi said. "I have Staci, Suri, Jenni, and Zozi at work right now. And there are other forces at play."

"What other forces?" said Lu. She dug her hand in the bowl of kale chips offered by another assistant and scooped out at least twenty or twenty-five of them. It was appalling.

"Forces that are different from the original forces," Candi said. That should have been enough to shut the woman up, but this was Lu.

"Okay, but *what* other forces? And what's the big deal about a cat anyway? What's Goodson want with it?"

"The search for the animal is not my only concern," said Candi. The woman was a nightmare. How did she even get this job?

Anniq came up behind Candi and fluffed Candi's hair. "You are stressed this morning?" she asked. "You seem tense."

"No more than usual, Anniq," Candi said. Unlike Candi, Anniq *was* looking luminous this morning, always looked luminous, but Candi couldn't bring herself to say it. "I'd like a bit of a trim, today."

"All right," said Anniq, agreeably. "An inch?"

"You know me so well, Anniq."

While Anniq washed and conditioned her hair, Candi thought about the cat. As much as she talked about how important finding the cat was, she thought the whole thing was ridiculous. Her talents were being wasted by chasing after someone's pet. Why not send Toni on this errand? Let the silly little twit believe she was doing something important. But when Candi had suggested it, Duke had given her that look. The baleful, empty look that told her not to push it.

She hated that look. She hated Duke, too, if she was being honest, which she almost never was. The man was downright creepy. Not as creepy as that doctor in the Bronx, but creepy nonetheless. She couldn't even imagine what Duke might say, might do, if she told him about the apartment building in Hoboken. What had happened, what she missed, what she was still missing.

A tiny voice spoke in the back of her brain: *Why not go over his head?*

She could do it, of all the blondes, she could do it. She could convince the big boss that Goodson had lost his touch. And *she* would be the fixer's fixer.

She closed her eyes and fantasized about starting up her own news station, her own consulting firm. The videos she could make! The things she could make people believe! Anything, anything. It was her particular talent, more than any of the other girls. Duke would come crawling back to her, begging to be a part of it, and she would slam the door in his face. Maybe even send him to a retirement home in Minnesota. The other blond ladies could follow him.

Candi would be the one and only.

"We're done," said Anniq. She wrapped a warm towel around Candi's shoulders and led her back to her chair. She combed out Candi's long hair and trimmed an inch off the bottom. It took Anniq an hour to do it, and another for her to blow-dry, curl, and spray the finished style. By the time Anniq was done, Candi's scalp ached and the lines in her forehead seemed worse somehow, the hair better on someone else, someone less aggravated. Maybe when she started her own consulting firm, she would get that pixie cut.

But she simply couldn't.

It wasn't what they wanted.

Candi fluffed the new curls but not so hard that she ruined their shape. "You're a wizard, Anniq. Thank you."

"You're so welcome," said Anniq warmly as ever. The stylist had put even more streaks of indigo in her own hair, along with some pink ones, too. Maybe Candi could entice Anniq and Belinda to come work for her. And if they wouldn't, she would have to ruin them, so that they could never work for anyone else, not even themselves. It would hurt Candi to do that, but if they were stubborn, if they had more ambition than was appropriate, what choice did she have?

A girl had to make a living.

Candi dug around in her tasteful leather bag, retrieved her phone, found the contact she was looking for. When a voice said, "Yes?" Candi said, "It's me. I want an update and I better be happy with what I hear."

CHAPTER TWENTY-NINE
Tess

When Tess and Theo joined Jaime in his living room, Cricket and her mother were standing there.

"Cricket!" Tess said.

"Yes?" said Cricket.

"You're here!"

"I know," said Cricket. She was wearing a subdued outfit, for her, anyway. A brown shirt, black pants. And a little black mask that covered her eyes.

Oh.

"I'm really sorry about Karl, Cricket."

"I dressed like him today," said Cricket.

"I see that. I like it."

Cricket looked down at the floor. "I'm sorry about Nine."

"Me too," said Tess.

"I know your mother is doing her best to find Karl and Nine," Mrs. Moran said. "But it is very nice to see you, Tess. And you, Theo. I think you've grown taller."

"That's just his hair," said Cricket.

"Cricket," her mother warned.

"It's true," said Theo. "Tess did get taller, though." He sounded grumpy about it. And then, astonishingly, he flexed his arm.

"Did you just try to make a muscle?" Cricket demanded.

"No."

Tess rolled her eyes. None of them were going to be able to skip the dense part.

"Are you visiting Mrs. Cruz?" Theo asked.

"We live here! Jaime's grandmother was gracious enough to get us a place," Mrs. Moran said.

"That's great. How do you like it?" Tess asked.

Mrs. Moran beamed. "We love it. So spacious. And new! Everything works, nothing leaks, and there's a pool and a gym. It's just amazing."

"Except for the NEFARIOUS ACTORS," said Cricket.

"Well, yes. Except for those." Cricket's mom pointed to the box that Jaime held. "Cricket noticed the bug problem. She's . . . she's been collecting them." She wrinkled her nose.

"Bugs? What kind?" said Theo. "Bugs are awesome."

"WIGGLE WORMS," said Cricket.

"Not familiar with those," said Theo. He opened one of the flaps. Tess peered inside. Silverfish.

"I broke them all," Cricket said darkly.

Tess stepped closer and touched one of the bugs. They looked like silverfish, but . . .

"Metal," Tess breathed.

"So metal," Cricket said. "And not in the good way."

"I know that you all are into science and insects and that kind of thing," Mrs. Moran said. "I thought maybe you would know what these are so that I can call management about the problem. We're going to have to get an exterminator here immediately."

"And the FBI," said Cricket.

"I'm not so sure we'll need the FBI, Cricket."

"The CIA, then." Cricket's eyes got big behind the mask. "Unless they did it."

"I don't believe the CIA infested our apartment building with bugs, Cricket," said Mrs. Moran. Cricket made a raspberry sound. Her mother ignored it. "Anyway, I'm going to leave that box with you. Maybe you can call me later, let me know what you think?"

"Sure, Mrs. Moran," said Jaime. "Happy to."

Mrs. Moran beamed again. "Come on, Cricket. Let's leave these guys to their experiments. I promised I would take you to the museum."

Cricket said, "We're going to see the dinosaur bones."

"The Natural History Museum?" said Tess. "My favorite. I love the megafauna exhibits, too."

"Hmmph," said Cricket.

"Bones of giant mammals that lived in the Pleistocene era," Theo explained.

"MEGAFAUNA," Cricket said, wonder in her voice. "Is Nine a MEGAFAUNA?"

"No, she's just big, not giant," said Tess. "And all those others are extinct."

"That's sad," said Cricket.

"Yeah," Tess said.

Jaime bent to look Cricket in the mask. "Thank you for collecting these bugs. I really appreciate it. I think you've found something very important and possibly nefarious."

Cricket smiled one of her rare smiles, one that transformed her whole face. "I'll keep looking for them when I get home."

"Good," said Jaime. "Have a great time at the museum and say hi to the giant sloth for me."

Once Cricket and Mrs. Moran were gone, Theo said, "I wonder what—"

But Tess cut him off. She shook her head and put a finger across her lips. Then, she pointed at the box.

Jaime placed it on the coffee table. Tess grabbed one of the bugs. Cricket hadn't lied; she'd broken them all. This one had tiny springs and wires hanging from its middle.

"A *bug*," said Theo, when he saw wires were connected to a microphone and a microcamera, a bug inside a bug.

They stood in Jaime's living room, trying to absorb what this meant. Someone had planted spying devices all throughout this apartment building. Maybe this very apartment. Hadn't one of these crawled out of one of Jaime's closets? They had mistaken it for a real bug at the time, but whoever made them could have seen and heard everything Jaime said, everything Tess and Theo had said today.

The clue! They'd been talking about the inscription from the island!

Ono popped his tiny head out from Jaime's pocket,

took in the box of broken bugs. "Oh no," he said.

Tess had to agree.

They searched Jaime's apartment and found three more silverfish, one behind the television in the living room, one under the sink in the kitchen, one under Jaime's bed. Jaime stomped on it as if it were poisonous. Which, in a way, it was.

But even though they'd found three more bugs, they couldn't trust that they'd gotten them all. On a piece of paper, Jaime wrote, "We have to get out of here. Go somewhere where we can't be overheard."

Tess nodded. For the benefit of any spies listening in, she said loudly, "You guys want to go to up to Central Park? We could rent some exos. Then come back here and swim again."

"Sounds good to me," Jaime said.

They packed up and headed out. Tess tried to keep her gaze focused straight ahead, tried to seem natural, but her limbs felt stiff and her lungs, tight. She couldn't guarantee that the bugs had been meant for them, but she had a feeling they had been and she couldn't shake it. Someone knew what they were looking for, or at least knew they were looking for something. Where else had been bugged? Aunt Esther's house? Grandpa Ben's room at the memory-care facility?

Who would do this?

Slant?

Who else would it be? Who else wanted all the Morningstarr buildings? Who else was babbling about progress every single day?

Who else would be so nefarious?

But another thought nagged at her, ate at her. What if the bugs were Morningstarr Machines? What if these machines, like the others, had minds of their own? What if the *Cipher* itself was listening in?

Who were the Morningstarrs? What was all of this for?

In silence, Jaime led Tess and Theo onto the ferry that would take them across the Hudson. They found a place outside against the rail where it was coolest and where the water churning against the engines might drown out anything they said. Not that they said much. All of them seemed to be lost in their own private reveries, their own private rages, their own private anxieties. Jaime tapped his fingers, Theo tugged on his lip, Tess yanked her braid and crossed her arms and couldn't get comfortable in her own body. She felt like a marionette with someone else pulling the strings. That blond woman. Slant. The Morningstarrs. And the Cipher itself.

She wished she knew what it wanted.

She wished she knew what *she* wanted.

She missed Grandma Annie. She missed Grandpa Ben. She missed Nine. She missed them all so hard she bit her tongue, and the tinny taste of blood flooded her mouth.

When she was little and plagued by nightmares, Grandpa Ben would sit up with her and have her tell him a story. A story that fixed all the nightmares, chased them away. If she dreamed of a monster under her bed, Grandpa Ben asked her what would make the monster less scary. So she would tell him a story about a monster that was scared and lonely because it lost its teddy bear. And if she dreamed she was swimming in the ocean and a shark came up beside her, she would tell Grandpa Ben a story about a shark that had decided to become a vegetarian and needed help with recipes. Angry ghosts turned into friendly ghosts who helped you empty the dishwasher; huge, faceless aliens with too many mouths transformed into happy little green Martians eager to share their knowledge of all the worlds in the universe.

Standing at the rails of the ferry, Tess told herself another story. One in which she and Theo and Jaime found the answer to the Cipher, and the answer was something so powerful and magical that could bring back everyone and everything that Tess had lost.

Tess almost laughed out loud. She would have said she'd been reading too many comic books, except she hadn't been reading any comic books lately.

And then the ferry was docking, and they disembarked along with everyone else telling themselves a story about how they would win that new client account, how they would impress the boss, how they would ace the audition or the tryout. Near Washington Square Park, a car stopped at a red light played music so loud that the bass was distorted. A bunch of kids walking across the street in front of the car started to dance to the music. They danced furiously all the way to the other curb, making everyone around them laugh. Tess too. It was as if the world didn't want her to be quite so sad, that her work wasn't done yet.

They got a couple of pretzels from a vendor and sat on a bench to eat them, and to talk.

"I knew there was something wrong with that place,"

Jaime said. "But I didn't think anyone had actually bugged it. I didn't know the Morningstarrs made those kinds of things."

"They didn't," Tess and Theo said at the same time.

"Not that we knew of before," Tess amended.

"Cricket tried to tell me about the bugs weeks ago, and I didn't pay attention. She called them wiggle worms."

"It's not your fault," Tess said. "How could you know?"

"I should have," Jaime insisted.

"Well, we know now," Theo said.

"They do, too!" said Jaime. "The people spying on us, whoever they are. We talked about the clue all morning!"

"We don't know who's spying on us," said Tess.

"Plus I'm not sure we gave ourselves away," Theo said. "We were researching it online, but did we say anything out loud?"

Tess went over their conversation in her head. "I don't think so. Not exactly."

"But those bugs didn't only have ears, they had eyes," said Jaime. "Maybe one of them saw the screen."

"So we have to get to the next clue first. And then we have to make sure that no one is on our trail, and there's nothing left of the clue for anyone else to figure out," Tess said.

"You mean, destroy it?" Jaime said. "What if it's valuable?"

A squirrel hopped in front of them, begging for handouts. Jaime eyed it with suspicion, as if it were a spy, too. He tore off a bit of pretzel and threw it. The squirrel ran after it.

"None of the clues have been especially valuable," Theo said. Ono beeped in protest. "Except for Ono."

"Before we talk about destroying anything, let's figure out where we're going." Jaime pulled his phone from his pocket, then stared at it. "What if the phone is bugged?"

"If it was," said Tess, "we would have been in Slant's dungeon a long time ago."

"You think Slant actually has a dungeon?" Theo asked.

"Oh, he definitely has a dungeon," said Jaime. "Back to the clue written on the wall of the haunted hospital. 'Bury me right next to Louis MG.' I saved the search we did before Cricket and her mom came over. We were trying to find out who Louis MG was, and we found that article about the most famous residents of New York

City's cemeteries. I'm betting this Louis guy is probably buried in one of them."

"There are a lot of cemeteries in New York City," Theo said, as if that wasn't obvious.

"So we might have to visit a lot of graves," Tess said.

"Cool," said Theo.

"Or at least a lot of cemetery websites," Jaime said.

Theo scrunched up his nose. "Meh."

They searched Trinity Cemetery, Woodlawn Cemetery, and Calvary Cemetery. Then they got more pretzels and few hot dogs. After they ate their lunch, they fed the relentless squirrel and searched the database of Green-Wood Cemetery. And that was where they found a list of famous Louises buried there, including one Louis Moreau Gottschalk.

"Louis MG," said Jaime, skimming the article he'd found. "Lot 19581 in the cemetery. An international musical star, brilliant pianist, and the first important American composer, born in New Orleans to a German-Jewish father and a Creole mother. His music melded all kinds of sounds, including Creole, black, mariachi, Cuban, all sorts of things. Plus he was a committed abolitionist. Seems like my kind of guy."

"And the Morningstarrs'," said Tess.

"Or the Cipher's," Jaime said.

"Green-Wood Cemetery," said Theo. "So we have to go back to Brooklyn."

"Yeah," said Tess. "But we can't go back in the daylight. Not if the clue means what I think it means."

"That we have to dig up something next to Louis," Jaime said. "I hope it's not a grave. Please, please, please let us not have to dig up a grave." He tossed a bit of hot dog bun to the enterprising squirrel, who chased the tumbling bit of bun to the base of a nearby tree.

A tree behind which two people in the most conspicuous trench coats that Tess had ever seen were trying to hide.

CHAPTER THIRTY
Theo

Tess gasped. Automatically, Theo gripped her arm. Jaime said, "Oh, sugar," except he didn't say *sugar*.

"What?" Theo said. "What is it?"

Jaime spoke out of one side of his mouth. "Two people hiding behind the tree. Three o'clock."

"What people?"

"Not so loud!" Tess said, too loud.

The people hiding behind the tree tried in vain to make themselves smaller. It was the most inept display of spy craft that Theo had ever seen. Not that he was an expert on spy craft, but he assumed that if you didn't want to be noticed, you shouldn't wander around in knee-length trench coats on a ninety-five-degree day. Also, you shouldn't try to hide behind a sapling.

"That's just ridiculous," Theo said.

"Shhh!" said Tess.

"It is pretty ridiculous," Jaime said. "But don't we know them?"

"Hard to tell with the giant sunglasses and the newspapers they're holding up. Ono would be a better spy."

"To the Land of Kings!" Ono burbled.

One of the spies dropped the newspaper for just a second. Tess gasped again, but this time in recognition.

"Omar Khayyám?" she said.

At the sound of his name, Omar Khayyám said, "Oh, sugar." Except he really said the word *sugar*.

Then he said, "Forget it, Priya. We've been made."

"Thank goodness!" said Priya. "I can finally take off this coat. It's hotter than Hades is out here."

"Hades isn't hot," Theo muttered. Tess gave him a look. "Well, it isn't!"

"Hades isn't real," Jaime said.

"I know, I'm just . . . oh, never mind," Theo said.

Priya Sharma and Omar Khayyám of the Cipherists Society, and old friends of the twins' grandfather Ben, stripped off the giant sunglasses and coats and put the newspapers into the nearest recycling can for the Rollers. Sheepishly, they approached Theo, Tess, and Jaime.

"Sorry, kids," said Priya. "We're not so good at this. Not as good as the others."

"Good at what?" Tess wanted to know. "And what others?"

Priya and Omar exchanged glances.

Jaime said, "Please tell us, Ms. Sharma and Mr. Khayyám. It's been a really confusing day and I don't think we can take any more confusion."

"Your grandfather asked us to keep an eye on you three," said Omar.

"But my grandfather is, he's . . ."

"We know where he is, dear Tess," said Priya gently. "A long time ago, he asked us that if anything should happen to him, we might look after you. Nothing intrusive or obvious. Observe from afar. And that's what we've been doing. Just checking in once in a while. Seeing that you're okay, especially after, well, Edgar, and 354 West 73rd Street. We did some walk-throughs of Jaime's building, visited your aunt's house in Queens a few times. Everything seemed fine. You even seemed happy, mostly."

Omar snapped a monogrammed handkerchief and used it to wipe sweat from his brow. "But then we heard about Nine. And your aunt called and asked us to step up the surveillance. So lately we've had to use three teams instead of one."

"You've been spying on us?" Theo said.

"No!" said Omar.

"Yes," said Priya. "But only to make sure you were safe, that's all."

"Who else has been spying?" said Tess.

"Delancey, Imogen, Ray, and Gino. Most of the society."

"But some of us are better at this clandestine stuff than others," Omar said. "We're the bottom tier, sadly."

"I told you the trench coats were a terrible idea," Priya said.

"This is an all-season coat!" said Omar.

Priya rolled her eyes. "Uh-huh. So what are you doing here in Washington Square? You seemed to be having a very intense conversation."

"You don't have listening devices?" Jaime asked.

"Of course not!" said Priya. "We wanted to make sure you were all right, not meddle in your personal business."

The very definition of spying was meddling in someone's personal business, but Theo didn't mention that.

"We assume you were hatching a plan to find Nine,"

said Omar. "Or that funny little raccoon who likes the cheese snacks."

This time, Tess gripped Theo's arm to keep him from blurting out whatever she was worried he'd blurt. "Yes, that's exactly what we were doing. I know my mom is looking really hard for them both, but we want to help."

"And you can't tell her that?" Priya asked.

"She doesn't know if the people who took Nine and Karl are dangerous. She doesn't want us hurt."

"Karl?" said Omar.

"The raccoon."

"Ah," Omar said. "Well. Maybe we can help. I'd like to get out of this heat for a while. Perhaps you three would like to come back to the society with us? Say hello to everyone there? We all miss you. And you can tell all about your plans."

"That sounds great, but we'd—" said Tess.

Again, Theo gripped her arm. "We'd love to. Would it be okay if we stayed the night? We don't want to be traveling home too late."

Priya beamed. "A sleepover! What a fabulous idea."

Omar said, "We're going to need extra toothbrushes."

After the twins called their parents and Jaime texted

his grandmother, they walked to the Cipherist Society, Priya and Omar keeping up a steady stream of chatter. Delancey DeBrule had taken up Edgar Wellington's role as president since Edgar's retirement and relocation to Boca Raton, Florida. Imogen Sparks was their chief fundraiser and political liaison, which meant she spent a lot of time yelling about local politicians. Adrian Birch and Flo Harriman were planning for the annual Cipherist convention that would take place in a month. But Auguste Dupin, their resident mynah bird, seemed to have fallen into a bit of depression since Edgar's retirement.

"He keeps reciting the poem 'Annabel Lee,'" said Priya. "I love that bird but I do wish he would learn more uplifting verse."

"When he's not reciting the poem, he sings songs from the musical *Hamilton*," Omar said.

"Only the sad ones," said Priya.

Omar shook his head. "Auguste can't rap."

They entered the building. Omar punched in some codes on the keypad, and a huge metal door opened onto the vast collection of the society. Even now, Theo felt a thrill when he first glimpsed all those shelves full of books and manuscripts, when they looked down four floors onto a cozy circle of chairs in and among precious artifacts encased in glass.

Auguste the mynah flapped on his perch. He said:

> *"For the moon never beams, without bringing me dreams*
> *Of the beautiful Annabel Lee;*
> *And the stars never rise, but I feel the bright eyes*
> *Of the beautiful Annabel Lee;*
> *And so, all the night-tide, I lie down by the side*
> *Of my darling—my darling—my life and my bride,*
> *In her sepulchre there by the sea—*
> *In her tomb by the sounding sea."*

"Mein Gott," said Gunter Deiderich. "Don't you know anything else, you daft old bird? Something by Taylor Swift, maybe?"

"Yes, Auguste," called Priya Sharma. "I would very much like to hear 'Shake It Off.'"

Everyone seated looked up. Imogen Sparks's grin was wide and welcoming as her outstretched arms. "Get down here right now, you three!"

"Don't squoosh them, Imogen," Gunter said, once they'd climbed down the stairs and Imogen gathered Theo into a hug.

"I will squoosh them if they will accept squooshes,"

said Imogen. "Will you allow me to squoosh you, Tess?"

"Squoosh away," said Tess. Imogen hugged her, and then Jaime as well. "It's been too long since you've visited."

"Only about a month," said Theo.

"Longer than that," said Gunter.

"Besides, the whole world can change in a month."

"Or a day," said Omar. "I'm afraid the kids caught us spying on them."

Imogen put her hands on her hips. "With those disguises? Shocking."

"See?" said Priya to Omar.

"Enough of that," said Gunter. "What's for dinner? These kids are too skinny."

"Gino is cooking up his pasta right now," Imogen said. "What are you doing over there, Mr. Jaime?"

Jaime, who had been murmuring to Auguste, said, "Trying to teach him the lyrics from a Nas song."

Imogen waved her hand. "Already tried that."

"*Whose world is this?*" Jaime said to the bird. "*It's mine, it's mine.*"

Auguste said, "*Who lives / Who dies / Who tells your story?*"

"What did I tell you?" said Imogen. "He's impossible."

They ate Gino's delicious tortellini with peas and mushrooms and listened to more happy banter between the Cipherists. It was good to be here with them, Theo thought, good to be back where his grandpa Ben had spent so much of his life, with the people he had loved most besides his own family. But then, these people were like family. Even the silly bird who couldn't stop singing his sad songs, reciting his sad poems.

But Theo couldn't help feeling a bit sad, too, sad as the bird. It used to be that the Cipherists knew everything; it used to be that his grandpa Ben knew the most of all. But now Grandpa Ben was gone, swirling in his own eroding memories in the care facility uptown and the Cipherists knew less than Theo himself. Once, that would have made Theo feel proud. Finally, he was the expert! He didn't feel like an expert. He felt like a lone pea lost in a soup of cream sauce.

But he didn't have time to dwell on sad things. They would have to sneak out in the middle of the night to get to Green-Wood Cemetery, or they would have to come up with some kind of story that would get the Cipherists to accompany them without understanding what they were really doing.

Stories were not Theo's thing—they were Tess's. And so far, she hadn't told any stories or offered any excuses or ideas. And Jaime, too, seemed lost in the banter of the Cipherists, or maybe he just looked as if he were.

They had been so focused on the clue and then the bugs that they hadn't had the time to talk about the woman in gray, the one who Jaime had been drawing for months. When Jaime had gone to answer the door back at his apartment, Tess had shown Theo the drawings on Jaime's desk. The likeness between the woman in gray and Jaime's superhero sketches was uncanny, unbelievable, inexplicable. If only they'd been able to talk to her, ask her where she'd come from, ask her why she'd saved them, ask her who in the world she was.

"A woman's been following us," Theo blurted. Tess kicked him under the table and Jaime looked as if he might flick a spoonful of peas at his face, but Theo soldiered on. "Two women, maybe more. All blondes."

"Blond women?" said Imogen. "What blond women?"

"I can't explain it; I don't know who they are. But they all have the same shade of blond hair; they all wear the same color red dress. We've seen them in a bunch of places."

"And one of them was the woman who accused Nine of biting her. She might be the one who took her," Tess added.

"We overheard them talking about a place in Brooklyn," Jaime said, catching on. "In Green-Wood Cemetery."

"I love the cemetery," Priya said. "So many important people buried there."

"And notorious people," Imogen said. "Boss Tweed for one. The Tiger of Tammany. Died in 1878."

"What did he do?" Jaime asked.

"What they all do. Steal from ordinary people," Omar said. "He held all sorts of offices including New York state senator. He used his positions to push through various building projects with overinflated prices so that he could skim off the top."

"More than skim," Imogen said. "The construction of the New York City courthouse was supposed to cost two hundred and fifty thousand dollars in 1858. It ended up costing twelve *million*, with all the extra going back to Tweed and his friends."

"Wow," said Jaime.

"New York City politics have always been ugly."

"Slant's going to run for office," Tess said.

"Ugh," said Gunter. "Don't remind us. Imogen will start yelling again and then Auguste will start another round of his sad songs and I will be forced to move back to Austria."

Adrian arranged his peas in a row on his plate. "Getting back to these blond ladies you mentioned. Why would they be talking about the cemetery?"

"We think they're hiding animals there," Theo said. "Hybrid animals. My mom suspects that someone must be collecting them for some reason. We think it's the blondes. We think that's why they were following us. To get to Nine and then to Karl."

"But hiding animals in the cemetery?" said Omar. "That doesn't seem like a good idea. Where would you keep them?"

"I suppose you could build a facility that resembled a tomb or mausoleum if you had the money," said Gunter. "Still, it seems very strange."

"Or smart," Imogen said. "Hiding in plain sight like that. Tourists go in and out all day. Who would notice a bunch of blond ladies or anyone else?"

"We were hoping to look around the cemetery," Tess said, "but we don't want to do it during the day. We don't want to be seen again. If we're caught on video or in photos again, my mom will have a fit."

Imogen clapped. "Ooooh. A midnight reconnaissance mission! I like it."

"I'm in," said Adrian.

"Me too," said Gunter. "Against my better judgment."

Gino and the rest also agreed to come. It had been too long since they'd had a real adventure, they said.

"But," Imogen added, pointing at Omar and Priya in turn, "this time, we lose the trench coats."

CHAPTER THIRTY-ONE
Jaime

When people talked about New York City being the city that never sleeps, they were often referring to the people who lived there.

But people were not the only things awake.

There were the gargoyles on the tops of buildings that seemed to watch as the cars passed by. The old portraits that seemed to glower at the guards who strolled museum halls, the skeletons of animals long extinct that seemed to move when no one was looking. Brownstones that looked like angry faces, or smiling ones, depending. The creaking of timbers and beams, wood and plaster, that everyone claimed was just "settling" but perhaps was something else. Something restless and fitful.

Unlike the people and the paintings and the very bones of the city, Jaime wished for a little rest. And, after the events of North Brother Island, a midnight trip to a cemetery sounded positively restful to Jaime.

Which could only mean that he had lost his entire mind.

He imagined what Mima might say if he were to tell her what he was doing. A stream of furious Spanish followed by swearing in five other languages, he guessed. And then a lecture about how he was acting a fool and she didn't raise a fool, etc., etc., etc. She would be right.

And yet, here he was, packed into a van with a bunch of eager Cipherists excited to creep around a graveyard.

They'd *all* lost their entire minds.

The city out the window drew his eye the way it always did. The lights twinkled and the people in the bars and the restaurants laughed, clinking glasses. A line of folks dressed in satin and sequins and artfully ripped-up jeans waited by a velvet rope for a bouncer the size of a giraffe-owary to let them into some exclusive dance club. He opened the door for a lucky few, and the music thudded like a heartbeat.

"Whose world is this? Whose world is this?" Jaime muttered, drumming his fingers on his knee.

His thoughts drifted to the woman in gray. Again.

He searched the streets for her, hoping that she was watching, that she was following. He hadn't felt safe with her, exactly, but he hadn't felt threatened, either. It was as if she'd had her own business to attend to on that island, and they'd messed up her plans, and she'd dealt with the situation as best as she could. He replayed her movements, spinning and kicking and punching her way through all those beefed-up dudes, and grinned to himself.

She'd dealt with the situation, all right.

The van reached the cemetery. It was hard to miss, with its ornate vampire-castle-looking gate, stone spires spiking the darkness.

"Creepy," Priya whispered. And then shivered as if she found the concept delightful.

Jaime unbuttoned his pocket, and Ono piped up. "To the Land of Kings?"

"Yes, we're in Kings County. My goodness!" Priya said, when she saw Ono. "Who is this?"

"Ono, Priya. Priya, Ono," said Jaime.

"Kings," said Ono.

"Is that all he says?"

"Oh no," said Ono.

"That's the other thing he says."

"Ah, simple but cute, your Ono," said Priya.

Ono made a buzzing sound that could have been annoyance or approval; Jaime couldn't tell.

They parked the van under a copse of trees some distance from the gate and walked the rest of the way. Outside, the spires seemed taller and spikier and even more vampire-castle-like. If he'd had the time, he would have sketched it, but the Cipherists were too excited to wait. Before they'd left the society, Jaime and the twins planned out their reconnaissance. Jaime had looked up the location of Louis Moreau Gottschalk's grave, but the Cipherists were focused mostly on the larger structures, mausoleums and the like all around the graveyard. He and Tess and Theo figured that they could split up once in the cemetery and find the next clue before the Cipherists were the wiser. It wasn't a foolproof plan. The Cipherists might have lost their entire minds, too, but they were the farthest things from fools. One or two or maybe even all of them might wonder where the kids had wandered off to. Or why the kids came back with dirt all over them. Or the Cipherists could stumble upon them right in the middle of the dig. But they would have to risk it. And even if they had to reveal their secrets to the Cipherists, Tess said, these people weren't like Edgar Wellington. They wouldn't turn on them, no matter what.

Jaime hoped Tess was right.

But Jaime didn't think any of them had counted on how dark the cemetery would be, how very much like the setting for a scary movie, maybe even more than the ruins at North Brother Island.

When they got to the gate, strange screeching overhead made Jaime and Tess and Theo jump.

"Don't worry," whispered Imogen. "It's just the monk parrots. They live in a nest on the highest spire. See?" She pointed. In the darkness, Jaime could just make out an enormous pile of twigs. Parrots, just parrots, he told himself, but his heart hammered.

"How did the parrots get here?" Tess asked.

Imogen shrugged. "Some people say a shipment of the birds escaped the airport. But nobody really knows. Could be pet owners who freed their birds."

"Or maybe the birds freed themselves," said Jaime.

"That too," said Imogen.

"If we get split up, we meet here at the front gate at three a.m.," said Gino. "Everyone okay with that?"

They all agreed. They entered the cemetery, at first sticking to the largest path snaking through the acres of graves. The whole group fell silent as they wended their way, as if they, too, were on their way to a funeral. So many people were buried here. Soldiers

and millionaires and artists and ballplayers and politicians and thieves. Some grave markers were small,
the names weathered away. Some were huge obelisks or
pyramids jutting out of the gently rolling hills. There
were statues of goddesses and statues of bears, statues
of sphinxes and statues of dogs.

But Jaime and Tess and Theo were interested in one
particular statue that marked Louis Gottschalk's grave:
The Angel of Music. According to the map on Jaime's phone,
it wasn't far from the main entrance, just off to the left.
The Cipherists had already spread out, taking pictures
and making grave rubbings, but they hadn't drifted far
enough for Jaime and the twins to slip away without
being observed.

Another screech shattered the night air, and Jaime
ducked instinctively. He thought he felt the *air* shudder
as with the furious beating of wings, but he could see
nothing. The twins ducked, too.

"Did you hear that?" Jaime whispered.

"I felt it," Tess whispered back.

The three of them stood back to back, all of them
trying to locate the source of the sound. Parrots?
Giraffe-owaries? *Jumbies?*

"This isn't as fun as I thought it would be," Theo
whispered.

"You thought it would be *fun*?" Jaime said.

"Shhh!" Tess hissed, as another screech cracked the sky open.

"Uh, where did they go?" Jaime said.

"Who?"

The three of them looked around. They could still hear faint chatter of barely suppressed voices, but the Cipherists had drifted out of sight.

"Well," said Theo. "Now's our chance."

"Yeah," Jaime and Tess agreed. But none of them moved until there was a long strange sigh somewhere off in the darkness. Wind in the trees?

Or something else.

Tess, Jaime, and Theo ran. Despite their fear, they didn't forget their mission. They went from one marker to the next, looking for Lot 19581.

"There she is," said Theo. In front of them stood the bronze angel high on her marble base. Louis's grave was fenced all around, with other graves nearby.

"'Bury me right next to Louis MG,'" Jaime quoted. "Right next to Louis. So I'm thinking we start digging on the right side."

"Inside or outside the fence?" said Tess.

"Inside," Theo said. "Right next to also means close to. So close to the grave marker."

"Makes sense to me," said Jaime. "Except we could be digging all night."

"Let's hope not," Tess said.

They hopped the small fence around the grave marker. Ono buzzed and beeped, the sounds comforting in this strange darkness, so Jaime set the robot on the marble stand at the foot of the angel. They got out small gardening trowels, the only digging equipment they could fit in their backpacks, and started to dig. First, they tried one place, and then decided that the three of them should dig in three separate places. The ground was soft, but the digging itself was hard work. Jaime could feel the blisters forming on his fingers and palms.

"How deep do you think we should go?" Tess said.

"Five feet," Theo said. "Standard graves in Brooklyn are three by eight feet, five feet down."

"I do not want to know how you know that," Jaime said.

"I hope we don't have to dig five feet down," said Tess.

They kept digging. Like the busiest part of the city, the cemetery seemed to be awake, too. The monk parrots' calls sounded eerily human, the wind like the whispers of ghosts. The angel seemed to watch them as they dug, her expression inscrutable. Jaime imagined her coming to life, her wings flapping, her bronze body rising up and up and up. He was so mesmerized by the vision of the angel taking flight that he didn't understand when his trowel struck something in the earth.

Clunk!

Jaime tossed the trowel aside, brushed away some dirt from whatever he'd hit. Not a rock. It felt like leather.

"I found something," he said.

"What?"

"I don't know yet. Help me with it."

The twins gave up on their own holes and helped Jaime dig. They cleared the top of what looked like an oversized leather box, about two feet square. Written on the top were the words JUNK TRUNK.

"'Junk Trunk'?" Tess said. "Doesn't sound too promising."

"One man's junk is another man's treasure," said Theo. "Kind of looks like one of Aunt Esther's old trunks. Or your trunk, Tess. The one you keep in your closet."

"Except The Magix isn't cured with grave dirt," Tess said. "And my stuff isn't junk."

"Are you ever going to tell me what you keep in there?"

"Nope," said Tess.

They dug all around the side of the trunk until they were able to heft it out of the ground. It wasn't large, and it wasn't buried five feet down, luckily for Jaime's sore hands. It also wasn't locked. Even though the cemetery was still creeping with jagged shadows, they grinned at one another before throwing open the lid.

Packed into the shallow trunk were all sorts of postcards and papers, little figurines and scribbled diagrams, all covered in dust and grime.

Tess leaned back on her heels. "It *is* a bunch of junk."

"Maybe not," said Jaime. He pulled a tiny copper figurine from the trunk. A woman wearing a robe and crown held a torch aloft. Along the bottom of the figurine were the words THE STATUE OF LIBERTY, 1886.

"Is this supposed to be the Liberty Statue?" said Theo. "But it wasn't built in 1886. And it doesn't look like that. Where's the eagle? And why is it green?"

Jaime set the figurine aside and hefted a small envelope. "Money!"

"Fake money," said Theo, unpacking it.

"Yeah," said Tess. "Andrew Jackson on the twenty-dollar bill? Where's Harriet Tubman?"

"And what are these?" Theo said, holding up some diagrams of strange machines.

"No idea," said Jaime. "But I recognize this one.

Solar glass. It's so wavy, though. Has to be ancient."

"Look!" Theo said, pulling a rusted solar battery out of the box. "It's enormous!"

They kept pawing through the trunk. They found a set of calculations on melting the polar ice caps, except the ice caps weren't melting as far as any of them knew and they couldn't imagine why someone would want them to. A book that said it featured extinct animals, but included pictures of polar bears and arctic foxes and tigers, none of which were extinct. An article on the dangers of oil rigs in the Gulf of Mexico, except they didn't know what an "oil rig" was. A printed blog piece about people continuously referred to as "illegals," except none of them knew how a person could be illegal. Prescription bottles for mysterious drugs. A magazine cover warning about the coming war in the Arctic. A business card for a firm called Trench & Snook.

"What *is* this stuff?" said Theo. "Some weirdo's apocalyptic cosplay props? This doesn't seem like Morningstarr material. . . . Who put it here?"

"Who cares?" said Tess, her patience fraying like her braid. "We have to figure out which one of these things is a clue."

"Maybe we should pack this whole trunk up and carry

it out with us," Theo said.

"What will we tell the Cipherists? That we just happened to trip over it?"

"Okay, then we stuff as much of this as we can into our backpacks."

"But what if the clue is on the trunk itself? Written on the bottom or something?" said Tess.

"We could bury it again and come back," Theo suggested.

"When will we have a chance to come back?"

"I don't know!"

"Maybe we should try to be a little quieter," said Jaime. "They can probably hear us up in the Bronx."

Beams of light blasted them. They held up their arms, squinting against the brightness. Ono squeaked, "Oh no!"

From the shadows, a voice drawled, "It's dangerous to go creeping around a graveyard in the middle of the night. Didn't your parents teach you children anything?"

CHAPTER THIRTY-TWO
Duke

It was a rare day—and a rarer night—when Duke Goodson showed up to do his own dirty work. But sometimes it was necessary. Like when your own people failed you, and you were forced to supervise so that nothing else would go wrong.

He would handle that unfortunate situation later. Right now, all he was interested in were these three children. A rather unremarkable lot, in his opinion. A shaggy boy in desperate need of a haircut, a girl who resembled her brother a lot less than she did a disgruntled owl, and another, larger boy also in need of a haircut. Didn't parents groom their children anymore?

"Candi. Toni. Zozi. Please take that item from the children and bring it here."

"No," said one of the children. The girl. Duke did not care for mouthy girls.

"No?" he said. "How do you plan on stopping me?"

"Who are you?" This from the big boy.

"That's not important," said Duke. "What's important is that trunk, or what's in it."

"It's not yours," said the other boy.

"True," Duke said. "It belongs to my client, who paid an absurd amount of money for anything you three should find. Did I say an absurd amount of money? I meant a truly ridiculous amount of money."

Candi, Toni, and Zozi went to retrieve the trunk from the children. When the girl saw Candi, she only gripped the trunk tighter.

"You!" the girl said through a fence of gritted teeth.

"Me," said Candi, her tone mild.

"You lying piece of—"

"Now, now," Candi said, easily tearing the trunk from the girl's grip. "No need to get hysterical." Candi glared at Toni and Zozi and carried the trunk back to Duke herself. Not that this would make up for anything, but Duke decided he would let Candi have her moment.

"Nine didn't bite you. How could you lie like that?" said the mouthy girl.

"Everyone lies when it suits them," said Candi.

"I don't!"

"Really? Where do your parents think you are right now?

The girl glowered impressively. "Where's my cat?"

Candi dropped the trunk at Duke's feet. She made her eyes wide, the very picture of innocence. "How should I know where your cat is? Didn't your own mother take her away?"

The girl actually hurled herself at Candi, but the two boys held her back. If the girl weren't so owlish, Duke would consider hiring her once she was grown. Spunk like that was useful. But she'd look terrible with blond hair, the poor thing. She should have arranged to be born into a more attractive family.

Speaking of family. "Where *do* your parents think you are?" Duke asked.

The girl said, "My parents think we're sleeping at Jaime's house. Jaime's grandmother thinks he's sleeping at ours."

"But you don't lie," said Candi.

"What we told them and what they believe are two different things," the bushy-haired boy said.

So no one really knew where the children were. Convenient. "I'm sure you'll make excellent lawyers one day," Duke said. "Or you would have. But I'm afraid it's time for us to go. And time for you, too."

The bigger boy stood. He did look rather like a budding rap star, not that Duke knew anything about rap, or cared. "We're not going anywhere with you," he said.

"Did I say you were going with me?" Duke said. "The ladies will escort you to your final destination."

Ashli, Tammi, Lori, Laci, and Lu came out of the shadows to join Candi, Toni, and Zozi. The blond women surrounded the children, backing them up against the base of the statue behind them. They did look magnificent in a group, Duke's ladies. Ash-blond hair bright as moonlight, red dresses dark as venous blood. Instead of their heels, the ladies wore black combat boots. But they could deal with these recalcitrant children with their hands tied behind their backs.

Most of them, anyway. Lu said, "They're just kids."

"I'm aware of that," said Duke.

"What do you want with a bunch of kids?"

Candi said, "Do shut up, Lu."

"I'm asking a question," Lu said.

"I don't pay you to ask questions, I pay you to do what I tell you to do," Duke snapped.

The girl muttered some string of nonsense to her

brother, something that sounded as if her lips were made of rubber: "Wabe caban't gabo wabith thabesabe gabuys."

"Stop that," said Duke.

The big boy said: "Whaby abaraben't thabe Cabipha-berabists cabomabing?"

"I said, stop."

"Mabaybe thabey're taboabo fabar abawabay tabo habeabar?" said the bushy-haired boy.

"*Stop.*"

"Whaberabe abarabe thabey, Tabexabas?" said the big boy.

"Knock it off!" said Duke.

"Staball abas labong abas yaboabu caban," said the girl. Then she said clearly, "What the heck are you ladies doing, anyway? Why would you want to work for this lying jerk?"

"Why not dream bigger?" said the big boy. "Open a self-defense school. Be bodyguards for movie stars. *Become* movie stars. I bet you'd be great in action films."

"Or any films," the girl said. "We don't want to limit them."

"Can any of you sing?" said the big boy. "You could form a band. That could be dope."

"At least find work that doesn't require you to

terrorize people," said the bushy-haired boy.

The girl said, "I'd still like to know where my cat is."

Duke's head was beginning to ache. Children were terrible, terrible little creatures. They should ship them all to a colony on the moon and let them raise themselves so that the adults could go to brunch in peace. "Can it, all of you. I've had enough of this bull."

"Mixed metaphors!" said the bushy-haired boy.

The bigger boy considered Duke. "Your accent is slipping."

The mouthy girl said, "Where's my cat?

The bushy-haired boy said, "Where are you from? Sounds like Long Island to me."

"I've always liked Long Island accents," said the big boy. "Why do you pretend you're from somewhere you aren't?"

The girl: "And where's Karl? I know you stole the other animals. I know you were keeping them on that island!"

Duke racked his brains but he couldn't think who Karl was, and then he was annoyed because he was wasting time trying to decipher the absurd babbling of preteens. "What are you talking about, you strange little girl? What island? Candi! What is she yammering about?"

Candi turned her wide, innocent eyes on Duke.

"Why, I have no idea, sir."

Duke longed for some antacids. A whole bottle of them. "Never mind. Round them all up and let's get out of here. I need some sleep."

Candi smiled. Too late, Duke realized that Candi was being far, far, too cheeky for a woman who must suspect by now that she was about to be shipped off to Minnesota and replaced with someone younger.

"It's so funny you should say that. I was thinking you needed some sleep, too," said Candi, right before she shot him with the fizz gun.

CHAPTER THIRTY-THREE

Tess

There was a strange, burbling noise, like water flowing over rocks. A spray of iridescent foam rocketed from the barrel of the gun, swallowing up the man's arms and legs. He toppled like a tree, yelling the whole time.

"Ouch," said the tallest blond woman. "I think that's what the kids would call a face-plant."

"I'll get you for this," the man said, wriggling under the mountain of foam.

"Don't fight it, Duke. Accept the loss gracefully."

"I . . . won't . . . accept . . . any . . . such . . . thing," the man said through gritted teeth as the foam swelled around him.

"No matter. In a minute, the foam will soak into your

skin and you won't be able to move, anyway. But you'll still be able to hear and understand everything we say." The woman laughed. It was the creepiest thing in the graveyard. Which was saying a lot.

Where were the Cipherists? Why weren't they coming?

The other blond women were nearly as stunned as the man on the ground. "Candi?" said one of them. "What did you do?"

"What did it look like, Toni darling? I know it's hard for you, but take your best stab at it."

"You fizzed him!" said Toni.

"That's correct," Candi said. "I fizzed him. And I'm taking his place."

"What does *that* mean?" another blond woman asked.

"It means that I'm working directly for the big boss," said Candi. "And you all answer to me, now."

"Why would we answer to you?" said yet another blond woman.

"Because I'm the one with the fizz gun, you silly twit," Candi replied. "And because you know I don't need it to fizz *you.*"

One of the blond ladies—Toni? Tammi?—looked as if she might want to test Candi's theory, but Candi only smiled wider. "Please, try it, dear. Here, I'll even put away the gun." She slipped the gun into her dress pocket and held up her hands. "See? Do your worst."

Toni/Tammi thought better of it and took a step back.

"Good girl," said Candi.

Tess pointed to the unconscious man. "Who is that?"

Candi shrugged. "That is someone who liked to imagine he was a fixer. The fixer's fixer." She nudged the man's hat with her boot. "Fixer's fixer, my butt. Fixed you, didn't I? In a few minutes I'll hit you with the eraser. You won't remember a thing." She swept her hand over her head and her long, stiff blond hair came away. A wig. Underneath, she was still blond, but instead of falling nearly to her waist, the hair waved around her shoulders.

"Layers!" gasped the other blond women.

Tess had to admit Candi looked a little better, except for the dead eyes and cartoon-villain smile. Morning-starr Machines were more cuddly. *Giraffe-owaries* were more cuddly.

"Now, children, we're going on a little field trip. Your kind likes field trips."

"*Our* kind?" said Jaime.

"Cultural elites," said Candi.

"Huh?" said Theo.

"She means nerds," said one of the other blond ladies.

Candi did not lose the creepily upbeat tone in her voice when she said, "Lu, if you do not stop talking, I will use the fizz gun on you. And the eraser. And anything else I can think of."

"You didn't mean nerds?" said Lu. "I always thought that meant nerds."

"You're the nerd, Lu," said another blond woman.

"Just because I like video games?"

Candi rolled her dead eyes. "Okay, we've all had our fun. Let's get the children and this trunk to the van and we'll head out."

An eerie hum filled the air, set Tess's skin prickling. Candi and the other blond ladies frowned, looked around for the source of the sound. The wind picked up, rustled the leaves in the trees, and the calls of the monk parrots blended into a long and tortured moan.

Ono, who had been perched quietly on the marble base of the angel, whispered, "Tabo thabe Laband abof Kabings!"

"Is your toy speaking Chinese?" said Toni/Tammi/Whatever.

"Zozi, Ashli, Lori. Fan out and go see what's making that noise," Candi said. "Could be one of their historian friends trying to distract us."

The blondes did as they were told, fanning out among the gravestones, blending into the darkness. The other blondes turned away from Tess, Theo, and Jaime so they could keep an eye on the surrounding grounds.

Which was when Jaime grabbed Ono and pitched the little robot at the nearest blond woman, buckling her knee and spilling her to the ground. Tess kicked the rear of the next woman and sent her headfirst into the hole they'd dug to find the trunk. Theo hefted the trunk and brought it down on the head on yet another blond.

A sudden burst of pain in her gut doubled Tess over, and another burst on her back flattened her. Theo and Jaime were dropped just as quickly. A couple of blond women tied Tess's, Theo's, and Jaime's hands behind their backs, and their ankles together.

Candi stood over them. "I wouldn't try that again."

Ono got to his tiny feet, marched slowly but resolutely toward Candi. When he reached her feet, one tiny arm lashed out and punched her in the kneecap. Candi reared back and kicked Ono. He spiraled like a football—

—right into the hand of a small black woman wearing a simple coat the color of thunderclouds, who caught him gently. Next to her crouched a large black cat.

Nine?

"This is no way to treat children," the woman said, in her low, raspy voice.

"Who are you?" said Toni/Tammi/Toto. "Candi, who is that?"

"A good question," said Candi. "What's with the Harry Potter coat?"

"I like this coat. What's with the red dresses?"

"We like these dresses. And they give us superpowers," Candi said.

The black woman grinned. "Fascinating. Did you use your powers on your boss over there?"

"Didn't need to. I used the fizz gun on him."

"Why?"

"I got a better offer. And a girl's got to make a living."

The woman in gray put Ono back on the ground. "If you're still taking orders, I don't understand how it's a better offer."

"You don't have to understand. You only have to forget what you saw here and go back to wherever you came from."

"Oh, but I've come too far," said the woman in gray. "And no matter how hard I try, I've never been much good at forgetting."

"A shame," said Candi, her tone airy, unconcerned. "Ladies?"

In a blink, the blondes had the woman in gray surrounded. The black cat lowered her head and growled.

"Nine," Tess said. "Please."

"Is that your kitty?" Candi said. "I remember her being bigger than that."

"Don't hurt her," Tess said.

"Tell that to your friend, here," said Candi.

"She isn't my friend!" Tess said.

"Good choice. I don't have friends, either."

"I have friends! But I don't know who that woman is!"

"A living mystery," said Candi. "Soon to be a dead one. Or maybe something quite a bit worse." She jerked her head and the blondes crouched, moving in on the woman in gray at the center. The cat suddenly sprang, banking off one of the blondes to swipe at another. The woman in gray bent in half, one leg planted, one leg kicking up like a switchblade to catch a blonde under the chin. Before the blonde fell, the woman in gray caught her, using her as a shield against the punches the blond women rained down. Then she thrust the blonde away. Coat swirling, she took out one blonde with a spinning backfist and the next with a roundhouse kick. The remaining blondes toppled like the rows of dominoes Tess and Theo used to set up around their old apartment.

The woman in gray stopped, stilled, not even winded. "Is that all you've got?"

Candi sighed. "You can't get good help these days."

"You haven't figured out that you're still the help," said the woman in gray, glancing down at the man in the cowboy hat. "You think you'll take his place but you won't. Another man will. And another after that. You think you're indispensable, but you're not. You think you have real power, but you don't."

"Oh, I have power all right," said Candi, her face twisting up into a snarl. "Would you like to see?"

"Show me," said the woman in gray.

Candi jumped, rearing back her fist and then catching the woman in gray in the cheek. She absorbed the blow and then head-butted Candi, rocking the blonde on her feet. The silvery coat swirled like a cape as the woman swept Candi's legs out from under her. Candi kicked out with both legs and managed to push the woman back, but only a foot or two.

As the two women fought, the big cat ran to Tess, circled all around her, rubbing and purring and explaining herself: "Mrrow, mrrow, mrrow."

"Nine! I knew it was you. Where have you been?"

Nine gnawed at the rope binding Tess's hands together, biting and sawing until she'd shredded them.

She left Tess to untie her own feet while she went to work on Theo's bindings. Tess freed her feet and then went to Jaime. But Jaime had help already. Ono. One of his little arms had split into a pair of scissors. It chopped through the ropes that held Jaime's feet. Tess undid Jaime's wrists.

In the middle of a thicket of gravestones, the women still fought. Candi was tall and quick and strong, but the woman in gray was stronger, faster, quick and brutal as a storm. She barely looked out of breath as she punched and kicked and punched again, her fists and feet a furious blur. With one tremendous kick from the woman in gray, Candi flew back and smashed into the *Angel of Music*, the sound nothing like music. She slid down the marble base and crumpled to the dirt.

The woman in gray straightened and turned an unreadable gaze on Tess and Theo and Jaime. She was so lovely and so strange that it was almost hard to look at her, but Tess refused to avert her eyes. She wanted to ask so many questions, say so many things. Who are you? Where did you come from? Where are you going? Thank you, thank you, thank you.

But what came out of her mouth wasn't thank you, and wasn't a question. "You stole my cat."

"I only borrowed her for a while," said the woman in

gray. "And I might have used a little dye to cover up her spots. It will wash out."

Tess winced at the sound of her own word coming back at her—*borrowed*. "You stole her," she insisted. "Why?"

"I was protecting her," said the woman. "And I needed her help."

"For what?" Theo asked.

"Nothing you need to worry about," the woman said. She crouched by the trunk. "What did you discover?"

"Nothing you need to worry about," Tess said.

The woman smiled. "You're your mother's daughter, Tess."

Theo said, "How do you know Tess's name? What do you know about our mother?"

"Not much anymore. I knew your mother a long, long time ago. People change. Maybe neither of you is like her at all. Was there something inside the trunk?"

Jaime was looking at the woman in gray as if he were seeing a ghost or something out of a dream. "Yes," he said.

"Jaime!" Tess said.

"We put all the stuff we found in our backpacks," Jaime continued, as if he hadn't heard Tess at all.

The woman searched the packs, her frown growing

deeper as she examined the papers and the money and the other items from the trunk. She held up the little green statue that looked so much like the Liberty Statue. "I don't understand."

"We don't, either," said Theo.

"I drew you," Jaime said.

"Pardon me?" said the woman in gray.

Jaime stood. He patted his pockets and pulled out a folded piece of paper. He held it out to the woman in gray. Though he was taller than she, he seemed utterly awestruck by her. His hand was shaking.

The woman unfolded the paper. Many moments passed as she examined it. Then she said, "An excellent likeness. I would not have thought you'd seen enough of my face that day on the island."

"No, you don't understand. I drew this before. I've been drawing you for months. Maybe longer."

"He has," said Tess. Theo nodded.

The woman in gray took two quick steps forward and gripped Jaime's arm. "How? Where else did you see me? The obelisk? Red Hook?"

"What? No. I imagined you."

"Did you see a picture? A photograph? I thought I made sure none were taken but maybe—"

"No! I . . . I . . ."

Another quick step forward. *"What? You what?"*

"I made you up."

The woman stepped back. Looked at the drawing, looked at Jaime. A kaleidoscope of emotions animated her face: rage, pain, and lastly a cool detachment. She held out the drawing to him. "As I said, an excellent likeness. Yet, you did not make me up. If anyone conjured me, it was I and I alone. You must have seen me somewhere before."

Jaime's face crumpled. "I'm sorry. I didn't mean to upset you, but—"

The woman put up a palm. *Stop.* Jaime did, though Tess saw his eyes welling with tears. At the sight of them, the cool detachment gave way. "What's your name?"

"Jaime. Jaime Cruz," he said.

"You are a very talented young man, Jaime Cruz, and I'm glad to make your acquaintance, even under these circumstances."

She held out a slim hand bloodied on the knuckles. Jaime hesitated, then shook it gently, so as not to hurt what had already been wounded.

"What may we call you, ma'am?" Jaime said, suddenly formal, as if he hadn't spent months drawing her in his sketchbooks, as if they had not just witnessed this woman outfighting so many other ferocious women, as if she weren't a dream made flesh.

But before the woman even had a chance to say her name, it came to Tess like a blast from a fizz gun, like lightning from a bruised and purple cloud.

"I've had many names," the woman said. "But you may call me Ava."

CHAPTER THIRTY-FOUR
Theo

Things that simply could not be done by humans: finding a word that rhymes with *orange* in English. Traveling faster than the speed of light. Living for nearly two hundred years without looking a day over twenty-five.

"You're Ava," said Theo. "But you're not *that* Ava."

Ava quirked a brow, amused. "There's another?"

No. Nope. Nuh-uh. "You can't be Ava Oneal. You can't be."

Ava didn't answer, but her silence was the answer.

He couldn't ask, he had to ask. "Are you a machine?"

Jaime sucked in a breath. "Theo!" Tess said, obviously horrified. But he needed to know.

"I'm always and forever a lady. And I'm as human as you are," Ava said.

"But that's impossible," said Theo. "Completely and totally impossible."

"I have been called impossible before," said Ava. She let go of Jaime's hand and held it out to shake Theo's, then Tess's. "And you are Tess and Theo Biedermann."

"How do you know that?" Tess said.

"Like I told you, I knew your mother once a long time ago."

"When? Where? How did you know her?" said Tess.

"Why show yourself now?" said Theo. "Where have you been all this time?"

"I'm sorry, I don't have the time to explain," Ava said. "*We* don't have the time."

"You knew the Morningstarrs!" said Tess. "But that means you've been alive for centuries!"

"Impossible," Theo repeated. The word bounced around his head like a shooting star. Impossible, impossible, impossible, impossible, impossible.

Tess ignored him. "You could tell us all about them! You can tell everyone how important they were! What they did! So Slant can't destroy any more of the city!"

"Technically, *we* destroyed a part of the city," Theo said. Tess stared at him as if he'd grown some glittery spider eyes all over. "What?" he said. "You know it's true."

"The Morningstarrs did that. Technically and otherwise." To Ava, Tess said, "We could go to the papers. We could go to the government. We could go to my mom."

"No one will believe it," Theo said. "*I* don't believe it." He didn't. He couldn't.

Impossible.

Ava shook her head. "It's late. Your friends will be here soon. And reinforcements from—" She paused, sighed. "Oh, dear. It seems we're missing a minion."

Theo turned. Candi, the tall woman who had been slumped at the base of the angel, was nowhere to be seen.

"That's unfortunate," said Ava. "I dislike doing the same task twice." She touched the moth pin on her lapel and the wings glinted in the moonlight.

As if Ava's words were the lines from a summoning spell, Theo heard the rustle of grass and leaves, a surge of voices, a flurry of footsteps. The Cipherists arrived, breathing hard, looking as if they'd just played a touch football game that got a little overzealous. Dirt stained their clothes.

"Oh, thank the Lord," said Imogen. "Where have you kids been? We've been calling for you."

Ava said, "We had a bit of trouble." She gestured to the blondes draped like boneless chickens all around.

Gunter said, "And you are?"

"This is my aunt," Jaime said, before Theo could blurt IMPOSSIBLE INCONCEIVABLE PREPOS-TEROUS like Cricket on too much Kool-Aid.

"Ava," said Ava. "Pleased to meet you all."

"We were exploring when the blond ladies came and started digging up that trunk," said Jaime. "We hid. I couldn't call for you, so I texted Aunt Ava. She lives in Brooklyn, not far from here. I knew she would come and help us."

"Well," said Omar. He spread his hands, gesturing to the bodies strewn about. "You seem to be a handy person to have around, Ms. Ava."

Ava shrugged. "They had a fizz gun. I simply turned it on them. Most people who carry such weapons believe such weapons themselves make them invincible. They are surprised to find it isn't true."

"The blond ladies who found us had no fizz guns," said Priya. "But we had Imogen. She knows kung fu."

"That wasn't kung fu," Ray Turnage said. "That was a good old-fashioned beatdown. The rest of us hardly had to lift a finger."

Imogen sniffed and flexed her wrists. "I didn't like their attitudes."

"They were rather irritating," Ava agreed.

"Is that who I think it is?" Priya said, pointing to the man in the cowboy hat slumped on the ground. It seems that Candi must have administered the eraser—whatever that was—because the man started to sing a tune. *"When the moon hits your eye like a big pizza pie, that's amore . . ."*

"That man should not be singing," said Ray.

"Who do you think it is?" said Imogen.

"That man who's always in the papers. The one who looks like a smug turtle. Luke Babson. Mike Goodstone. Something like that."

Gunter knelt by the slumped man. "Mein Gott, it's Duke Goodson. I've read about him, I've seen him on TV. A nasty fellow. Likes to pretend he's a good old Southern boy, when he's about as Southern as my great-grandmother Brunhilde. He works for all sorts of horrible people."

"Like Slant?" Tess said.

"Like Slant," said Gunter. "But he mostly works to enrich himself."

"That's a lot of people in this city," Imogen said.

"I like pizza," said Duke Goodson.

Gunter stood. "I suggest we call your mother, Tess. Anonymously. Tip her that Mr. Goodson here was seen digging up graves in Green-Wood Cemetery."

"That might get him a whole different type of news-paper write-up," Imogen said.

"I'll call after we're done here," said Omar.

"Won't they be able to identify your number?" Tess said.

"I have a scrambler phone," Omar said.

"You do?" Ray said.

"I thought everybody did."

"What were they looking for, anyway?" said Gino. He crouched beside the hole Theo and Tess and Jaime had dug by the *Angel of Music*.

"No idea," said Jaime. "They were mad when they found the trunk empty."

"Then they would make abysmal Cipherists," said Priya. "Even an empty box can be a clue. Everything is a dead end until it's not."

"Dead ends," said Ray. "Nice."

"What?"

"Dead ends? We're in a graveyard?"

"You and your puns," Priya said.

"Hey! You were the one who said it!"

"Not intentionally."

"Do you think they were trying to solve the Cipher?" said Priya.

"Doubtful," said Gino. "I can't imagine this lot

finding steps in the Cipher that we haven't. And why bother trying to solve a Cipher when you can simply buy or steal anything and everything you want?"

Theo winced at the things he and Tess and Jaime had stolen: Ono and the book from Kingsland Homestead. And how much damage had the eagles caused at Station One? Someone would have to pay for that. Maybe they'd made it easier for Slant to buy the station, too, and charge everyone a skillion dollars just to ride the Underway.

Omar inspected the trunk. "This appears to be old. Perhaps early nineteenth century, perhaps even earlier than that. No identifying markings that I can see right now. But we can take it back to the society with us. Inspect it properly."

Tess opened her mouth, probably to argue, but Imogen had spotted Nine. "Is that . . . ?"

"Yes!" said Tess. "The blond women brought her, maybe to help sniff out the trunk, I don't know. They dyed her so that she wouldn't be recognized. But I knew her. I would always know her."

"Mrrow," said Nine.

Theo was glad Nine was back but, at the same time, outraged that Tess and Jaime were so comfortable telling these lies when a woman who claimed to be *the* Ava

Oneal was standing here, chatting as if she hadn't been delivered straight from the pages of a history book. Or the pages of Jaime's sketchbook.

Theo's head spun. He needed some water. He needed some crackers. He needed a nap.

"I'm so glad that you found Nine, that you're not hurt, that your aunt was able to come for you," Imogen said.

"I feel awful that this little trip put you in danger," Priya said. "We were so excited to have our little adventure we didn't think about the risks."

"We don't often think about the risks," said Gino.

"Some of us think too much about them," Tess said. Nine nudged her fingers. Tess scratched the cat between the ears. Despite the living mystery, the breathing impossibility standing in front of them, Tess seemed calmer than she had in days. Once again, it seemed as if Theo and Tess had traded places, and that Theo was the anxious one, and Tess, the logical. He would have to have his own therapy animal. Considering his spinning head, his roiling gut, it would have to be a big one. A wolf named Pink. A giraffe-owary named . . . Giro.

Help.

"Enough talking. We need to tie these people up and leave them for the police," Gino said. "It's better than they deserve, attacking a bunch of children."

The Cipherists got to work tying up Duke Goodson and the blond ladies, with the aid of Ava and Jaime and even Nine, who twirled around Tess's legs and mrrowed and purred so loudly that Theo would have heard her from Manhattan.

But while everyone else was tying up villains and criminals, Theo looked over the now-empty trunk. The other clues were so sophisticated, numerical puzzles and riddles hidden in monuments. The "Junk Trunk" was a silly name for an antique that could hold a clue to the Morningstarr Cipher, and such a crude and random way to hide a clue, but maybe that was the point. To hide the trunk's importance, to throw people off. Theo felt all along the inside of the trunk, looking for anything they missed. A false bottom or lid. A fake side panel.

As he ran his fingers over the lip of the trunk, he felt something pointy. He picked at the point, pulled out an old photograph that had fallen between the lining and wall of the trunk.

Theo squinted at the photo, willing his overwhelmed brain to process what he was holding, what he was seeing, besides one impossible thing too many.

CHAPTER THIRTY-FIVE

Jaime

While Tess chattered happily and Theo dissolved into the sludgy swirl of his own thoughts, time collapsed for Jaime. First, he was wandering in a grave-yard, tying up comic-book supervillains, talking to bunch of puzzle hunters as well as a walking figment of his imagination; next, he was reliving his sixth birth-day.

Jaime's father didn't take him to any of the places other fathers take their sons on their birthdays. They did not go to Ruggles Field to see the Starrs play the Cubs, they did not have a party at the exo arena at Chelsea Piers, they did not go for pizza and cake, they did not invite a group of kids for a rousing—and chaotic—game of bubble soccer, in which the participants dressed in giant inflatable balls and bashed into one another for fun.

Instead, Jaime and his father went to a museum to watch a man fold paper.

It was not just any man. And he wasn't folding paper airplanes. This was an origami master, and the things he created from single sheets of paper were magical. Butterflies and beetles, fiddler crabs and crickets, scorpions and dragonflies. Abstract polyhedra and polypolyhedra. An allosaurus and a pegasus and cat after cat after cat.

"The Japanese have been perfecting the art of paper folding for four hundred years," explained the tour guide, as the man quietly folded and pinched a piece of shiny bronze paper at a table behind her. "One of the most famous and accomplished was a man named Akira Yoshizawa, renowned for everything he did, but especially his gorillas."

Once the tour had moved on to view said gorillas and the rest of the exhibit, Jaime and his father stayed to watch the man fold. This artist was not Japanese, but a white man with a tidy beard. To Jaime, he looked like a schoolteacher or maybe a librarian. His fingers looked too big to make such delicate things as the paper cranes that people could buy in the gift shop.

"Did you always do this?" Jaime asked him.

"I worked as a scientist a long time ago," said the man.

"Oh! What kind of scientist?" Jaime's father asked.

"A physicist," said the man.

"My mom was a physicist," Jaime said proudly. "She did lots of important things. She loved it. Why did you give it up?"

The man laughed. "I didn't. Not exactly."

"Huh?" said Jaime.

"What I mean is, folding paper is a lot like math, a lot like science."

Jaime was doubtful. "Really?"

"Sure. NASA scientists are interested in the art of folding because they have to find ways to fit large things in small spaces. There's another scientist whose art is displayed here, a man named John Montroll, who has made models of Platonic solids and Archimedean solids."

"I don't know what those are," said Jaime.

"Beautiful," said the man, in that dreamy way Jaime's father might talk about his mother. "Origami is a lot like magic, too. No matter how many folds you make or if you end up with a cat or a crane or a mantis or a fish, you still have only one sheet of paper. The paper stays the same. It never loses its essence."

"What's essence?"

"Its spirit. Its soul."

"Paper doesn't have a soul."

"No?" The man held out a tiny paper figure. Jaime took it. It was a bronze woman in a long elaborate bronze dress.

"Who is she?" Jaime said.

"I'm not sure. She might be many things. But I think she's a scientist."

"And also an artist?"

"Why not?" said the man. "But maybe you can ask her."

Jaime still had the tiny woman. Every once in a while, he would ask her what she was. Sometimes he imagined she said she was a scientist, sometimes he imagined she said she was an artist—a particle artist, a star artist. Sometimes when he asked her who she was, he imagined she said she was his mother and she was all of the other things, too. Everything at once.

She was also a piece of paper. The paper remained the same.

So how could he be standing here talking to someone he'd drawn? Someone who looked a bit like his mother but wasn't his mother, someone he was sure he'd never seen anywhere but in his own head and flowing from his pencil? How had he conjured up a woman who had lived in the past? Was she the same woman who had teamed up with the Morningstarrs? Was she an entirely different person? Was her soul the same?

"Hey, Theo!" Tess barked, cracking Jaime and Theo out of their respective reveries. "Are you going to sit there all night or are you going to help us?"

Theo, who had been crouching by the empty trunk, said, "Yes."

"Yes, you're going to sit there all night, or yes, you're going to help us?"

"What?" said Theo. He looked as if someone's great-auntie had whacked him upside the head with a giant pocketbook.

"Are you okay?" Jaime said.

"Yeah," Theo said. "Fine. I'm great. Good. Sure."

"Uh-huh," said Jaime.

Theo stuck his hand in his hair. "You take a lot of pictures. Do you know when was photography invented?"

Jaime was used to the twins' non sequiturs, Theo's especially. "Hmmm," Jaime said. "I think daguerreotypes were the first kind of photos. Maybe 1830s or '40s?"

"Okay," Theo said, the arm dropping. "Thanks."

"Why do you want to know about photographs?"

"No reason."

"You always have a reason. You're the king of reason."

"No, I'm not," Theo muttered. "I never was."

"Right," Jaime said. Jaime couldn't blame Theo for his confusion. That same metaphorical pocketbook had whacked Jaime upside the head, too. He was surprised they all weren't careening around the cemetery, keening like ghosts who had seen a ghost. Would a ghost be afraid of a ghost? These were the kinds of things he was thinking now.

"Oh no?" Ono burbled.

Jaime patted Ono's little metal head. "Kings, Ono, Kings."

And this was the kind of thing he was saying, the kind of thing he was doing. Nine, sensing the general and pervasive anxiety, went to Theo and to Jaime in turn, nibbling on their fingers and rubbing against their legs.

"Kings, Kings," said Ono, and imitated the cat's soothing purr.

Imogen dusted off her hands. "Evil people tied up. Hole filled. I think we're done here."

Omar hefted the trunk. "I'll take this to the van and call the police on my way back."

"What about the rest of us?" Priya said.

Omar's grin was like another flashlight in the dark. "I arranged for faster transportation for all of you."

"What do you mean?" said Imogen.

"Look up, my friends," Omar said.

Above their heads, quietly hovering, was a dirigible the same color as the night sky. A ladder unfurled from the cab and dropped to the ground.

Imogen clapped. "It's such a clear night. The views will be spectacular. Kids, why don't you go first? We'll be right behind you."

Ava said, "That is, as they say, my cue. It was a pleasure meeting you all. I will take my leave now."

"Take your leave?" said Imogen, grabbing Ava's hands. "Oh, please don't. We would love for you and Jaime to come back with us. Any family of his is a friend of ours. I could show you our Morningstarr collection at the archive. It's extensive, as you probably know."

The woman in gray smiled, as a teacher might to an eager student. "I'm sure it is."

"And we have cookies!"

Imogen's warmth was hard for anyone to resist. And no one could resist cookies. "All right," Ava said. "Thank you."

Each of them climbed the ladder in turn. Nine consented to be draped around Gunter's neck so that she,

432 ◆ LAURA RUBY

too, could ride the airship to Manhattan (as long as she agreed not to unsheathe her claws). From the cockpit, Delancey DeBrule greeted them all. She even gave a warm welcome to Ava, a welcome that surprised Jaime considering that the twins had once compared Delancey to a stick bug. (Which they thought was a compliment because, twins.)

"Everybody ready?" Delancey said.

"Get a move on, Delancey!" said Imogen. "I don't want to end up in a newspaper article with Luke Son-good."

"I think you meant Schoomp Sonfluke," Priya said.

"Nein," said Gunter. "Doof Flukenfluke."

"Good old Doof," said Ray. "I hope they bury his career in the dirt."

"No pun!" said Priya.

Ray's laugh was like happy music, a trip down the piano keys. "Puns all day."

They pulled up the ladder and the dirigible began its slow rise up and up. Below them, the cemetery got smaller and smaller. Soon, the tiny red lights from the coming police cars lit up the darkness below, but the dirigible was already too high to be visible from the ground. They saw the glinting black water of the river and, if they leaned out of the cab just so, the stars overhead. Up here, between earth and sky, Jaime's head gradually cleared. The confusion fell away and there was only the glinting river, the sparkling city, and the stars twinkling. He thought that God must be an artist—a star artist, a particle artist—to have made such a pretty sky, such interesting people. He wasn't even worried about the Cipher. They would figure out the clue, they always did. And it would take as long as it took. And they would find Karl for Cricket; maybe Ava would help them. He remembered Theo talking about his grandfather, saying his grandfather believed that solving a puzzle was about the process rather than the result; and though Jaime liked results, he felt comfortable with what was in process right now. The Cipherists were doing what everyone seemed to do at the sight of such magnificent stars, they pointed out the various constellations to one another, even though they all seemed to know them: Big Dipper, Little Dipper, Hercules, Cassiopeia, Cygnus, Lyra, Lynx, Hydra, Gemini. Ava joined in with a story about the constellation Orion. Some said that Poseidon was Orion's father, she told them, but that the great huntress Euryale of the Amazons was his mother. Orion inherited her talent and became the greatest hunter in the world. But if Orion had inherited his mother's hunting skills, he had also inherited his father's ego. He claimed he could kill the largest and most ferocious creatures on the earth, any creature he wanted. As punishment, Gaia, the earth, sent a single small scorpion to sting and kill him.

"That sounds like a story Grandpa Ben would tell," said Tess. "Right, Theo? Theo!"

"Sure," said Theo, clearly not listening. He sat alone on one side of the dirigible cab, alternately tugging on his lip and stuffing his hand in his bushy hair. Theo was quiet the whole ride back to the society, quiet through the landing of the dirigible, quiet through the tour of the Morningstarr Archive that Imogen gave Ava. And he was quiet when various Cipherists said good night and left for their own homes, quiet when Gino and Imogen puttered around the kitchen putting the last of the cookies away, quiet when Imogen showed them where they could catch a few hours of sleep before morning, and quiet when Imogen herself fell asleep, snoring softly in one of the leather chairs in the farthest corner of the great room.

It was not normal for Theo to be so quiet.

After everyone else was asleep, Theo got up from the sleeping bag the Cipherists had laid out for him. Jaime watched as Theo prowled the exhibits—stopping at the centuries-old egg in the case, letters from Benedict Arnold and Mary, Queen of Scots.

Jaime sat up, whispered, "Are you okay?"

Theo's lips moved but found no words. Behind him, Auguste broke into song, soft and low, *"Who lives / Who dies / Who tells your story?"* Theo jumped as if poked.

"What is it?" Tess said, awake, too.

Theo pulled out a white square from his back pocket. "I found this in the trunk." He gave the square to Jaime.

Jaime used the light from his phone to see it. The white square was a photograph, a Polaroid of all things. His parents had some of these types of photos, taken in the 1970s with a special camera that was no longer in use. In the photograph, a dark-haired young man and woman in nineteenth-century dress sat at the foot of a tree, laughing. Along the bottom edge of the photo, someone had written, *"The Morningstarr Twins, 1807."* Jaime flipped the photograph. On the back were the words, *"Now you know."*

Jaime stared at the image, the date, the words.

"Jaime?" said Tess. Nine crept over to him, nudged at his knees, but he barely felt her.

"What is the trouble?" Ava said. Her dark eyes told him that she hadn't been sleeping, either.

Tess said, "What are you looking at, Jaime?"

Jaime was looking at picture taken with a camera that didn't exist in 1807. He was looking at a picture of the

Morningstarrs when they were young and strong, doing something people had claimed they never did—laugh. And he was looking at their bright open faces, filled with hope.

Now you know.

Time folded, unfolded, folded again.

"Jaime!" said Tess. "What are you looking at?"

Jaime tore his eyes away from the photo. He glanced from Tess to Theo, Theo to Tess.

"You," he said. "It's a picture of you."

Sunrise in Gotham Senior Living Center
1953/1972/1979/2005/2007/?
Grandpa Ben

If you wanted to visit the Sunrise in Gotham Senior Living Center from Manhattan, you had to make your way up through the city to Marble Hill, the only Manhattan neighborhood on the mainland instead of the island. Unlike the streets of much of Manhattan, and more like the streets of the Bronx, Marble Hill had houses with porches, spacious lots with lawns and trees. The center itself was nicely situated on the top of a knoll overlooking the Hudson, high enough that the center's numerous windows were filled with sunlight from sunrise to sunset. The people at the Sunrise in Gotham Senior Living Center believed in the power of the sun to brighten moods and illuminate the dustiest corners of the mind. They also believed in daily exercise, good nutrition, lively entertainment, clean, comfortable quarters, and pleasurable company. It was the finest memory-care center in all the five boroughs, or so the brochures said.

Benjamin Adler found it pleasant enough. He enjoyed the large sunny rooms, the "Bop to the Beat" exercise classes, the plentiful, if a tad bland, food. The center had a variety of pets—therapy animals—that visited the residents, including four dogs, three miniature ponies, two very large and floppy cat-rabbits, and Norma the Llama, who had spit on only one resident during her tenure so far, old Mr. Mitchell. (Since many of the residents and even some of the staff were tempted to spit on old Mr. Mitchell, no one got too worked up about that.) They also had a small Morningstarr Machine, a miniature Roller that cleaned up the trash, that the residents called Simon. "Hello, Simon!" they would say, and Simon would do a strange but charming whirl before cleaning up the crumbs and debris. Sometimes the center brought in cover bands to play Chubby Checker or Beatles tunes, and the residents would twist and lindy on creaky knees. Other times, the center brought in a violinist or a singer, and the residents would close their eyes and remember long-ago concerts with husbands and wives, dance performances of children and grandchildren who could never visit enough, even if they came every day.

Now Benjamin sat in his favorite spot by the window, watching a rather determined squirrel drag an entire bagel across the lawn outside. The people at the Sunrise in Gotham Senior Living Center did their best with the food, but the bagels, oy. Not so good.

"Good afternoon, Mr. Adler!" said one of Benjamin Adler's favorite aides. Her name began with a *G*. Gloria? Gracie? Gwendolyn!

"Good-bye!" he said, pleased he'd remembered her name.

"Good-bye, already? I've got a few more hours yet," Gwendolyn replied cheerfully. She tapped the puzzle book in front of him. "How's the puzzle coming?"

His mind scratched for the word he wanted, his tongue twisting. Sometimes the words came easily; mostly they didn't. And when the words did come, they weren't always the ones he was searching for. This frustrated and saddened him, but he tried to live with it as best he could, as he'd been forced to live with so many things.

"It's a kindly puzzle," he said. "Thank you."

"That's good to hear," said Gwendolyn. "I hope you're excited for your visitors."

"Apples and oranges," he said, which was not what he meant to say at all. Once upon a time, he said what he meant. Years ago, in 1972, he'd bumped into a beautiful girl named Annie in the middle of a delicatessen, spilling his matzo ball soup all over himself. He'd gazed into her beautiful dark eyes and asked her to marry him right then and there. She'd laughed, but he was never more serious.

"Would you like an apple?" said Gwendolyn. "I can get you one."

"1972," he said.

"What happened in 1972, Mr. Adler?"

"It's all stuff and nonsense," he said, another thing he hadn't meant to say. He meant the opposite of stuff and nonsense; he meant that he'd fallen in love with his Annie at the first glance he'd ever had of her; he meant that she was everything and everything was her.

"A song," he said, trying to correct himself. "*La-la-LA-la, la-la-la-LA-la-la.*" Annie was a singer and a song.

"1972 is a song? I didn't know that."

There was a little girl, also a song. What was her name? *M, M, M.* Miriam! A tiny replica of her mother, but with his eyes. Born in 1979 in the middle of the night. Never slept. Always yelling. She had something to say before she could say it. Benjamin could sympathize with that now. *Hush, little baby, don't say a word / Daddy's going to buy you a mockingbird.* The birds sing, too.

"We put her bed in the bathtub so she wouldn't wake up the neighbors," he said.

"Who was in the bathtub, Mr. Adler?"

"The little song," said Benjamin. The words weren't coming out remotely right, but it didn't matter. He had entire film reels of his past that played on and off in his mind, and watching them was more soothing than talking. And though they didn't play in order—in one reel he was four years old and riding a horse for the first time; in the next he was fifty-eight and Miriam was having her own little songs; and then he was twenty-three and all the wedding guests were dancing the horah, and he and Annie were lifted in chairs at the center of the circle; in the next, he was sixty and Miriam's little songs were singing, "Grandpa! Grandpa!"

"Mr. Adler? Would you like me to take this lunch tray away? And maybe bring you an apple?"

"Far kinder tsereist men a velt." He didn't remember exactly what it meant, but he knew it was the truth.

"I'll bring you an apple," Gwendolyn said, scooping up the tray. She hurried off.

On the other side of the table, a small, wizened woman sitting in a wheelchair wrung her hands. "What do I do now? Am I okay?"

"You're okay. You don't need to do anything," said Benjamin.

The woman smiled. "Thank you. I just like to ask."

The right words sometimes came, and when they did, it was like a puzzle piece snapping into place. Benjamin smiled back. He pointed at the squirrel outside. "They do their best, but the bagels here, oy."

"Oy," the woman said. "Not so good."

"Good for the fuzzy tails, though," he said.

"Fuzzy tails," the woman agreed.

"The little songs are coming to sing," he informed her.

"That's nice," she said. "I like music."

They sat in companionable silence for a while, enjoying the sun on their faces, the view of the fuzzy tail and his precious but obviously terrible bagel, the films unspooling in their own minds. There was another bird that sang, not a mockingbird, but a . . . a . . . crow? No. A talking bird. Big and black. You could teach him things, and he would remember. He would tell you what he knew, if you asked the right question.

"Here, birdy-birdy-birdy," Benjamin said.

Gwendolyn appeared next to him. "Your first visitor is here now," she said. "A surprise visitor!"

Benjamin turned. A woman with warm brown skin and black hair piled on her head stood there. She wore a pair of small sunglasses with blue lenses and a long silvery-gray coat that settled around her ankles.

"It's the summertime," he said. "Isn't it?"

"Yes," said the woman. "But I don't want to get too hot."

This made sense and also did not, but Benjamin wouldn't dwell on the contradiction.

Neither would Gwendolyn. "I'll let you two visit for a while. Come on, Mrs. Feingold. Let's go for a walk outside."

"I want to see the fuzzy tails," said Mrs. Feingold.

"And they want to see you," Gwendolyn said.

"Don't baby me," said Mrs. Feingold. Then she said, "Am I okay?"

"You're perfect, Mrs. Feingold."

"Feh."

The visitor sat down next to Benjamin. "Do you know me?"

"I think I should," said Benjamin. The right words. But also the wrong ones, because he didn't know her. At least, he didn't know her name. But she was familiar to him, as if someone had described her to him long ago and here she was. Like the answer to a clue in a crossword. Annie loved her crosswords.

"My name is Ava. I knew your daughter," said the woman.

"You did?" he said, but as soon as he said it, another film unspooled in his head. His little song, telling him all about this woman, what she looked like, how she would sometimes brush her hair away from her forehead at night. Her imaginary friend. *T, T, T.* Tara, Tabitha, Tiffany—

"Trixie!" he said.

"Yes, she did call me that. She thought I was magic."

"I thought you were a ghost," he said, not what he meant. He tapped his temple.

"I am no ghost," said Ava. "And I am always and forever a lady." She took his hand. Her fingers were warm.

"A lady," he repeated. "Yes."

She said, "I stayed away for so long. I wanted to. But a person gets curious despite herself. And as far away as I'd gotten, word of you came to me. I heard that you had some interesting theories about the Cipher and the people who had created it. That the Morningstarrs liked to laugh."

"The world is a funny place," he said. The right words.

"They did like to laugh. In the beginning anyway. Your Miriam liked to laugh, too. She reminded me of them. Of Tess. So I would visit occasionally, after everyone else went to sleep. I have spent much of my life watching everyone else sleep. In beds. In graves."

Benjamin tried to make sense of what she was saying, but the words and their meanings got tangled in his head. Everything seemed to be backward, or upside down.

"I have a question for you," she said. "And I need you to try and answer, though I know it might be difficult."

"Yes," he said. Yes, it might be difficult; yes, he would try.

"Did you know?" she said. "Did you know who the children were?"

The children? The children. *Far kinder tsereist men a velt.* For your children you would tear the world apart. Maybe he had.

But he couldn't answer the woman's question because the children were the children, no more, no less. Who else could they be but themselves?

He shrugged helplessly. Her smile was so sad it almost broke his heart. He hadn't known there was so much of it left to break.

"I thought I was too old to be angry," Ava said. "I thought too much time had passed, too many people had come and gone. I thought I was numb. But . . ." She hesitated. Her dark eyes were filled with pain and grief and rage and loneliness and something else he was sure he wouldn't have been able to name even before he'd lost everything, even before all the words had gotten scrambled in his head.

"I'm not numb after all," she said, not to him, but to herself.

He wasn't, either. He squeezed her hand, and she squeezed back.

"All the little songs will be here soon," he said, both an invitation and a warning.

"Is it all right if I sit with you till then?" she asked. "It's peaceful here. And I like the sun."

"Me too," he said.

They sat by the window of the Sunrise in Gotham Senior Living Center, two old and weary souls, hoping the light was enough to bring them back to life.

TO BE CONCLUDED

ACKNOWLEDGMENTS

This book is dedicated to my late father, Richard Ruby, who spent much of his youth as an ironworker in his grandfather's construction company. He, along with many others, helped to build bridges and buildings around New York City. He is gone, but also with me every day.

In the middle of writing this book, I was diagnosed with an illness, so I could not have finished this without a massive amount of support. Thanks to my agent, Tina DuBois; my editor, Jordan Brown; Debbie Kovacs at Walden Media; art director Amy Ryan; designers Aurora Parlagreco and Laura Mock; Renée Cafiero, Mark Rifkin, and Josh Weiss in the managing editorial department; and everyone else at Walden Pond Press for their faith and patience.

Many thanks to the Hamline MFAC students and faculty who sent cards and jokes and food and gifts that helped keep me going.

I'm eternally grateful for the amazing women of the LSG, the Shade, my beautiful Harpies, and my writing group (you know who you are).

Thanks also to Miriam Busch, the original Aunt Esther, knower of all the things; and Annika Cioffi, keeper of the Nines.

Love to all my family, every Ruby and Metro who called and visited even when I was too sick and cranky to speak, as well as to Anne Ursu, the Tess to my Theo, and the Theo to my Tess.

And finally, thanks and love to Steve, without whom I would be just a ghost, lost and untethered in the world.

LAURA RUBY

is the author of books for adults, teens, and children, including the Michael L. Printz Medal winner and National Book Award finalist *Bone Gap*, the Edgar Award nominee *Lily's Ghosts*, the Book Sense Pick *Good Girls*, and *York: The Shadow Cipher*, the first book in the York trilogy. She is on the faculty of Hamline University's MFA in writing for children and young adults program and lives in the Chicago area. You can visit her online at www.lauraruby.com.